The Ascendi

MW01241287

PURSUING
TRUTH

Karen Ann Bulluck
#1 International Best-Selling Author

PURSUING TRUTH
The Ascending Ladders Series Book 2

Copyright © 2023 by Karen B. Heine

Inspired Legacy Publishing is a division of (DBA) Inspired Legacy, LLC
PO Box 900816
Sandy UT 84090-0816.

ISBN 979-8-9882276-3-2 (paperback)
ISBN 979-8-9882276-4-9 (hardcover)

Printed in the United States of America.

What People Are Saying

"Captivating story, believable dialogue and a group of characters that just about anyone could easily identify with. Well done, Ms. Bulluck... well done."
Brian Hilliard
Popular Speaker & Coach

"A thoroughly enjoyable and suspenseful read."
Lisa Coletta
Founder/Managing Director, The Governance Collective

"Another masterful story that rings so true to life that you feel the emotions of the characters!! You can't help but be drawn into the story!"
Misti Mazurik
Director of Operations, Your Purpose Driven Practice

"Sheryl Simmon's journey poses some vital questions, highlighting the complexities of human relationships and decision-making dilemmas. Pursuing Truth will make you take a second look at your own journey!
Dr. Kasthuri Henry, PhD, CTP - Founder, Ennobled for Success Institute
International #1 Best Selling Author

"*Pursuing Truth* pulls you into the story immediately and keeps you guessing right up until the end...
Rich in storytelling and intrigue, this book was an absolute delight to read!"
Krista Mollion
Founder of From Zero 2 Six Academy

"Great characters, powerful story, exciting read. Karen Bulluck has done it again with her new book *Pursuing Truth: Book Two of The Ascending Ladders Series*. I loved the book."
Maureen Ryan Blake
Maureen Ryan Blake Media

"It's got it all: dynamics around communication, responsibility, account-ability, professionalism, trust, mutual respect, pushing the limits. The title sums it up: *Pursuing Truth*."
Sally Anderson
World Class Coach Intuitive
Sally Anderson International

"With exceptional storytelling, Bulluck keeps readers engaged, skill-fully unraveling mysteries while leaving a lasting impression. A gripping must-read."
Brigitte Bojkowszky, PH.D.
Global & Personal Branding Strategist
BridgetBrands

"As an avid reader, I love books that combine intrigue with life lessons and redemption. In *Pursuing Truth*, author Karen Ann Bulluck gives us this and more."
Dr. Lori Leyden
Developer of The Grace Process®, Founder of Create Global Healing

"*Pursuing Truth* is a real page-turner."
Susan K. Younger
Relationship Architect – Engaging Humanity in the Workplace
Codebreaker Technologies Pro Certification

"I hope *Pursuing Truth*, although a fictional book, can make a non-fiction impact on how leaders see their role and responsibility of being more human and understanding in times of crisis."
Nikki Green
Life & Business Resiliency Expert, 4x Best-Selling Author
Green Chameleon Collective

Dedication

Dedicated to Paul C. Tinnirello and the late Laurie Schapp Coleman. I have been supported, encouraged and inspired by your belief in me for many years. My journey to this book would have been vastly different had you not been in my life.

Table of Contents

Chapter 1

Dave Simmons smiled when he saw the caller ID on his ringing phone. *Alisha.* She would be a nice distraction on this gray, tedious Monday. He scooped up the phone.

"Hey Alisha," he said heartily. "How was your holiday?"

It was the Monday after Thanksgiving, and Dave was in the office. Due to his heavy travel schedule, he didn't have a permanent office or cubicle in LSM Consulting's corporate headquarters. He had grabbed a desk in the open pod on the second floor of the four-story building that was reserved for staff without assigned seating.

Tucked in the back corner with windows on two sides, it was brighter than most of the other pods and had a view over the suburban corporate complex. Plus, its corner location gave it a semblance of privacy. The location also gave him more space to spread out, an important consideration given his six-foot-one-inch height.

"Hey, Dave! It was good. Thanks for asking. How was yours?" Alisha's cheerful voice sang in his ear. He pictured her long blonde hair carelessly pulled into a ponytail and her blue eyes with their customary sparkle of mischief.

"Good," he answered, though without much enthusiasm. "My wife's family was here for the holiday. Her mother, her two brothers, and their families. It was nice." A reluctant smile tugged at his lips. "Sheryl's mom is a great cook. I'm still stuffed from all the wonderful food."

"That's nice," Alisha said, a touch of longing in her voice. "It was just me and Mom again this year. What about your family? Why weren't they there?"

"Mom and Dad went to be with my sister Belinda and her family this year," he said. "We rotate. We'll get to see them at Christmas." He idly twirled a pen in his free hand, thinking about the holiday pattern set early in his marriage with Sheryl. For some reason, he and his wife rarely intermingled their families. *Perhaps that would have been different if we had had children,* he thought suddenly, the pen pausing in his hand.

Distracted, Dave tightened his grip as he began tapping the smooth brown laminate surface. It was fake wood, a vain attempt by the corporate decorators to make the workspace less sterile. The rapping noise was loud in the quiet pod. Startled, he shifted the pen onto a pad of paper to mute the sound.

". . . Christmas," he heard Alisha say, realizing that he had missed some of her words.

"Sorry, what about Christmas?"

"Dave, you weren't listening," Alisha scolded playfully.

The crow's feet around his dark brown eyes deepened as he grinned. He loved that she never got annoyed when he was distracted. "Sorry."

"So, Christmas," Alisha went on. "I'm probably going to be in New Jersey for Christmas this year."

"In New Jersey? Why in the world would you come here for Christmas?" Dave sat up in his chair. "Unless you are going to New York? You and your mom?"

"Well, I'll be in New Jersey—maybe—because I'll be living there by then, I hope."

Dave dropped the pen. "Living here?"

"Yeah, my transfer to headquarters just came through. I got the call this morning," Alisha chirped. "I'm so excited."

"Transfer?" Dave echoed, struggling to grasp this unexpected news.

"Yes, transfer. You know, we've been talking about it."

Dave swallowed hard. Yes, they had discussed the idea, but it had seemed more like brainstorming than a viable option. He knew that Alisha Carson was unhappy working for Liam Moriarty, her current boss. Liam was one of the reasons that he and Alisha had grown close. Dave had observed Liam's behavior with Alisha and found it very disturbing. Wanting to protect and support the younger woman, Dave had offered advice at times. Alisha moving to New Jersey, clear across the country from Liam, was one possibility they had briefly discussed. But Dave hadn't thought she would go through with it.

It isn't that moving to headquarters would be bad for Alisha, Dave thought, his head still spinning. He knew from experience that people in the home office were chosen for promotions and internal opportunities more often than those in the field. Although LSM's business spanned North America and much of Europe, it was an elite consulting firm with just over eight hundred employees across all its locations. They didn't have a huge staff, but the people they did have were the best in the business. Alisha was very good. If she was going to grow in her career, New Jersey was probably a smart choice.

"Yes, we have," Dave finally conceded, his voice a little rough. "I just didn't think you'd ever leave California. You're not going to like the winter weather here."

Alisha paused. He heard her take a deep breath. "I thought you'd be happy about it," she said, her voice more subdued now.

Dave ran his free hand through his thick, light-brown hair, sending it into disarray, and swiveled his utilitarian chair toward the window. He looked out at the sterile gray office building, striped with darkly tinted glass, that sat about five hundred yards away across an expanse of leaf-strewn grass, a clone of the one in which he was sitting. The grass was a mottled green and tan, no longer the rich green of summer but not yet faded into a dull winter brown. The trees encircling the lawn were already in full winter mode; their limbs were bare and stark, empty.

Dave pitched his baritone voice lower, glancing around to see who might be listening. The low frosted glass dividers between the pod desks didn't provide any real privacy. He had to be careful with his words, especially if someone in the sales organization was nearby. Alisha's boss was a regional sales manager. He, or one of his counterparts from other regions, was often in the headquarters building.

"Of course I'm happy for you," he said. "It's great that you're getting away from Liam. Is the job here a step up?"

"No, it's a lateral move," Alisha replied, "but the company will pay my moving expenses. I was planning on flying out there later this week to look for apartments or condos. I was hoping that you'd help me this weekend?"

"Uh, *this* weekend?" Dave hesitated. "I'm not sure what plans we have this weekend. I . . . um . . . I'll have to check with Sheryl."

"Oh, I thought the two of you did your own thing," Alisha said, her voice now cajoling. "I'm sure you can make time to help me. She won't mind. How many times have you told me she's always busy with her work? I'll let you know when I've scheduled my flights, and you can pick me up from the airport."

Grimacing, Dave recognized that this was why Alisha was such a good salesperson. She didn't take no for an answer—at least not very often. He admired her use of the "presumptive close" with clients, but he was less than thrilled to be on the receiving end of it. Plus, what *would* he say to Sheryl? Somehow, he didn't think his wife would like this very much.

"Dave?" he heard Alisha again. "Where did you go?"

Spinning back around toward the desk, Dave refocused on the conversation. "I'm here. I was just thinking."

"Okay then, I'll let you get back to work. I'll text you with the details later today. Talk soon!" Alisha hung up before he could say no.

Dave let out a deep sigh and slumped forward, dropping his head into his hands. His hands covered his eyes and the burgeoning streaks of silver at his temples. He could almost feel the crisp blue dress shirt that he wore tucked into tan khakis wrinkling as he folded his torso over the desk. Usually preferring to be neat and professional in his appearance, he didn't care just then. He could barely stop himself from groaning.

He felt rather than saw a head pop up over the low wall separating him from the next desk.

His friend and colleague Robert Coleman spoke softly, his voice full of concern. "What was that all about?"

Dave finally looked up and frowned. "You heard?" he asked. *At least it's Robert. He can be trusted.* He hadn't realized Robert was also in town today, but it wasn't surprising. Robert had a similar role to Dave's, although his expertise was in artificial intelligence (AI) rather than network engineering, Dave's specialty. They both were technologists who had been drafted into front-line sales support roles because they were good in front of customers.

Robert nodded. "Some of it. Couldn't help it."

"And you're not curious or nosey, now, are you?" Dave grumbled.

Robert grinned. "One of my best traits."

At nearly six feet seven inches tall, Robert didn't even have to stand up to peer over the low cubicle partition. He was a handsome man, with dark ebony skin and wide-set brown eyes. He kept his black hair closely cropped, unlike Dave who tended to let his hair creep over his collar.

"Alisha is moving to New Jersey," Dave said, shaking his head.

"She is?" Robert gave a long, low whistle. "Well, that's going to make things interesting around here." His deep bass voice was full of dry humor.

Dave made a face at him. "Shut up," he said. "I don't need input from the peanut gallery."

Robert laughed. "No, you need input from a good psychologist," he said. "You've really got a mess now, my friend. What are you going to do?"

"What do you mean, what am I going to do? I guess I'll help Alisha get settled, a little, but there's only so much I can do."

Robert arched a single eyebrow, a skill Dave admired under different circumstances. "And what about Sheryl?" his friend asked.

"What about her? She won't mind me helping a friend," Dave replied defensively. "I've helped friends transferring to New Jersey before, including you, you idiot."

"Yeah . . . but I'm not an attractive, single blonde, who is, may I remind you, twelve or more years younger than your wife," Robert retorted. They had speculated previously that Alisha was probably in her mid-thirties, while both he and Dave were in their early fifties. Sheryl, at fifty, was only a couple of years younger than they were.

Dave scowled. "Crap!"

"Pretty much," Robert agreed cheerfully. "I think you're going to be in a heap of trouble, my man." Chuckling softly, Robert sat all the way down and turned back to his laptop.

Dave glared at the back of Robert's head for several moments before turning back to his own computer. *Robert's right,* Dave thought, *Alisha is a lot younger than Sheryl, who probably isn't going to be thrilled about me helping Alisha, even if she is only a colleague and friend.*

He rolled his shoulders and pulled the proposal he was supposed to be finalizing for an account rep here in New Jersey up on his screen. As he dug into the document, he couldn't help the nagging feeling that Alisha moving here was going to be even more complicated than he thought.

Chapter 2

Sheryl Simmons dropped her fork while finishing up the last of the salad she had brought back from the cafeteria. Bits of salad dressing flew across the desk and onto her light wool suit jacket. *Phew!* she thought wryly, dabbing at the navy fabric with her napkin, *at least it missed my silk blouse. Salad dressing on my blouse doesn't fit my idea of the polished, professional Chief Information Officer at The Diamante.*

Sheryl's office did. But even after two months of inhabiting it, the larger office and fancier desk that had come with her promotion to Chief Information Officer at the boutique investment firm still made her uncomfortable. For one thing, it was too isolated, too cavernous compared to her smaller office that had been close to the cubicle rows. For another, she still thought of it as "Carl's office" and "Carl's desk." After all, it had been Carl Schmidt's space for so long before his sudden resignation in the wake of the extensive layoffs . . . and the nightmarish problems with the Portal Project. She missed Carl's presence, although she was grateful for the occasional conversations they still had.

Sheryl pushed the rest of her salad away, no longer hungry. She had always been lean, but she had lost a bit of weight in recent months, and now her clothes were a little loose. She knew she needed to eat, but she was just too on edge. The holiday weekend with her family had been nice, but things with Dave . . . well, they still hadn't had a chance to talk.

A voice at the door interrupted her thoughts.

"Got a minute?"

Sheryl looked up and saw that it was Keisha Smith. Smiling broadly, she waved her in.

"Sure," she said, glancing at the time on her computer screen. "I've got twenty minutes before my next meeting."

Keisha nodded, slipped into the office, and carefully closed the office door behind her.

Sheryl's eyes widened. It wasn't unusual for the younger woman to stop by with news or questions, but she didn't often close the door. "What's up?" she asked.

"Well, I think we have a bit of a problem," Keisha said quietly, as if there still wasn't enough privacy. Quickly crossing the ten feet or so to the desk, she slid into one of the simple but elegant burgundy chairs in front of her boss.

Keisha didn't seem bothered at all by the imposing bulk of the ornate mahogany desk, although Sheryl still was. If it wasn't so expensive—and tied to Carl—Sheryl would have gotten rid of it on her first day. She would have preferred something simpler and less intimidating both for herself and most of her visitors.

"Another problem with the Portal Project?" Sheryl asked. The Portal Project was a key company initiative that Keisha was assigned to. It was also the project that had nearly cratered Sheryl's career, and it had been the culminating blow in Carl's. Keisha had been instrumental in bringing the problems with the project to light and, thank God, in helping to solve them. Still, the portal's release had had to be postponed by almost a year, much to the chagrin of the company's president and the head of sales.

"I hope we're not talking more delays," Sheryl added warily.

"No, not really," her protégé answered.

"Not really? I don't like 'not really.' We can't afford more delays, Keisha. We're skating on thin ice as it is." Sheryl couldn't stop the edge that crept into her voice.

"I know." Keisha dipped her head somberly. She was wearing her hair loose today, but she had straightened the natural curls into a smooth, sleek wave that fell below her shoulders. When Sheryl looked more closely, she could see that Keisha's café-au-lait skin was paler than usual, despite the artful makeup she wore.

"You look upset," she observed.

"I am," the programmer affirmed quietly, then cleared her throat. "I found something that I don't know what to do with. I've been worried about it all weekend."

"You could have called me."

"Yeah, but I didn't want to disturb your holiday. You had family in." Keisha's voice was soft and gentle.

Sheryl nodded. "Thanks for that. So, what did you find?"

"Well, remember when we were having trouble accessing the CRM system?"

"Sure," Sheryl said. "You couldn't connect to that system because the outside vendor had created some kind of firewall to prevent API calls, right? But we got that resolved."

"Yes, that's right," Keisha agreed, appreciating Sheryl's terrific memory. "But it looks like we didn't solve *all* of the problems."

"What do you mean?" Sheryl asked, leaning on her forearms, her hands clasped tightly together.

"Well, it seems like we have access to most of the system like we should . . . but I'm not sure we can access all of it. I ran across some sections of the database that look like they are encrypted and not visible in the application," Keisha explained. "I'm not sure. I can't really see into it, but the index files showed some fields that I'm not seeing."

Furrows appeared under the wispy bangs of Sheryl's dark brown hair. She clasped her hands together in front of her chin.

"Could they just be fields that were indexed and aren't there anymore?" she asked, going into problem-solving mode. "Are the index files corrupted or out of date?"

"I thought of that, too," Keisha said, drawing her eyebrows together. "But I don't think so. The dates are current. I think the fields are real."

"So, what does that mean?"

"I don't know," Keisha said, "but something feels off. Like, umm, someone's hiding something."

Sheryl took a deep breath and tucked her chin-length hair behind one ear. The pale-blue silk blouse she wore under her suit jacket made her hazel eyes look more blue than gray but couldn't hide the fatigue in them. A thin gold chain hung around her neck, and small gold hoops dropped from her earlobes. Conservative adornments compared to Keisha's, reflecting the difference in the two women's positions and personalities.

Keisha waited expectantly.

"What could someone be hiding and why?" Sheryl asked, almost to herself.

"I don't know, boss lady," Keisha responded, with a bit more of her normal sassiness. "That's why I'm talking to you."

Sheryl made a face. "Gee, thanks," she said dryly. "What makes you think I have all the answers?"

"Because you usually do, and if you don't, you know where to find 'em," Keisha replied promptly, then hesitated. "Umm . . . I mean, I got the goods on the technical stuff, but you know the lay of the land around here better than I do."

Sheryl smiled. Yes, Keisha was a brilliant software designer and programmer, and each woman respected the fact that the other had earned her position through hard work, strategic thinking, and sheer tenacity. "I'm a bit stumped on this one," Sheryl admitted, feeling her already taut shoulders tighten further. "I guess I'm going to have to think about it."

Keisha nodded, her eyebrows sliding back into a more relaxed position. "Okay, then, I'll leave you to your thinking."

"I'll probably have more questions," Sheryl warned.

"I'll answer what I can." Keisha smiled a little. She started to rise from her chair but hesitated. "Should I keep digging to see what else I can find?"

Sheryl frowned. "I guess so," she said slowly, "but be careful. If someone really is hiding something . . . we don't want to make them nervous." Then she let out a self-deprecating chuckle. "That sounded like something out of a spy novel." She gave Keisha a crooked smile.

This time, Keisha didn't smile back. "I'm not sure you're too far off with that."

Sheryl stiffened and leaned back in her seat. "You think it's that serious?"

"Yeah, it might be. I *do* think I should be careful. There's something about this whole thing that ain't right."

Sheryl bit her lower lip, unsure of how to respond to that. She had started encouraging people to pay attention to their intuition after her own experiences that fall, but the idea that someone might be hiding something nefarious seemed far-fetched to her. There were so many checks and balances in the investment world, most dictated by the Securities and Exchange Commission (SEC). And, The Diamante had its own internal safeguards and protocols everyone was trained to follow, although they were not as robust as those in larger, more prominent firms. *How could anyone create hidden fields, much less keep them hidden? And why?*

Sheryl looked appraisingly at Keisha. The younger woman didn't seem hysterical or overwrought, although she was clearly worried. For all her youth and flamboyance, Keisha had a good head on her shoulders.

Or does she? The image of Keisha screaming at her a few months ago popped unbidden into Sheryl's head. *Keisha hadn't been rational then, had she?* Sheryl flushed a little at her own thoughts; she knew full well that Keisha had had good cause for her anger then.

Watching their colleagues being unceremoniously marched out of the office by security guards during the layoff was enough to make anyone furious. It had even enraged Sheryl, who rarely allowed herself to get angry. Still, Keisha was the one who had yelled at her and then stalked out of the office, staying away for three days. It had been hard for Sheryl to convince Human Resources to let Keisha even keep her job after that, especially in the midst of such severe layoffs. *Could it be that Keisha is being a bit overdramatic again?*

Looking at Keisha carefully, Sheryl didn't believe that her associate was. Keisha's eyes were clear and focused. She was dressed with her normal flair in a bright turquoise blouse tucked into black pants with a wide, shiny black leather belt encircling her tiny waist. Her jewelry was big and bold, matching her makeup perfectly. Other than the faint shadows under her eyes, which showed her sleepless weekend, she looked perfectly in control.

"Okay, be careful, then," Sheryl finally said. "I don't want you to get in any trouble, but try to see what else you can figure out. Right now, frankly, we don't have enough information to even ask reasonable questions."

Keisha nodded, looking relieved that Sheryl was taking her seriously. "Got it, boss," she said, rising from the chair.

Sheryl noted that Keisha's step was lighter as she headed toward the door, and she sighed silently as she watched her walk toward the wooden office door. But Sheryl's mind was racing ahead. *What now? Don't I already have enough problems without adding this mystery?* She exhaled deeply, a feeling of dread snaking up her spine.

Chapter 3

Alisha Carson slammed the cell phone down on her desk a little too hard. She winced, hoping she hadn't damaged it.

Damn it. She'd thought Dave would be happier about her moving— or at least more supportive. After all, it had been his idea to apply for a job at Corporate, to get away from Liam.

Alisha's frown deepened. *Liam sure isn't happy.* He had accused her of bailing on him when he first heard she had requested the transfer. She was certain that he had tried to stop it, but apparently he didn't have as much sway in the company hierarchy as he thought. Thank goodness for that!

She looked around the small apartment in Lexington Hills, California, that she called home. Yeah, it was reasonably close to San Jose, her office, and her customers, but it was tiny and not particularly nice. She had tried to spruce it up with bright paint and cheerful pillows and lamps, but it was old and small. The furniture was mostly hand-me-downs or thrift shop fare and was tired.

When she first rented the place nearly ten years ago, she hadn't been able to afford something more luxurious. And by the time she had worked her way into a more lucrative role, she had been too busy with work and its related traveling to bother to move. She'd definitely get a more comfortable and attractive place in New Jersey. The question was where.

She felt the tiniest twinge of guilt when she thought about how she had manipulated Dave into picking her up at the airport. She hoped that he would follow through. She was almost certain that he was too nice a guy not to, as long as he was in town. Alisha made a mental note: she'd have to check his travel schedule before she booked her flights. She knew from experience that would be easy enough to do on the team's calendar.

By now, Alisha had worked on enough accounts with Dave to have access to that information, though technically they were on different teams—for now. She had been hoping to get assigned to the same territory as Dave, his primary one, but that hadn't happened. Yet.

The sales territory that had been open for her lateral move was in the mid-Atlantic region, not the New England one where Dave was officially assigned. Still, technical sales staff supported larger areas, often crossing territory boundaries. That's how she met Dave in the first place. He wasn't assigned to California, nor was Robert, but they had both been needed on a big Silicon Valley project that she had initiated. Alisha was very technical herself, but sometimes it helped to bring in the big guns, so to speak.

And Dave and Robert were the top engineers at LSM in their respective areas of expertise. They weren't restricted by territory, as she was now and would continue to be in the East. She secretly hoped she'd be given some accounts that would require Dave's expertise. *And if not, I'll find them.*

Shaking herself out of her reverie, Alisha pulled up the team schedule in one browser window and her flight options in the other. Good. Dave was available on Thursday afternoon. He only had day trips this week. Working quickly, she locked in the flights and sent an immediate meeting request to Dave for the pickup timeframe. Perfect. He couldn't get waylaid by another meeting. Now, she just had to tell her mother.

She tugged on the end of her ponytail, which held her naturally blonde hair away from her face when she worked. Alisha's hair was exceptionally long, falling nearly to her waist. It was also thick and wavy, which meant that it almost always had to be contained in some way. She knew she had a bad habit of playing with it, especially when she was nervous or upset. She'd learned to control that tendency in front of customers. Still, it had always been her unconscious "tell" when playing poker with her father and half-brothers.

Sitting at the small white desk she had tucked in a corner of the open room of her living space, she stared out the window. Across the apartment building's parking lot lay a small park. Empty now, the park would be full of moms and toddlers later in the morning and school-age children in the afternoon. Watching the children play was both enjoyable and bittersweet. A look of irritation swept across her face. She didn't need that distraction now, even if her own biological clock was ticking away.

Alisha glanced down at her phone. Her mother had to be told. *Should I call her now and get it over with?* Her mother would be at work at this time of day. Denise Carson worked at an insurance agency, although she wasn't an agent. Alisha had never been exactly sure what she did. It seemed like an admin role to her, but her mother insisted it was more complicated than that.

What Alisha did know was that her mother hadn't wanted to put the time and energy into taking the necessary tests to become an agent, despite having every ability to do so except will. Her mother had held few ambitions in life other than to be a wife.

Not a mother, a wife.

Not that she had been a bad mother. After all, Alisha was all she had after the divorce, but still . . .

Deciding that it would be better to call her mother at work, where she was less likely to make a fuss, Alisha picked up the phone and dialed her mother's cell.

As usual, Denise Carson picked up the phone right away. "Alisha! So nice to hear from you. Is everything okay?"

Alisha rolled her eyes. Her mother started almost every conversation this way. Was everything okay? It irritated her that the older woman thought there was something wrong all the time. She always expected the worst.

"Hey, Mom. I'm fine. Everything is fine. I just wanted to share some news with you."

"Oh, good," Denise answered. "What's the news? Do you have a new boyfriend?"

Alisha stifled a groan. That was another thing. Her mother was always interested in her love life. Even though Denise had been divorced from Alisha's father for more than thirty years, she never gave up on romance for Alisha. Or for herself, for that matter, except that Denise would never marry again. She didn't want to give up the Carson name nor the generous alimony that Samuel Carson still paid. Not that the Carson name meant anything special, but her mother seemed to think it did.

"No, Mom, I'm not calling about a boyfriend. I wouldn't bother you at work for that!" Alisha gently scolded her mother.

"Oh, it's no bother, honey. I'm always happy to talk to you," Denise answered in the well-modulated tone she used at the office. "So, what's your news?"

"I got a new job, Mom," Alisha began.

"Ooohhh, that's great, honey! I didn't know you were looking."

"Well, I wasn't looking, Mom, not really," she replied carefully. "But an opportunity came up for a new role within LSM Consulting that I wanted to check out. I applied, not thinking for a minute that I would get it . . . and I got it!" Alisha tried to inject the appropriate amount of enthusiasm into the words, but she could tell that her voice was tight and a little higher than usual. She tugged on her ponytail again.

"That's great!" her mother cooed into the phone. Alisha could picture her mother's bright smile, the same one she saw in her own mirror. "Another promotion!"

"Uh, no, not a promotion," Alisha quickly corrected. "A lateral transfer, to a different region."

Alisha could almost hear her mother frown. She knew what was coming. Despite her full-time job and an active social life, Denise Carson was inordinately involved in Alisha's life. Alisha had dinner with her every Sunday and spent every holiday with her. Sometimes one or more of her mother's friends would join them, but usually it was just the two of them. After the divorce, Alisha was all that Denise had. Sure, her mother dated, but casually. She never let anyone get too close.

"A transfer?" Denise's voice wobbled suddenly. "A transfer to where?"

Alisha's head dropped back in exasperation. She let out a breath. This was going to be the bad part. "To New Jersey, Mom."

"New Jersey . . ." Her mother's voice trailed off. Alisha could visualize the tears forming in her eyes. Denise was a first-class crier.

Here it comes . . . three, two, one—

"—But you can't move to New Jersey, Alisha. What about me? What about our Sundays? You can't leave me here alone."

With each sentence, the pitch and volume of Denise's voice had risen so that the last words came out in a wail, albeit a soft one. Alisha pictured her mother, smartly dressed in business casual attire, perfectly coiffed, sitting at her desk in the posh agency office, now starting to cry.

"Mom," Alisha hissed urgently. "Calm down. You'll make a scene in the office!" Now she regretted calling her mother at work. Of course this was how her mother would respond. Her hope that being in the office would have toned her mother's drama down evaporated.

"You're right. I will make a scene," Denise's voice firmed, taking on a steely note that Alisha knew all too well. "I can't do that. I'll call you back after work. Better yet, you will come for dinner tonight, and we'll get this all sorted out. New Jersey. Hmph."

Alisha shook her head. *Oh boy.* She was in for it now. Denise's emotions could turn on a dime and often did. She recognized that her mother had shifted into attack mode. *Ugh!*

"Mom, I can't come over for dinner tonight," she hedged, pausing for a moment before realizing that her mother had hung up. Alisha's face scrunched into a rueful smile. She knew where she had learned some of her own tricks. *I'll guess I'll be going to dinner at Mom's.*

She turned back to her computer. It was early enough to go into the office, not even 9:00 am, but she decided against it. *Liam won't be happy, but who cares about him anymore?* She laughed at herself. *I should care. Liam could still find a way to retaliate.*

But she could work faster and more efficiently from home. She had some proposals to finalize. These were deals she'd been working on for weeks and, in one case, months. She wasn't about to hand them off as easy money to Liam or another associate. No, she couldn't leave for New Jersey without finishing them up. Plus, she needed at least one of them to close to make her quota for the year.

Alisha pulled up the first file and started reviewing it. It was not a deal that she had worked on with Dave. *Just as well*, she thought. She needed to focus on her own stuff. There would be time enough to worry about Dave when she got to New Jersey.

Chapter 4

By the time the end of the workday arrived, Sheryl's eyes hurt. They burned from the lengthy time in front of the computer screen, but she resisted the urge to rub them. She didn't want to smear her eye makeup. From the activity outside of her door, she could tell many of the fifty or so people on her floor—all of them part of her team—were shuffling down the corridors and into the classy, mostly glass elevators to descend the three stories back into the real world.

Sheryl glanced through the report she had prepared on The Diamante's pending infrastructure upgrade. Rick Sutton, Vice President of the network engineering group, had done the heavy lifting on this one, but she had worked hard to make it coherent for the aggressive and savvy president Todd Fisher and, eventually, the demanding members of the board. As good as he was at other aspects of his job, Rick was no writer. As his supervisor, Sheryl often found herself cleaning up his work before it could be passed along to anyone else, much less Todd.

And this was an important document. Sheryl could not afford to forget that infrastructure, particularly security, had been a major part of Carl's downfall. A significant security breach last summer had upset everyone within the organization as well as many of the customers who had been impacted. Fortunately, no money had been lost and few sensitive details had been leaked. Still, it had been extremely embarrassing.

Even though Todd had fired Rick's predecessor, that incident, followed by the delays on the Portal Project, had accelerated Carl's "retirement." Sheryl was very well aware that she was herself on a short leash; her age, sex, and the fact that she was Carl's protégé all were factors against her.

It didn't matter that Sheryl felt young, healthy, and energetic. It mattered little that she worked out and generally took care of herself. Sheryl had turned fifty in May, and the fifties were a precarious time in the corporate world. Companies were always looking for someone younger, brighter, and less expensive. Sheryl strongly suspected that she was, for now, a beneficiary of being less expensive. She was certain they weren't paying her nearly what they had paid Carl. Not that her experience warranted it, but she secretly wondered if she was being paid less than a male in her position would be, whatever their experience.

She shook her head, reminding herself not to focus on things she couldn't control. *Stay positive!* She had certainly been happy with her compensation package when it had been offered to her—definitely an upgrade. So had her husband, Dave.

While in the process of turning off her computer and packing the evening's work in her briefcase, she felt a presence at the door. Her smile faltered a bit when she saw Jim Leaders.

Jim was one of Sheryl's peers, the head of Client Services, which most other organizations called Sales. He was responsible for the team that brought new clients into The Diamante as well as the support teams that kept them happy. Most of his subordinates were financial advisors or administrative people who handled the minutiae of customers' portfolios. Jim had been brought on board by Todd, shortly after he had joined the firm three years ago.

Sheryl mostly got along with Jim, but there was something about him that made her vaguely uneasy. Still, she made sure the corners of her mouth curled upward as Jim smiled at her.

"Hey Sheryl," he said in his deep, booming voice that reminded her of her high school's football coach.

"Hey yourself, Jim," she replied evenly.

"I was on my way out when I noticed you were still here," he said. Sheryl observed he wore a gray wool overcoat and a matching herringbone scarf around his neck. He held a stylish black leather briefcase in his left hand, while his right was propped against the metal frame of her office doorway.

"Oh, I can see that," Sheryl said uncertainly. "What's up?" *Why is he here, and today of all days?* she thought. *He rarely stops by my office anymore.* Although he had checked in almost daily for the first few weeks after the project deadline had been postponed.

"Just thought I'd check and see how the Portal Project is coming along. I've heard good things from my staff, but I wanted to hear it from the horse's mouth."

"You calling me a horse, Jim?" she said lightly.

Jim chortled. "You're a funny one, Sheryl!"

Jim's appearance was often very sophisticated. His dark blond hair was carefully groomed with, she guessed, either gel or hairspray. He had a handsome face with strong features, gray-blue eyes, and a nose that was slightly bulbous at the end. But sometimes, like now, his demeanor didn't quite match his outward appearance.

"Maybe you should trust your team . . . my team tells me the project is coming along nicely," she answered. "On schedule and within the new budget."

Jim's eyes narrowed, as if he didn't believe her. But he quickly gave her another one of his big salesy smiles and nodded. "Great! Great!"

Sheryl all but shuddered. While she had learned to like Jim much of the time, he occasionally had a false joviality that sometimes made her skin crawl.

"Yup, it is great!" she said, matching his overly enthusiastic tone. "I am in touch with the team almost daily. We'll get there. No need for you to worry. I'll let you know if anything important comes up."

"Good. Good." Jim's head bobbed in time with his words. "I'll be on my way, then. Have a good night!"

Dropping his hand from the door frame, he gave her a brief wave and disappeared down the hallway, without waiting for her response.

Sheryl gazed thoughtfully after him. That had been an odd visit. *Maybe he was just checking, but . . .* her thoughts darted back to Keisha and her suspicions. *Was the visit a coincidence?* The uneasy feeling pervaded. She was glad she had been preparing to leave, even though it was earlier than usual. She wanted to get out of the office.

She stood up and smoothed the front of her wool skirt. Gathering her black leather purse and matching briefcase, both gifts from Dave, she walked to the small closet to grab her burgundy scarf, camel coat, and a few other personal belongings. It was another perk of inheriting Carl's office.

She paused at her office doorway, looking down the long aisle that separated the cubicles and smaller offices along the outside wall. She relaxed when she saw that Jim was nowhere in sight, and she hurried out of the building.

By shortly after seven, Sheryl was home in her sweatpants, a fleece top, and cozy slippers, sipping a glass of her favorite Pinot Noir in the kitchen. The drive to her home in Lebanon, New Jersey, took just shy of thirty minutes in her comfortable Lexus sedan and had helped her relax a bit. Sheryl always listened to music when she drove, tonight choosing a mellow channel on SiriusXM radio. Enjoying the latest bit of warmth that the wine brought down her throat, she wondered what she could put together quickly for dinner.

It dawned on her that she didn't know whether she was getting dinner only for herself or if Dave would be there, too. They hadn't talked that morning. In fact, they hadn't talked much all weekend. She sighed and idly rubbed the back of her neck with her free hand.

I guess it doesn't matter. I'll only worry about feeding myself.

But Sheryl didn't move. She sat at the kitchen island, her thoughts bouncing irrationally between Keisha, Jim, and Dave. *What if Keisha is right? What if someone is doing something illegal? It could bring down the whole firm. Why isn't Dave talking to me? Is he hiding something? Is everyone hiding something?*

It was only slightly past seven, but the late November sky was already fully dark. The only light in the room was a single lamp, dimly lit, that hung above her head, and the stove clock's blue light. The darkness suited her mood. She couldn't quite summon the energy to rise.

She stared at the clock.

7:12.

7:17.

7:23.

Sheryl heard the thrum of the garage door going up. *Ah, he is home. But . . . will he talk?*

Dave had been avoiding conversation for weeks now, ever since they had started arguing about her work and how she was handling the repercussions of the layoffs. He had strongly disagreed with her decisions to acknowledge and recognize the feelings of the remaining staff, and she had been hurt by his lack of support and understanding. He'd been happy with her newly achieved salary, but that was about it.

Of course, some of the tension may have started before that. Sadly, Sheryl wasn't quite sure, but she did know that some of the distance in their marriage was her fault. She got caught up with work; they both did. Sometimes, that didn't leave a lot of room for their relationship. It hadn't been as much of a priority.

She wondered, as she waited for the inside garage door to open, where they were headed now. *Can we make this work?*

Her gaze idly shifted toward the adjacent room. Even in the dim light, she could see the collage of pictures on the wall that stretched between the kitchen windows and the French doors in the great room. She knew the contents of those pictures well. Some of her favorites, nearly twenty-five years old now, were of their wedding. She and Dave had been so hopeful, so *in love* with each other and with life. Other pictures chronicled their various vacations, everything from ski slopes in the Canadian Rockies to hiking in Hawaii. They had always been athletic and active, and despite both being in their fifties now, they still were adventurous.

Just not as much with each other.

The rest of the great room was filled with comfortable furniture arranged between the tall stone fireplace on one side, the French doors on the other, and a gigantic entertainment center in between two tall windows on the side wall. She smiled inwardly as she thought about the entertainment unit. That had, of course, been Dave's idea. He had only convinced her that they should buy it after ceding space on the shelves for her books and other decorative items. It had worked out, though. The room was a lovely blend of their personalities, both individually and as a couple. It showed the best of both of them, she realized.

Just then Dave stepped into the house, carrying a leather computer backpack over one shoulder and his phone in his hand. He stopped abruptly when he saw her, seemingly surprised.

"You're here," he said needlessly. "What are you doing sitting in the dark?"

"I'm here . . ." she echoed softly, "and it's not so dark."

"You're early. I was surprised to see your car."

Sheryl shrugged. "Yeah, I'm a little earlier than usual. I guess I was hoping that you'd be home. I wanted to see you, to talk."

A look crossed Dave's face so quickly that she couldn't quite categorize it. *Was it guilt?*

He shook his head. "I'm beat," he huffed. "It's been a long day after a long weekend. Can't it wait?"

"Wait?" Without her meaning to, Sheryl's voice abruptly rose in pitch and volume. "I've been waiting for weeks, Dave. We haven't really talked since that last big argument almost two weeks ago. We haven't settled it. We haven't done anything. I don't want to keep going on like this, avoiding one another, only talking about things that don't matter."

"Just let it go, Sheryl. Why do we have to rehash everything?" Dave sounded utterly disgusted. "I didn't agree with your decision to hold that damn memorial service, but you did it anyway. It worked out okay, so do you have to say 'I told you so'? Is that what you want to talk about?"

Sheryl recoiled at the vehemence of his voice. The "damn memorial service" had been one of the ways that Sheryl helped her staff cope with the loss of a large number of their colleagues during the layoffs. It had been a forum to remember and honor the people who were no longer there. The idea had been controversial but also hugely successful. The productivity on Sheryl's teams had rebounded much faster than other areas of the company, so much so that her peers had ended up holding "memorial services" of their own . . . with Sheryl's guidance.

"Really?" Sheryl responded sharply. "That's all you think I want to talk about, to say I told you so? Come on, Dave. I've never been like that. We have a lot more to talk about than that one argument, even though it was a big one." She paused, thoughtfully, her voice lowering. "I think it was a symptom of something else, but I can't figure out what. It's almost like . . . like you are pushing me away."

Her breath caught in her throat.

Yes, that's it. He HAS been pushing me away.

Dave started to shake his head when his wife cut back in.

"—No, you *are* pushing me away," she followed up firmly. "And I want to know why, and how we can fix it."

Dave glared at her, anger filling his dark brown eyes. "Geez, Sheryl." His tone was an exasperated sneer. "It's so nice to be welcomed home at the end of the day by a loving wife. Great to see you, too." Giving her a long glare, he marched past her, unslinging the backpack from his shoulder. His eyes shifted straight ahead, his posture rigid. Clearly, there would be no talking that evening.

As he stalked away, Sheryl felt the heat spiraling up her spine as her shoulders and jaw tightened. Tears welled in her eyes, for underneath the anger was the pain, the great gaping pain of rejection.

It took every ounce of her self-control not to run after him, to scream at him, to make him feel her pain. She knew deep down that it wouldn't help, that it wasn't the right thing to do. She needed to calm herself down. She had already been wound up because of the new developments at work, and now this. Somehow, she had to keep the two separate.

Calm. Breathe. Slow, deep breaths.

Sheryl sat for several minutes, struggling to take in great, rhythmic belly breaths. Tilting her head back slightly, she gazed upward. She closed her eyes, trying to summon her higher self, to feel the connection of that wise, inner knowing. It was still a new process for her. She had deepened her spiritual journey during all the chaos at work during the last few months, needing to feel anchored and supported.

As she grounded herself, she was simply yet powerfully reminded that through expanding her meditation, prayer, and journaling practices, and incorporating breath work into her routine, she had found support and comfort. She had discovered just how powerful that connection to her higher self was. She just wished she could turn it on like a faucet. *Someday.*

She drew in a few more calming breaths with long, slow exhales in between.

Four counts in.

Eight counts out.

Stay in the light.

Sheryl started to come back to herself, feeling her feet tucked against the rung of the counter stool. Her jaw loosened a bit. She felt her hands slowly unclench. She hadn't even realized that they had been balled into tight fists. She heard her breathing become smoother, easier.

Other sounds intruded on her awareness: Dave banging doors and drawers, rustling as he changed his clothes. The gentle whir of the refrigerator.

Food. I need food, she thought. *He'll need to eat, too. I might as well get something out.*

She smiled at her last thought. *Progress!* A few months ago, she wouldn't have considered for a moment getting food out for him after his display of anger and what felt like contempt. She had to admit that she was reluctant; it still seemed like rewarding bad behavior. She hadn't quite gotten her head around that. Her newfound mindfulness, encouraged by her dear friend Cindy, taught her not to lash out in anger, not to punish, but how did one communicate then that some behavior was not acceptable?

Taking one last deep breath, she got up from the stool and headed to the freezer. She and Dave shared the cooking duties, and they always made more than one meal at a time. It made dinner during the week so much easier. All they had to do was pull something out of the freezer and reheat it.

Bending over the drawer-style freezer, she pulled out a container of turkey chili big enough for both of them. After sliding it into the microwave, she went back to the refrigerator for salad fixings and cheese.

As the microwave chimed, Sheryl heard Dave come downstairs and go into his office without acknowledging her.

She glanced at her glass of wine, nearly empty now. *Another glass won't hurt,* she thought fiercely, and she grabbed the bottle. After filling it only halfway, she focused carefully on the task of dinner, not allowing her mind to wander back to the conflict. She practiced her mindfulness, paying full attention to what she was doing. She used the simple chores to further de-escalate her emotions.

When the meal was ready, she put Dave's chili and salad on a tray and walked to his office. The door was closed. Usually that meant "Do not disturb." She hesitated but knocked anyway. She thought she heard a mumbled invitation to enter, and, carefully balancing the tray, she swung the door open.

"I brought you—" she started, then she stopped when she realized Dave was on the phone. He hadn't told her to come in.

". . . a real bitch!" her husband was saying.

Sheryl gasped. *Is he talking about me?*

Her husband swung around, realizing that she was in the room. His face darkened, and his mouth opened. She knew she didn't want to hear what he was going to say.

"I brought you dinner," she explained. She slid the tray onto his desk and practically ran out of the room.

Chapter 5

Dave glared at the hastily closed door.

". . . Dave, what was that?" He heard Robert's voice from a distance and realized he had pulled the phone away from his ear.

Pushing his hand back up, Dave tried to return his mind to the conversation. "It was Sheryl, bringing in my dinner."

"That was nice of her," Robert said cheerfully.

"No, it was manipulative of her," Dave retorted. "She's trying to make me feel guilty."

There was a pause before Robert responded. "Really, that doesn't sound like the Sheryl I know."

So, Robert thinks he's now an expert on Sheryl, having met her a few times? Of course, Robert and his wife had also joined Dave and Sheryl for dinner and had been to their home a few times. Still, that wasn't enough to *know* someone.

"Ha!" Dave said with a snort. "That's what you think."

"What do you have to feel guilty about?" Robert tried another tack.

"Nothing," Dave answered abruptly. "I'm just sick of manipulative women."

"More than one manipulative woman?" Robert's voice was knowing. "Let me guess . . . Alisha."

Dave groaned. "Do you know what she did? She actually scheduled time on my calendar to pick her up on Thursday!"

"I assume we're talking about Alisha now, not Sheryl?"

"Why would Sheryl need to be picked up on Thursday?" Dave snapped. "Of course Alisha."

Robert whistled. "Are you going to do it?"

"What else am I supposed to do?" Dave asked. "She asked me to . . . I didn't say no."

"But you didn't say yes, either," Robert supplied, quickly filling in the gaps.

Dave hesitated, then sighed. "You're right, but you know how she is," he said defensively.

"I sure do," Robert laughed. "I've seen her in action. She's good. Maybe too good? Sounds like she's got you boxed into a corner."

"It's just a ride from the airport," Dave countered. "No mountains, no molehills, no boxes. What were we talking about, anyway?"

Robert chuckled. "The Rayburg account? We have to deal with Pauline somehow. She's pissed about the scope change."

"Forget it. I'm not in the mood to talk about any more difficult women!" Dave growled. "Let's regroup in the morning. We don't have to reach out to Pauline tonight."

"No, but if that's the case, it should be handled first thing tomorrow. She does deserve an answer, even if it's not one she's going to like."

"I know. I know," said Dave irritably. "We need more time to solve the latest glitch in her project. I'll think about what that will take, and we can compare notes in the morning."

"Gotcha," Robert replied. "Try to have a good evening . . . and enjoy your dinner."

Dave scowled again. He knew Robert was taunting him. "Yeah, yeah, funny guy. I'm hanging up now."

He heard Robert laughing as he disconnected the call.

Dave sat back in his ergonomic leather chair, looking at the cooling chili, the cheese perfectly melted on top, exactly the way he liked it. *Damn it.* Sheryl was trying to make him feel guilty, but he was hungry. He dug in. He knew he would have to talk to her sometime, but not tonight. *Definitely not tonight.*

He finished his meal within ten minutes, practically inhaling the chili and salad. He hadn't realized how hungry he had been.

Satiated, he relaxed into his chair, enjoying the look and feel of his office as he usually did. It was a small room nestled off the foyer, close to the front door. It had only one tall window that looked out over the lawn and street beyond it. A row of built-in bookcases and cabinets lined the back wall.

His matching mahogany desk, not overly large, sat perpendicular to the hallway door about halfway down the interior wall. It faced the window, and he could easily spin his chair around to reach the shelves and cabinets behind him. The walls were dark green, his favorite color, and a rich area rug covered the hardwood floors. This was one place in the house where he could escape uninterrupted.

Except for tonight. *Why had Sheryl walked in like that? And what had she heard?* It was unusual for her to barge in. She always respected his privacy, as he did with her office in the smallest of the upstairs bedrooms. He shifted uncomfortably in his chair. He knew he had been an ass earlier. It was just . . . what? There really wasn't an excuse, except he hated that she had been lying in wait for him to get home, for the sole purpose of nagging him again.

He looked at the tray and empty dishes. *I could at least say thank you.* He picked them up and, juggling them carefully, opened the door and headed to the kitchen. He expected the room to be empty. It wasn't.

Sheryl was sitting on a kitchen stool, much as she had been when he got home except the wine was put away. Her hands were wrapped around a steaming mug, the tangy aroma of peppermint tea gently permeating the room. She looked up in surprise when he walked in but quickly ducked her head and avoided his gaze. He noticed her knuckles whiten.

Placing the tray next to the sink, Dave turned toward her. "I'm sorry," he said quietly. "I shouldn't have snapped at you like that when I came in."

She glanced up. Her eyes, just visible in the dimly lit room, looked red-edged. *Has she been crying?* She nodded but didn't speak.

He turned back to the sink and quickly dealt with the dishes and tray. "Thanks for making me dinner and bringing it in," he said over his shoulder.

He felt, more than heard, a soft snort.

"What?" he asked.

There was a long pause.

"To whom were you calling me a bitch?" she finally said, her voice slightly hoarse.

Yup, she's been crying, he thought. He shook his head but didn't turn around. "No one. I wasn't calling you a bitch. I was talking about some-one else. A client. To Robert."

"Oh," Sheryl responded warily. "I thought . . . well, I thought you were talking about me."

"You shouldn't have barged in like that," Dave shot back.

Sheryl stiffened. "Oh, of course it's my fault," she said, her voice dripping with sarcasm. "Heaven forbid I barge into your sacred space with your dinner. Honestly, I thought I heard you say to come in."

Dave clenched his fists but took a deep breath. He really didn't want to fight more tonight. "You're right. I'm sorry. I do appreciate you bringing my dinner in. You didn't have to do that."

He could see her chest expand as she took a long breath. Then she let it out with a long sigh.

"You're welcome . . ." Her voice trailed off.

He could tell she wanted to say something else. He waited for a few seconds, giving her the chance, but she remained silent.

"Look, I know we need to talk, but we're both tired now," he said quietly. "It's not a good time."

She gave him a measured look. "It's never a good time, Dave."

He looked uncomfortable but nodded. "I'm not sure . . . No, let's not get into it. Can we just plan to talk this weekend?"

"It's only Monday. Are you out of town this week?"

"No, I'm in town, although I have a couple of day trips, tomorrow and Wednesday. I might be late getting back," he answered, hoping that was enough to forestall her.

Her lips thinned. "Hmph. What about Thursday?"

He grimaced, feeling his stomach drop. "Umm, I have to pick up a colleague from California at the airport Thursday," he said.

Sheryl raised her eyebrows. "Really? Why wouldn't she get her own car?"

It took a second for Dave to realize Sheryl had said "she." He quickly debated challenging her assumption, then thought better of it. He was wary enough about Alisha and her presumptuous behavior that he didn't want to sound defensive. *Thank you, Robert, for putting* that *idea in my head.* He should be happy that Alisha was getting away from Liam. He hated to see her—or any woman, for that matter—treated like that. No, he *was* happy about it.

Mentally shrugging, he focused on Sheryl.

"*She* asked me to pick her up so we can go over a few things about a project at Apple," he said. "I assume she'll get her own car on Friday."

Sheryl looked at him with narrowed eyes. She hesitated. "Odd time to come in from California," she observed. "Thursday? Why would she need a car on Friday? Is she staying the weekend here?"

"Yes, she's staying the weekend. She's actually transferring to the home office soon," he answered cautiously. He kept his face and eyes carefully impassive. He watched as Sheryl slid off the counter stool.

"And will you be seeing her over the weekend?" Sheryl asked sharply, leaning slightly toward him.

"Uh . . . not sure yet," he said.

"Is this the same 'colleague' that you've been playing golf with in California?" Sheryl snapped.

"One of them," he answered, not quite truthfully. He had played with others—Liam and Robert—but he had played alone with Alisha a couple of times while she tried to help him with his game.

He could tell that Sheryl didn't quite believe him. She looked at him assessingly, as if to determine whether or not he was lying. He never lied to Sheryl, or . . . rarely. They had always been honest with each other. He felt, well, he just wasn't quite comfortable telling Sheryl too much about Alisha. *She might take it the wrong way.*

Sheryl's fingers tapped the countertop in a rhythmic pattern. Finally she nodded, apparently deciding to accept what he said.

"Okay. Well, I guess we'll have to wait until the weekend to talk," she said. "Unless there's something more that you want to tell me about *her* now?"

"There's nothing *more* to tell," he said irritably. "She's a colleague and a bit of a friend. We're working together on a few projects. She's asked for my help. That's it."

I hope I didn't sound too defensive, he thought.

Sheryl was looking at him again, probing with her eyes. He saw the alertness, her caution, in her posture. Her fingers kept drumming.

Finally, she nodded. "Okay, I'll accept that. You've never lied to me. We don't do that. But I suspect that *she* is something else to talk about this weekend."

He rolled his eyes. "I told you it's nothing."

"Good, then it won't be a problem to talk about her," Sheryl said crisply. "You're welcome for dinner, by the way. I guess I'll head on up and get ready for bed. As you said, I'm tired."

He frowned, unhappy at the implication behind her words.

He turned back to the sink. "Okay. I'll finish cleaning up the kitchen and be up in a bit. I have to respond to a couple more emails, but I won't be long," he answered.

"Good night, then." He heard Sheryl slide the stool into place and pick up her mug. Her rubber-soled shoes squeaked quietly as she pivoted. He barely heard her leave.

Dave stood stiffly at the sink until he heard the water in the master bathroom start. Then, and only then, his shoulders sagged. *Robert was right. Sheryl is certainly not happy about any of this.* Of course, he didn't know if he was happy about any of this either.

He had a bad feeling that things were about to get a lot more complicated.

Chapter 6

Alisha arrived at her mother's home promptly at 6:30, grateful that she had been able to navigate the traffic in only forty minutes. On a weekend, she could make it in about twenty-two minutes. With afternoon rush hour traffic, it could have taken a lot longer. It wouldn't do to be late. *Not tonight.*

She even had made time to drop by a grocery store on the way and grab some fresh, cheerful flowers. She knew her mother would love that.

Her mom lived in a small, tasteful house at the edge of Saratoga, a town in the heart of Silicon Valley just a few miles from the Apple campus at Cupertino. It was the same home in which Alisha had grown up, that Denise had formerly bought with her ex-husband.

At that time, it had been a modest house in a modest neighborhood, but with the skyrocketing prices in the area, it was now worth a small fortune. Alisha had always thought her mother should sell as the property taxes were a significant expense, but her mother insisted on staying put.

As Alisha breezed through the front door, her mother was bustling around in the tiny galley-like kitchen, putting the finishing touches on dinner. Her mom always plated the food before serving it, ensuring a pleasing presentation for her excellent cooking. It was a skill that Alisha had not learned, nor had she wanted to. After kissing her mother lightly on the cheek, she pulled a vase from a cabinet, filled it with water, and arranged the flowers as artfully as she could. She knew her mom would "fix" them as soon as possible.

Alisha sat down at the table, which was already set with blue and yellow placemats and matching napkins, while she watched her mother. Observing her closely, she couldn't help but see that her mother's eyes were slightly red-rimmed and a bit shiny. Tears. One of her mother's favorite weapons.

Denise was an older version of Alisha. The blonde in her hair was aided by monthly trips to the local salon, and she wore her hair short so it curled around her face. Her blue eyes were a bit more gray than Alisha's. She was still trim and fit, thanks probably less to her gardening than to her regular visits to the Pilates studio. The woman still easily attracted male attention, as did Alisha.

Maybe me moving away will be a good thing for her, Alisha thought. *Maybe she'll make more of a life for herself now.*

She started slightly when her mother put a plate of food in front of her. It smelled wonderful: chicken enchiladas with salsa verde. There was also a large salad with a variety of vegetables that had probably come from the stamp-sized garden her mother kept out back.

Alisha watched as her mother took her own seat and put her napkin in her lap. Her mother had changed out of her work clothes and now wore a pair of jeans and a light long-sleeved sweater. Of course, the sweater was blue. Her mother almost always wore blue to try to make her eyes look more blue than gray.

Inwardly, Alisha cringed, knowing that her mother was dressed better than she was. She had merely thrown a 49ers sweatshirt over her somewhat ratty jeans. *I wonder if Mom will comment on that, too.*

After waiting for her mother to pick up her fork first, Alisha grabbed hers and began to eat.

"So," Denise said, an edge in her voice. "Tell me about this ridiculous notion that you're moving to New Jersey."

Alisha paused, her fork halfway to her mouth, "Mom, it's not a ridiculous notion. I am moving to New Jersey," she said firmly. "Hopefully before the end of the year."

"The end of the . . . ? Now, Alisha Jane, you are most certainly not going to move before the end of the year. There's not enough time, for one, and I know you wouldn't leave me here alone for the holidays. Now, tell me why you think you have to move. I assume it has to do with that boss of yours . . . Liam, right?"

Alisha practically bit her tongue. She hated when her mother took that tone with her, the condescending one as if Alisha were still a child. She had the urge to get up and stomp out, but she stopped herself. It wouldn't help.

"Yes, Mom," Alisha replied with exaggerated patience. "It does have to do with Liam. I need to get away from him. Plus, moving to headquarters will be good for my career."

"Well, I understand why you want to get away from that nasty man, but seriously, how can you leave me? Surely you can get another job in this area. The technology sector is expanding like crazy out here. Why aren't you doing that?" Her mother paused abruptly, narrowing her eyes. It was a look she often used to get at the truth. "What else is in New Jersey? Is there a man involved?"

Alisha tried to keep her eyes and voice steady. This was one conversation she absolutely did not want to have with her mother. "No, Mom, it's about my career."

Her mother shook her head. "No, it's not. I can tell, and I always know. What else? Better yet, *who* else?"

"Mo-o-om . . ." Alisha drew out the word into multiple syllables. "Stop! Why can't you believe me?"

"Because I know when you are holding things back, girl; I always have. Even though you are thirty-four years old, you can't fool me. Now talk."

Alisha felt her resolve crumbling. Her mother could always pull things out of her. After all, she had been her confidante most of her life. Alisha had never made girlfriends easily. She'd naturally just turned to her mother. "Well, there is someone who has been very kind to me, very helpful. It was his idea for me to move to headquarters."

Her mother sat up straighter in her chair, her eyes gleaming with renewed interest. "A boyfriend?" she asked hopefully. "Oh, that's nice."

"Well, he's not exactly a boyfriend, Mom. He's just a good friend. He's older than me. He's been kind of, well, mentoring me, helping me. I think he likes me, but it's a little, um, complicated."

"Complicated how?" Her mother's eyes narrowed. "Alisha . . ."

"Yes, Mom, he's married," Alisha said, guessing what Denise was really asking. "But he's not happy with his marriage. He talks to me about that."

Her mother gave her a hard stare. "Alisha, you should not be messing around in that. You know how much it hurt me when *that woman* took your father away from me. It'd be awful for you to do that to someone else. You're playing with fire, and you need to stop," she ended sternly, her blue-gray eyes suddenly cold.

Alisha gulped. She knew this. This reaction was exactly why she hadn't wanted to tell her. Her mother always took things the wrong way, blowing them way out of proportion and making them sound worse than they really were.

"Mom, I really like Dave. He is one of the good guys, one of the few nice men that I've met. Too many guys are like Liam. They only see my blonde hair and boobs. Dave sees me—really sees me. He talks to me and treats me like a real person." Alisha's voice thrummed with passion as she talked, probably more than she realized.

Her mother's look turned sad, but her voice remained stern and pointed. "Alisha, I'm sorry about that. I know that men—"

"But it's more than that," Alisha rushed on, interrupting what she didn't want her mother to say. "He *protected* me. He saw that Liam wasn't treating me right that day at the golf course, and he jumped in to try to help. That's how we became friends, because he cared enough to help me."

Denise looked at her thoughtfully, the silence stretching out for a long moment. "Maybe you ought to tell me about that," she finally invited.

Alisha looked at her, surprised. *Why is Mom asking me about this now? Is this some kind of trick?* But she nodded. "Okay, but let's get dinner cleaned up and get some coffee—or tea. It's kind of a long story."

Her mother looked at her closely, then stood up and started clearing the table.

Once the kitchen was cleaned and tidied, Alisha made cups of herbal tea for both herself and her mother. They went out to the little deck in the back of the house. It was no more than eight by six, barely enough to fit the two patio chairs and the small table between them. Her mother had pulled bright red-and-white-striped cushions from a closet inside the house. Alisha sank into the one farther away from the door and waited for her mother to settle in.

"Alisha," the older woman said somberly, holding her teacup with both hands. The evening was cool. In the dim light of the tiki-style lamps her mother had lit, Alisha could see the steam rising from the cup and evaporating in the dry air. "I'm concerned. Tell me about this outing. Was this when you went to Pebble Beach?"

"Yes, Mom." Alisha was surprised that her mother remembered. Golf, and sports in general, were not her thing. "It was. Someone set Liam up with a Friday afternoon tee time for four. He invited Dave and Robert, who were out here that week working on the Soltang project. Liam asked me to go because he couldn't find another guy to fill out the foursome."

"Yes, I remember that," Denise murmured. She knew what a great golfer Alisha was and how hard she had worked to become good. Alisha was good at a lot of sports. It was one of the many things she had done to get her father's attention, but sadly, Sam had remained mostly interested in the boys. Alisha had been allowed to go along with her father and half-brothers only if she could keep up, so keep up she had.

Alisha continued. "So, we had a good afternoon, but Liam had beer with him. He started drinking around the 9th hole. Robert had one with him, but Dave didn't. Dave was having enough trouble keeping his ball on the course. He's not a great golfer."

Alisha smiled at the memory of how frustrated Dave had been. She and Robert had both tried to give him some pointers, but it had been clear he didn't play much, if at all. His golf had improved a bit now, since she had dragged him out to play a few more times that fall.

"I thought you had to be very good to play that course," Denise said with a bit of confusion, interrupting Alisha's thoughts.

"Yes, you do, or you should be," Alisha agreed. "It's a tough course, but so beautiful. Dave was kind of caught up in that, too, the sheer beauty of the place, the ocean, the rocks, the seals. It is spectacular. Robert was too, but he's a better golfer. Liam was just being Liam, drinking, focused on winning, and acting like the big hero because he brought everyone there. Toward the end of the match, Liam started picking on me, giving me grief about my shots, and generally putting me down in front of everyone near the green because I'm a girl."

"That's not fair!" Denise said indignantly. "You're a good golfer. Even your father says so!"

Alisha snorted. "Yes, Mom, even Dad has to admit that I can golf. But anyway, I could see Robert and Dave getting annoyed at Liam, but it was Dave who jumped in and told him to knock it off, that it wasn't appropriate."

Denise nodded. "That was kind of him. I take it Liam's still upset because you wouldn't go out with him?"

Alisha nodded. "Yeah, that's one way of putting it." Liam had more or less propositioned Alisha a month or so before the golf match. It hadn't been the first time, but that time had been the most aggressive. Liam was usually careful not to do anything inappropriate in front of other people. He was careful about protecting himself. But after the last time Alisha turned him down, he had become more openly derogatory.

Denise frowned. "Didn't you ever report him? I thought we talked about that."

Alisha grimaced, twisting her ponytail around her fingers. "Yes, we did, but it would have been my word against his. I didn't think anyone would listen."

"But you could have tried," her mother insisted.

"Yeah, and if no one believed me? Or worse, if Liam convinced people I was making it up? It would have tanked my career . . . and not just at LSM." Alisha's voice rose and cracked slightly. *Damn, why am I letting myself get so wound up?*

"Okay, honey, calm down," her mother soothed. "I know these things are tricky. But why didn't this Dave say something then?"

"Because I asked him not to, him and Robert both. I didn't want to come off as a hysterical female," Alisha said, defending herself, but the words sounded a little weak even to her.

"But surely with two witnesses . . ." Denise's voice trailed off.

"No, Mom, I wasn't going to go there. You know what Dad always said. You have to tough these things out. No whining."

Alisha saw the tears form in her mother's eyes, genuine ones this time. Talking about her ex-husband almost always did that. On one hand, she got upset that Samuel didn't treat Alisha well. On the other, well, Alisha knew that her mother still, ridiculously, wanted to be married to him.

Impulsively, she reached over and gave her mother a hug. "It will be okay, Mom. You'll see."

Her mother pursed her lips and shook her head.

"Not if you move to New Jersey, it won't."

Chapter 7

Dave glanced at his watch again. 3:15. He needed to leave for the airport soon, but he didn't want to be too early. Surprisingly, he'd heard little from Alisha since Monday except for a few business-like emails about their joint California projects and a short text that morning, reminding him to pick her up. He didn't know what to think about her texting instead of calling, although he guessed that she didn't want to give him a chance to back out of his "commitment" today.

He wasn't sure if he would have. Either way, it was too late now. Checking the time once more, he realized that he needed to get going. He shut down his laptop and started gathering things up from the desk he was utilizing at Corporate.

Robert glanced up at him as he stood. "You're going to get Alisha now?"

Dave made an exasperated face. *You dog. You know full well that I am,* he thought, irritated.

"Yeah, I'll see you tomorrow," Dave replied shortly.

Robert raised an eyebrow but said nothing more. Dave, irritated by the taunt on Robert's face, turned abruptly and walked away. He quickly crossed the hundred yards or so to the elevator, weaving between the cubicle pods on the floor. He could feel Robert's gaze still on him. He felt like *everyone's* eyes were on him. It was ridiculous. He was just giving Alisha a ride. It was no big deal. Or was it?

As he slid into his SUV a few moments later, he couldn't shake the dueling feelings of anticipation and dread. He *liked* Alisha. She was smart and funny and full of energy. He loved her enthusiasm. He was happy that she was getting away from Liam, and he reluctantly admitted to himself that he was flattered by her interest in him, her willingness to ask for his advice and to take it. If he were to be honest, it was nice to have her admiration. It made him feel, well . . . special.

And she was an attractive woman, very attractive. He'd have to be blind not to notice that. He was a guy, after all. *It's normal to notice women, maybe even be slightly attracted to them, right? It doesn't* mean *anything.*

He grimaced and focused his attention on the road. Navigating the traffic on Route 78 in New Jersey required concentration, he reminded himself as he merged onto the highway. It was a short drive to Newark airport from the office, no more than twenty minutes even with a bit of traffic. Turning on his blinker, he smoothly changed lanes, guiding the black Ford Explorer into the fast lane.

His phone dinged. Alisha.

Her plane had landed, and she was on her way to baggage claim. His timing would be good as long as there wasn't a delay with the luggage. It wasn't raining, so he figured there wouldn't be. He wondered where she was staying tonight. She hadn't sent that information along.

Fifteen minutes later, Dave pulled up next to the curb of the busy pickup section of the terminal, overcrowded with travelers all jostling to find the right vehicle that would take them away. After a few moments, he spotted Alisha and jumped out to help her with her bags. She was toting a large one. It seemed much too large for just a weekend. Frowning slightly, he lifted it easily into the back of the Explorer while she slid into the passenger seat.

He noticed she was dressed casually in jeans, low boots and a soft teal sweater that clung gently to her curves. Her coat was slung over her arm even though the temperature was in the low forties. He still wore his business attire of a striped dress shirt and khaki-style navy pants. He did have his coat on, a dark brown leather jacket that had been a gift from Sheryl.

Alisha was sliding her hand appreciatively across the supple leather seat when he got back into the SUV.

"Nice," she said. "This is the fancy model."

Dave grinned. "You bet!" he said. "I do enough driving; I want to enjoy it."

"You don't have a company car?" Alisha asked. He realized that she must have one.

"No, I don't do that much driving for work anymore. I've been under the annual mileage requirement for the last few years because I started doing so much work outside my region," he said.

"Oh, that kind of stinks," she said. "Having a company car saves a lot of money."

He nodded. "It does, but I like getting to pick my own car."

"Typical guy," Alisha laughed. Dave sensed her watching him as deftly pulled through the airport traffic and back onto the highway.

"Where are we going?" he asked. "You never said."

"Oh, I made a hotel reservation at the Marriott Courtyard, the one near the office," she replied. "It's convenient, and I get more points."

"That's right," he said, grinning. "You're a Marriott girl." Dave usually stayed in Hilton properties, except for the couple of times he had traveled with Alisha. She'd insisted on Marriott.

"I made reservations for dinner at that Mexican restaurant you and Robert are always talking about, Conchita's," Alisha continued. "I know you like Mexican food, although I'm sure it's not as good as we get in California."

"It's not," Dave agreed, "but it's not bad. Robert and I go there for lunch once in a while."

"Great," she said brightly. "I made the reservation for 5:30. I figured I could check in at the hotel and drop my bags off before we go. I'm sure it won't matter if we're a little early."

"Uh, no, I'm sure it won't," he said uncomfortably.

He saw Alisha slide a sharp look at him out of the corner of his eye. "It *is* okay to have dinner tonight, right?" she asked. He heard a hard edge in her voice, even though he could tell she was trying to sound like she was teasing.

"Of course," he said, a bit reluctantly. "I told Sheryl I would be out for dinner."

"Does she know it's with me?" Alisha asked.

"Yup, she does," he said shortly, turning his full attention to the increasing traffic. They were driving directly into the setting sun even though it was not even 4:30 yet. He could barely see the brake lights ahead of him as traffic slowed.

"She doesn't mind?" Alisha pressed.

"Not really," he said, then quickly switched the subject. "Where are you looking for places tomorrow?"

He could almost hear Alisha's curiosity, but she allowed him to steer the subject away from his wife. She went down a list of towns, all close to the office, where she had found condos that might meet her needs. Dave listened with half an ear, his mind on the traffic and on Sheryl. *Does Sheryl mind that I'm having dinner with Alisha?*

Fifteen minutes later, Dave pulled up at the hotel. He got out and pulled Alisha's bag out of the back and handed it to her.

"I'll wait out here while you get settled," he said.

"You don't have to sit out here in the cold," she protested. "You can come in with me."

He shook his head. "No, I'll wait here. I have to check on some emails anyway. I can keep the car running."

Alisha shrugged. "Okay. I'll be quick." She disappeared into the hotel lobby, bags in tow.

Dave called Sheryl.

"Hey," he said when she picked up. "I just wanted to remind you that I won't be home for dinner tonight."

"I remember," Sheryl said dryly. "You're picking Alisha up at the airport and entertaining her for the evening."

Dave shifted uncomfortably in the seat. "Yeah, although I'm not sure I'd call it entertainment. We're going over potential real estate for her. She doesn't know the area."

"Yeah, you said that," Sheryl said flatly.

Dave couldn't read her voice. "You okay with that?" he asked cautiously.

"Ha! You're asking me that now? Aren't you with her already?" Sheryl replied. Her tone was definitely biting.

"Umm . . . I'm sorry. I guess . . ."

"You guess what? You guess that you should have asked? It would have been nice, but you know you don't need to ask my permission. When have I ever been like that?"

"You haven't," he said quickly. "You know it's just business."

"Do I?" Sheryl snapped. "I'm not sure what to think sometimes, Dave. You said it was nothing the other day. Why are you calling now? Guilty conscience?"

"No, of course not," Dave responded quickly. "Alisha just asked if you minded, and I thought I should check. That's all."

"Well, that's so kind of you," she retorted sarcastically. "It's too late even if I did mind, isn't it?"

Dave didn't know how to respond to that.

Finally, Sheryl sighed. "Dave, go and have dinner. It's fine. We'll talk more this weekend, like you promised."

Dave felt like a heel. He should not have made this phone call. *Had it been out of a guilty conscience?*

"Okay," he finally answered. "I won't be late."

"I'll see you at home," Sheryl said and hung up.

I guess she does mind.

He started when the passenger door opened, and Alisha jumped in.

"All set," she said brightly. "Ready for dinner?"

Struggling to keep up with the abrupt change, Dave nodded. "Uh, sure," he said as he put the SUV in gear. "Let's go."

Dave looked around as they walked into the familiar restaurant. He hoped no one from the office would be there tonight. The restaurant was small, the room not much bigger than the great room in his home. About a dozen tables were scattered around the room, most in close proximity to one another. He was relieved when he didn't see anyone he knew.

As if sensing his mood, Alisha kept the conversation light and focused on her condominium hunt as they settled at their table. He had to give her credit. She had done a lot of research already and had a good list of places to look at. She had even connected with a real estate agent, one referred by the Human Resources department at LSM. It sounded like his help wouldn't be necessary. *Thank goodness.*

". . . So, will you come with me on Saturday to look at these places, Dave?" Alisha was saying.

He snapped his attention back to her. "What? Why do you need me?" he asked. "You've done your homework. You can handle this."

Alisha pouted, just a little. "But I'd love to have a man's perspective. You'll see things that I'd miss."

Dave frowned. "Come on, Alisha. You're a smart, capable woman. Why do you think you need a man?"

"Oh, I don't *need* you," she said firmly. "But that doesn't mean I don't appreciate another opinion. There's no one else here to help me."

"I can't on Saturday. I promised Sheryl I'd spend some time with her."

"But Da-ave, you said you'd help me."

Dave rubbed his hand across his forehead as if to ward off a headache. He looked around the restaurant, avoiding her gaze while he gathered his thoughts. He became aware that they were seated in one of the three booths along the back wall, next to the kitchen door. It created an intimacy that he suddenly felt was, well, weird. He always sat at a table up front with Robert.

Turning back to Alisha, he realized that she was looking at him expectantly.

"I can't on Saturday. I promised Sheryl," he repeated.

"It doesn't have to be the whole day," she said quickly, leaning toward him. She pushed a piece of hair that had escaped her ponytail back from her face, then slid her hand across the table to tap his hand lightly. "My realtor isn't even available until after lunch. Just a few hours, please?"

Dave calculated the timing in his head. He could have breakfast with Sheryl. They could have their talk. Surely that wouldn't take more than an hour or so, then he could meet Alisha after lunch. *That would work, right?*

He shook his head. He'd already blown it a couple of times this week with Sheryl, including today. As irritated as he felt with her, he needed to show his wife some respect. "I need to talk to Sheryl," he repeated firmly. Alisha pulled her hand back.

They were interrupted by the waitress, who placed a large bowl of chips along with two types of salsa on the table. She took their order: a margarita and chicken enchiladas with salsa verde for Alisha and a chicken burrito with a beer for him.

"How about meeting me in the afternoon?" Alisha continued doggedly, once the cheerful server left. Her hands were now clasped in front of her on the table, almost in supplication.

Dave leaned back. "I don't know. Saturday's not going to be easy."

"How about tomorrow? During the day? Or Sunday? I could do a preliminary look on Saturday, and we could go back together on Sunday to see the ones I like best," Alisha enthused, sitting up straighter and gesturing with both hands.

Inwardly groaning, Dave ran his hand through his hair. *This woman does not take no for an answer.* "I don't know, Alisha. I'll have to see. Maybe."

"Great," Alisha said brightly. "I'll tell the realtor the new plan."

"Alisha," he warned, although there was no growl to his voice. "I said I don't know."

"But you'll make it work for me. I know you will, Dave."

Alisha was nothing if not confident, at least on the outside. He sometimes wondered how much she was faking it. There was a bit of desperation in her manner once in a while that puzzled him.

Thankfully, the food arrived, claiming their attention. Alisha chattered brightly while they ate, mostly about work projects. He listened with half an ear, trying to figure out how to manage this latest request of hers. *I don't want to spend Sunday with her. That's my time to relax. I'll have to make something work on Saturday.*

Finally, the meal came to an end. When Alisha suggested another round of drinks, he shook his head. "I need to get going. You must be tired from the trip, and I told Sheryl I wouldn't be late."

Alisha smiled, but it didn't seem as bright as it had been a few moments ago. He signaled for the check. Alisha didn't protest. Nor did she push the weekend plans any further. From experience at work, Dave knew she had good instincts about when to back off. She only said a cheerful goodnight when he dropped her at the hotel.

He watched her walk into the lobby, then glanced at the clock on the dashboard. Thanks to the early start, it was only just after seven. His commute was a bit longer than Sheryl's, around forty minutes. *Good, I'll be home before eight.*

Dave knew Alisha wasn't happy that he hadn't committed to her weekend plan. Clearly, she expected support and help. Wouldn't he do that for another colleague? *I can't deny her that,* he thought. *After all, she's moving someplace where she doesn't know many people, at least not well. Nor does she know the area.*

But somewhere in the back of his mind, a little voice reminded him that there were several women at the home office that Alisha knew—and possibly knew pretty well. *Why couldn't she ask one of them? Instead of me?*

Chapter 8

Sheryl was in her home office, reviewing the latest status report Patrick Kerrigan had provided on the Portal Project, when she heard the garage door open. She glanced at her watch. 7:45. Not too late. At least Dave had kept *that* promise.

She leaned back in her chair, a white ergonomic contraption with a mesh back. It wasn't pretty, but it was comfortable. She loved her office. Located in the smallest of the four bedrooms in their home, it overlooked the backyard and the small stream that marked the edge of the property. It was her favorite view in the entire house. At her best friend Cindy's suggestion, she had decorated it in subtle shades of blue and cream for a calming effect. Heaven knew she needed that, especially now.

There was no mention in the report of the potential issues Keisha had found. Sheryl was still hoping that would turn out to be nothing, because the rest of the news on the project was actually very good. In fact, Patrick, the director in charge, had even implied the project could come in ahead of schedule. *I wish I could fully trust that projection.* After all, Patrick's false reporting on status had been a major issue just a few months earlier when she and her boss had been blindsided by the news of a significant delay in the Portal Project. Carl had lost his job, and hers had been on the line. Thank goodness Keisha had spoken up.

Sheryl sincerely hoped that Patrick had learned his lesson, but she would not allow this bit of information to go outside her team until she was certain. Patrick was in his mid-thirties but still inexperienced in leading projects. He had only been a director for a short time. *I want to trust Patrick, but I can't quite yet.* She sighed. *And, there's no sense in raising anyone's expectations until we're one hundred percent sure.*

Sheryl heard Dave come in and enter the hall, his loafers tapping against the stone tiles. It sounded like he was headed straight to his office. It was funny how they both used their home offices as a retreat, even from each other. She debated getting up and going to greet him. She was mostly finished with her work for the night, or she could be. Maybe she *should* be, with how tired her eyes were once again.

Shrugging, she reached for the power button on the laptop and shut it down. She doubted she could concentrate on work anymore, knowing Dave was home. Her mind shifted to the reason he was late. She couldn't block the thought that had immediately come into her mind, unbidden.

Had he only *been having dinner with her?*

As Sheryl shook her head, she heard Dave's footsteps on the stairs. Her heart skipped a beat. *Is he coming to see me? Or is he going straight to the bedroom?* The sound of his feet on the wooden treads stopped. It sounded like he was at the top of the stairs. She wouldn't know if he had stepped onto the runner that spanned the length of the upstairs hall, which muted any noise. Suddenly, she sensed his presence behind her. She swiveled around in her chair.

"Still working?" Dave asked, his tall frame filling the doorway.

Sheryl swallowed. "Just finishing up," she said briskly, or as briskly as she could manage given the jangling of her nerves. *I wish I didn't feel so uncomfortable and helpless with Dave.*

Dave hesitated. "Anything special going on?"

Sheryl eyes widened with surprise. It had been weeks since he had asked about her work, not since their last huge argument about her actions at the board meeting—especially when she had taken on the powerful Hank Turner and his cohort Anthony Russo. *Dave was so angry, so . . . hurtful. He didn't even try to understand how I felt.* She shook her head to cover her astonishment and sought to even her tone as she replied, "No, only reviewing the latest report on the Portal Project."

He nodded. "How's that going?"

"Good. I think. Patrick thinks we may be ahead of schedule, but it's too soon to tell."

"That's good. It would be great if you could bring it in a bit early," Dave said, his voice a little too hearty.

"Mm-hmm," Sheryl murmured in agreement. She saw the tension in the set of Dave's shoulders. He wasn't hiding his feelings very well, and she suspected that her tension was apparent to him, too.

Their eyes met and held briefly. Dave looked away.

"How was your dinner?" she asked. *Might as well put it out there.*

"Um, good," Dave replied, looking at the floor. "We went to the Mexican place near the office. Her hotel isn't far from there."

"Conchita's?"

"Yeah, that's right."

"Could you look at me?" Sheryl asked pointedly.

Dave looked up. "Sorry. I, uh, I . . . Sorry."

"Sorry about what?" Sheryl's tone was snippier than she would have liked.

"Geez, Sheryl," Dave said. "I'm trying to make conversation here."

"It shouldn't be this hard, Dave."

He rotated his head the way he always did when he was tense. "I know. It's that, well, I feel like anything I say is going to be wrong."

Sheryl felt herself soften. She leaned toward him. "I'm not trying to make you wrong. You seem so uncomfortable. Why?"

"It feels weird," he replied. "It was just dinner with a colleague, a young woman I'm trying to help, and . . . I don't know. You are acting like I'm doing something wrong."

"Me?" Sheryl's voice was incredulous. She let out a huff of air. "I *just* asked a question. Maybe you feel like you're doing something wrong?"

His face hardened. "I'm not," he said emphatically.

Sheryl put both hands up in surrender, palms facing him. "Okay, okay. You're not. What does she need help with?"

"Can we sit down?" Dave asked, looking around the room. Other than her desk chair and a daybed full of pillows, there was no place to sit.

Sheryl sighed. "I could use a cup of tea . . . Or maybe a glass of wine. Let's go downstairs."

"Sounds good. I could use a drink myself," he said.

He waited at the door while she took the five or six steps to reach him. Stepping back into the hall, he gestured for her to precede him. He always was a gentleman, something she appreciated even when some of her friends thought the gestures demeaning. They had always been genuine with Dave.

He turned as she went by, and they walked the short distance in the hall and down the stairs, side by side. By tacit agreement, they meandered into the great room instead of the kitchen. Dave headed to the wet bar tucked neatly in the far corner, while Sheryl sank into the deep, comfortable leather sofa. She curled herself against the arm at one end, where she usually sat. Dave didn't bother to turn on the lights, allowing the darkness to relax them both a little more as he poured a small glass of cognac for each of them.

She looked up in surprise as he handed her the snifter but then smiled softly in thanks. Drinking cognac together had always been a way they unwound together in the past. It was nice that he remembered. She was also glad she had changed into comfortable sweatpants and a fleece pullover. The room was chilly.

She watched curiously as Dave plopped onto the sofa, too. He normally sat in the adjacent recliner. He slid one bent leg onto the sofa and leaned back against the other arm.

Sheryl waited for him to speak first.

After several moments of silence, Dave said, "Alisha needs, um, *needed* my help because she was having a bit of trouble with her boss, Liam Moriarty."

"I don't think I've met Liam," Sheryl said. "Although I know you've mentioned him once or twice."

"No, you haven't met him. He's the regional sales manager in the West, mostly California. He doesn't come out here often. I've probably only mentioned him in passing because I don't like him much."

"Alisha is in sales, then?"

"Yes, she's the sales rep—whoops, account manager—in the San Jose area," he said.

Sheryl chuckled softly. She knew how much account managers hated to be called sales reps.

"Liam, well, he likes the ladies," Dave went on, leaning toward her a little as he confided. "A little too much, even though he's married. He was being somewhat aggressive with Alisha. I've been trying to help her out."

"Dave, that's awful!" Sheryl blurted, sitting up in shock. A wave of anger shot through her. She had had a couple of men treat her inappropriately earlier in her career. It had been so hard to deal with. "How is he getting away with that? Has she reported him to HR? They would be able to help her more than you, wouldn't they?"

"Yeah, they would," Dave acknowledged. "But Alisha doesn't want to go to HR. 'He said, she said,' you know. She was afraid that it would hurt her career."

Sheryl rolled her eyes and leaned back. "Come on, Dave. In this day and age? Men are generally guilty until proven innocent. You know that."

"Not always," Dave said defensively. "Especially because Liam is slick. I don't think her fears are totally unfounded, although I did encourage her to report him."

"So, how are you involved?"

"I offered her some advice, listened, that kind of thing."

"Was one of the pieces of your advice the suggestion that she move to New Jersey?" Sheryl asked. She could hear the edge creeping into her tone, although she tried to minimize the bite as soon as she heard it. She was so happy that Dave was actually talking, even if she wasn't crazy about what he was saying. She didn't want to risk shutting him down.

"No, yes, uh, maybe." He sighed. "It was an idea that came up. I don't know whether I suggested it or she did."

Sheryl sipped a little too much cognac, feeling the liquid burn down her throat as her hands tightened around the glass. The only light in the room poured gently in from the kitchen. She tried to see the expression on Dave's face, but it was hard to make it out, silhouetted in the dark as he was. She wanted, *needed*, some clue as to what he was really thinking.

She heard the soft swoosh of cloth sliding against leather as Dave shifted in his seat.

"Does it matter who suggested it?" he asked, breaking the silence.

"I don't know," Sheryl said. "Does it? Do you want her here?"

Dave sat up again, his back ramrod straight. "What does that mean? What are you implying?" he demanded.

"I'm not implying anything. I just asked a question, Dave. Do you want her here? It's a simple question." Sheryl didn't try to keep the sarcasm out of her voice this time.

"Well, it doesn't sound simple to me," Dave's voice had taken on a hard edge. "The only possible way I could answer that is 'No, I don't,' but that wouldn't be the whole truth."

Sheryl was stunned. She pushed back into the cushions as if she had been struck. Unbidden, her friend Cindy's words, spoken just two weeks ago, crossed her mind. *As in you think he might be . . . cheating?*

Dave stood up. His face was tight, his posture rigid. He took a step toward her and turned to face her. She barely kept herself from cringing. With the kitchen light now shining on his face, she could see that it was contorted in anger. But Dave had never, ever hurt her physically.

He pried the nearly empty glass from her fingers and stalked the fifteen or so feet across the room to the wet bar. He slammed both glasses on the counter, but they didn't break. He poured a generous amount of cognac in both glasses and put the bottle down hard. He paused then, leaning against the bar with both hands, his head bent. She could see him taking deep breaths, even in the dim light.

Finally, he turned and walked back, his posture less rigid although by no means relaxed. He handed her a glass, hesitated, then sat back down where he had been.

Sheryl watched as Dave sank even farther back into his corner of the sofa. They weren't close. The couch was oversized and at least eight feet long. Despite being on the same piece of furniture, the distance felt more like a mile. *What should I say now?* she worried.

It was Dave who finally broke the silence. "I don't know why I said that," he began. "I . . . I guess I have no idea what I think about her moving here. I do know she needs to get away from Liam. And yes, she should report him to HR. Maybe I should, although frankly she's begged me not to. She's a smart woman, very smart, very good at her job. She will have more opportunities based near the home office." He paused. "You know how that goes."

Sheryl nodded.

KAREN ANN BULLUCK

"We've become friends."

As Dave continued, Sheryl sensed he was looking out into the room instead of at her.

"I like her. I enjoy talking to her, and she's great to work with. She knows when to bring the technical team in, and she doesn't get in our way."

Sheryl swallowed. Her hands tightened on the snifter again. She curled herself deeper into the sofa, not sure that she wanted to hear any more. Dave became silent.

"But . . ." Sheryl reluctantly prompted.

Dave's head jerked up, as if remembering she was there.

"But," he echoed. "I don't know. I don't know what she wants from me."

Sheryl bit her lower lip. "Does that matter? What she wants?"

She heard the slither of cloth against the leather sofa, indicating some movement on his part. *A shrug?* "Yes and no. She could make things uncomfortable . . . Or . . ."

Sheryl felt him take a deep breath. She heard the exhale, the faint whir of the refrigerator in the next room, the heavy thudding of her own heartbeat. Every nerve in her body seemed to tingle.

"Or what . . . ?"

Dave's whole body jerked. "Or nothing," he snapped. "Nothing. She could just make things uncomfortable. That's it."

Taken aback by his abrupt change of tone, Sheryl sat up and leaned toward him.

"I don't think it's nothing" she said firmly. There was no anger in her voice. She didn't feel angry. She felt dread, fear. She knew with every fiber of her being that this was not "nothing."

Dave stood up. "Look. I told you what I know. Can't you leave it at that? It's not a big deal. She's a friend, a co-worker. I'm helping her out. There's nothing more to it than that."

"Then why are you so upset?" Sheryl asked.

"Because you're acting like I'm doing something wrong!"

"I'm sorry that you feel that way," Sheryl said more calmly, falling back on her conflict management skills. "That's not my intent. I'm trying to understand the situation."

"For God's sake, Sheryl. Don't patronize me. I'm not one of your minions at work."

"I'm not patronizing you, Dave. I'm trying to have a constructive conversation, something you seem to be incapable of these days."

"Ahh, there you go. Start with the accusations. I'm always the bad guy, aren't I?"

"No, you're not," Sheryl shot back. "I'd be perfectly happy if you'd tell me what I'm doing wrong, what I've done wrong, to the point where we can't even talk. We've always been able to talk. I don't know why we can't now."

Sheryl could feel the tears forming in her eyes. Her breathing turned ragged. *I do not want to cry. I should be angry, not crying.*

"Damn it. Don't cry. I can't stand it when you cry."

Sheryl heard Dave's voice from a distance. She tried to hold back the sobs, but the pressure was too much. Suddenly, everything hit her at once—the continuing disagreements with Dave, the pressure to perform, the Portal Project, and now this. She knew she should be screaming mad, but as so often in the ancient way of women, her anger, hurt, and frustration dissolved into tears.

She heard Dave groan, and then he pulled her into his arms. She buried her head against his chest, letting the torrent sweep over her. She had been holding herself together for so long.

Dave held her as she cried, patting her back and murmuring comforting words in her ear, although she couldn't have repeated any of them for the life of her.

After several long minutes, the sobs subsided. Her tears began to dry, although the front of Dave's shirt was soaked. He held her away from him a little so he could look at her face.

"Are you okay now?" he asked gently.

Sheryl nodded. "I'm sorry. I guess it was just . . . everything."

"Everything?"

"Yeah, everything. You know. Us not talking. All the work stress.

Everything that's been building up over the last few months, and even this week."

"What's happened this week?" Dave asked. "Besides our little mess."

Sheryl wrinkled her nose. "'Our little mess'? That's an interesting way of phrasing it. But there's something weird going on at work, too. Something Keisha found. I don't know yet, but it could be bad . . . really bad," she admitted.

"Do you want to tell me about it?"

"No, not now. I can't think about it right now." She sighed. "I'm tired." The release of emotion had left her completely drained.

"I'll bet," he said. "That was quite a cry. Let's get you to bed. I guess we can continue this conversation—if it needs to be continued—another time."

Sheryl raised her eyebrows but didn't argue. "Yeah, let's go to bed," she agreed.

Dave picked up the snifters and took them into the kitchen while Sheryl headed upstairs.

She felt better after the cry, but the edginess and tension weren't completely gone. She was grateful to have felt such tenderness in the way Dave had held her, much more than she'd felt from him in a long time. He certainly hadn't held her that way a few months ago, when she was crying about the layoffs at work.

She now felt, well, connected to him. She sighed deeply.

But what about Alisha? The thought nagged at her. *What does Dave really think about her moving here?* Despite the closeness of the last few minutes, the residual tightness in Sheryl's gut demanded more answers.

Still, she'd have to try to put it out of her mind if she was going to get any sleep. She hoped she could.

Does Dave even know what he thinks—or feels—about Alisha? Sheryl wondered as she drifted off to sleep. *I'm not sure he does.* And perhaps that made her most uncomfortable of all.

Chapter 9

Friday, December 3

Even though her eyes were glued to her screen, Sheryl didn't see a single word in front of her. Her mind had slipped back to the early morning. She had been in her post-workout high, her tension eased, when Dave had unexpectedly and wonderfully asked her to dinner that evening. Okay, maybe *wonderfully* was too strong a word, but she felt hope for the first time in a while. Until that hope had rushed through her, she hadn't been fully aware of how much she had lost it. Sighing, she tried to focus on her work again.

This is just one small step, she reminded herself. *The problems with Dave are hardly solved.* But the soft smile lingered upon her face.

Turning back to her work, an uneasy feeling riffled through her stomach. She knew instinctively this had nothing to do with Dave. Biting her lip, Sheryl sent a quick message to Tina, her administrative assistant, to remind her when the Portal Project meeting was about start. Something was nudging her to attend today, even though she usually didn't. She was making it more of a priority to listen to her intuition, especially after seeing how much it had helped her in the last few months.

Opening her inbox, she saw there was an email from Todd, marked urgent. He wanted another update on the Portal Project. Sheryl frowned.

What? He had heard the update at the board meeting just over a week ago. What made him think that something was different in that short time frame?

She reread the email carefully. The language was terse, only two sentences, although that wasn't unusual for Todd. His tone was . . . irritated, maybe? It was hard to tell, although the urgent flag was a clue that something was bugging him. She wondered if Anthony Russo, an influential member of the Board of Directors, was hassling him again. After all, he and Hank Turner had been very upset about the delay in the Project at the November board meeting, her first one.

Sheryl shuddered. She had made a mess at that meeting, held only two weeks ago, by voting against the Chief Financial Officer candidate—Layla Arch—that everyone else had chosen. This in turn had led several other board members to change their votes. After that, well, Anthony and Hank were even more angry than they had been about the project delay.

Picturing Hank's angry face during their last encounter, she was grateful that she'd never have to deal with him again. Todd had forced him to resign because of his behavior, but Anthony, along with Hank's replacement, was still there, still putting pressure on them all—and especially Todd—to reduce costs and deliver projects more quickly.

Frowning, she put Todd's email aside, wanting to give herself a chance to absorb it and consider her answer. She went quickly through a number of other emails, clearing her inbox of the new messages in less than thirty minutes. That done, she sighed and turned back to Todd's email. She still didn't know how to answer it.

She sat for a moment, her hands poised over the keyboard, struggling to compose an appropriate response when all she wanted to say was, "Why are you bothering me with this?" She was interrupted by a knock on the door. Tina poked her blonde head in.

"You asked me to remind you about the team meeting for the Portal Project," Tina said briskly, her tone cheerful, as always. "It starts in five."

Sheryl nodded appreciatively. "Thanks, Tina. Your timing is perfect."

"You bet," came the quick reply.

Tina vanished again. Sheryl smiled. She loved the younger woman's energy. She had been a group administrative assistant for Sheryl and her peers prior to Sheryl's promotion. Now, she was solely Sheryl's admin, having been promoted when Carl's secretary decided to retire when he left.

Frowning at the screen, Sheryl deleted the still blank reply to Todd and minimized her email. She gathered her tablet and phone and stood up decisively. She trusted the team to handle the day-to-day aspects of the work, but given her instincts and Todd's email, there was no way she was going to skip today. She worried about Keisha's findings, but there was something else that needed her attention. She just didn't know what it was . . . yet.

The team met in a conference room across the floor from her office. She walked along the aisle separating the cubicles from the offices and conference rooms along the outside walls. The floor was quiet. She could hear the tapping of fingers on keyboards and the occasional murmur of low conversation. Several people were wearing headsets, their heads nodding along to the rhythm of music she couldn't hear. Everything seemed normal and, thankfully, undramatic.

She slipped into the conference room a few minutes early, garnering somewhat nervous greetings from the five people who had already gathered. Patrick Kerrigan smiled his welcome, clearly comfortable with her attendance. She greeted everyone by name, even those attending from Sales. She was familiar with everyone in attendance, even if she didn't know many of them well. Keisha slid into a chair near Sheryl just before the meeting was scheduled to begin. She raised her eyebrows and smiled, as surprised as everyone else that the CIO was there.

A moment later, Rachel Solowitz walked in and took the seat at the other end of the table from Patrick. Now it was Sheryl's turn to be shocked. She kept her expression open and friendly, grateful that she had decided to attend the meeting. Although Rachel was a step below Sheryl in the corporate hierarchy as she reported to Jim Leaders, Rachel was significantly higher in rank than Patrick. It felt ironic to Sheryl and just a little strange still that just a few months ago, she and Rachel had been peers.

Sheryl noticed that Patrick's eyes widened under his coppery eyebrows at Rachel's entry, although he greeted her cheerfully. He had a naturally sunny disposition, red hair, and blue eyes that fit his Irish name. Still, Sheryl's unease grew. Clearly, Rachel didn't normally attend the status meetings either. *So, why is she here today?*

Sheryl had deliberately chosen to sit on the side of the large faux-mahogany table that stretched nearly the length of the bland conference room, not wanting to usurp Patrick's authority in any way. She watched as he started the meeting, ignoring the projector hanging from the ceiling and the miniature computer on the side credenza. *No demonstrations today, then.*

Sheryl glanced out the two picture windows on the outside wall, then turned her attention to the eleven people sitting in the institutional black chairs surrounding the table. All were in fairly casual attire, even Patrick, who sported a long-sleeve polo shirt with blue stripes tucked into the ubiquitous khakis.

Everyone seemed comfortable except for Rachel. She was dressed more formally in a black silk blouse and was leaning forward, almost as if waiting to jump into the conversation. Sheryl knew Rachel fairly well. They were of a similar age and had worked together on a few projects before, but none as vitally important as this one. A tall woman with dark brown hair and deep-set brown eyes, Rachel was Jim Leaders' right-hand person. She often was his representative at meetings, and Sheryl appreciated the fact that she was much easier to deal with than Jim. Rachel was more straightforward, more open.

There was no printed agenda for the meeting. Patrick confidently talked through the project plan, noting any areas that were deemed yellow by the team. Yellow indicated that an item was "at-risk," and there were only a few of them. Better yet, there were no red items, which would have signified a serious problem.

Finishing the review, Patrick sent a questioning look to Sheryl, checking to see if she wanted to say anything. She subtly shook her head. It had not been her intention to interfere, but simply to observe so she would feel more confident in her reply to Todd. After a mere fifteen minutes, Patrick moved to close the meeting. That was when Rachel pounced.

"Patrick, excuse me," she said. "You haven't addressed the real issue that we are facing."

Patrick looked shocked. His face flushed, an unfortunate side effect of his fair, freckled skin. "What real issue?" he blurted.

Rachel frowned. "You're not aware that the integration with our CRM program isn't working?"

Patrick hesitated, still looking dumbstruck, but then shook his head. "I know it's not complete, but it's not behind schedule." He looked at Keisha to elaborate.

"Yes, Rachel," Keisha agreed. "I'm still working on it, but there are no major issues at this point."

"That's not what I understood," Rachel said firmly. "I had my monthly call with representatives of the SalesTeam software just yesterday, and they indicated that you had placed several calls to them for support."

Sheryl saw Keisha stiffen, but she answered Rachel calmly, her face deliberately impassive. "Yes, I have placed a few calls, but my questions have all been answered."

Leaning back, Sheryl watched Rachel's reaction. She was puzzled by Rachel's attitude. She knew from experience that the woman could be intense, but she was usually more congenial about it. Today, her attitude was quite aggressive.

Rachel held Keisha's gaze for a moment before dropping her eyes. "Well, if you say so," she conceded. "I guess I got the wrong impression from the SalesTeam folks."

"Yes, you must have," Keisha agreed with a touch of deference. "But I'll let you know if I have any problems with them. I know you are the main liaison for them."

Sheryl smiled inwardly. *Well done, Keisha!* She did, however, make a mental note to follow up with Rachel and make sure there was nothing else going on. She liked and respected Rachel. More importantly, she trusted Rachel's instincts. Perhaps there was something missing, something that Keisha wasn't seeing.

She turned her attention back to Patrick, who had wrapped up the meeting. Glad she had attended, she stood up and thanked him. Then she turned to speak to Rachel, who greeted her with a warm smile.

"Hey Sheryl," Rachel said. "I didn't expect to see you here."

Sheryl smiled back. "My calendar was open, so I decided at the last minute to sit in. I like to pop in once in a while."

"I'm glad to see that," Rachel said. "There's a lot of pressure on this project."

"Don't I know it," Sheryl agreed easily. "I'm glad you are staying involved, too. The team needs all the support they can get."

Rachel laughed. "Yes, they do. Your team and mine. But we've both got good people on it. That helps."

"Yes, it does." Sheryl, sensing that the conference room was now empty, asked bluntly, "What did your contact at SalesTeam say that made you so upset?"

Rachel glanced around the room, checking visually to see if they were alone, then looked back at Sheryl. "Oh that. Well, she said that Keisha had asked a lot of questions about the database and implied that she might not understand the structure. I guess her questions seemed kind of basic to them. I told her Keisha was very bright, so I thought I'd better ask myself."

Sheryl nodded. "Keisha's very thorough. She was probably just double-checking."

Rachel shrugged, tucking a lock of wavy hair that had escaped from her sleek chignon behind her ear. "I'm sure. Keisha is doing amazing things with the user interface. We are all impressed."

"Oh good. I really like what I've seen so far, too, but it's your team that has to be happy—and the customers, of course."

Rachel glanced down as her phone chirped softly. "Hey, I've gotta run to another meeting. Let's catch up another time."

"Sounds good," Sheryl replied. "Maybe we could grab lunch sometime soon."

"Great, let's do that," Rachel called back over her shoulder as she hurried out of the room.

Sheryl chuckled softly. That was more like Rachel, always running off to the next thing. Still, she stared at Rachel's diminishing form before she turned and headed back to her office. She had another meeting of her own to attend.

By the time mid-afternoon rolled around, Sheryl had attended three more meetings, including having a quick salad with her friend Janine from Human Resources in the cafeteria, and responded—carefully—to Todd's email. After hitting send, she leaned back in her chair and looked out the window at the sun slowly sliding behind the trees on the edge of the property. It felt like the sun set too early in December.

She contemplated the day's events. First Todd's email, then Rachel's odd appearance at the meeting, and her sense of unease that had prompted her to attend the meeting in the first place. It seemed evident now that something *was* wrong, and that something had to do with the database for the SalesTeam software. She thought back to Rachel's questioning of Keisha. *Does Rachel know anything about this?*

Sheryl made a mental note to schedule time with Rachel the following week and sound her out. She wasn't sure she would mention Keisha's concerns directly, but perhaps Rachel could give her some insight on how things were being viewed by The Diamante's sales team. Jim Leaders was unlikely to have any details, and Sheryl didn't feel comfortable approaching anyone else on that particular team—not under these circumstances. At least she and Rachel had a good working relationship.

Sheryl's thoughts turned to Patrick. He was doing a good job with the project, but he wasn't equipped to deal with someone like Rachel or, worse, Jim. That had been obvious at the meeting today, although he had had the sense to turn the conversation over to Keisha. *I really ought to have someone more senior supporting Patrick,* she thought. She didn't have the time since her promotion to mentor him as much as she would have liked, especially since he had been so off-track a few months ago. He was doing much better, but now with these potential issues, Patrick was likely to need help.

She had been mulling over how best to reassign her direct reports in the wake of the layoffs and Carl's unexpected resignation, because right now she had more direct reports than she could adequately handle, even without the high visibility of the Portal Project. What she really needed was someone to take over her old role, but who?

Jose Rodrigues and Yvette Champlaign were the most obvious candidates. Both had years of experience with The Diamante and were strong leaders. Jose was more technical than Yvette, but Yvette was a bit older and had a nice touch with people whereas Jose's temper could get the best of him at times. *Yet, Jose handled the layoffs better than I had expected. He's making significant progress in his leadership.* She sighed. She didn't have to make that decision today, but she would have to do something, and soon. Patrick wasn't experienced enough to bring this project home by himself, especially if her and Keisha's suspicions had any traction. In the back of her mind, she was a little concerned that a change in management might demoralize Patrick, but she guessed he wouldn't be totally surprised. She sighed again. *That's a lot for a Friday afternoon. Time to think about going home.*

Turning back to her computer, she quickly dealt with the remaining items in her inbox, motivated to finish up so that she could leave a little early. She wanted time to unwind a little and change her clothes before her "date" with Dave. She wanted to wear something a little more attractive than her work clothes tonight, something Dave would appreciate. *Oh boy, I'm acting like a teenage girl.*

She was mentally reviewing her wardrobe when her instant messenger chimed. It was Keisha, asking Sheryl to come to her cubicle, yet another unusual occurrence. Frowning, Sheryl typed "Yes" and stood up. She walked quickly to the door and out into the aisle.

Keisha's cubicle wasn't far, and the light scent of her dramatic perfume reached Sheryl's nose seconds before she slipped into the small space. Keisha had already pulled a spare chair up next to hers, and she politely signaled for Sheryl to sit.

Despite her casual dress, Keisha's demeanor was very intense.

"Hey, what's up?" Sheryl asked very softly.

"Hey," the younger woman whispered. "What was Rachel doing at the meeting this morning?"

Sheryl looked closely at Keisha's slightly flushed face before answering carefully, also in a whisper. "I'm not sure. I talked to her briefly after the meeting. She said the people at SalesTeam had been concerned about your questions."

"She said that at the meeting," Keisha said disdainfully. "I don't buy it."

"It could be true," Sheryl said mildly. "Rachel's usually very upfront about things."

Keisha all but snorted. "Well, maybe. But she isn't now."

Sheryl tilted her head, assessing. "You seem pretty sure about that."

"Look, Rachel doesn't ever come to our status meetings, and now she shows up after what I told you earlier in the week? Yeah, I did call the SalesTeam support line a couple of times, but so what? I've called them before. Why would she be all worried about it now?"

"Good question," Sheryl said carefully.

"I want you to see for yourself what I've found," Keisha went on, still speaking in a hushed voice. "It's easier to show you here." She tilted her screen a little more toward Sheryl.

"Look at this," Keisha said as she pointed to a PDF document on the screen. "That's the database structure I was given by SalesTeam. Do you see all the fields numbered 78 through 99?"

Sheryl nodded. The field descriptions were blank, leading her to believe that they were available for custom information.

Keisha minimized that document, switching to a visual of a database record. "Now, look at that," she said in an urgent whisper. "It skips from 77 to 100, and only then do the fields continue in sequence."

Sheryl looked at the screen carefully, confirming for herself what Keisha had pointed out. "Those look like custom field holders," she said. "Maybe we just didn't use them when we implemented the software."

Keisha shook her head. "Now, look at this." She pulled up what looked like a database schema with various record lengths. "Most of the customer account records have a record length of about 185 fields. See?"

Sheryl nodded.

"But then there are a bunch of records that have over 200 fields . . . 206, to be exact."

"Exactly 21 more fields," Sheryl said, her head suddenly thrumming with a burgeoning headache.

"Exactly," Keisha whispered triumphantly.

Sheryl shot her a dark look. "This is not good news," she admonished her.

Keisha grinned, like a cat who had its quarry trapped, but quickly sobered. "I know. The question is, what are we going to do about it?"

Sheryl leaned back, quietly motioning for Keisha to close the documents on the screen. "I don't know, but it's going to be me doing something, not you," she said firmly, wanting to keep Keisha out of the line of fire as much as possible.

"That's fine by me," Keisha quickly agreed.

"Is this what you asked SalesTeam support about?"

"Not directly," Keisha said quickly. "I just asked them to confirm the field sequencing protocol they are using. It shouldn't be a big deal unless they know there is something off. Do you think Rachel knows?"

Sheryl considered her own earlier thoughts, then shook her head. "No, Rachel's always been straight. Maybe that's why she's concerned. Or Jim asked to check after she reported the issue to him. That's more likely."

Keisha shrugged. "I don't know. You know Rachel and Jim better than I do. I thought it was weird that she showed up today."

"I'll talk to her again," Sheryl promised. "I'll see if I can get any more info about her concerns."

Keisha nodded gratefully, then glanced furtively around. "You'd better go before someone wonders why you're here for so long."

Sheryl nodded, rising from the chair.

"Thanks, boss," Keisha said cheerfully and loudly. "Have a great weekend."

"You, too," Sheryl replied, stepping into the aisle. She noticed a few people glance up briefly, but no one seemed surprised or concerned. Thankfully, she stopped by Keisha's cubicle frequently enough that this visit wouldn't raise too many questions.

Keeping a pleasant expression on her face, she nodded at those with whom she made friendly eye contact as she made her way back to her own office.

Deep inside, however, her mind was reeling. She had no idea what to do with this new information or even if it meant anything at all. *There could be*, she reminded herself hopefully, *a simple explanation*. But even as the thought crossed her mind, she knew it was wrong. When her intuition was this strong, it was never wrong, and if it had been nudging her earlier in the day, it was clamoring now. She just wished she knew what to do.

She renewed her vow to talk to Rachel next week. Early next week. Rachel was the obvious choice, and she had given Sheryl an opening by showing up at the discussion today. Well, there was nothing she could do about it at this moment. Besides, maybe she'd come up with a brilliant plan over the weekend.

Seated back at her desk, she stretched her shoulders, trying to ease the tension in her neck and alleviate her headache. She also took an ibuprofen tablet for good measure. She stared out the window. The sun had set, and darkness was closing in. She shivered, feeling a different kind of darkness falling inside. *What am I going to do?*

Chapter 10

Dave finished up the proposal and hit the save button with a satisfied smile. Robert would still have to give it a once-over before they submitted it to the account representative for final approval, but Dave was very pleased with his work. The prospective client, a large multinational bank, had been looking for a different way to secure the company's intranet and increase network speed considerably at the same time. He knew he had come up with an innovative design, something he had been thinking about for a while. He just hadn't had the right opportunity to try it out until now.

Still smiling, Dave glanced at his watch. It was only 3:30. He had time to review the document with Robert and still leave with plenty of time to get home, change, and be ready to go to dinner with Sheryl. He had surprised himself, and her, this morning with his impromptu invitation, but it felt good. Finally, after so many missteps with his wife in recent months, he felt like he was doing the right thing. Just seeing the smile that lit up her face was reward enough. It had been a long time since he had managed to have that effect on her. It almost made up for the frostiness between them. Almost.

He shook his head to release those thoughts, attached the file to an email, and sent it off to Robert who, as usual, was parked in the cubby next to him. Wanting to expedite his departure, he stood up and leaned over the low glass divider toward Robert.

"Hey," he said urgently. "Can you take a look at the proposal I just sent you? I need to get it off to Desean before I head home, and I want to get on the road soon."

Robert looked up, blinking as he pried his focus from his work to Dave. "Sure," he said distractedly. "Just give me a sec."

Dave murmured agreement and sat back down, mentally pushing Robert to hurry. He glanced out the window at the darkening sky. The setting sun reflected off the windows on the adjacent building, wrapping it in strips of shimmering gold. He heard his computer ding with a notification of an incoming email. He ignored it. He didn't want to get pulled into anything that would delay his departure. He'd made reservations at the Tewksbury Inn for dinner, requesting a quiet upstairs table. It was a restaurant that he and Sheryl used to frequent and enjoy. *Under the circumstances, I have no intention of being late.*

Turning back to his workstation, he straightened the desk and tucked his notebook and pens in his backpack. He had everything ready, except for his laptop, when he felt a hand come down on his shoulder. It was too small to be Robert's.

"Hey there!" he heard Alisha say, close to his ear.

He straightened and swiveled his chair, forcing her to back up a step. Seemingly undeterred, she sat down on the edge of the desk and smiled. Dave noticed that she looked especially attractive today in black pants, high heels, and a crimson top. Her hair was pulled up into its customary ponytail, emphasizing her youth.

"What are you up to?" she asked pertly.

"I'm getting ready to leave as soon as Robert finishes reviewing my proposal," he said.

"Oh." He watched Alisha scan the desk and realize he was nearly ready to go. "Where are you off to? Are we going out for drinks?"

Dave shook his head. "No, I'm headed home. Sheryl and I are going out to dinner tonight."

Alisha stiffened, her lips thinning. A flash of emotion crossed her face before she quickly donned a cheerful smile.

"Ah, that's nice," she said, although there was little enthusiasm in her voice. "But I need you to help me with *my* proposal before you head out for the day. It's the first one that I'm doing for Katrin, my new boss. It's important that I get it right, and you know what Katrin looks for."

"Alisha, I don't have time for that today."

"You can look at it while you're waiting for Robert," she insisted. She glanced over at Robert. "Hey, Robert, you can take your time with that," she said in a teasing tone.

Dave raised his voice a notch. "No, I'm sure Robert's almost done now," he said firmly.

"It will take too long for me to review yours. If you send it to me, I'll look at it when I get a chance over the weekend," he offered.

Alisha pouted; there was no other word to describe it. Dave inwardly winced. He wasn't a fan of the "little girl" act she used at times.

"But I promised! I'm supposed to get it to her before the end of business today. It won't take you very long to look at it, I promise," she wheedled.

Robert stood up, imposing with his height.

"Hey Dave, I just sent that proposal back to you. I had a couple of small suggestions. Shouldn't take you but a minute to tidy it up and get it off to Desean," he said calmly.

Dave looked up and nodded. "Great. I'll jump right on it." He swiveled his chair back toward the laptop, effectively turning his back on Alisha.

"But what about me?" Alisha said. "I really, really need your help, Dave."

He heard Robert sigh. "I can take a look at it," he offered. "I know Katrin, too."

Dave slanted him a grateful look. He felt Alisha shift closer to the laptop on his desk, where she was still sitting. There was a long pause.

Finally, Alisha made a soft harrumph of frustration and answered Robert. "Well," she said, taking a deep breath, "if Dave won't help me, I guess it wouldn't hurt for you to look at it."

Robert laughed. "Alisha, I don't need to look at it. I want to leave early, too."

Dave felt Alisha hop off his desk. "Okay, okay. I get it," she replied to Robert with a resigned sigh. "I would appreciate your help. I'll send you the file."

"Okay then," Robert said and sat back down.

"I'll see you tomorrow at ten." Alisha directed her words back to Dave. "You'll pick me up at my hotel."

As usual, she didn't leave room for dissent.

"Okay," Dave said without turning around. "I'll see you then. It might help if you sent me the list of places we are going to see ahead of time, just so I have a sense of where we're going and how long we're likely to be."

"Great, I'll do that," Alisha said, a smile back in her voice. "We'll have time to get lunch in between appointments, so you don't need to worry about food."

Dave whipped around, but Alisha had already sashayed out of the cubicle, heading toward the elevator. Her new boss had an office on the third floor, just above the visitor pod where Dave and Robert sat. Alisha had wisely chosen a cubicle up there for the day.

Dave frowned as he heard Robert laughing out loud.

"I repeat: you've got your hands full with that one," Robert said, smirking. "I'm glad I'm not her type."

Dave rolled his eyes. He stood up and looked at Robert. "Thanks, man. I do appreciate your offering to look at the proposal."

"Yeah, you owe me one," Robert grinned. "I'll tally up your tab. But I doubt she'll try to keep *me* here too late."

"I'm sure she won't," Dave agreed, sitting back down.

He quickly read through and inserted Robert's changes, added one additional point of his own, and saved the document. Ignoring other emails in his inbox, including two new ones from Alisha, he sent the proposal off to Desean and quickly shut down his laptop. He wanted to escape before Alisha came back.

He tossed a quick "Good night" to Robert as he slung his backpack over his shoulder and headed toward the stairwell, hoping to avoid meeting the woman anywhere near the elevators. He made it to his SUV without running into her. Throwing his backpack quickly into the passenger seat, he buckled up and drove rapidly, but safely, out of the lot.

Phew! He let out a huff of relief. It was already dark, but fortunately, he wasn't too much later than he'd planned.

Dave made the normally forty-five-minute drive in just under forty minutes. Thankfully, traffic had been light, and the state police officers who often patrolled Interstate 78 seemed to be somewhere else on this cold December night. And it *was* cold. The outside temperature indicator on his car's instrument panel read a mere twenty degrees. The dashboard clock confirmed that he'd have barely enough time to change and—he ran a hand along his jaw—shave the day's stubble from his face. He hurried out of his vehicle and into the house.

The kitchen was empty. As he walked toward his office to drop his bag, he heard faint rustling coming from the master bedroom. *She must be changing, too.* Buoyed by that thought, he quickly rid himself of his work stuff and headed upstairs.

Sheryl was just coming out of the bathroom when he walked through the double doors. His breath caught. Yes, she had just finished changing, and she was stunning. She wore a snug, V-neck cashmere sweater over a knee-length brown leather skirt and high boots. The sweater was heather purple, which was reflected beautifully in her hazel eyes. She'd taken extra care with her makeup, and the overall effect was simple, sophisticated, and, in his eyes, sexy. Classic Sheryl.

He drew in a breath, noticing the hesitancy in her eyes. "You look amazing," he said with a smile. "Wow."

She visibly relaxed before him. Her lips curled into a shy smile. "Thanks."

"I'd better get going if I'm going to live up to that!" he said. "I won't be long. Promise."

He leaned over and kissed her cheek as he walked by. Sheryl smiled again.

She was in the kitchen when he went back downstairs, clad now in a maroon cashmere sweater over a tan turtleneck and wool slacks. Sheryl looked at him and grinned. "Not bad, Mr. Simmons. Not bad at all."

He flashed a smile in thanks. "Shall we?" he said. "Our reservation is at 6:00."

"I'm ready," she said, sliding into her coat. He followed suit and added his scarf and gloves, and they headed out to his still warm SUV.

Twenty minutes later, they hustled into the restaurant, where they were escorted to a nice corner table in the back of the upstairs dining room. Due to the odd shape of the room, the table was set in a little alcove, slightly apart from other tables. It was exactly the privacy Dave had requested. He was glad he had made the reservation early enough to be accommodated, as he knew the place would fill up later in the evening, but he and Sheryl never minded eating early, even though they rarely did.

Sheryl slid into the chair that Dave held for her, after handing her coat to the maître d'.

"Rough day?" he asked. They hadn't spoken much on the car ride over.

"Yeah, is it that obvious?" she replied.

"Only to me," he said. "You seem a bit tense in the shoulders."

Sheryl rubbed her right temple. "I've got a potentially huge problem at work," she confided. "I don't know how huge, though." She paused and looked at him, her eyes troubled. "If it's as bad as I think it could be, well . . . it could bring the whole company down."

Dave's eyes widened. "That's quite a statement," he said. "I'm not sure how to respond to that. Want to tell me what's going on?"

Sighing, Sheryl shook her head. "Not tonight. I do want to tell you, but, I don't know, I need to get my own head around it. Plus," she added, laying a hand warmly on his arm, "I don't want to spoil our dinner. It's been a while since we've gone out like this."

Dave nodded. "Okay for now. But let's be sure to talk about it before the weekend is over."

He noticed the surprise in Sheryl's eyes, the way she tilted her head and looked more closely at him. Was she really that untrusting of him? He inwardly winced. *Yeah, she probably is.* Of course, he wasn't totally trusting of her either, not after all the crazy things he felt she had done earlier that fall. Things like going against the entire Board of Directors when they had unanimously voted to hire the infamous Layla Arch. She was darn lucky that Janine and some of the others had subsequently backed her. Otherwise, she would have been out of a job with a big black mark on her record.

He realized she was staring at him with a puzzled, almost fearful look. Some of his lingering disdain over her actions at work must have been showing on his face. *Gotta put that stuff outta my head for tonight.*

He picked up the menu. *Time to focus.*

By the time they ordered and got their drinks—wine for Sheryl, Scotch for Dave—and placed their food order, they both settled into a more relaxed state. They talked easily about Dave's new proposal, caught up on what Robert was doing, and stayed, by mutual agreement, on neutral topics. It wasn't until they had nearly finished their entrees that Alisha's name came up.

"So, what are your plans for tomorrow?" Sheryl asked.

Dave hesitated. "I'm going condo hunting with Alisha," he said cautiously.

Sheryl's lips tipped down. "Yeah, you told me about that earlier this week, didn't you? I guess I forgot."

Dave knew that Sheryl rarely forgot anything. Either she had put it out of her mind, or she had been hoping that he wouldn't go. Probably the latter.

"Yes, I did. I promised to help her with her transition. She wants another set of eyes when she's looking at places. Plus, she doesn't know the area very well. I can help with that."

"Why you?" Sheryl asked him plainly. "Doesn't she have any women friends here in the home office who could help?"

Dave paused. "I honestly don't know. I've never seen her hang out with anyone from headquarters. She doesn't get here very often . . . She also said she'd like a male perspective."

"Of course she did," Sheryl muttered, loudly enough for Dave to make out the words.

"Sheryl, come on. I'm just helping her out."

"I guess I don't understand why she needs so much help. I thought she was a salesperson. I know at your company they have to be extremely savvy. Isn't she capable of taking care of herself?"

Dave tilted his head to the left. "Really?"

Dave watched Sheryl bite her lip. Her hands clenched around her utensils. He could see her struggling to control her emotions. *Anger? Frustration? Was that sadness?* He couldn't get a handle on them.

Gathering herself, she took a deep breath. "Okay. I know you said she was having trouble with Liam, right? Why don't you tell me more about that? What has she told you?"

"You really want to know?" Dave asked.

When Sheryl nodded, he continued. "It started when we all played golf. Remember when I stayed in California to play at Pebble Beach?"

Sheryl gave him a sharp look but nodded.

"Well, that was when we, Robert and I, started noticing how Liam was acting. We'd seen him with women before. He, uh, likes women, even though he is married. Anyway, he was drinking a bit and started coming on to Alisha, but in a weird way. Every time I turned around, he was trying to touch her. When she tried to back away, he'd make little nasty comments about what a tease she was. We could tell Alisha was getting upset, but Liam is her boss. She tried to put him off as firmly and politely as she could, but Liam just kept going."

"Did you or Robert say anything to him?" Sheryl asked, her eyes wide.

"Yeah, we both took him aside and told him to knock it off, but he more or less told us to stay out of his business. After the game, it got worse. At one point, I got a chance to ask her if he was always like that. She acknowledged that he often was, but she told me to leave it alone, so I did. But the whole thing made me uncomfortable. I don't like to see women treated like that."

"That's horrible!" Sheryl exclaimed. "I'm surprised that you and Robert didn't take more action. Poor Alisha."

"Exactly, poor Alisha," Dave agreed. "We really did everything we could short of bodily restraining him. So . . . I called her on Monday to make sure she was okay and to see how I could help. I felt so bad for her."

Sheryl looked at him thoughtfully. "You always did like coming to the rescue," she said softly.

"Hmph. Is that a compliment?"

She laughed. "Probably. You are very sweet that way."

Dave made a face, not sure that he liked being called "sweet." Yet, he was glad Sheryl appreciated his protective nature. He had learned it the hard way, trying—mostly unsuccessfully—to protect his mother from his father's occasional outbursts of temper. He had vowed never to treat women badly, no matter how angry he got. That thought stopped him in his tracks. *Have I broken that vow with the way I treated Sheryl in the last few months?*

"Anyway," he continued, pushing that disturbing thought aside, "Alisha and I started talking more regularly after that, even if we weren't involved in a sales deal together. I guess she started using me more as a sounding board. Liam's behavior has only gotten worse, and it's not only Alisha. He hits on other women, too, although he's generally very careful about how and when. I don't think he does it much at work. Alisha might be the exception there."

"Is she very attractive?" Sheryl asked.

"Yes, she is," Dave replied frankly. "She's blonde and blue-eyed. Very fit, and she has a great figure."

"Just what I wanted to hear," Sheryl murmured.

"She's young—well, young to us. Probably thirty-five or so. Obviously, younger than Liam. She is in a tough spot," he added, his expression somewhat pleading. "You can see that."

He saw Sheryl melt. He had known she would. Sheryl always had a big heart. It was one of the things he loved about her.

"Yeah. I can see that," she said, her voice now full of kindness. "It sounds like you're being a nice guy. I do feel bad for her, but she really ought to go to HR. Guys like that need to be stopped, and thank God it's so much easier today than it was even a few years ago."

"I know, but it's still a hassle, and Liam does have a lot of influence in the company. I'm not sure why he let his guard down with Robert and me there. He doesn't ever do that. I don't think there's a lot of evidence, other than that one time."

"That should be enough!" Sheryl cried.

"Yes, it should be, but I can't do anything without Alisha agreeing, and she isn't. So, I'm just trying to help her get away from him at this point."

Sheryl nodded. He could see that she was upset; mostly, he hoped, about Alisha's situation.

"Yeah, I get it," Sheryl finally said. "It is good of you to help her. You are a nice guy. I just hope . . ."

"You hope what?" Dave asked.

"I hope she doesn't take advantage of you, that's all."

Dave laughed. "Nah, she won't," he said confidently.

Sheryl looked skeptical but didn't say anything.

"How about dessert?" Dave asked, anxious to get the conversation back on safer ground. No sense in going further down this road, not when Sheryl was being so sympathetic.

Sheryl smiled. "Sure, why not? We deserve it!"

He laughed. "Great. What should we get?"

They decided on sharing the Decadent Chocolate Cake, which turned out to be as good as its name. They also splurged on two glasses of cognac along with their decaf coffee. Sheryl seemed more open and receptive now that the whole situation with Alisha was out in the open, and Dave was very glad about that. It helped him relax, too.

He glanced at his wife over his cognac, realizing he admired Sheryl for listening, trying to understand, and being sympathetic toward Alisha. He knew not all women would, even if Sheryl was not entirely convinced about Alisha's motives. Neither was he, truth be told. Still, he felt better after talking to her, hearing her perspective. He felt much closer to her.

Dave held her hand as they walked to the SUV in sync, both of them sated and comfortable. He bent to give her a brief kiss as he opened her door, but his lips lingered. Sheryl's mouth softened under his, inviting a deeper intimacy.

He broke it off after a moment. "Hold that thought," he said, enjoying the return invitation in her eyes. Then he smiled to himself as he walked around to the driver's side. It had been a good evening, and it looked like it might just get even better.

Chapter 11

Waiting in the hotel lobby, Alisha checked her phone again. Dave was late. Not too late, less than five minutes, but she was ready to get going. They had their first appointment with the realtor at 10:30. There was still time, but . . . She glanced at her phone. No change.

She glanced down at her outfit. She wore tight jeans tucked into boots. Her sweater was snug, highlighting her curves, but it definitely wasn't too provocative. *Yeah,* she thought, *I look good, but still, well, respectable.* After all, she and Dave were looking for what she hoped might be their future home.

Alisha took a deep breath.

I need to calm down. I don't want Dave to think I'm too anxious.

But today was important. She wanted to take the budding relationship between her and Dave to the next level. They had been flirting with more than friendship in the last few months, more so recently. Professionally, and even personally, he confided in her. And she trusted him more than she had trusted anyone before. There hadn't been many men like Dave in her life. Her father certainly wasn't any kind of role model for reliability. Today was the first step in making him hers and hers alone.

Dave's black Explorer pulled into the hotel parking lot, and Alisha felt her tension ease. She had been surprised when he agreed to go condo hunting with her today instead of Sunday. But she was glad. If she was lucky, she could convince him to help her again tomorrow. *He must have blown Sheryl off today.* She smiled, satisfied at that thought, zipped up her down jacket, and hurried out into the cold wind.

Settling into the plush leather seat, Alisha gave Dave a big grin. "Good morning!" she said cheerfully as he turned off the radio.

Dave smiled, but with much less enthusiasm. "Good morning," he said calmly. "Where are we headed first?"

"We're meeting the realtor at Bracing Place, which is in Berkeley Heights. According to Google Maps, you'll need to get on the highway."

Dave nodded. "Okay, I think I know roughly where that is."

She studied him as he navigated onto 78, hearing the faint squeak of his leather jacket as he moved. The day was gray and overcast, but she could see that Dave himself wasn't very gloomy. In fact, he looked more relaxed today, a bit tired, but he seemed . . . content. *He must be relieved to be with me instead of dealing with Sheryl.* She knew how upset he had been when Sheryl started doing crazy things at work. He had told Alisha all about it, about how he felt that he didn't know Sheryl anymore. Now, he was with her, feeling content. Alisha beamed.

He obviously felt her gaze, because he shot her a quick, questioning look.

"You seem more relaxed than usual today," she said, answering his unspoken question.

He smirked. This time, she couldn't tell if the expression was smug or not. "Yeah," he said, his voice deepening. "I'm good today."

"Glad you're here?" she said playfully.

He shot her a surprised look. "I'm glad to be able to help you out," he said carefully. "But honestly, there are things I'd prefer to be doing than looking at condos . . . although it is too cold for golf."

Alisha sat back, feeling rebuffed despite the friendly tone in his voice. She tucked her thumbs beneath her fingers, stretching the bright blue gloves she wore. "Well, I'm sorry that I'm wrecking your weekend," she said huffily.

Dave sighed. "You're not wrecking my weekend, Alisha. It's fine. I know you'll feel better with a second opinion. I get that. Is this where I turn?"

Alisha looked at the map on her phone. "Yes," she said. "Make a right. We're almost there."

She concentrated on telling him where to drive. His response wasn't exactly what she had been hoping for. He was being friendly, but she sensed a distance she didn't like—one she was not used to. First the report he refused to go over, and now this . . . *What happened with Sheryl last night? Is he no longer angry with his wife?* She didn't really want to bring Sheryl up, but maybe she should. She would have to remind Dave why he was better off with her than Sheryl, as he had been hinting before Thanksgiving. The SUV pulled to the curb. *Too late to remind him now. Damn!*

The realtor was waiting out in front of a newish two-story condominium. Alisha greeted her warmly. She had felt a good connection with Beatrice over the phone. A chic-looking woman in her early fifties, Beatrice had great credentials and a friendly manner. She had impressed Alisha with her intuitive understanding of Alisha's needs and quick responses to her questions. It didn't hurt that she had come highly recommended by the head of Human Resources.

Alisha saw Beatrice eye Dave appraisingly and quickly introduced them. "Beatrice, this is Dave. He's a very good friend who was nice enough to give me a second opinion today," she said, throwing a flirty look at Dave.

Dave politely shook Beatrice's hand. "Yeah, she said she needed a guy's perspective," he elaborated. "Although I'm not sure why."

Beatrice laughed. "Well, of course she did, honey."

Alisha saw Dave frown, and she quickly steered Beatrice toward the condo they had come to see. The exterior was pleasant but not exciting, with white aluminum siding and a neutral gray trim. However, in Alisha's mind, the true selling point for this one was that it was an end unit with an extra garage bay. Beatrice wasted no time extolling the virtues of the neighborhood while she unlocked the door and ushered them in.

Beatrice efficiently led Alisha through the home, with Dave trailing behind. Alisha liked it, but it seemed a little dark and closed in. *It could use a few skylights on the second floor,* she thought as they climbed the carpeted stairs.

The master bedroom in the back of the unit had a balcony that overlooked a playground area. Leaning over the railing, she noticed Dave's eyes sweep over the jungle gym and swings, his face tightening ever so slightly. She gently touched his arm, conveying her understanding and comfort. That would be a nice reminder for him that she was still young enough to have children—and willing. But Dave turned away abruptly without acknowledging her touch. Puzzled, Alisha followed him into the master bath.

The en-suite bathroom was a pleasant surprise, with both a dual-zone shower and a deep soaking tub. There was plenty of room for her to spread out her things and still have space for someone else to share.

She turned to Dave. "What do you think?" she asked, smiling with pleasure.

He shrugged. "It's nice. Lots of room. The construction seems solid from what I can see." He turned on the faucet in the sink closest to him. "Good water pressure. That can be a problem with so many condos close together. Do you like it?"

"It's okay," she replied cautiously. "But there's not a lot of light, and the space might be a little tight for me and . . ." She let her voice trail off, leaving the implication hanging in the air. She held her breath. This was it. Her first real hint to Dave.

Yes, Dave had made sure she was safe from Liam. And he was helping her today. But this . . . it sent a thrill through her spine. She needed someone like him, and he needed her. And here she was, looking for the space where they could be happy together. Where he could get away from Sheryl as much as she was getting away from Liam.

Dave stiffened. Alisha knew immediately she had made a mistake when he turned off the water, then quickly backed out of the bathroom. "I'll go check out the kitchen while you finish up in here," he said and quickly headed toward the stairs.

Beatrice glanced at her speculatively, but all she said was, "There's more to see downstairs."

Alisha paused, then nodded and followed her out. But the bounce had gone out of her step.

By the time Beatrice and Alisha finished going through the rest of the condo, Dave had slipped outside and was waiting by his vehicle. He was engrossed in something on his phone and didn't look up as the two women approached.

"Dave?" Alisha gently called his attention to her.

He slid the phone into his pocket and looked at her. His face was grim, but he quickly smoothed it into a neutral mask.

Beatrice, giving the ring on Dave's left hand a sharp look, turned her attention to Alisha. "Well, what did you think?"

"It was nice," Alisha said slowly. "There were things I liked, but I think I'm looking for a bit more."

"More what?" Beatrice probed.

"I don't know. More exciting, I guess. It was nice but a little bland, and the neighborhood seems a little, hmm, sedate?"

Beatrice nodded. "Okay, let's go onto the next one. You'll like it better, I think." She smiled at Dave. "You can follow me. It's not far."

He nodded and walked around to the driver's door, leaving Alisha to fend for herself. She climbed in, feeling disgruntled. So far, things were not going according to plan.

The next condo showed more promise. Like the first one, it was an end unit, but it had a larger garage and a garden area in the back. The rooms were bigger with more natural light, and there was not a playground in sight. That suited Alisha. Even though she was prepared to have Dave's children, she didn't need to listen to the neighborhood kids screaming outside all day.

However, Dave noticed a few cracks on a bedroom wall that looked like there might be a structural issue. They were well-hidden behind an oversized armoire, Alisha noted with a tiny nod. *Good, Dave is really taking an interest in scoping out the place. Maybe he's just being cautious because of Beatrice.*

Looking around, she felt that this condo suited her more than the first. She could envision living here, the rooms lavishly decorated, entertaining friends with Dave by her side. She turned to share her excitement, but he had already headed back downstairs. She frowned. *He's here and helping, but he doesn't really seem present today like he normally is.*

She realized Beatrice was watching her, a knowing look in her brown eyes.

"Nice-looking man," Beatrice commented. "But didn't I see a ring on his hand?"

Alisha glared at the older woman for a moment. "Let's see the rest," she said abruptly, and she followed Dave out of the room.

Outside again, she admitted to Beatrice and Dave that she was far more interested in this unit than the first one. Beatrice agreed enthusiastically; after all, the asking price was a bit higher on this one, too.

Dave nodded but didn't comment. Alisha started to push him for an opinion and was shocked when Beatrice interrupted.

"Alisha, dear," she said sweetly but with an undertone of pure steel, "why don't you ride with me to the next place? It's only about five minutes away, and based on your feedback so far, I'd like to review our plan for the day. Dave can follow us."

Alisha was stunned when Beatrice grabbed her elbow and propelled her toward the car.

"Dave, is that okay with you?" Beatrice called over her shoulder.

Alisha barely heard Dave's agreement as Beatrice slammed the passenger door and hurried around to the driver's side of her late-model Cadillac. The luxuriousness of the car barely registered as she turned to confront the realtor.

"What did you do that for?" she stormed. "I need to talk to him, to get him back on the same page!" Alisha was appalled at herself for sharing so brazenly. She usually held her cards closer to her chest, but things were getting so far off course, and the nerve of this woman!

Beatrice calmly put the vehicle in drive and pulled away from the curb. "I did it for your own good," she said firmly. "I don't know what's going on with you and that man, but honey, you are making a mess of things. Give him a breather. He needs it. He's clearly not ready to think about moving in with you." She paused as she glanced at her GPS. "And what about that ring? Are you sure you know what you are getting yourself into? From the paperwork you sent me, you surely can afford these places on your own. You don't *need* a man."

"Of course I can afford it," Alisha snapped. "That's not the point. I'm moving here to be with him. I want to be with him."

"I thought you were moving here for your job," Beatrice said mildly, clearly unaffected by Alisha's rage.

"I am, damn it!" Alisha's voice rose in frustration. "But you're missing the point."

"No dear. At the risk of losing this commission, *you* are missing the point."

"And you are going to lose this commission!" Alisha cried. "Who do you think you are? You're not my mother!"

Beatrice glanced at her and sighed. Her voice softened. "No honey, I'm not, and you're right. I shouldn't be interfering. I just can't help myself. I have a bad habit of giving advice when it's not wanted," she conceded. "But I do have your best interest at heart, my dear, whether you believe that or not. I have two daughters of my own, and close to your age. I'd like to think that someone else would give them sage advice when I'm not there."

"Well, you're right. You should butt out," Alisha grumbled, feeling somewhat mollified by Beatrice's concession. Plus, she knew Beatrice was right about Dave, and she had no idea what to do about it. She had been so sure that he was ready to take their relationship to the next level. He had been so protective of her, which had left her feeling warm and safe, and so unhappy with Sheryl. *What the hell had happened?*

Beatrice drew her attention to the schedule for the rest of the day. They both knew that the condo they had just left was perfect for Alisha—with or without Dave. Alisha's thrifty living in California had given her a sizeable nest egg that would provide a terrific down payment, making the monthly payments more than manageable.

Beatrice bluntly told her that there was only one more property that she felt Alisha would like and there was no point in visiting the others. The next stop would be the last. Beatrice also encouraged Alisha to think about making an offer quickly. It was a seller's market. Both properties were recently listed, and they wouldn't be on the market for long.

Alisha drew a deep breath as they pulled up to the final home. Beatrice was right about one thing: she had to calm down. She had a mission to complete. Smoothing her hair and her feelings, she zipped her jacket up before she got out. By the time Dave walked up beside her, she had already donned her professional face. If that was where he was drawing the line today, she could adapt. Maybe she'd pushed it too far, but that didn't mean she couldn't adjust her tactics and recover gracefully.

"I have good news," she said in a pleasant voice. "Beatrice and I decided to curtail the list of properties today. That last condo was really great, and now that she knows what I like, she's eliminated all but this one. So, this is the last stop. Sound good?"

Dave's look of relief was almost comical. Alisha ground her teeth as he replied, "Yeah, sounds great," much too happily. He added, "But you don't have to cut it short on my account."

"Oh, we're not," she said, her tone light and neutral. "It's all good. I want to see these other two places to compare, but I kind of fell in love with that last place."

"Oh, good. It was a really great place. I'm sure you'd be happy there. And I only saw that one red flag. Maybe the inspection will show that those cracks are only superficial. You do know you need an inspection?"

"Yes, I know. I once looked at properties near home, and Beatrice has already talked me through all that. I'm glad she's so experienced, me being a first-time homebuyer. She's really helpful," Alisha said brightly, thankful for her sales training. She could fake enthusiasm with the best of them.

"Excellent," Dave replied. "I'm sure she knows her stuff."

Alisha smiled. "Let's go check this one out," she said, and followed Beatrice up the walk, Dave by her side. She caught a whiff of a woodsy cologne as they entered the house. It was a scent she loved, although it was one he'd never worn in the office.

Did he put that on for me before heading out this morning? She felt her spirits lift briefly, until another thought crossed her mind. *Or is that Sheryl's favorite?*

Alisha, despite her ire with Beatrice, had observed that they had traveled into a more congested area during the drive. This condo was close to the Short Hills Mall, a high-end shopping center she had heard mentioned by the women in the office. She asked Dave and Beatrice about the location as they walked up to a pretty unit with a partial brick façade and a small front porch. They both agreed that Summit had easier access to shopping and restaurants, and the development looked newer and even more upscale than the last one.

"It's farther from the office," Dave observed. "But that probably won't be a big deal to you since you won't be there that often. Summit is closer to the airport and the trains to New York. That could be a saving grace."

"Hmm, that could be a plus."

Beatrice opened the door and began to guide Alisha through the downstairs rooms. Dave followed for a bit, but when they headed upstairs, she noticed that he had drifted away. Alisha frowned inwardly but focused on what Beatrice was saying. *Did I really scare him that much that he won't even walk into a bedroom with me now? Does that idea repulse him all of a sudden?*

They discovered that this end unit was about the same age as the last one they had seen and had similar features inside. All the rooms were smaller, but only slightly, and the light was excellent. Alisha especially liked the layout of the master bedroom, and there was no playground in sight here either.

Alisha, staring out the bedroom window at a row of trees on the perimeter of the property, sighed. The branches looked so bare and stark against the gray sky. The whole scene suddenly seemed as bleak as she now felt. Getting together with Dave was clearly going to take longer than she hoped. *In the meantime, it might be nice to be closer to the social activities that Summit has to offer.* She frowned, not liking that line of reasoning. She shook her head, her ponytail swinging. She had a lot to think about.

When the two women headed downstairs, they found Dave in the den, leaning against the desk, lost in his phone again. He gave Alisha a guilty look when they walked in and shoved the phone back in his pocket.

"All set?" he asked.

"What do you think of this place?" Alisha's voice was upbeat and friendly.

"Uh, it's nice. Looks well-built, and the fixtures seem a little higher quality. I didn't see any red flags," he offered.

Alisha gave him a quick smile. "Thanks. I agree."

"So, what's next?"

Alisha glanced at Beatrice, then back at Dave. "Well . . ."

"Why don't we go back to my office and discuss your options?" Beatrice interrupted. "If you're serious about either of them, you'll want to think about getting an offer in right away."

Alisha hesitated, looking at Dave, willing him to suggest that they needed to discuss her options together first. He didn't.

"Oh, well, yeah, I could do that," Alisha finally ground out.

Avoiding her gaze, Dave straightened and turned to Beatrice. "Is your office far?" he asked. "I mean, would it be okay for you to drop Alisha back at her hotel when you're done? She won't need me for this part."

Alisha's heart dropped even as her whole body tensed. *Really?* She wanted to scream at him. *Yes, I do need you. I want your help!* But she kept her mouth shut, finally resigned to the fact that he was intent on escape. She had seen it before, with her father. She had hoped it would be different . . .

"Oh, that's no trouble, dear," Beatrice was telling Dave. "My office isn't far, and Alisha and I will do quite fine on our own."

Alisha didn't bother to smile. "Of course, that makes sense," she agreed calmly.

"Great! I'll leave you ladies to it, then," Dave said, seeming more cheerful than he had been all day. "Beatrice, it's been a pleasure. Alisha, good luck. You'll have to give me all the details on Monday when we're back in the office."

Giving them a quick wave, he practically raced out the door. Alisha stood stock-still, utter humiliation and rage rolling through her in waves. *Monday? In the office on Monday? How dare he? After all we've been through, he's going to treat me like I'm only a co-worker? Monday?*

"Take a deep breath, honey," Beatrice said in her ear. "Tomorrow is another day."

Alisha glared at her. "Well, you just gave him the perfect way out. Thanks a lot. I should find another realtor," she rasped.

"But you won't," Beatrice said cheerfully, turning toward the door. "Because you know I'm the best one to help you. Let's go, honey," she added gently. "I promise, if you are serious, you'll want to get an offer in today—before anyone else has a chance to make a bid. The question is which one."

Still fuming, Alisha followed her out. She might have had to retreat today, but this was far from over. She wasn't moving all the way to New Jersey, of all places, for nothing. *I'm going to figure out what's going on with Dave and fix it—one way or another.* She thought about the playground at the first condo and suddenly smiled. *Ha! I still have cards up my sleeve. Sheryl is not going to win this one.*

Chapter 12

Monday, December 6

Sheryl pushed her bangs back from her face, sighing as she closed her journal. It was time to shower and get to work. Her day had started early with a workout followed by her morning practices, her connection time. It was a habit she had started only a few months ago, and it paid off in spades, but there were days she'd rather have that extra fifteen or twenty minutes of sleep.

Today was one of them, but then Mondays were always hard. It had been a good weekend. She smiled an inner smile as she thought about the intimacy that she and Dave had shared on Friday night and his tenderness the next morning. It had been a few months since they had done more than simply share a bed, and she was relieved that Dave had initiated sex. She had been beginning to wonder if . . . well, "they" said that lack of sex was a sign that a man was having an affair. Of course, one night didn't necessarily mean that he wasn't, but . . . The night had gone a long way to making her feel a lot more hopeful about their relationship.

It also helped that Dave had seemed quite annoyed when he returned from house-hunting with the woman on Saturday. He hadn't said much, but she had gotten the distinct impression that Alisha had irritated him in some way. Sheryl allowed herself a small smirk. Maybe Alisha wasn't as much of an issue as Sheryl had thought.

She looked at the journal she was holding, running a hand over the rough faux-leather surface. This, *this* was still hanging over her head, over her relationship with Dave, and they hadn't talked about it.

It wasn't the journal itself, she thought, as she slid it into the desk drawer and blew out the candle that she had lit for meditation. It was her spiritual practice as a whole, or rather its impact on her work. Dave hadn't mentioned it, but she had seen his face at the dinner table on Friday. He was still angry about how she had handled things at The Diamante, even though he had pushed it aside. *We still need to talk about that.*

Still, her mood was buoyant as she drove her dark blue sedan with its calming beige interior toward the office thirty minutes later. They had made progress, and the lump of dread that had been lodged in her stomach for weeks felt smaller and more manageable. She tuned the radio to an upbeat SiriusXM channel, feeling ready to face the day.

Sheryl was startled when her personal cell phone rang, the blare of the ringtone cutting sharply through the car. She was even more surprised when she saw that the caller was Keisha, from *her* personal phone.

"Why do I think this is not good news?" she asked without preamble.

"It's not," Keisha said, her voice dark and heavy. "I think I figured out what's going on."

"Did you work all weekend?" Sheryl asked, concern threading her voice.

"Yeah, but it's okay," Keisha said. "I just . . . I just couldn't stop once I started unraveling things."

"So, you're calling before we get to the office for privacy, I assume?"

"Yeah, although I'm not sure I should tell you while you're driving. Is there somewhere you can stop?"

Sheryl heart skipped a beat and her chest tightened as she looked more closely at where she was on the highway. "I'm about a mile and a half from the next exit," she told Keisha. "I'll call you back when I find somewhere to park." *This doesn't sound good at all.*

Forcing herself to focus on the road, Sheryl kept her breathing as even and deep as she could. By the time she had taken the exit and pulled into the gas station/convenience store lot, a full five minutes had passed. Parking in front of a scraggly row of evergreen bushes which she barely noticed, she called Keisha back. Keisha answered on the first ring.

"Okay, so here's what I found," she said quickly. "The fields haven't always been missing."

"What? What do you mean they haven't always been missing?"

"Well, I had Danielle pull a few of the old backup database files for me," Keisha explained, referring to one of the database administrators

KAREN ANN BULLUCK

on Sheryl's team. "I told her that I wanted to do some testing and wanted to see different data. I think she was skeptical, but she gave me some backups from six months ago and a year ago. Those fields were in both of those databases! Both of them!"

Sheryl cocked her head, listening intently. "That's weird. What's in the fields?"

"Okay, that's where it gets really strange, because the data in those fields makes no sense. It's like random numbers and letters that have no apparent meaning. But the really interesting thing is that not all the customer records have those fields. Only a few do. There are more that have them in the six-month-old database, but the year-old one has a few."

Sheryl gripped the steering wheel, her fingers stretching against her leather gloves, her mind racing. "Go on," she said. "But what happened to the fields? Why are they missing now?"

"Well, it looks like someone took them out. Someone from SalesTeam, most likely. They were customizable fields. A lot of people don't use them. It could be that they weren't needed anymore, but somehow, I don't think so."

"What?" Sheryl interjected. "What do you mean by that?"

Keisha drew in a deep breath. "Because the field labeled 'Options' looks like it might have held dollar amounts. And, well, I'm really guessing here, but it looks like those dollar amounts are not invested with The Diamante. It looks like they may have been funneled out."

"Funneled out?" Sheryl cried, latching onto the most dangerous information. "They're taking money out of The Diamante accounts?"

Sheryl tried to assimilate the information and the consequences. If someone was funneling money out of the company, it was, first of all, illegal. That in itself was a huge problem, but the company's reputation would be ruined. *Wow. What a scandal. It could put us out of business.*

". . . No, no," she heard Keisha saying. "I didn't say anyone is taking money out of The Diamante accounts."

"Then what money is being funneled out?"

"Well, maybe that's the wrong word." Keisha paused. "Maybe *redirecting* is a better word."

"Redirecting? Keisha, you're not making sense."

"I know. Just listen," Keisha answered impatiently, her voice rough with fatigue.

Sheryl wondered briefly if she was coherent.

". . . So, I looked at the accounts that had data in those fields," Keisha continued, sounding tired and frustrated. "And I noticed a pattern. First, all the accounts belonged to just two financial advisors. Second, all the accounts had high initial investment projections in the normal part of the prospect profile. Very high. Third, none of the accounts ended up putting that whole initial investment projection into The Diamante funds. Usually, they only invested about a half to two-thirds of what they said they were considering investing initially."

There was a long silence while Sheryl tried to take it all in. She rubbed her temple with one gloved hand, while the other tapped on the steering wheel.

"So, what does this mean?" she finally asked. "They could have decided just to put part of their money with The Diamante. That doesn't seem like a huge issue. I'm sure it happens."

"It's just two financial advisors, Sheryl."

"Okay, I'll bite," Sheryl responded, irritated now with Keisha's pace. "Who are the two financial advisors?"

"Suni Chung and Gregor, uh, the one with the unpronounceable last name."

"Aren't they both pretty new?" Sheryl asked, thinking back to what she knew about them. "Gregor has been here a bit longer than Suni. Maybe a couple of years?"

Sheryl didn't often interact with the financial advisors, nor did Keisha. Anything they knew came from the company newsletter or the grapevine. Sheryl couldn't remember anything outstanding about either of them. They both had good reputations, and Sheryl was pretty sure they were among the firm's top performers.

Suddenly grasping Keisha's implication, Sheryl filled in the blank. "And you think they are steering the money into investments outside The Diamante? Do you have any proof?"

"Yes, that's what it looks like," Keisha answered, her voice sounding satisfied and relieved. "I'm glad you came to the same conclusion. But no, I don't have proof. Just patterns. From what I can see, the dollar amounts in the Options field is the difference between the initial discussion and what shows up on the client investment reports . . . And I could be wrong. I don't know for sure what those numbers are. But someone inside has to know. After all, Suni and Gregor couldn't have changed the database."

"Wow," Sheryl said, her mind churning. *Besides the scandal, what else could happen? Is there any way that Keisha could be blamed? Or me? Would I be in trouble with the SEC too? Or the database administrators? How far would this go?*

Pushing those thoughts aside, Sheryl refocused on responding to Keisha. "I don't even know what to say, but you're right about the database. So, who could have helped them inside?"

"That's hard to say," Keisha answered carefully. "I've thought about it, but you remember that IT wasn't involved when the SalesTeam software was set up. They didn't even want us to access the database for the Portal Project, remember?"

"Yeah, I remember." Sheryl rolled her shoulders in a vain attempt to ease the tension that was gripping them. *What else do I know about those advisors . . . ? Did Jim bring them on? They were hired after he started. Or Rachel? She had a vague sense that they had worked with one of them at another company. Which one . . . ? Was that even right?*

"Is it illegal? Steering money to different investments?" Keisha's anxious question interrupted her thoughts.

"I don't know," Sheryl said, bringing her focus back to the conversation. She was very unsettled by what Keisha had told her. "It may be, and it's certainly unethical. For one thing, it has to be against The Diamante's policies." Sheryl sighed deeply, shaking her head. "I don't even know what to think, what to say."

"I know," Keisha said. "It's pretty surreal. And I don't know how we'd even go about proving it. What do we do, though? Don't we have to report something to someone?"

"I have to think about this," Sheryl said quickly, wanting to protect Keisha as much as she could. Reassurance in her voice, she went on,

"You were right to call me privately. I'm honestly not sure what to do or who to talk to, but I'll figure it out. For now, just keep all this to yourself, and don't ask any more questions about those fields."

"No, of course, I won't," Keisha replied, sounding relieved. "I'll just ignore this whole thing until I hear from you."

"Sounds good," Sheryl said distractedly.

"Okay, see you at the office," Keisha said. "Drive safe."

"Uh, you too," Sheryl replied, then realized Keisha had already hung up. She sat in the car, staring blindly through the windshield. *Who do I talk to about this? Alex? He's the Chief Investment Officer. Or the compliance officer? Or Todd? No, I don't want to talk to Todd, not yet. Todd has no patience when it comes to revenue and money. He'll have my head . . . or Keisha's—or the whole team's! I don't want her to get caught in the crossfire. This is a nightmare. A total nightmare.*

After several minutes, Sheryl realized that she was still sitting there, the car running. She had to get to the office. Putting the car in reverse, she carefully navigated out of the parking spot. She paid extra attention merging back onto the highway, not wanting to get into an accident because of her distraction. The morning sun in her eyes was challenging enough.

Thirty minutes later, she was safely ensconced in her office, her computer on, going through her emails. But her mind kept going back to the conversation with Keisha. What should she do? There was no proof, but it seemed obvious that *something* wrong, something that needed to be investigated. Her only choice seemed to be Compliance. She paused. *But maybe I should talk to Rachel first. Follow up on last week's meeting. Maybe she can give me some insight, point out something I'm missing. Even though I can't ask her directly.*

Sheryl immediately called Rachel and asked her to go out to lunch. She didn't want to meet her in the cafeteria. She was relieved when Rachel agreed. Blocking her calendar accordingly, she turned back to her email with a clearer mind.

Not ten minutes later, an unfamiliar man's frame filled her doorway. Tall and very slender, he had thinning gray hair, brown eyes, and one of the warmest smiles she had ever seen.

"Sheryl?" he asked hesitantly, stepping into her office.

"Yes, and you are . . ." *Blake Jones!* Sheryl realized in an instant, remembering the picture that she had seen on the Internet while researching the CFO candidate. Blake was the alternative applicant to Layla Arch, Hank Turner's choice, at that fateful November board meeting.

"Blake Jones," he confirmed, confidently crossing the room to hold out his hand. "I understand I have you to thank for my position here at The Diamante."

Flushing, Sheryl rose and shook his hand warmly. "Well, I wouldn't go that far," she demurred.

He chuckled, taking the seat in front of her desk that she indicated. "That's not what I've heard," he replied, quirking one eyebrow. "Especially since you took on Hank Turner to do it. That's *really* impressive. He's a tough old codger."

Sheryl's blush deepened. "I only did what I thought was the right thing," she responded humbly.

"Well, thank you," Blake said firmly. "I'm happy to be here, and I'm truly looking forward to working with you." He paused before adding wryly, "Even *if* I'll have to deal with Anthony Russo and whoever replaced Hank."

Grimacing in sympathy, Sheryl wanted to assure him that it would be fine, but she didn't actually know that. So, she changed the subject and asked about his initial impressions of the firm. After all, today was his first day. He had clearly made visiting her a top priority, which was flattering. They chatted pleasantly for several minutes before he excused himself and hurried off, promising to schedule more time with her soon.

Reflecting on the visit, Sheryl was happy that her first in-person encounter with the new CFO affirmed her controversial vote. He seemed intelligent, competent, and astute—just as she had expected from seeing his credentials. *He also seems like a really nice man, kind of like Alex Thompson.* She smiled, hopeful that she'd now have two friends and allies on the executive team and board. *Given where things might be headed, that could be a really good thing.*

A knot in her stomach, Sheryl headed to the lobby to meet Rachel at noon. She didn't quite understand her trepidation, but she vowed to keep all her senses alert—including her intuition—during this lunch meeting.

Rachel was already waiting near the door with her black coat and gloves on. Her associate greeted her with a friendly smile, looking surprisingly pleased and enthusiastic. Sheryl smiled in return, relaxing a bit. She usually enjoyed Rachel, even though they didn't spend much time together. Rachel was always funny and quick-witted, with an eye for the absurd.

She and Sheryl had commiserated about being women in the male-dominated investment world, although both were relieved that was rapidly changing. Rachel had been among the first to congratulate Sheryl on her promotion early in the fall. Sheryl knew that Rachel hoped it would open more doors for herself in the future.

The two women chatted easily as Sheryl drove to a nearby restaurant, one frequented by The Diamante staff but not usually on Mondays. They grabbed a table near a side window, taking advantage of the nearly empty dining room. Putting the white linen napkin in her lap, Sheryl observed with relief that none of the other diners were from the company.

It wasn't until after they had ordered that Rachel brought up the Portal Project.

"I'm glad that we have some privacy to talk," she began. "I wanted to tell you how glad I was to see you at that meeting last week. We've been very concerned about the project, especially since your promotion. We weren't sure that you would have enough time to really pay attention to it."

Sheryl cocked an eyebrow. "Really? Who are 'we'?"

"Well, Jim and I, of course."

"Ah, yes. Jim. Well, I know how extremely important this project is. I promise I'm keeping it high on my radar," she said agreeably.

Rachel smiled. "Of course. I knew that, but you know how Jim worries."

Sheryl didn't know anything of the sort. She knew Jim was ambitious and that he had made a big deal about the Portal Project—but worried?

"I'm sorry that you and Jim have been worried," Sheryl responded evenly. "I'll have to make sure that I touch base more often and let you know that I'm keeping an eye on things."

"That would be great!" Rachel replied enthusiastically. "Plus, it gives us a chance to spend more time together."

"Absolutely. That is a nice bonus. So, how do you think the project is going from your end?"

"Oh, good, I guess. We do love the new interface, but it's taking an awfully long time," Rachel said, softening her barb with a pleasant tone.

"Yes, I'm sorry about that," Sheryl empathized. "We all want it done sooner, but we'll also be happier with the result of taking the extra time. Making that interface so simple and elegant requires extra work on the backend."

"I know. I know," Rachel concurred ruefully. "It will be worth it. Right?"

"Yes, it will be," Sheryl said firmly, feeling another trickle of unease. "I promise." But she wondered if she could keep that promise. After all, Sheryl was not going to allow the release of a project when there was a possibility that it would cover up illegal or unethical activities by the financial advisors.

Rachel laughed, but it seemed a little disingenuous to Sheryl. "You're right. I need to have more faith in you and your team. Keisha is so talented with the interface. It's too bad her database skills aren't as strong."

Sheryl nodded thoughtfully, playing along. "Well, she's not a DBA, but she can hold her own. She's learning quickly."

Rachel tugged at the colorful scarf around her neck. "Yes, I'm sure she is."

Sheryl hesitated. *I have to be careful not to tip my hand here. I don't want Rachel to suspect what we know, just in case she is involved. I don't want to give her the chance to cover anything up or raise alarms . . . or tip the real culprit off accidentally.*

"Do you know who designed the database?" Sheryl asked, trying to sound nonchalant. "You were involved with the installation of SalesTeam, weren't you?

"Oh, I was a little," Rachel said, biting her lip. "But we didn't do that much customization at the beginning."

"Really?" Sheryl asked curiously. "It was only installed a couple of years ago. Right after Jim started. But that's when you started, too, isn't it?"

"Yes, it was," Rachel said, a bit of impatience slipping into her voice. "I knew Jim from a previous employer. When he started at The Diamante, he wanted to have a few familiar people on his team. I was lucky enough to be one of them."

"Oh, I remember that now," Sheryl said, keeping her voice light. She took a sip of her water, glancing out the window at the bare slate patio.

The server arrived with their food. Both women had ordered salads. Sheryl had added salmon to hers. She wondered where to take the conversation next. Despite her casual attitude, Sheryl sensed real discomfort beneath Rachel's veneer. *What does she know about the database?*

"So, if you didn't change much at the beginning, when *did* you guys add customization to SalesTeam?" Sheryl asked, trying to match Rachel's casualness.

"Oh, I'm not sure," Rachel said, frowning a little. "I don't think much customization was ever done. I only took over as the liaison for SalesTeam a few months ago. Jim was handling it himself before then."

"Ah, that's right," Sheryl agreed. "You only took over when the Portal Project started."

"Yes, around then. I'm not sure what was done before then. Jim didn't mention anything special."

"Well, it doesn't matter now," Sheryl said, stumped about where to go next. "Are there any other concerns that you have?"

Rachel didn't have anything else, and the conversation turned to the latest industry scandal at one of The Diamante's competitors and other industry news. Sheryl barely tasted her food as she weighed what little information Rachel had given her while maintaining the conversation.

Seeming more relaxed by the time they got back to the office, Rachel waved cheerfully when they parted in the lobby. Sheryl watched in surprise as Rachel headed down the corridor toward the cafeteria rather than joining her in the elevator or taking the stairs. Rachel's office was on the floor above hers. *That's odd. Where is she going?*

Sheryl watched for a moment before choosing to take the stairs to the second floor. The lunch hadn't given her any new information . . . or had it?

I guess I'm going to have to try talking to Jim. If anyone ordered the database altered, it would have to be him. But what is Rachel so worried about that she's keeping it from me? And where the heck did she go just now?

Chapter 13

Her computer chimed, indicating an incoming email. Sheryl glanced up, surprised, and yet not, to see a message from Jim. No, it was a meeting invitation. For that afternoon. Rachel must have gone directly to his office upon returning from lunch. *Ah. Well, that didn't take long, did it? That explains why she didn't ride the elevator with me.* Jim was on the same floor as Sheryl, not Rachel.

She glanced at the time. The meeting invite was for only twenty minutes from now. Unfortunately, Sheryl couldn't claim she would be in another meeting; her calendar showed that she was wide open. Jim, or his admin, would have seen that when scheduling the meeting.

Damn, I should have seen this coming. Jim always takes the bull by the horns. Sheryl paused, rolling her shoulders in a vain attempt to ease the tension that suddenly tightened them. She forced herself to take a deep, deep breath. The next step had been taken out of her hands. She wasn't happy. After all, she had just been debating whether to go directly to Compliance or talk to Alex Thompson, the head of investments, about her concerns.

Shaking her head, Sheryl realized that she had no choice now. She preferred and had planned to confront Jim at some point on *her* terms, not his, but she'd have to make the best of it. Turning back to her email, she sighed loudly, irritated but also vaguely relieved that her next action was clear.

Thirty minutes later, any sense of relief was long gone. Sheryl had taken the time to freshen her makeup and spent a few minutes picturing herself surrounded with white light before walking slowly and calmly down the long corridor to Jim's office. Since it was on the opposite side of the building from her office, she had time to give herself a mental pep talk on the way. *Something is wrong, but I'm not at fault and neither is Keisha,* she reminded herself. *I'm not going to make accusations, either. We're just gathering information.*

She entered the lavish office calm and centered, ready to take on whatever Jim was dishing out without getting defensive. Jim had stood when she entered the office, although not out of politeness. He was at least six feet tall, and he used every inch of his muscular build to tower over Sheryl's shorter frame.

Blindsided by his threatening stance, Sheryl forced herself to stand her ground, looking him squarely in the eye. He immediately barraged her with accusatory questions from behind his massive desk:

"Why did you ask Rachel about the database? What does that Keisha girl think she found? Why do you have such incompetent people working on such an important project?" he blustered, barely pausing to take a breath.

Stunned by the ferocity of his attack, Sheryl took a deep breath to steady herself. "Are you finished?" she asked. She kept her voice calm but met Jim's gaze with fire in her hazel eyes.

Jim took a slight step back, his gray-blue eyes narrowing.

"No, I'm not finished," he growled, though with a bit less aggression in his voice. "But I want to hear what you have to say for yourself."

Outraged, Sheryl moved closer to the front of his desk, squaring her shoulders and pulling herself up to her full height. *This is a nightmare. I should have gone to Compliance, but he's not going to intimidate me!*

"I'm answering your ridiculous questions about my team," she said firmly, still maintaining her poise. "They are highly qualified, and how dare you suggest otherwise? I merely asked Rachel a few questions about some anomalies we found in the database. I was going to ask you next, but here we are."

Jim glared at her before glancing at the heavy Rolex on his wrist.

"Well, you *are* going to have to answer my questions, and not just for me," he sneered. "You and your incompetent staff are creating problems that you *are* going to have to answer for."

He paused, an almost gleeful look crossing his craggy face.

"I've asked Todd and Janine to join us," Jim announced with a smirk. He put on a great show of sitting back down behind his desk, which filled the back corner of his office.

Shocked, Sheryl stared at him. Jim crossed his arms and leaned back. His bright green golf shirt almost glowed against the somber brown leather of his chair, she noticed incongruently, and his slicked-back, blond hair was slightly mussed. He looked quite pleased with himself.

"What? Todd, like the president of the company Todd?" Sheryl finally managed to ask, completely appalled by Jim's boldness. "Why?"

"Weren't you listening?" Jim chided, his green eyes hard and accusing. "Your girl Keisha has been sabotaging the database, and she's trying to blame it on Rachel, or worse, me! She's pulled the wool over your eyes, Sheryl. We've got to get her out of here and *now*, before she does any more damage."

Sheryl sank down one of the chairs near Jim's desk. Her hands clenched the arms as she fought her inclination to scream. Instead, she forced herself to breathe, to bring her scrambled mind to rest. Only minutes ago, she had been trying to figure out her offensive strategy, and now she was completely on the defensive.

Watching Jim, she could feel the hot color rising from her neck into her cheeks at his absurd accusations about Keisha. Sheryl's comfortable navy pants suddenly felt constricting around her waist. *Sure, Jim has every right to question me about Keisha's findings—but sabotaging? Keisha? It's ridiculous. And then calling Todd? Plus Janine from HR?*

"You have no evidence of that," Sheryl found herself replying sharply. "What are you talking about, Jim? These are wild accusations, and unfounded at best."

"No wilder than the accusations you threw at Rachel," Jim shot back.

"What? I did not shoot any accusations at Rachel," Sheryl denied hotly meeting his gaze directly. "I just asked a few questions." She raised a finger, pointing to the ceiling. "Questions, Jim, questions. Not accusations."

"Well, Rachel didn't like the tone of the questions, and neither do I. I'll not have you maligning me or my staff." He huffed. "And that Keisha. She's put you up to it. I can't believe you *trust* someone like that."

Anger shot through Sheryl like a bolt of lightning. She had never come close to striking someone, but she would have liked to slap the man's smug face at that moment. Instead, she closed her eyes and counted to ten, desperately working to regain her center—and her composure. *Help me!* she pleaded in silent prayer, feeling her energy moving both upward and inward.

Opening her eyes, she looked directly at Jim. "Someone like what?" Sheryl countered, her voice icy, hoping that Jim was not implying something negative about Keisha because of her mixed race.

She watched Jim flinch ever so slightly at her tone and question.

"You know what I mean," he blustered.

"No, Jim, I don't think I do," she responded, her tone even but threaded with steel.

They both started at a loud rap at the door, which was immediately flung open. Todd strode in, and Sheryl immediately noted a look of concern on his handsome face. He was as disheveled as Sheryl had ever seen him, as if he had dropped everything he was doing and raced to Jim's office. The sleeves of his blue button-down shirt were rolled up, navy tie slightly askew, and his nearly black hair looked like he had been running his hands through it. *What in the world did Jim tell him?*

Janine Sanders, the head of Human Resources and Sheryl's friend since Janine had started with the company six years before, followed him in, shooting a questioning look at Sheryl. Sheryl acknowledged her look with a nod and a sideways glance at Jim, still furious with the man's gall.

Jim unfolded his large frame from the deep leather chair, walked around his desk, and shook Todd's hand vigorously. He gestured to Todd to take a seat at the head of the conference table that lay perpendicular to the right wall of the room. Jim's office was enormous, second only to Todd's in size.

Janine slid into the chair next to Todd, and Jim moved to his other side and sat. Sheryl hesitated, then took the chair next to Janine's petite form. She felt she was somehow supposed to take the chair at the other end of the table but refused to be put in a position of being interrogated.

Todd settled into his chair and looked carefully at Sheryl, then Jim, his bright blue eyes shrewd and alert.

"Okay, Jim," Todd said, his deep voice graver than usual. "You said this was an emergency, that the whole company was being put at risk by Sheryl's team. Explain."

"Todd, Janine, thanks for coming on such short notice," Jim started out, his voice echoing Todd's serious tone. "We do have a *big* problem with someone on Sheryl's team—someone who I understand has caused problems before. I want to take care of it sooner rather than later, which is why I wanted you both here."

Even as Sheryl's fists clenched under the table where no one could see, she watched Todd as he raised his eyebrows. "If the problem is on Sheryl's team, how is it that you are involved, Jim?"

"Sadly, it seems that Sheryl had been taken in by this person. She doesn't see her for what she really is," Jim said solicitously.

Sheryl couldn't stifle a sharp gasp of outrage.

"Really?" Todd said, his head tilting to the side. "That surprises me."

"I know," Jim agreed smoothly. "It surprised me, too. But Sheryl made some terrible accusations to Rachel today, at the behest of the programmer Keisha. So, I can only conclude that she must believe whatever stories Keisha is telling her. She's a real danger to the company, Todd."

All the foreboding that Sheryl had been feeling since before this meeting shot to the surface, but she kept quiet as Janine stepped in.

"A danger, how?" Janine interrupted, leaning toward Jim.

"Well, she could bring the whole company down!" Jim stated, waving his hands in an overly dramatic gesture.

Janine shot another glance at Sheryl, clearly not buying Jim's display, to Sheryl's relief. Sheryl turned her gaze to study Todd. He looked skeptical but concerned as he turned toward her.

"Sheryl, this sounds serious. What kind of accusations has Keisha made?" Todd asked, a deep V forming between his eyebrows.

"She accused Rachel of tampering with the CRM database!" Jim roared, jumping in before Sheryl had a chance to answer.

"Is this true?" Todd asked, deliberately directing his question to Sheryl.

Sheryl shook her head. "No, it's not true, Todd. There *is* a discrepancy in the database that Keisha discovered," she said, letting her voice be cool and direct. "I simply asked Rachel what she knew about the database design. There were absolutely no accusations made."

"But—" Jim blustered.

"—A discrepancy?" Todd asked Sheryl, ignoring the older man.

"Yes, there is a discrepancy. Todd, I've seen it myself," Sheryl answered evenly, shooting a quick, angry glare at Jim. "I don't know what it means at this point. I was just trying to get some background information from Rachel, since I've had a good working relationship with her in the past. She apparently misinterpreted my questions or overreacted to them, because Jim asked for this meeting just minutes after Rachel and I got back from lunch."

"She didn't overreact!" Jim burst out. "You practically accused her— or someone in Sales—of tampering with the database design."

"No, I didn't!" Sheryl said hotly, before reining in her temper again. "I merely asked her who had been involved in designing the data structure when SalesTeam was installed. I *never* expected this kind of reaction."

"Well, you must suspect something, Sheryl," Todd said. "Or you wouldn't have asked the questions."

Sheryl took a deep breath.

"Of course she does," Jim interrupted again. "That girl Keisha is just covering up her own incompetence . . . or worse."

Sheryl trembled as the rage and worry that had been building all afternoon washed over her. *Jim set this whole meeting up with the sole purpose of shifting the focus off Rachel and himself onto me. How does he think he's going to get away with that?*

"I know she is trouble," Jim continued, his voice insistent and growing steadily louder. "I just know it."

Todd and Janine both turned to Jim. "What do you mean, 'trouble'? How do you know it?" Janine asked.

"Well, uh, you can just look at her and see that she's trouble. And then, she's been asking all these questions about the database. She should know the answers to these questions—she's a programmer!" he explained emphatically, as if Keisha was stupid.

"What do you mean you can *look* at her and see that she's trouble?" Janine said, her voice like cold steel. Her chiseled features tightened, lending a very severe look to her face. Her short salt-and-pepper hair further enhanced the harshness.

"Oh, you know what I mean," Jim said.

"I think you'd better be explicit," Todd said, his voice now tight and hard, and Sheryl was somewhat relieved at his and Janine's response. She hoped they were as irritated by all of this as she was.

"Oh, never mind," Jim said, waving his hands dismissively. "The database issues. She's just not able to handle them, and she's trying to cover her own ignorance."

Janine leveled a long look at Jim, but then turned to Sheryl.

"What do you think about that, Sheryl?"

Sheryl bit her lip. *I guess it's time to put my cards on the table, whether I want to or not.*

Jim started to respond again, but Todd held up his hand. "Enough, Jim, I get your position. I'd like to hear from Sheryl."

"Well," she admitted carefully, sitting up straighter. "I really wanted to get more information before I brought this forward, but from what Keisha has found—and showed me—it looks like there were some custom fields in the SalesTeam database that have since been hidden . . . and the data erased."

"Hidden? Erased? What does that mean, Sheryl?" Todd asked sharply.

"It doesn't mean a damn thing," Jim snarled, leaning into the table. "See, I told you that Keisha is making stuff up."

"Enough!" Todd snapped, slamming his hand on the mahogany table. Jim jumped back and then slumped somewhat into the conference table chair as Todd returned his gaze to Sheryl's.

"Todd, I really think we should have Joaquin Gonzales here for the rest of this conversation," Sheryl said. "It's possible that the situation has compliance implications. I was actually planning on talking to him next, if Jim hadn't jumped the gun and called this sudden and unprofessional meeting without having all the facts."

Todd recoiled, his frown deepening. "That bad?"

"Maybe. I don't know. I believe, at this point, it is in the company's best interest, in case a formal investigation is warranted," Sheryl said.

"Is she kidding?" Jim erupted, rising suddenly and waving his arms wildly. "A formal investigation into what? A blind supervisor believing a seriously incompetent and malicious programmer?"

They all looked at Jim in astonishment.

The man is clearly not acting rationally, Sheryl thought. *What is wrong with him? Could he be behind what we found?*

"Is it safe for me to assume that this is no longer a Human Resources issue?" Janine asked.

"Actually . . . I'm not sure that's true," Sheryl said slowly, thinking about the two financial advisors but unwilling to disclose any more information in front of Jim without this next vital step. If the company was being compromised—either ethically or with clear violations—she knew full well how documenting each step was vital to maintain integrity before the SEC.

Todd nodded. "Janine, you should stay. Let's get Joaquin in here, and see what Sheryl has to say."

He stood up and pointedly directed Jim to sit back down. He did, with a huff. Todd then strode the fifteen feet or so to Jim's desk, grabbed the phone, and then paused, looking directly at Sheryl.

"You're sure this is the correct next step?" he asked sternly, as if warning her to rethink her demand.

Sheryl nodded decisively. "Yes, Todd. Absolutely."

Todd dialed the phone. "Okay, then. I hope you know what you're doing."

Sheryl nodded again, hiding her inward cringe. She understood why Todd didn't want to get Joaquin involved. It was a point of no return. *The question is for who: Jim? Rachel? Or me?*

Chapter 14

Dave inwardly groaned as he noticed Alisha hurrying across the parking lot toward his car. *I almost made my escape, damn it, but I can't pretend I don't see her now.*

He pulled his hand back from the door handle of his Explorer and put it in his pocket, leaning back against the car. Alisha's pace slowed as she approached him. She was slightly out of breath, her ponytail a bit disheveled, her cheeks red from the effort of chasing him in what he thought of as ridiculously high heels. Dave was amazed at how she managed to stay upright in them.

"Hey, Dave," Alisha said cheerfully. "If I didn't know better, I'd say you've been avoiding me today."

Dave smiled cautiously. "Hi, Alisha. I've been busy today. Hitting the road early tomorrow."

Her smile faded a bit, but she nodded. "Of course, Mondays are always rough," she concurred. "I wanted—"

"—Alisha, I really need to get going," Dave interrupted brusquely, wanting to end the conversation quickly. He straightened, ready to turn back to the door. "Is there something you need?"

Alisha frowned. "Well, not specifically. I'm going to be here through the end of the week. I was hoping we could sit down together. I've missed talking to you," she said hopefully.

"Yeah, I know. I've been busy and so have you," Dave responded, a little more soothingly. He cursed inwardly. *Why is this so awkward? We work together, and I thought we were friends. I'm almost afraid to talk to her.*

"I guess you don't have time for a quick drink now? Seeing as you'll be gone the rest of the week?" she pressed, tilting her head to the right.

He shook his head. "Sorry, I really don't. I still have a proposal to polish up tonight,"

"Ah, I get that," she said. "Where are you off to?"

"Just up to Connecticut for a couple of days," he said, turning slightly toward the SUV.

"I'll see you later in the week, then? I'm not flying back until Friday afternoon. Maybe—"

"—That'll work. I'll see you later in the week," Dave interjected quickly, forestalling her likely attempt to get him to drive her to the airport. "Let me know if you hear about the condo."

Sliding his hand out of his pocket finally, he turned and reached for the door handle.

"Oh, I will," Alisha said brightly, but he detected a certain roughness in her voice. "I'll give you a call when I hear."

Dave nodded over his shoulder, opening the door and swinging his computer bag across to the passenger seat.

"Have a great evening," he said as he slid in.

"You, too!" Alisha smiled again, but Dave saw the tightness in her face and the sudden stiffness in her posture. He watched as she tugged on her ponytail. He gave her a quick wave as he closed the door and pressed the button to start the car.

Alisha waved and turned toward the building. Dave waited only long enough for her to be safely away before turning toward home.

During the drive, he replayed the conversation in his head. He knew that Alisha was hurt by his distance, but he didn't know what else to do. After Saturday's outing and her comments in certain living areas of the condos, well, he was afraid that she had other ideas about their relationship. Ideas that he wasn't comfortable with. He liked Alisha; he found her refreshing, and, as much as he hated to admit it, he had enjoyed receiving attention from such an attractive woman. But after Saturday, he had taken stock of the situation, of their relationship, and he was very much afraid that he might have been giving Alisha mixed signals.

Dave *had* complained about Sheryl a lot to Alisha, especially when Sheryl was taking such big risks at work that he just didn't understand. He rapped his fist against the steering wheel. He had been frustrated that Sheryl wouldn't listen to him, and he had vented to Alisha. It seemed like a fair exchange when she was talking to him about Liam and her father. *We were sharing personal concerns like friends and colleagues sometimes do. Was that so bad?*

A rapid movement in the corner of his eyes caught his attention, and he hit the brakes sharply as a battered red Toyota drove right in front of him. A quick glance in the rear-view mirror assured him that the person behind him had plenty of space to slow down, a rarity on 78. He breathed a sigh of relief and quickly accelerated again, chiding himself for his lack of attention. One never knew what could happen on New Jersey highways, or any highway, for that matter.

I'll have to think about Alisha later—or not. The whole situation with her has gotten way too complicated, and Sheryl is complicated enough.

Sighing, he focused his vision on the road and mirrors, but his mind still wandered. He did have a proposal to work on, and he also hoped to have dinner with Sheryl. He had been encouraged by their date night on Friday, and they had had a pleasant day yesterday, even though they had only been doing chores around the house. Dave suddenly smiled as he remembered Sheryl curled against him on the sofa as they had watched television last night. She had seemed more open and relaxed than she had in a while. He realized how much he had missed that.

Her car wasn't in the garage when he got home. Not that he was surprised; he had left earlier than normal. Most days, he would have finished up the proposal at the office, but he had felt a strong urge to see Sheryl before he left for his business trip. Grabbing his backpack, he crossed the empty garage space and went into the kitchen with sudden determination. *I can get dinner ready. Maybe that'll make up for what an ass I was last week when Sheryl made dinner for me.*

It was nearly ninety minutes later when he finally heard Sheryl's garage door go up. Dave pulled the two generous servings of lasagna that he had defrosted earlier and Sheryl's salad out of the refrigerator. He had eaten his own salad nearly an hour ago. He had been ready to gnaw his arm off, so he was very relieved that she was finally home. He was just putting the lasagna in the microwave when Sheryl walked in.

Glancing over his shoulder as he pressed start, he stopped abruptly and turned toward her.

"What happened to you?" he asked, concerned by the pallor of her face and her sagging shoulders. "Are you okay?"

He tugged her briefcase out of her hand and set it down, reaching to help her with her coat.

She shook her head. "Actually, no. I'm not okay."

Dave pulled her into a comforting embrace. He felt her shudder against him, but she stepped back after a minute or two.

"I need to get changed, and do I need to get dinner?"

"Dinner's in the microwave," he said quickly. "You get changed. I'll have a glass of wine for you when you come back."

She smiled tiredly. "Okay. Sounds good."

His wife walked out of the room, her heels clicking wearily on the hall tiles.

Dave grabbed a fresh bottle of Pinot Noir from the kitchen rack and poured two generous glasses. He lightly dressed her salad and set two places at the kitchen table, even though they usually just ate at the counter. He was putting a plate with the lasagna at her normal seat as she shuffled back into the room, her feet now in soft slippers that scuffed the floor.

She had washed her face, removed her makeup, and put on cozy fleece pants and a sweater. He always thought she looked better that way, more natural, except for the strained look in her eyes.

"Thanks," she said softly as he held the chair for her. He picked up two glasses of water from the counter and put them on the table next to the wine glasses.

She paused for a moment, bowing her head, and he joined her in a silent prayer of thanks for the meal. They had always said grace together in the past, but he realized they had gotten out of that habit recently. *And help me support her tonight,* he added silently for good measure.

When he looked up, he noticed Sheryl smiling at him, her face gentle.

"Thanks," she said.

Dave shrugged. "So, tell me what's going on. Or do you want to eat first?"

128

Her smile faded. "I can talk while I eat," she answered, taking a drink from her wine glass. "This will help."

Dave watched as she ate a bit of lasagna, clearly gathering her thoughts.

"Honestly, I'm not sure how much I can really tell you," she said, shaking her head. "It's a big mess, but there could be some legal stuff involved."

"What?" Dave's face contorted in a half-smile, half-frown of disbelief.

"No, I'm not kidding," Sheryl responded.

He listened intently while she described the events of the last few days, culminating with the day's drama.

Astounded, Dave stopped eating. His hands were still wrapped around his utensils but lying on the table next to his plate. He leaned forward, staring at Sheryl as if trying to figure out exactly what she was saying.

"I know. It's unbelievable," Sheryl said, obviously reading the expression on his face.

"I don't even know what to say," Dave said. "If Compliance is involved, it has to be serious. No wonder you don't think you can talk about it. Not that I'm going to say anything, but still. Geez, Sheryl. This is crazy stuff."

"Tell me about it," Sheryl said. "And I thought what happened last fall was crazy. This . . . this makes it look like child's play."

"But Keisha, how is she involved?" he asked. He leaned back against his chair, his face hardening. "She's always involved when you are having problems at work."

"Dave," Sheryl said sharply. "It's not about Keisha. She just happened to have discovered the discrepancy."

"She's nothing but trouble for you," he said hotly, his mind racing back to the time when Keisha walked out on the job for three days and Sheryl had defended her. He felt his blood begin to boil. *She's a flighty girl who thinks that Sheryl will let her get away with anything!*

"She's not! She's talented and smart. It's not her fault that she found this problem!"

"Well, why is she always in the middle of things, then?"

"Dave, she's not. She was only involved in one aspect of what happened last fall. Don't you go blaming her!" Sheryl said angrily and loudly.

Dave reeled back. He saw a red flush stain her cheeks as she half rose from her chair. His stomach suddenly tightened into a huge knot. *Damn it, I stepped in it again.*

"Stop, sit down," Dave said, careful now to use a more conciliatory tone. "Please."

Sheryl sat and took another long drink of her wine. She was still glaring at him.

"I'm sorry," he said, placing his hand over hers. "I didn't mean to make you angry. I just . . ."

"You just what?"

"I just wanted to . . . Hell, I don't know. I just heard her name and saw red. I jumped to conclusions and shouldn't have."

"You're right. You did. I don't know why Keisha's name upsets you so much."

"I guess I still associate that mess in the fall with her," Dave grudgingly admitted.

"But very little of it had anything to do with her, if you remember correctly—which you obviously don't," Sheryl's voice was bitter and still angry.

Dave released his breath with a sharp huff. Some of the fire went out of him. "You're right. You're right. I'm sorry." He took a gulp of wine, too.

Sheryl's shoulders relaxed some. She picked up her fork but looked him straight in the eye.

"You've got to stop doing that," she said firmly. "We never resolved what happened between us because of all the stuff I did at work that you didn't agree with. You're going to continue to get angry until we do, and that's the last thing I need right now." She leaned toward him, hitting her flattened hand on the table. "I need you to support me, not get angry. If you can't do that, then we need to stop talking about this."

Dave dipped his head. *Damn. I know she's right, but . . .*

"Why are you so angry about all that, Dave? I really don't get it. Why?" Sheryl's voice was weary and frustrated. He could see tears forming in her eyes. She clearly didn't get what he was upset about.

"I was upset because you were putting your job at risk," he explained quickly.

"So? Why does that matter so much to you? It's not like we'd starve if I lost my job."

Dave looked at her, suddenly unsure of himself. *Why am I so upset?*

"I, uh, just know how important your job is to you," he said, the words sounding lame even to his ears.

"Dave, that can't be it," Sheryl said in disgust. She put her fork down, pushing her plate away. "If you can't tell me honestly why you have been so outraged by what I've done at work, then I don't know what there is to talk about."

She stood up, picking up both the water glass and the wine glass. She refilled both before turning to look at him.

"I'm going up," she said, her voice heavy. He could see the disappointment and hurt in her eyes. "I'm exhausted, and I need to get my head out of this so that I can sleep. I'll be in my office, but I need some time—alone."

"Sheryl," Dave started.

"Don't, just don't," she snapped, but there was more weariness than fire in her voice.

"I'm sorry," he said, raising his hand in defense. "I'll take care of the dishes."

"Thanks," she said, turning toward the hallway, but halfway there, she paused and looked back, her face resolute. "And Dave, you really need to think about the answer to that question. I think our marriage depends on it."

Stunned, Dave watched her turn and walk out of the kitchen. His face hardened as he felt his whole body tense. Waiting until she was out of earshot, he slammed his fist on the counter.

So, she's resorting to threats now. Maybe I shouldn't brush Alisha off so quickly.

But, even through the anger, he felt the sharp prick of his conscience, that little voice he liked to ignore. *Damn it. But maybe she has a point, too.*

He turned to the dishes, handling them a bit more roughly than he should. His mind whirred. *Why am I so angry?*

He suddenly wished he knew.

Chapter 15

Alone in her hotel room, Alisha paced with rapid, jerky steps. Things were not working out as planned. Her emotions were all over the place. She yanked back the dark gray curtain and looked out onto the brightly lit hotel parking lot, hoping irrationally to see Dave's SUV pull in. Anger, disappointment, hurt, hope, and fear tumbled over each other in rapid succession, leaving her confused and exhausted. The dismal view, with no Dave in sight, only emphasized her pain. She needed to do something, take some action to get things back under control.

Beatrice's advice about being more patient flashed through her mind, but she instantly dismissed it. *What did she know? I see Dave slipping away. I have to somehow get his attention again, get him focused on helping me. But how?*

Her phone buzzed, startling her. Hoping it was Dave, she snatched up the phone, only to realize it was her mother—again. Denise had been calling nonstop since Alisha had arrived in New Jersey, alternately railing at her daughter's decision and pleading with her to change her mind. Alisha had been beyond irritated with her, but now she stared hard at the phone, unsure if she wanted to answer it.

Maybe Mom is right. The thought floated across Alisha's mind involuntarily, and she impatiently pushed it away. *No, she's not. This will work. I'll figure it out.*

But, really. What were her options? She was out of ideas at the moment, which was why, for the life of her, she couldn't stop pacing in her rage and agitation.

The phone stopped ringing. She had missed the call. She bit her lip. Despite her aggravation with her mother, she didn't want to alienate her. Mom had always been her biggest supporter. Sighing, she called her back.

"Hey, Mom," she said brightly, not wanting her mother to hear her frustration. The last thing she wanted to hear was 'I told you so' if she gave her mom any hint that things weren't working out the way Alisha had wanted them to. Her mother was prone to throw those in her face at the slightest provocation.

"Hi, darling. How was your day?" Denise said sweetly.

Alisha pulled the phone away from her ear and looked at it in disbelief for several seconds. Putting it back to her ear, she rolled her eyes and told her mother that her day had been great.

"Did you get the condo you offered for?" her mother asked.

"I don't know yet. I haven't heard. I was just going to call my realtor."

"Oh, well, I'll let you do that," Denise responded cheerfully. "Call me back and let me know what she says."

Alisha wondered whether aliens had taken over her mother. This was a new tactic. She shrugged. *It's better than her crying.*

"Sure, Mom," she said, echoing the cheery tone.

"Okay, dear. Call me right back." The call ended.

Weird.

Shaking her head, she pulled up Beatrice's cell number and called. The realtor picked up immediately.

"I'm sorry, dear," she said without preamble. "I haven't heard anything. I just tried to call their realtor, but she didn't answer, which is odd for Patricia." From their lengthy chat on Saturday afternoon, she gathered that Beatrice knew everyone in the real estate business in New Jersey. She apparently was old friends with the seller's realtor.

"Is that good or bad?" Alisha demanded, uncomfortable with yet more uncertainty.

"I don't know," Beatrice said matter-of-factly. "I can only guess they have more than one offer, and they are evaluating them."

Which is exactly what Dave said.

"So, what do we do?" Alisha asked impatiently.

"Be patient, my dear," the older woman said calmly. "I know that's not what you want to hear. You don't seem to have learned patience yet, but that's all we can do now. The ball is in their court. I'll be in touch as soon as I hear anything."

Alisha audibly groaned, tugging at her ponytail. *Is this woman trying to kill me? Her and her patience.*

"I know, dear, but I'm sure we'll hear soon."

"Fine, fine," Alisha said sullenly. "I'll wait."

Beatrice chuckled, and Alisha felt a bloom of heat flare on the top of her head. She flopped onto the bed. *How dare she laugh at me?*

"Just call me when you hear something," she growled and ended the call.

Grrrrr. When are things going to start going my way?

Still sprawled across the king-size bed, she called her mother back. "No news, Mom."

"Oh, I'm sorry, honey. The waiting is always so hard. Maybe this whole move wasn't meant to be. Have you thought of that?" Denise said, but with more gentleness than Alisha expected.

"Mo-om!"

"I know it's not what you want to hear, sweetie."

"Are you and Beatrice coordinating your conversations?"

"What do you mean, dear? Of course I'm not talking to Beatrice."

"Well, you two sure sound like you are in sync," Alisha grumbled.

"Maybe because we are both wise women with plenty of life's experience," Denise replied pertly.

Alisha rubbed her temple with her free hand, exasperated by her mother's upbeat chatter. "Really, Mom? Your life's experience?"

She paused, but her mother didn't respond. "Okay, then. I'll call you when I hear something. Gotta go now."

"Bye, dear." She hesitated. "But please let me know when you hear something."

"Yeah, I will," Alisha said, hitting the end button, letting her arm flop back on the bright white duvet cover.

I'm tired of being treated like a child by everyone. I'm thirty-four years old, for God's sake.

Invigorated by her sense of indignation, she jumped up and went back to her pacing. *What can I do to get Dave's attention back? Since I can't do anything about the condo, I must be able to do something about him.*

If Dave was going to be out of town for a couple of days, she had time to plan. But plan what?

Her phone buzzed again. Excitedly, she grabbed it, experiencing disappointment along with a twinge of guilt when she saw that it was Juliet, a close friend and sometimes confidante from childhood. She and Juliet hadn't been in touch much in recent months, ever since she had become closer with Dave. Her friend had been supportive and comforting when Alisha talked to her about Liam, but like her mother, Juliet hadn't been a fan of her growing crush on Dave. So, Alisha had been avoiding her.

"Juliet, I'm surprised to hear from you," she greeted her.

"Yeah?" Juliet's voice held an exquisite dollop of sarcasm. "I got a feeling I should check in on you."

Alisha collapsed into the uncomfortable gray chair next to the window, tugging the curtain open again. "Well, as usual, your timing is perfect," she admitted, the irony not lost on her.

"What's going on?" Juliet asked, her voice softening. "You can talk to me. I promise not to get all judgy on you this time."

Alisha sighed, curling her legs under her. "Thanks. I'd appreciate that. Things aren't going well here. Dave is, well, kind of pushing me away . . . or it feels like that, and I put a bid on a condo, but I haven't heard back yet." The words came out in a rush.

"Hey, slow down," Juliet protested. "That sounds like a lot. Tell me about the condo first."

Alisha dutifully told her friend about the condo-hunting excursion on Saturday, focusing mostly on the condos they looked at and the one she had picked. She left out the details about Beatrice's comments and most of Dave's reaction.

"That sounds like a great place, the kind of place you deserve for all your hard work," Juliet responded cautiously. "Why don't you sound more excited about it?"

"Well, for one thing, I haven't gotten it yet," Alisha shot back.

"Oh, you will . . . if you really want it."

"What does that mean? Of course I want it," Alisha snapped. She had little patience when Juliet got metaphysical on her.

"Yeah? It doesn't sound like it to me. There's not much energy in your voice when you talk about it. Is that because of Dave?"

Alisha grimaced. This is why she hadn't been talking to Juliet recently. The woman she sometimes chose to call her friend was much too perceptive.

"Yeah," she admitted, now sighing and giving in to her need to talk to someone. She shifted in the chair to get more comfortable. "It probably is. He was helpful but not very enthusiastic on Saturday. Beatrice said . . ." She trailed off, not wanting to share Beatrice's observations, which would only fuel Juliet's objections.

"Beatrice said what?" Juliet prompted.

Silence.

"I'm guessing that Beatrice noticed that Dave is married? And you didn't like that?"

Alisha growled. "Yeah, pretty much. She said I was pushing too hard."

"Are you?"

Alisha stiffened. "No. I'm not. I'm just taking things to the next natural level," she responded defensively, although even she could hear the doubt that crept into her voice.

"Oh Alisha," Juliet said sympathetically.

Tears pooled in Alisha's eyes, and she wiped them away with the palm of her hand. *I'm not going to cry. I'm not.* But she was so . . . discouraged. Juliet's sympathy hit at the heart of her doubts about Dave's feelings for her, doubts that she didn't want to acknowledge.

"Alisha? You okay?"

"Yeah, I'm here," she answered hoarsely.

"Are you crying?"

"No. I don't cry," Alisha protested, but without any heat.

"Oh honey, I know you've been pushing me away because I told you I don't agree with you about Dave, but that doesn't mean I don't love you. You know that, right?"

Sniffling, Alisha whispered a short "Yeah."

"What's really going on? I know you've been upset about Liam, and you should be. But you should be *angry*. You should do something about it through official channels, not by chasing Dave. And hey . . . not judging. Just stating facts, my friend."

"You know I can't do that," Alisha argued hotly, feeling all the anxiety of the last several months wash over her. "Juliet, I'd lose my job! Or, worse, I'd be forever labeled a troublemaker."

"Not if you're right. That doesn't happen these days. Women are believed by default. You have everything on your side. All the things you told me about that bastard and what he kept doing and never listening to you…" Juliet's voice was calm, but Alisha heard the fire behind her words.

"Yeah, yeah, I know you believe that, but my dad told me otherwise. He said that men have no respect for women who whine and complain," Alisha said. "I don't do that."

She heard Juliet muttering on the other end of the phone.

"What are you mumbling about?"

Juliet sighed. "Just that sometimes I'd like to give your father a piece of my mind—a big one!"

"—Hey, he's my dad!"

"I know, and I know you love him and admire him and respect him. What I don't understand is *why* sometimes. He hasn't been exactly supportive of you. Think of all the times he told you that he was going to see you, to take you golfing or whatever, and then blew you off and took your half-brothers instead. He's always putting them ahead of you. It's not acceptable! It gets you so upset . . . and it make me angry for you."

"Well, maybe, but . . ."

"But what? You're still chasing his approval? You're still trying to get him to show you he loves you? Alisha, it's not going to happen," Juliet said bluntly. "And I think that's why you're chasing Dave. Honestly, I think he's become some kind of twisted father figure to you."

Alisha bolted out of the chair, seeing red. Juliet was always harping about her father. That ticked her off enough. Alisha could complain about him, but no one else in her life could—and now Juliet was saying these insane things about her relationship with Dave?

She pulled the phone away from her ear, holding it far out in front of her like it was poison.

"Okay, that's enough. I'm hanging up now. And you don't need to call back. I don't need friends who are calling me twisted," Alisha yelled, loud enough for Juliet to hear her. She gathered her anger around her like a shield and disconnected the call before Juliet could respond.

But the anger fizzled as quickly as it came. Her rigid spine collapsed as tears and wrenching sobs overcame her. *Everyone is against me. Everyone. This is not about my father. It's not! He loves me. He just shows it like a guy.*

She allowed the tears to fall for several minutes, sobbing out her fear and frustration. But then she remembered her father's words.

I am not going to become that kind of weak, sniveling woman, she scolded herself. Blowing her nose, she pushed the sadness and fear down. She went into the bathroom and rinsed her face in cold water. Staring at herself in the mirror, she looked hard into her own eyes and made a promise to herself.

You are going to figure this out, girl. You are going to win. No matter what. You are going to show them all, including your friend—ha!—Juliet. I'll get Dave. One way or another.

She thought of her favorite movie character, Scarlett O'Hara. *Yes,* she reminded herself, *"tomorrow is another day."*

Chapter 16

"What the hell are you doing?" Sheryl cried indignantly, stalking into her office and catching Jim Leaders sitting behind her desk with his hands poised on her keyboard. Shocked, she was returning from a meeting with the team about the suspension of the Portal Project and their interim assignments when she walked in to see this invasion at her own desk.

Jim stood up quickly, sending her desk chair crashing against the credenza behind it. He glanced back for a moment at the loud bang but then scurried around to the front of her desk like a crab scrabbling across the sand to its shelter.

"Uh, I'm, uh, waiting for you," he blurted, straightening his shoulders.

"Behind my desk?" Sheryl asked, feeling more curious than angry, although she purposely kept her tone harsh. She wanted Jim to think that she was angry and off-balance.

"Uh, yeah, um . . . you were gone a long time."

"I was in a meeting," she said, walking briskly around to stand behind her desk and glared at him. "Why did you feel like you could wait in my office—behind my desk?"

"I need to talk to you about this whole fiasco!" he cried. "You've created a huge mess!"

"I created a mess?" Sheryl asked, suppressing a bizarre urge to laugh. The combination of yoga, journaling, and meditation that morning had given her an incredible feeling of being centered, which was lasting well into her workday. Now, she consciously controlled her breathing so she maintained her calm. Thank God, or she would be lashing out at this man and his violation of her privacy.

"Yes! You and that Keisha!"

She stared at him. "Keisha and I didn't create a mess. I think that was you or someone on your team. We just uncovered it."

"Me? You're blaming me? Are you crazy, woman?" Jim, still standing, threw his arms up in the air.

Sheryl raised her eyebrows, unable to keep a small smirk from crossing her face. It was almost a miracle how calm she felt today. Especially since she had shocked herself as much as she had Dave with her pronouncement last night. She hadn't expected to say it, hadn't even thought about telling him that their marriage was at risk before something deep inside had prompted her to turn and do just that.

Remaining standing and steadfast, she refocused on Jim.

"No. I'm not crazy. Are you?"

Jim looked confused as she turned the tables on him. "What? No, what are you talking about?"

Sheryl sighed, deciding to stop tormenting him. "Jim, what are you really doing here?" she asked authoritatively.

The confusion on his face gave way to a guilty look as he flushed slightly at her tone.

"Sheryl, this whole situation is a real mess," he said, for the first time sounding like the seasoned executive he was. "I mean, Compliance! That could involve the SEC, you know. It could be a disaster."

Sheryl sat down and motioned for Jim to do the same. She was very well aware that the Securities and Exchange Commission, which regulated The Diamante and all investment firms, could make or break the company.

"Yes, Jim. I know that. That's why I was trying to do a bit more informal investigation *before* I brought Joaquin and Todd in. You were the one that called them, if you remember."

Jim's face turned red as he shifted in the chair. "Yes, because I didn't expect things to escalate like they did."

He paused and looked down, as if uncertain what to say next. Sheryl watched carefully, trying to gauge what he was thinking about, where he was going with his comments, but he seemed to be struggling to gather his thoughts.

"You mean Joaquin initiating a formal investigation?" she finally prompted. The compliance officer, after listening carefully to Sheryl's recitation of the facts, had agreed with her recommendation to start a formal investigation immediately. Jim had been apoplectic and apparently still was.

He started in his chair, raising his eyes. "Yeah, that," he said, some emotion in his voice that Sheryl couldn't place. *Regret? Frustration?* "I didn't mean for it to go that far. I thought Todd would just tell you to knock it off. I mean, I didn't think Keisha was credible."

"Yes, you made that clear yesterday," Sheryl said, an edge to her voice, thinking back to Jim's wild accusations before the compliance officer had arrived.

"Joaquin shouldn't have shut down the project," he said bitterly. "That's just going to mean more delays."

"What else could he do, Jim?"

Joaquin, with Todd's support, had frozen the databases associated with the Portal Project, ensuring that no further changes could be made during his review. Todd has also been furious about the shutdown but very resolved to see the investigation handled properly.

Jim shrugged and sank back deeper in his chair, seemingly defeated.

"You still haven't told me why you were trying to get on my computer," Sheryl said with an edge of steel to her voice.

Jim shrugged and his eyes widened slightly. He looked like a five-year-old caught with his hand in the cookie jar.

"I was just trying to see if there were any emails, anything that showed that you and Keisha made this up," he finally conceded. "I mean, no one on *my* team would do what you've implied—no one would steer money out of The Diamante. That's just crazy stuff. You could go to jail for that!"

Now it was Sheryl's turn to be puzzled. Jim seemed sincere, despite his attempt to break into her computer. *Is he bluffing? Is he that good of a liar? Or is he as bewildered as he appears?* She frowned and made up her mind. *Whatever the case, I don't trust him.*

"Why are you frowning at me?" Jim asked impatiently.

"Because I don't whether to believe you," she answered in a calm voice. "All I do know is that this is in Joaquin's hands, and frankly, I don't know what you want from me at this point."

"Hrmph. What I want is for this to go away," Jim said, clenching his fists.

"Yeah, me, too," Sheryl agreed flatly, "but that's not going to happen now."

"I know. I know. Okay, I'll leave . . . but you let me know if there's anything else that comes up." He rose and started toward the door. Then, stopping abruptly, he turned around to look at her. "Maybe we can work together to get this fixed."

"What? A moment ago you were trying to break into my computer to find dirt on me and my team. Now you want to work together?" Sheryl's voice rose as she stood up, too.

Jim had the grace to look a little sheepish. "Yeah, I know that sounds ridiculous, but, well, shouldn't we try to cooperate?"

Sheryl laughed out loud. "Jim, you need to make up your mind. Am I on your side or against you? One minute you're treating me like the enemy, and now you want to cooperate? I thought you were a better guy than that."

Jim recoiled at her bold words. "Wow, that's harsh."

Sheryl shrugged off his comment. "So, which is it?" she demanded, expecting an answer.

Shaking his head, Jim retreated toward the door. "I don't know, Sheryl. You tell me."

Sheryl smiled softly, but there was an undeniable edge to her voice. "Jim, I'm only the enemy if you've done something wrong."

She stood straight and tall behind her desk, watching as Jim eyed her distrustfully one more time, then turned on his heel and left without responding.

Deciding that the whole encounter was beyond her ability to analyze, she sat down and turned toward her computer. She entered the password that had prevented Jim from accessing it and pulled up her email. She had plenty of other things to get done. At this point, Jim and the investigation could wait.

An hour and dozens of emails later, Sheryl sat at the conference table in Joaquin's office, with Todd present and Keisha beside her, as they reviewed again—this time, step-by-step—the information that Keisha had uncovered. A tall, thin man with dark hair and eyes, Joaquin was serious and intense, befitting his position as the Chief Compliance Officer.

It was an important role. Even though The Diamante was smaller and had a less robust compliance program than the larger investment firms, his role and relationship with the SEC were critical to the firm. Compliance with the appropriate laws and regulations was essential and had always been taken very seriously by The Diamante's leadership, which Sheryl appreciated. It was why she felt she could work here in good conscience.

Keisha was understandably nervous. Feeling the younger woman's leg bouncing under the table, Sheryl did her best to provide a calming and reassuring presence.

Sheryl sat across from Joaquin and reviewed again the details of what she and Keisha had discovered. Unlike yesterday, she gave him the facts but also elaborated on possible causes for the discrepancies in the database, the missing data, and the way the data appeared only in the profiles of the two specific financial analysts.

Joaquin listened carefully, making copious notes in his leather-bound notebook, interrupting now and then to ask clarifying questions of her or Keisha.

Todd paid close attention to the questions and answers but didn't interfere. Sheryl respected his restraint, because she could see by his shifting that he was itching to jump in. However, his face grew grimmer with each fact or conjecture that was revealed.

Sheryl did intercede when she felt Joaquin was pushing Keisha too hard, although she understood his need to get as much detail as he could. Keisha patiently walked him through the database incidents on her laptop, having been granted temporary access to the files for the meeting.

Finally Joaquin sat back. "Why didn't you bring this to my attention sooner?" he asked, directing the question to Sheryl.

"Because I wasn't sure," Sheryl said, making it clear that it was her decision, not Keisha's. "I wanted to see if I could get some sense of what might be going on before escalating it. I didn't want to make a big deal out of something innocent."

Joaquin eyed her assessingly. "It seems pretty clear from what you've laid out here. I'm not sure I understand the hesitation. Are you sure that's all?"

Sheryl's heart fluttered with nerves, but she met Joaquin's gaze squarely. "Yes, I'm sure. This has all happened very quickly. I've been trying to be as proactive and responsible as possible. I felt that things should be handled with discretion until I was certain of the facts," she said confidently. "I went to lunch with Rachel to get clarification— and to ensure that Keisha didn't get blamed." She had informed him earlier of the two meetings in which that had been implied, and now she cocked her head, looking at him directly. "I didn't want her to become the scapegoat."

Joaquin nodded, understanding her wish to keep the specifics from the younger woman in her presence. Todd shifted uncomfortably again in his chair.

"Okay then," he said, looking back toward Keisha. "I guess that's all for now. You understand that you can't discuss this with anyone—inside or outside the company?"

Keisha swallowed and nodded. "Of course."

Joaquin turned to his superior. "Todd, do you have anything else for Keisha?"

"No questions, but I do want to thank her for her diligence in this matter. Other people might have missed it or ignored it. Keisha, I greatly appreciate your integrity," Todd said gravely.

Keisha blushed at the praise from the company president but managed to say a gracious "Thank you." Sheryl felt a surge of pride for her young protégé.

"Yes, thank you, Keisha," Joaquin added with a rare but kind smile. "Todd's right. Your integrity is to be commended. I think that's all we need from you for now."

Keisha whispered another quick "Thank you," nodded to both men and Sheryl, and walked out of the office quickly but with dignity.

"She is an impressive young lady," Todd said to Sheryl. "It's hard to find fault with her logic—or yours—but I guess that's up to Joaquin to decide."

Joaquin nodded. "I have to admit that I'm very concerned, Todd. I was yesterday, after listening to Sheryl, but seeing the evidence, I'm going to recommend that we hire a forensic database expert to validate all of this and try to determine how it came about."

Todd frowned but nodded. "You do what you think is best, Joaquin. I'm not going to interfere with an investigation that is this serious. Do you plan on notifying the SEC?"

It was Joaquin's turn to frown. He glanced at Sheryl, as if assessing whether she should be privy to that information.

"My lips are sealed," she said, knowing that it was important to keep any SEC involvement from becoming public knowledge before it became official.

"I think I'm going to have to, Todd. They might step in and investigate themselves, but I don't want to give the impression we're hiding anything. I'll tell them our plan and maybe get a recommendation from them on the database expert. That might keep them at bay for a little bit."

Todd nodded. "Okay, I'll have to notify the board members then too. Do you want to be there?"

Joaquin nodded. "I'd better be. I think I should tell them, with Sheryl there to fill in any details."

Sheryl inwardly cringed. *Oh no, not the board!* She wasn't anxious to be the center of attention in *that* arena again—especially when Anthony Russo could still be angry. Plus, she had no idea how the new director, Hank's replacement, would act. She hadn't even met him yet.

"Of course, Sheryl would be there anyway," Todd agreed, oblivious to Sheryl's discomfiture. He stood, nodded to them both, and strode out the door.

Chapter 17

Thursday, December 9

It wasn't until Dave was driving back from Connecticut on Thursday afternoon that he allowed the question Sheryl had asked to come to the forefront of his mind.

"Why am I still so angry about how she handled things at work?" he grumbled to himself. The words seemed to mock him as he said them aloud.

The question had surfaced quite a few times, but he had ruthlessly suppressed it, shifting his focus to his design work, client meetings, and proposals. Dave had worked well into each evening since, stopping only long enough in advance of sleep to unwind a bit with the ESPN app and the latest sports news.

He felt a bit guilty, since he hadn't talked to Sheryl much, but then she hadn't been very talkative in their brief conversations, either. It was clear that she felt that the ball was in his court. *And I guess it is, for all I know what to do with it.* He snapped off the radio, irritated by the upbeat tones of the sports announcers.

Why am *I so angry with her about her actions at work?* He thought again. *After all, they have nothing really to do with me. It's not like she always took my advice in the past—she hasn't. And even when she ignored it, it's never upset me all that much.* He sighed aloud. *She's always had a mind of her own.*

Just as he glanced at the navigation screen on his Explorer to double-check his ETA, it lit up with an incoming call. *Alisha. Someone else I've managed to avoid so far this week.*

Reluctantly he answered. "Hey, Alisha. What's up? I'm driving, so this will need to be quick."

There was a company policy against talking on the phone when driving on company business, but most of the salespeople, including

Alisha, ignored it. Dave complied with the policy most of the time. But occasionally he would answer an incoming call, always keeping it short.

"Oh, Dave," Alisha teased. "You are such a rule follower sometimes."

"Yeah, yeah," Dave responded. "Was there something important, or can I call you back?"

"I haven't heard from you since Monday," she whined, her pitch rising ever so slightly. "You didn't even check to see whether I got the condo or not."

"I've been busy, Alisha, working," Dave said impatiently.

"Okay, okay, I got it," Alisha said. He could picture her waving her hand as she often did when he told her something she didn't like.

There was a pause.

"So, Alisha…did you get the condo?" Dave dutifully asked.

"I did!" Alisha crowed with glee. "I'm so excited."

"That's great. Congratulations!" Dave said, working hard to inject genuine interest into his voice while his stomach clenched.

"Thank you! We'll have to celebrate," Alisha enthused. "When are you back in the office? Today? Can we go out this evening?"

This time it was Dave who hesitated. "Umm, I should be back in the office in about an hour," he said. "But I just need to drop something off, and then I was going to head home and finish up the day from there."

"Oh." He could hear Alisha's pout. "Wait. I could leave a little early, and we could grab a quick drink before you go home. That way you won't be late getting home, and we could have a little time to celebrate. You've been blowing me off since Saturday. I'd really like to talk. There are a few things I could use your help with. Please?" she begged.

Dave sighed, looking at the time. *I probably could squeeze in a drink with her, and I have been avoiding her.* He did a rapid calculation in his head. *As long as it's quick, I could still be home before Sheryl.*

"Alright," he said reluctantly, "but it will have to be short. No more than an hour."

"Thank you, Dave," Alisha said brightly. "I promise I won't keep you too long."

"I'm going to hold you to that," Dave said firmly.

He disconnected the call before she could say anything else. *Might as well take a page out of her playbook and not give her a chance to argue.*

It was closer to ninety minutes before Dave reached the office because of heavy traffic through the White Plains area. It was going to be tight to have a drink with Alisha and still get home at a reasonable hour. He debated calling Sheryl and letting her know that he would be home for dinner but decided against it. *Just in case Alisha really does need something that could take a while.* He sighed. *After all, I did promise to help her.* The problem was that he wasn't sure what kind of help she wanted any more. And he was still puzzling out this problem with Sheryl in his mind.

Dave trudged across the parking lot into the office building, his backpack slung over his shoulder. Alisha was waiting in the lobby. Her eyes lit up when she saw him.

"You got here!" she exclaimed with a big smile, bouncing slightly on the balls of her feet. "Traffic must have been tough."

He nodded. "Yeah, White Plains can be a bear. Let me drop this folder off with Susan Hall, and then I'll be ready to go," he said, waving a file folder in her direction.

"I'll be here," she said cheerfully.

Dave resisted the urge to roll his eyes and headed toward the stairs. Susan's cubicle was on the second floor, and it would feel good to stretch his legs after three hours in the car. He took his time going up the stairs, then laid out the information the client had sent back with him for Susan. She was a recent technical school graduate, one of the entry-level network engineers that provided support for Dave's team. He carefully explained the analysis he needed and made sure she understood before returning down the stairs to the lobby.

Alisha, absorbed in her phone, didn't see him at first. He studied her as he crossed the fifty feet or so across the wide lobby. Her hair was in its customary ponytail, and she was dressed more casually than usual. Dave noticed that her shoulders seemed a bit hunched and there was an unusual rigidity to her posture.

She looked up as she heard his footsteps, and he saw her relax, her face brightening with a smile, her shoulders lifting and straightening as she rose from the bench. The lights overhead created the impression of a spotlight on her, illuminating her against the deepening twilight beyond the floor-to-ceiling windows behind her. He was struck once again by how much vitality she exuded. *It's too bad things have gotten weird with her, because I've always enjoyed her company.*

"Ready?" she smiled. He was surprised that she didn't comment on the length of his absence.

"Sure," he said evenly. "Where are we going?"

"We could go back to Conchita's," she suggested. "Or someplace else. You tell me."

Dave shook his head at the thought of the small, intimate Mexican restaurant. "There's a TGI Fridays not far from your hotel. Let's meet there," he said quietly, conscious that a few other employees were headed out through the lobby.

"You don't want to drive together?" she pressed.

"No, it would be out of my way to come back here," he said, his tone brusque.

Alisha searched his face for a moment before acquiescing to the plan.

"Okay, I'll follow you there," she said, picking up her oversized purse and laptop bag.

Alisha stuck close to his side as they walked out to the parking lot together. Dave, looking around, caught at least one sidelong look from a colleague observing them together. He inwardly cringed. The two of them together had different implications here in New Jersey than when they were in California.

He stepped away from her, edging in the direction of his SUV. "Just pull up behind me when you get in your car," he said quietly.

Seemingly unaware that they were being observed, Alisha gave him a big smile and headed toward her car. Dave walked quickly in the other direction.

By the time they settled at a high-top table in the bar area of the restaurant, it was much later than Dave had wanted to be. He sent Sheryl a quick text, explaining that he had been held up and not to wait for him for dinner. He would get something for himself when he got in. Satisfied that he wouldn't cause Sheryl extra work or worry, he turned his attention to Alisha.

She was ordering a drink for herself and his favorite beer for him. He grimaced at her presumption but let it slide, asking the server to bring a glass of water as well. He was thirsty after the afternoon of driving and didn't want to gulp the beer.

"So," Alisha said after the server left. "Isn't it great that I got that condo?"

She leaned forward across the table, and Dave was suddenly and uncomfortably aware of how much of her cleavage was revealed by the deep V of her brightly colored top. He flushed and leaned back, carefully bringing his focus to her face.

"It is," he said. "Did you have to raise your offer?"

She wrinkled her nose. "Yeah, a little, but I was the more qualified buyer, so not by much. Beatrice said I still got a good deal."

"That's great. When do you close?"

"Not until after the holidays. Mid-January is the tentative date. I'm kind of bummed. I was hoping that we could close more quickly."

"Mid-January is still pretty fast," he observed coolly. "And you'll want to spend the holidays with your family anyway, won't you?"

She shrugged. "Yeah, I guess. My dad will probably go away someplace with his wife and my brothers, though." Dave saw the hurt cross her face before she brightened. "But Mom will be happy to have me there."

"She must be upset about you moving," he said, knowing how much Denise clung to Alisha from previous conversations.

"Yeah, she is," Alisha agreed. "But she'll get over it. Maybe it will even be good for her."

Dave looked skeptical but didn't argue. The server appeared with their drinks. He noticed that Alisha had ordered what looked like a Cosmopolitan.

"Good thing you're not driving far," he said, nodding to the stiff drink.

She grinned. "Yup, but I thought it was a good celebratory drink. To my new condo," she said, raising her glass toward him.

He tapped his beer mug against the more delicate cocktail glass, raising it in salute, and took a small sip.

"So, what did you need help with?" he asked, anxious to get whatever she needed out of the way and get on the road home.

"Oh that," she said. "I really just want to celebrate tonight. That can wait." She leaned forward and tapped his arm playfully. "We don't have to be so serious all the time. Let's just enjoy."

Dave stiffened, glancing around the bar to see if there was anyone he knew. The area was crowded, as it usually was, and the tables weren't very far apart. He and Robert occasionally had drinks here, as did other members of the LSM team. It wasn't too far from the office. But it wasn't just co-workers that were making him nervous.

"Who are you looking for?" Alisha asked, taking a long swig.

"No one in particular," he said. "Just seeing who might be here."

"Do you see anyone you know?" she asked curiously, looking around herself.

"Nope. Not a one," he answered, his face relaxing a little.

She smiled back. "So, I've already started thinking about how to decorate. What do you think about turning that little room downstairs into a beautiful den? I could put a little desk in there and a set of comfy chairs, make it a cozy little place to hang out."

"Sure," he shrugged, "if that's what you want. That sounds like it could work."

"Dave, you could be a *little* more enthusiastic," she chided.

"Hey, decorating's not my thing," he said, putting both hands up. "You should talk to your mom or one of your girlfriends about that."

She pouted. Again. "But I want *you* to like it, too," she said.

Dave frowned. "I doubt I'll be spending much, if any, time there," he said. "There's no reason for me to like it."

"I want you to come visit, Dave. We could have drinks there after work instead of having to come to a bar like this."

Dave's discomfort ratcheted up several notches. He shifted uneasily on the bar stool. He noticed a determined gleam in her eyes, even though her tone was light and playful.

"I don't think that's a good idea," he said carefully. "I don't think Sheryl would like that."

"Oh, who cares?" Alisha said, shrugging one shoulder. She leaned forward conspiratorially. "She doesn't worry about what *you* like, but I do."

Dave abruptly pushed back from the table and stood up, his suspicions about her intentions quite suddenly confirmed beyond any doubt.

"Alisha," he said quietly but urgently, "what's gotten into you? I thought we were friends. I thought I was helping you. But all of a sudden you seem to think...well, that there's something else. I'm still married to Sheryl, you know. That hasn't changed, even if we have been going through a bit of a rough patch."

He felt a pang of guilt as he watched Alisha's eyes flood with sudden tears. She reached out and grabbed his forearm.

"But Dave, you've been so wonderful to me, so caring, so supportive. I thought you wanted me to be here. I thought you wanted . . ."

"Wanted what, Alisha? We've never talked about anything else I wanted."

"You said you wanted children," she whispered, her fingers tightening. "Sheryl can't give you that."

Dave's shoulders sagged. He let out a long breath. *Oh God, yes, I did say that!* He shuddered as a sense of dread shot through him.

He swallowed hard. "Yeah, I did, but, well, I didn't mean . . ."

"What did you mean? I thought you cared about me!" she cried, her voice rising again.

Dave became aware of the people around them, especially when the occupants of the nearest tables were suddenly quiet. He picked up his coat.

"This is not the time and place," he said very quietly. "Let's go."

He pulled some bills from his wallet and put them on the table, anchoring them with his empty beer mug. He slid into his leather jacket, busying himself with zipping it while Alisha slowly gathered her things. He waited while she preceded him out of the bar.

As they crossed the well-lit parking lot, she suddenly stopped, turning toward him. He stopped too, careful to stay out of arm's reach. They faced each other uncertainly, halfway between the restaurant and their cars.

"Let's go back to my hotel room and talk," she suggested in a subdued tone.

"No, not a good idea," he said, shaking his head firmly and shoving his hands into his coat pockets. "I need to get home."

"To her," Alisha said bitterly, her face twisting in a grimace.

"She *is* my wife, Alisha. You've known that all along."

"But I thought you were unhappy with her, angry with her!" she snapped, her voice sharp as she stepped closer to him. "You've said really awful things about her. How can you say things like that and still want to go home to her?"

"Couples fight, Alisha," he said, defending himself, but he suddenly saw how Alisha could have interpreted his words. *She's right. I have said some awful things about Sheryl. Obviously more than I should have.* He suddenly felt queasy. *Oh boy, I think I've been really stupid.*

"Look," he said, his voice softer. "We can talk another time. I think maybe . . . well, maybe I said stuff I shouldn't have."

Alisha stared at him. He could see the pain in her eyes, the usual bright blue dulled by tears and . . . was that betrayal? His lips thinned, but he remained silent. *If anything, I've betrayed Sheryl, not her.*

Alisha seemed to realize that he wasn't going to discuss more. Her gaze dropped.

"Okay, okay," she said, her voice hardening. "But this isn't over. We need to talk again soon."

He thought he heard a thread of anger in the words. He definitely heard bitterness.

"I thought you were different," she said, almost under her breath. "But I guess you're just another typical, selfish guy."

He watched her shoulders slump.

"Alisha, don't say that," he begged quietly. He started to lift his hand toward her but quickly dropped it back to his side.

She looked up at him sharply, her body straightening. "Why not? Tell me how it isn't true."

"I never promised you anything. I only ever just wanted to help you. I still do."

"Well, if this is helping, I'm not sure I want it."

She turned suddenly, marching away from him toward their vehicles, still parked a hundred feet away, side by side. Dave could hear the staccato tap of her heels ring loudly in the cold, quiet night air. He stood still and watched as she slid into her rental car, slammed the door shut, and wheeled almost recklessly out of the parking lot. Only then did he let out a breath.

I hope she gets to her hotel safely.

Dave walked slowly the last few yards to his Explorer, feeling thoroughly weary.

I hope I get home safely, too.

He started the engine and paused, abruptly dropping his forehead onto the top of the steering wheel, his hands clammy. The queasiness blossomed into full-fledged nausea. He barely managed to contain it. Dave suddenly felt with every fiber of his being that Alisha wasn't going to let this go. He had witnessed what a bulldog she was once she sank her teeth into something—or someone. *I'm pretty sure I'm going to pay for my stupidity somehow, some way.*

He raised his head as another thought shot through him. He slammed his fist hard against the steering wheel.

And crap, crap, crap . . . how the hell am I going to explain this *to Sheryl?*

Chapter 18

Friday, December 10

Dave glanced at his Rolex for probably the twentieth time since lunch. It was 2:45 pm, and he hadn't seen or heard from Alisha all day. He sighed. He knew she had been angry last evening, really angry, but it wasn't like her to stop communicating with him entirely. Well, to be honest with himself, he had never seen this side of her before. He really couldn't say how she responded when she was angry. *Is she going to completely cut off our friendship?*

Shrugging his shoulders, he muttered to himself, "It really doesn't matter. She'll get over it."

Robert's head popped up from the other side of the cubicle wall. "Talking to yourself now?" he teased cheerfully, his tone matching the bright blue-and-white-striped sweater he wore.

Dave looked up and rolled his eyes. "What does it matter to you?"

"You should talk more quietly," Robert shot back. "Who's getting over what? Sheryl or Alisha?"

Dave grimaced. "Do you ever mind your own business?"

"Sure, just not with you."

Dave could have sworn that Robert winked.

"Gee, how did I get so lucky?" Dave asked sarcastically.

"That's what friends are for!" Robert lowered his voice conspiratorially, glancing around although the nearby cubicles were nearly empty. "So, Alisha or Sheryl? I'm guessing Alisha, since she hasn't stopped by all day today. What did you do to piss her off?"

Dave harrumphed and ignored him, unwilling to confess that it was actually both of them he was worried about. *I still haven't figured out what to tell Sheryl about that scene.* He had managed to avoid discussing it when he got home, but he knew he couldn't put it off forever.

"Come on, man," Robert pressed him. "You're my daily dose of—"

Robert stopped as Dave's cell phone buzzed loudly against the laminate surface of the desktop. Dave glanced at the number and frowned. It was the office number. Odd. Very few people had or used desktop phones.

"Dave Simmons," he answered briskly.

"Hi Dave, it's Elizabeth Curtis."

Dave blinked. Elizabeth was the head of Human Resources. "Hello, Elizabeth . . ." Dave responded cautiously. "How are you?"

Robert, still watching and listening over the cubicle wall, widened his eyes.

"I'm fine, Dave. Thanks for asking. But this isn't a social call," she answered, her moderately pitched voice professional. "I'd like you to come down to my office, please."

Dave's stomach knotted instantly. "Yes, of course, Elizabeth. I have a meeting with George at 3:00. I'll stop by afterward?"

Dave rarely had meetings with his boss, George Hansen, and he didn't want to blow this one off.

"No, Dave. I really need to see you right now. I'll let George know you'll be with me," Elizabeth said firmly.

"Um, well . . . okay, then. I'll be there in a few minutes," he said, his hand clutching the phone tightly.

"Thank you." She clicked off the call before Dave could say anything else.

Putting his phone carefully back on the desk, Dave wiped his suddenly clammy hand on the navy-blue khaki of his pant leg. He looked at the proposal on his computer screen, absently reaching over to hit the save button. His mind whirled. *What in the world does Elizabeth Curtis want from me? And on a Friday afternoon?* He rolled his shoulders, trying to ease the tension that gripped them.

A sudden thought struck him. *Did Alisha finally decide to report Liam?* He took a deep breath, realizing he would have to prepare himself mentally during the short trip to Elizabeth's door if that was the case.

"What was that all about?"

Dave flinched at Robert's voice. "I don't know. She wants to see me."

"Elizabeth from HR? Now?"

"Yeah."

"What does she want?"

"How do I know?" Dave snapped impatiently. "You overheard the conversation. She didn't say."

"I hope you're not in trouble."

"Why would I be in trouble?" Dave asked roughly.

"I dunno." Robert narrowed his eyes. "What did you do?"

Shaking his head vigorously, Dave stood up. "I didn't do anything, you idiot."

"Okay, sorry," Robert said, with more sympathy in his voice.

Dave tugged on his burgundy sweater to straighten it and ran a hand through his hair. A worried frown formed between his eyebrows as he looked over at Robert.

"It'll be okay," Robert said, his voice soft. "I'll wait here until you get back."

Dave swallowed hard and nodded. "Thanks."

He headed out of the cubicle and wove his way through five cubicle pods toward the stairs. Human Resources was on the first floor, only a flight down. He didn't feel like standing in the elevator or, worse, running into anyone who wanted to chat. He felt Robert's gaze on his back as he walked, as well as the other man's concern. It echoed his own.

His mind churned as he walked. *Did Alisha finally report Liam? What did she say specifically about his actions? I'll guess I'll tell Elizabeth about the golf game. I saw that firsthand.*

He reached the Human Resources department less than five minutes after Elizabeth's call. He was immediately ushered into her office by her administrative assistant, a friendly woman named Carol. Elizabeth was seated at her conference table, which was situated near the door. Another woman, whom Dave didn't know, was seated beside her.

Elizabeth's office was in a corner for maximum privacy. Her furnishings were modest and efficient, made of the same faux wood as the cubicle surfaces. However, she had a number of plants lining the windows and cheerful art on the walls, giving the room a more personal flavor. Still, it did nothing to ease his tension.

Dave slid into the seat that Elizabeth indicated, across the table from her.

"Elizabeth," he said, acknowledging her with a nod.

"Dave Simmons, this is Barbara Montgomery," she said, gesturing to the diminutive woman with dark blonde hair and green eyes beside her. "She'll be taking notes."

He nodded politely to Barbara but quickly turned his attention back to Elizabeth.

"Notes?" Dave asked, drawing his brows together. "What's this about?"

Elizabeth's brown eyes regarded him seriously. As usual, she was dressed more formally than most of the LSM staff in a black jacket over a black-and-white print blouse. The typical office attire was the more casual look that Barbara and Dave wore. Elizabeth's nearly black hair was pulled back away from her lightly tanned face, and large silver earrings hung from her ears.

"You don't know?" she asked.

Dave shook his head, not wanting to make a misstep by talking about Liam until he was sure what Alisha had said. "I have no idea. What's going on?"

Elizabeth exchanged a look with Barbara before turning back to Dave. "Dave, some serious accusations have been made against you. Barbara and I are conducting an investigation, and I expect you to cooperate fully and be completely candid during this interview."

Dave stared at her, his jaw dropping.

"Investigation? Into me?" he asked incredulously.

"An investigation into allegations of sexual harassment and misconduct that have been made against you. Alisha Carson has filed a formal complaint with some very serious and concerning information. We're here to gather your side of the story."

Dave's mind spun and his throat went dry. *Is she serious? Sexual harassment?*

"Dave." Elizabeth's sharp voice cut through his agitation.

He shook his head vigorously. "Yes, Elizabeth. I'm sorry. I'm just stunned. This is crazy. I have no idea what in the world you are talking about. Alisha and I are friends. At least, I thought we were. This makes no sense whatsoever!" he cried, his voice rising in disbelief and outrage with each word.

Elizabeth looked concerned. She leaned toward him, enunciating her words clearly. "Dave, you need to take this very seriously."

Something about her tone penetrated his rising panic. He took several deep breaths, then nodded.

"Of course," he said, more calmly, but his voice was rough and deep with emotion.

Elizabeth, after giving him an assessing look, continued briskly. "Okay then, let's go over the events in question."

Dave swallowed hard. He glanced at Barbara sitting rigidly beside Elizabeth. Her eyes, unlike Elizabeth's, were hard and unsympathetic. "Okay," he said.

"Why don't you start by telling us what happened last evening with you and Alisha?"

"Last evening? Uh, sure," Dave responded uncertainly. He hated that his voice shook. *What has Alisha told them? I wasn't inappropriate last evening. If anything . . . it was Alisha that was!*

He leaned forward, resting his forearms on the table, his hands clenched together. He began to recount the events of last evening, starting with Alisha's invitation to go out for a drink. He spoke carefully and thoughtfully, trying to recall and relay the details as accurately as possible, stumbling over the more uncomfortable parts of the encounter. Elizabeth interrupted occasionally to ask for clarification, but Barbara remained silent, typing furiously on the keyboard of the laptop open in front of her.

"And then she drove away, kind of recklessly," Dave concluded. "I watched until she was out of sight, then got in my own car and went home."

He leaned back in his chair, steepling his hands in front of him, but gazing steadily back at Elizabeth. It took everything in his power not to try to look over at Barbara's computer screen.

"And that's it?" Elizabeth asked. "You went home?"

"Yes, that's it," Dave responded firmly.

Elizabeth glanced at Barbara, who shrugged slightly.

"What time did you get home?"

"I don't know exactly. Maybe 7:30 or so? Traffic was pretty light."

"Was anyone at home with you?" Elizabeth asked.

"My wife got home shortly after I did," Dave answered, feeling slightly relieved that this was the case.

"Do you mind if we call her to confirm that?" Her words were more a statement than a question.

A bolt of indignation shot through him. "Mind? Hell yes, I mind. Why in the world do you need to confirm that with her?" Dave demanded. "What in God's name did Alisha tell you?"

"Dave, there's no need for that kind of language," the HR executive reprimanded sharply.

Dave paused and pinched the bridge of his nose. "I'm sorry," he said with genuine remorse. "You're right. I just . . . I just don't understand any of this."

Elizabeth nodded. "I can see that," she said, her voice calm. "But I do need to call your wife. Sheryl, right?"

"Yes, Sheryl," he answered, slumping defeatedly in the chair. "Do you need her number?"

"I assume what we have on file is accurate?" She read the numbers off a sheet on the table.

"That's correct," Dave told her grudgingly.

Elizabeth walked the five feet or so to her desk. Dave noticed that Elizabeth wore a muted red skirt and shoes, belying the more sober appearance she had when she was sitting down.

Rounding the desk, she picked up the phone and dialed, keeping her eyes on Dave as she did. Her conversation with Sheryl was brief. She explained that she couldn't go into detail, then asked if Sheryl could confirm that Dave had been home when Sheryl arrived around 7:30 the prior evening. Thanking Sheryl politely, Elizabeth demurred to provide any further information, saying only that she was sure Dave would update her as appropriate, and hung up.

"Barbara, you can make a note that Dave's wife confirmed his approximate arrival time at home," she said calmly to the younger woman as she walked back to the table.

Barbara stiffened but dutifully started typing again.

"So, Dave," Elizabeth spoke as she eased into her chair. "It appears we have a bit of a 'he said, she said' situation. We're going to have to expand the investigation."

Dave's fists clenched as they rested on the table. He saw Elizabeth take note. He knew Barbara was, too.

"What does that mean?" he asked, his voice tight. He couldn't quite keep the edge of anger out of it. "You just confirmed at least part of my story."

"It means that we're going to need to get more corroborating information," Elizabeth said simply. "But in the meantime, I'm going to have to ask you for your badge, cell phone, and computer. You are suspended without pay until this is resolved."

Dave lunged up out of his chair. "Suspended? You've got to be kidding me!" he all but shouted.

"Dave," Elizabeth barked. "Sit down and control yourself."

Dave sat, but he glared at her. "How would you react?" he ground out. "I've done nothing wrong except try to help a young woman out of a difficult situation, and now you're suspending *me*? Of course I'm angry, and I have every right to be."

"What do you mean?" Elizabeth asked, suddenly alert. "Helping her out how?"

"Ha! She didn't tell you about Liam and the real reason that she's here in New Jersey, did she?" he asked, his voice full of disgust. "Why don't you ask her who the real perpetrator of sexual harassment is? Because it damn sure isn't me!"

Elizabeth and Barbara exchanged another long look. This time, Barbara's eyebrows were raised, and Dave saw a flicker of doubt cross her face for the first time.

Both women focused on Dave with renewed interest.

"You'd better tell me everything you think we need to know," Elizabeth said.

Sighing, Dave went through the whole story of Alisha, Liam, and himself, starting with the golf match in Monterey. Barbara typed steadily throughout the recitation. Elizabeth regarded him thoughtfully, her face carefully neutral.

"So, if anyone should be accused of sexual misconduct, it's Liam, not me," Dave finished emphatically.

Elizabeth paused, scrutinizing his face. "I'm curious as to why you didn't bring this to our attention earlier."

"Because Alisha didn't want me to. In fact, she was *adamant* that I not. With Robert, too."

"Is Robert in the office today?"

"Yes," Dave said. "We were sitting together when you called. He knows I'm here."

Elizabeth's eyebrows shot up for a moment, but she nodded to Barbara, who got up abruptly and left the room, moving quickly and quietly across the carpet in her low-heeled shoes.

Dave gave Elizabeth a questioning look.

"She's going to contact Robert," she answered matter-of-factly. "In the meantime, I will need your phone and badge. We'll retrieve your computer from your desk. You are not to touch it."

"Really? I'm still suspended? Is Alisha?" Dave asked bitterly.

Elizabeth sighed. "Yes, it's protocol. I have no choice about that. And no, Alisha isn't suspended, since she's the one who submitted the complaint."

Dave felt a hot fire of rage rush through him. It was all he could do to sit quietly and not jump up again and scream at the woman sitting so calmly in front of him. He clenched and unclenched his fists on top of the table, struggling to control himself.

"I know it doesn't seem fair," Elizabeth finally said, after watching him steadily while he labored to control himself. "But the standard is to believe women who make these accusations." She looked at him pointedly. "They rarely lie."

Dave snorted. "I told *her* that," he snarled. "I just never thought—"

Barbara poked her head in the door. "He'll be right here."

Elizabeth held out her hand. "Dave?"

Dave pulled the badge and phone off his belt and handed them to her.

"Do you have anything you need at your desk?"

"My coat, car keys."

Elizabeth looked at Barbara, who turned away and hurried out again.

"Okay, you can wait outside my office while your personal items are retrieved," she said. "I trust you can leave quietly and without trying to see Alisha?"

Dave's lips tightened, but he nodded. "I'm not happy, but I won't cause any trouble."

"I'm sure you're not," she said, sympathetically. "I'll be in touch."

Dave nodded again and stood up. He gave Elizabeth a long look before turning and walking out of the office.

His mind whirled and his fingers drummed against his knee while he waited in an uncomfortable chair outside of Elizabeth's office. *Just what exactly does Alisha think she's going to accomplish with this maneuver?*

Suddenly his fingers stopped drumming. *Now my boss knows all about this . . . And what am I going to tell Sheryl? She must be beside herself after that phone call. I can't even text her.* He dropped his head in his hands. *Damn, I wish I had a personal cell phone.*

Chapter 19

Sheryl slowly put her cell phone down on her desk. Disconcerted, she stared at it, willing it to reveal answers that were clearly beyond its capabilities. *Why did Elizabeth Curtis call me to ask when Dave got home last evening? What kind of trouble is he in?* Because she was sure her husband was in trouble. Every fiber of her being told her that, on top of that cryptic phone call.

She was still staring at the phone when she became aware of someone hovering at her office door. Looking up, she saw Keisha standing there uncertainly, as if unsure of her welcome. Sheryl waved her in.

"Hey Keisha," she said, trying to infuse warmth into her voice. "How are you doing?"

"Are you okay?" the younger woman asked bluntly. "You look . . ."

Sheryl, seeing Keisha's concern, felt a lump swell in her throat. *Man, I'd love to have someone to talk to right now, and Keisha is smart.* She subtly shook her head. *No, she's not the right person to confide in. Too awkward with all the work stuff we already have going on, not to mention that I'm her boss's boss.*

"Are you okay?" Keisha asked again, interrupting Sheryl's thoughts.

Sheryl's head bobbed in a semblance of a nod, and she swallowed. "Yeah, I'm okay. What's up?" she asked.

Keisha bit her full lower lip. "I was just wondering, um, if there's any news on the Portal Project," she began. She shut the door, crossed the room slowly, and sank into the chair in front of Sheryl's desk.

Sheryl straightened her shoulders. "Uh, no," she answered, struggling to shift her focus off that disconcerting phone call. "Everything is still on hold."

"I'm sorry if I caused this problem," Keisha said, her face pale. "I . . . I didn't want the project to be stopped. I know it's important."

Keisha's tone, apologetic and uncertain, caught Sheryl's attention. She frowned. The tone and demeanor were quite unlike Keisha. *Something must be wrong.*

"I know you didn't, Keisha. Why would you think you caused that problem?" Sheryl asked, puzzled but wanting to reassure her. "You only brought it to our attention. That was the right thing to do."

"Are you sure? Rachel doesn't seem to think so."

Sheryl's already tense muscles tightened further. "What? When did Rachel talk to you?" Sheryl asked sharply.

"This morning," Keisha said, dropping her gaze. "I wasn't going to tell you, but, well, it's been bugging me. Making me, I dunno . . . question myself? She told me it was all my fault, that I was creating problems for everyone. She said, um, that I would 'pay for it.'"

Sheryl rose from her chair as a wave of fury washed over her. "What? How could she say that to you? Why?"

Keisha looked at her boss fearfully. "I don't know, Sheryl. She approached me!"

Sheryl took a deep breath and sank back down. Closing her eyes, she centered herself. When she was back in control, she looked up. *At least this is a problem I can do something about.*

"I'm sorry. I didn't mean to snap at *you.* This caught me by surprise. If Rachel approaches you again, you tell her to talk to me. She shouldn't be accusing you."

"Well, I did tell her to talk to you already," Keisha responded, sitting up straighter in the chair. "She just walked away. I guess this means she didn't come to you."

Sheryl shook her head. "No, she didn't." She let out a huff of air. "She must have been trying to intimidate you." She squeezed her forehead with her thumb and index finger. "But why?"

"I don't know. I just thought I should tell you," Keisha said. "I mean, I should tell you, right?"

"Oh, yes, you should tell me. I'll talk to her . . . Or maybe Joaquin is a better idea." Sheryl mused, half to herself. *What is the best way to play this? And when?* She glanced at her watch. It was already after three. *I don't know what Rachel is up to, but given that she went right to Jim the last time . . . No, I think Joaquin is the right choice, but it can probably wait until Monday.*

Keisha's soft cough interrupted her thoughts. Sheryl gave her a wry, apologetic smile.

"Sorry, just thinking. But Keisha, please try not to engage with Rachel again, even if she comes to you. Walk away and come to my office. I don't want you to have to deal with that. It's not fair," she said firmly.

Keisha smiled more broadly, much closer to her normal, cheeky grin. "Thank you. I really don't *want* to deal with her."

"I'm sorry you had to," Sheryl said sympathetically. "I'll see what I can do to make sure it doesn't happen again." She paused. "You know, you should head out for the weekend now. It's been a rough week. Try to relax and get some rest, and most importantly, try not to let this stuff bother you."

"I'll try," Keisha responded, but Sheryl heard a bit of hesitancy back in her voice.

"Hey, it's going to be okay," she comforted the younger woman. She stood up, walked around the desk, and laid a hand on Keisha's shoulder. "You've done everything right. You're truly to be commended. Something is going on, and we're not even close to getting to the bottom of it, but we will."

"Okay then," Keisha said, rising. "I will take off." She flashed a quick grin. "Thanks, boss."

Sheryl smiled distractedly but didn't answer, her mind already shifting back to Dave and Elizabeth Curtis.

Keisha started to turn toward the door but paused and gave Sheryl another assessing look. "Are you sure *you're* okay? I don't mean to be rude, but you're not looking like yourself."

Sheryl gave her a rueful smile. "Yeah, I'll be okay. Thanks for asking," she said, although her tone was hardly convincing, even to herself.

Keisha looked doubtful, but after a moment, she finally headed toward the door. "Okay, boss, if you say so. Let me know if you need something. Have a good weekend," she said over her shoulder.

"You too," Sheryl answered, watching Keisha stride out much more confidently than she had walked in, but her gaze snapped right back to her cell phone. *Should I call Dave?*

Walking back to her chair, she picked up the phone but didn't dial. She held it in her hand, contemplating. *If Dave is there with Elizabeth, he can't answer anyway. I guess I'll have to wait.* She put the phone back down and turned to her computer, flipping through the emails that had come in while she and Keisha talked. But she couldn't ignore her growing sense of unease. *Something is very, very wrong.*

She glanced at the time. It was nearly 4:00. *I should work a little longer. It's still early.* But she couldn't bring her focus fully to her work. *I have to go home,* she thought with increasing urgency. *I have to find out what's wrong with Dave. The only reason Elizabeth Curtis would call me is that Dave is in some kind of trouble.* She stopped, stiffening as a single name reverberated loudly in her head: *Alisha!*

Her lips set in a tight line, she closed the email program, shut down her computer, and tucked it into its bag. She double-checked that her file drawers were locked, a new habit following Jim's intrusion, and headed toward the door. Whatever was going on, she needed to be home. She needed to be there for Dave.

The thirty-minute drive home seemed interminable. She put on the LeAnn Rimes chanting music that usually soothed her, but even that didn't lift her spirits. A sense of dread permeated the car. The relief when she reached the driveway and opened the garage door was palpable, but Dave's vehicle wasn't in there. *He must still be at work. That's good, isn't it?*

She parked her car in the garage, gathered her purse and laptop bag, and headed into the house. Her footsteps echoed in the empty kitchen as she crossed the room and headed upstairs to change. She dropped the laptop bag in her office first, shedding her low-heeled pumps before walking to the bedroom and into the walk-in closet. *What to wear? I guess we're not going out tonight. Should I just be comfortable?*

But putting on sweats somehow felt wrong. She grabbed a pair of well-worn jeans and a soft sweater and pulled them on. She ran a brush through her hair and wiped the faint smudges of mascara from under her eyes. Then, grabbing her phone, she sent Dave a quick text, asking him to call when he could.

Now what?

Back downstairs, she looked around the kitchen, restless and jumpy. Needing to do something, she pulled some Brie from the refrigerator and a box of whole-grain crackers from the pantry. Rinsing a sprig of grapes, she placed it, the cheese, and the crackers on a decorative cutting board and set it on the island counter. She turned to the wine refrigerator at the end of the counter and selected an earthy Pinot Noir, which she opened and left to breathe.

Quarter to five. I wonder when will Dave get home? She was a little surprised he hadn't called yet.

Just then she heard the garage door open. She waited. Dave walked in moments later, his hands empty, which shocked her. *Where is his computer?*

"Hey," he said, stopping just inside the door. "I, uh, didn't expect you here quite yet."

"You're early, too," she replied.

"Yeah, I, uh . . ." His voice trailed off.

Their eyes met and held. There was a long moment of silence. Sheryl wasn't sure what to say.

"I guess you're wondering about the phone call from Elizabeth Curtis," he said finally, his shoulders sagging beneath his black leather jacket.

Sheryl nodded; her eyes creased with further worry. "Yes, I am. Something is wrong, isn't it?"

He shrugged. "Yeah. Something is wrong." His voice was as defeated as she had ever heard it.

Her heart swelled with compassion. Walking over to him, she gave him a quick hug. "Why don't you take your coat off and change? I made us a snack. I'll pour some wine—or do you need something stronger?" she asked quietly.

He grimaced. "I want something stronger, but I should probably stick with wine. Thank you. I'll be right back."

Sheryl watched him walk out of the kitchen, his head hanging. He looked like he had the weight of the world on his shoulders. Feeling helpless, she took the plate into the great room and set it on the coffee table. By the time Dave returned, she had poured two glasses of wine, set one on the table next to the food, and settled herself in the corner of the sofa, wine glass in hand.

Dave gave her a weak smile and settled on the opposite end of the sofa. He took a gulp of the Pinot and sighed.

Sheryl was unable to contain herself any longer. "What happened? What's going on? Why did Elizabeth call me?"

Dave shook his head. "Man, I don't even know where to start," he said, his voice rough but quiet, almost as if he were talking to himself.

Sheryl leaned forward. "Dave, just tell me," she pleaded.

He looked up and met her eyes. "The bottom line is that I'm suspended without pay—"

"—Without pay? Why?"

"Because Alisha accused me of . . ."

He took another gulp of wine, looking away from her. He seemed to be struggling with some emotion that she couldn't place. Sheryl felt a frisson of fear snake down her spine.

"Accused you of what?" Sheryl finally spoke into the silence, her voice raspy.

Dave closed his eyes and ran a hand through his hair. He cleared his throat. "Accused me of, uh . . ." His breath came out in a long whoosh. He inhaled deeply. "God, I don't want to even say the words out loud."

Alarmed, Sheryl slid across the smooth leather and touched his arm, dread coiling through her stomach. "Dave? You're scaring me. Just say it."

Staring into the wine glass, Dave's words came out in a rush. "Accused me of sexual harassment."

Sheryl recoiled, her back stiffening. All the doubts she had had about Alisha and Dave came flooding back. *Were they more than friends? Are they having an affair? But why would she accuse him . . . ?*

"How can that be?" She blurted out, her tone demanding. "You said you weren't involved with her, that you weren't having an—"

"I'm not!" Dave broke in angrily, his eyes flashing as he met her gaze for the first time. "I'm not! I told you that."

"But then how? Why would she say something like that?" Sheryl's tone was harsh and bewildered at the same time. The dread solidified into a hard knot of anger in her gut, but there was something in Dave's expression that kept her from lashing out at him. She could see that he was angry and hurt.

"I don't know why," Dave ground out, standing up and striding across the room.

Sheryl leaned back, her eyes filling with tears. "I don't understand, Dave. *Something* has to have happened."

Dave threw up his hands. "Yes, damn it. Something happened, but it was her, not me!" he exclaimed, pacing back and forth between the fireplace and the French doors. His movements were jerky and abrupt. She could feel the heavy thud of his steps reverberating through the carpeted floor.

She watched him warily. Clearly, he felt he had been wronged. *But why would Alisha accuse him if nothing happened?*

Tamping down her own fears and anger, she waited while Dave gathered himself. Finally, he turned to face her again.

"Dave, sit down and tell me the whole story. Help me understand what's happening," she coaxed, her voice more soothing.

"Okay, okay," he muttered, but he retreated to the kitchen to refill his wine glass first. Returning half a minute later, he sank down next to her but didn't touch her.

"I think I screwed up," he started, his face twisting with self-condemnation.

Sheryl stiffened and drew back.

"No, Sheryl, I didn't have an affair with her," he said impatiently. "I told you that. But I think Alisha got the wrong idea about our relationship anyway."

Sheryl took a big drink of her wine. She looked at him encouragingly but didn't relax her posture. "Go on," she said.

Dave stared at his wine for a moment, then went through the same story he had told Elizabeth about the previous evening. "So, that's why she called you," he finished. "To make sure that I was where I said I was."

Sheryl released the breath she hadn't realized she was holding. "Wow," she said. "I'm not sure what to make of all that." She paused, thinking back to the previous weekend. "Is that why you were upset when you came home from condo-hunting with Alisha?"

"Yeah," Dave agreed, a wry smile on his face. "Pretty much. That's when I started to get an inkling that she was headed down a road that I wasn't."

"But why would she think that you were?" Sheryl asked, confused. She rubbed her temple with her left hand, gripping the stem of the wine glass with her right. *This isn't making sense. What would Alisha think that Dave was interested . . . or available?*

Dave ran his hand through his hair, again, and looked away. She could feel the tension pulsing in him. He seemed ready to bolt.

"Dave?"

He cleared his throat. His voice was rough when he spoke. "Well, uh, I might have told her that I was upset with you."

Sheryl jumped up, tears flooding her eyes. "You did what?" Her voice rose in pitch and volume. "Just what did you tell her?"

Dave stood up, walking away from her toward the French doors. He stood staring out into the darkening sky. She saw him inhale deeply. When he turned, once more he didn't meet her eyes.

"Sheryl, I was angry with you. She was sharing personal things with me—it seemed only natural to share with her, too. I was just venting, but . . ." His voice trailed off.

"But she took the venting as a sign that you were *leaving* me? That must have been some venting, Dave," Sheryl spoke sarcastically into the silence. Trembling, she walked into the kitchen. Tears threatened again as she pressed her lips together and swallowed hard. She didn't know whether to cry or throw something. Neither seemed appropriate, and yet both seemed appropriate.

She carefully set her wine glass on the island counter and leaned against the hard, marbled granite with both hands. Dropping her head, she struggled to control the feelings of betrayal, hurt, and anger that were coursing through her. *Stop it!* she told herself. *Don't make it mean something it doesn't. Don't make it mean anything about you.*

"Sheryl?"

She felt Dave come up behind her and ignored him until she felt him rest his hand hesitantly on her shoulder. Suppressing the urge to push his hand away, she turned to face him.

"This feels really bad, Dave," she said, searching his eyes for his reaction. "I know things weren't going well between us, that you didn't like what I was doing, that you felt I wasn't listening to you, but I don't understand why you had to share all that with another woman."

A flicker of shame crossed Dave's face. "I can see that now," he said. "But I thought she was a friend, just a friend."

"Did you really?" Sheryl retorted sharply before she could stop herself.

He dropped his hand to his side. "Mostly," he answered with a husky voice. "If I'm honest with myself, mostly. I guess there was some part of me . . . I mean, she was listening to me. You weren't. I don't know." He sighed heavily. "I'm sorry. I didn't think."

Sheryl snorted. "No, you didn't think," she snapped, gripping the countertop tightly with her left hand.

"I guess it comes back to the question you asked me, doesn't it? Why *was* I so angry with you?" he said, almost to himself.

"You think?" Sheryl said, not bothering to hide the sarcasm. "Did you ever figure that out?"

"No, yes, I, uh, I guess what I just said was part of it. I felt like you weren't listening to me . . . that you didn't . . . need . . . me." His voice held a hint of wonder, as if he was just coming to that realization.

"Dave, we've never been super dependent on one another. Why would that bother you now?" Sheryl said impatiently.

"I don't know," he said defensively. "I think it just felt different, like you were different. You had this big new role. You were forging ahead against my advice. I felt like I was beneath you, not important enough to listen to, I guess."

"Are you making that up now to make yourself feel better?" she asked incredulously.

"No, Sheryl. No, I'm not. Come on. Give me a little break here."

"Like you did for me?" she snapped.

He stepped back, his face flushing as if she'd slapped him. He took a deep breath. "I guess I deserve that," he said. He looked away.

"I'm sorry. I shouldn't have said that," Sheryl said, regretting her sharp words. She softened her tone. "That's not helping. I guess I can kind of understand why you were feeling that way. But why didn't you talk to me about it?"

"Thanks, but you weren't exactly receptive to my suggestions and thoughts."

"Hmmm," she murmured, considering his comment. *Is he right about that? Was I being that intractable?*

A tense silence stretched across the room. Sheryl picked up her glass again, idly twirling it in her hand. Dave shoved his own hands into his pockets, as if he didn't know what to do with them. After several minutes, Sheryl broke the silence with the real question that had been haunting her since she first heard about Alisha.

"Dave? *Were* you thinking of leaving me? Did she *really* read the signals all wrong?" she asked urgently.

"What? No! No, no, no! I wasn't thinking about leaving you. Yeah, I was pissed at you. Yeah, I felt like you were operating on your own, without me. But I *never* considered leaving you," he replied passionately, stretching his hands out in front of him.

Relief flooded her. His voice was too raw, his gestures too real for her to disbelieve him.

"Then why? Why would she think you were?" Her voice rose with confusion and concern.

Dave turned away. Putting his half-full wine glass down, he headed for the wet bar in the corner of the great room. Pulling out a glass, he poured himself a hefty shot of Scotch. Sheryl felt the knot of dread reestablish itself in her stomach.

"Well, there's one more thing I might have mentioned," he said cautiously.

"And that is?" Sheryl asked after a moment had passed.

Silence. Suddenly, Sheryl wasn't sure she wanted to know the answer.

"Well, I might have hinted that I still want to have a child," Dave finally said, his voice barely above a whisper.

Sheryl stopped breathing as she felt the blood drain from her head. The wine glass slid from her suddenly nerveless fingers, shattering on the tile and spraying red wine in a wide arc across the floor.

Chapter 20

Alisha paced across the small space available in her hotel room. Her agitation grew with each little lap, back and forth, back and forth. She couldn't manage more than about ten steps in each direction. It wasn't very satisfying. Maybe she could walk outside, or, better yet, run.

She crossed to the window, lifted the curtain, and looked out. The weather hadn't changed. Dark gray clouds hung low in the sky, and sheets of rain whipped across the parking lot in waves. She knew from the temperature on the weather app that it was a cold rain. Not a day to walk or run outside. *At least it isn't snowing.*

She flung the curtain back down in disgust and resumed her pacing. She should be in California, enjoying sunshine and warmer weather. But she was stuck here now, in New Jersey, in this hotel room, for who knew how long. All because of Dave.

She gritted her teeth as she thought back again to their last evening out. Every time she thought about his callousness, his rejection, she grew more furious. *How dare he? He's no better than my father, than Liam, than any of the other assholes in my life. And I trusted him!*

She threw her hands up in the air. "But what the hell am I going to do all weekend?" she muttered aloud. "In this weather?"

She thought about calling her mother, but she had already explained to her that she had to stay in New Jersey. Her mom had inexplicably gone back to whining about the move and Alisha's being so far away, so Alisha didn't want to put herself through that again. She never knew what she was going to get from Denise. She even briefly considered calling Juliet, but she didn't want to hear Juliet's opinion of the latest developments with Dave. Yet another "I told you so" from her friend was the last thing she needed.

So, where does that leave me? Damn it, Dave. If I can't be in California, I should be able to be with you. But nooooo, you're probably home snug and warm with Sheryl! Damn, damn, damn. I wonder if anyone in Human Resources has even talked to you yet. Do you know what kind of trouble you are in?

She felt a twinge of guilt with that thought. *Anything that happens now, Dave deserves, right?* Barbara Montgomery had been clear about that, and Alisha had been very grateful for her support. Finally, someone had listened to her.

Barbara had been so kind and sympathetic when Alisha had talked to her Friday morning. She had called to see how Alisha was doing with her condo search and if there was anything that Barbara herself could do to help. Alisha, still feeling raw and rejected by Dave, had welcomed the call, welcomed the kindness and concern that suddenly seemed so scarce in her life. She had been only too happy to open up to Barbara and tell her how Dave had betrayed her.

Alisha had to admit that she hadn't expected Barbara to react quite so strongly. She had been confiding in Barbara the way one would to a close friend. In her misery, she hadn't quite realized that Barbara was calling in an official capacity . . . and Barbara had reacted the way any Human Resources professional would—with sympathy, concern, and severe condemnation of Dave's behavior.

It wasn't until she said the word "investigation" that Alisha recognized that she was on the verge of lodging a formal complaint, almost whether she wanted to or not. Barbara had been adamant about wanting justice—for Alisha and all the other women out there who were "mistreated by arrogant, misogynistic men." She insisted that this couldn't be allowed to continue.

Alisha had tried, half-heartedly, to backtrack, to tell Barbara that she really didn't want to file a complaint, but Barbara was appalled that she would allow Dave's behavior to go unchecked. Barbara had been so insistent that it was not acceptable, not the kind of behavior LSM condoned, that Alisha had felt obligated to formally proceed.

So, instead of going back to California to start packing and get ready to move, she had been told to stay in New Jersey until the matter was resolved. Barbara would ensure that Dave was investigated and, most likely, suspended, if not even fired immediately. Barbara had been totally outraged on Alisha's behalf, which was gratifying if a little disconcerting.

But Alisha had also been told not to call Dave under any circumstances. That didn't mean he couldn't call *her*, though, did it?

Alisha started when her phone rang. She stopped pacing and grabbed the phone eagerly. *Dave? No, ugh, Juliet.* She stared at the phone, not sure if she should answer it. She finally slid her finger to answer just before it rolled over to voicemail.

"Hey Juliet," she said, trying to keep her voice calm and casual. "What's up?"

"Hey yourself," came the cheerful response. "Are you back in CA? Wanna grab dinner tonight? It's been a while since we got together."

Alisha frowned. Juliet was nothing if not loyal. She should be thankful, but, well, sometimes it just made her feel bad about her own lack of initiative in the friendship. She rarely called Juliet. Juliet was the one who made most of the effort.

"Alisha?" Juliet's voice rose a little.

"Yeah, yeah, I'm here," she said, not quite keeping the irritability out of her voice.

"Great, and dinner?"

"No, I'm here on the phone, not here in California. I ended up having to stay over the weekend," Alisha clarified, resuming her pacing.

"Oh, that's too bad." Juliet sounded genuinely disappointed.

"Yeah, the weather here sucks," Alisha grumbled. "I'd rather be home."

Juliet chuckled. Alisha could see her tucking her long red hair behind her right ear as she did. "Yeah, well, it's hard to beat California weather, that's for sure. How come you had to stay? Problems with the condo?"

"Nah, problems at work," Alisha responded evasively.

"Oh no, with the new job?"

"No, no. That's fine. I like my new boss, and everything seems to be going well with that," Alisha said frankly. *I* am *much happier with my new boss. Such an improvement on Liam!*

"Oh, excellent. I'm glad to hear that. So, what's the problem then? Does it have to do with Dave?"

Alisha groaned.

"I guess that's a yes," Juliet said, sighing a little into the phone. "What happened?" She paused. When Alisha didn't answer, she continued. "Or is it what *didn't* happen?"

Alisha let out a huff of air. "How do you do that?" she asked, pausing by the window and lifting the curtain again. *Still raining, dammit.*

"Do what? Guess what's going on? It doesn't take much, Alisha. So what's going on?"

"Do I have to tell you?" Alisha asked flippantly.

"No, you don't. I can just hang up," Juliet offered seriously.

"No, don't hang up. I'll tell you," Alisha said in a rush, the words popping out of her mouth almost before she knew it. Then she paused. *What should I tell Juliet? She's not going to be happy about this.*

"Hey, you don't have to tell me. We can talk about something else. I really just wanted to see if you were free for dinner. We can catch up another time," Juliet said, clearly sensing Alisha's reluctance in the long silence.

Alisha sighed. "You're not going to like it . . ." she began. She walked over to the bed and plopped down, sprawling out with her head on the pillow, one arm tucked behind it.

"Oh, Alisha, what did you do now?"

Stiffening, Alisha snapped. "Why do you always assume that I did something?"

Alisha could tell that Juliet stifled a laugh. She pulled the phone away from her ear, contemplating hanging up.

"I'm sorry. I shouldn't do that," Juliet said, her voice distant and muffled.

Alisha returned the phone to her ear. "No, you shouldn't," she retorted. "But it wasn't me. It was Barbara."

"Who's Barbara?"

"Barbara's the HR woman that's been helping me with the transfer. I told you about her."

"Oh yeah, I remember now. So, what did she do?"

Alisha paused, then gave Juliet a very sanitized version of what had happened and Barbara's response, presenting her side as favorably as she possibly could. She carefully omitted some of her more obvious overtures to Dave. In her mind, Dave had been even more of the aggressor than he was in the version of the story she told Barbara.

". . . and then, he shook me and told me that I was a tease. I got in my car and got away as fast as I could," Alisha finished defiantly.

"Oh Alisha," Juliet said, her voice shocked but somehow soft and soothing, too. "I *am* sorry. I know I was pretty vocal about you not pursuing Dave, but I didn't want you to get hurt like this."

"Thanks, Juliet," Alisha said gruffly, her voice taut with emotion.

"But Alisha . . ."

Uh oh. Here it comes.

"Are you sure about what Dave was saying? What you said doesn't sound like the Dave you've described before, you know, with Liam and everything . . ." Juliet said cautiously.

Alisha sat up, crossing her legs and leaning forward. "What? Are you calling me a liar?" she said indignantly.

"No, I'm not, but it sounds like it was a very emotional conversation. Are you sure you are remembering it correctly?" Juliet's voice was tentative and low.

Alisha growled. "I should have just hung up. I should have known you wouldn't believe me!" she cried, jumping off the bed. "I just can't talk to you about Dave. You're always making me wrong. Well, I'm NOT WRONG!" she shouted.

She clicked the end button and threw the phone on the bed. "I'm not wrong," she repeated firmly to herself. "I'm not."

But the little voice inside her head contradicted her. *Yes, you are . . . and you'd better do something about it before it's too late.*

Alisha wished she could hang up on the little voice as easily as she had hung up on Juliet. She sighed deeply. She knew she needed to get her act together. If she was going to go through with this complaint—and she was—she had to be credible. She had to believe in herself and her pursuit of justice.

She decided to find the hotel gym. It was the best way she knew to work off this energy and get herself back in the game . . . and silence that damn little voice.

Chapter 21

Sheryl mentally ran through the questions—again—that had been swirling in her mind after Dave's bombshell last evening. *I am fifty years old, nearly fifty-one. Dave is two years older. He can't really be serious about starting a family now, can he? And where did this idea come from? Did Alisha plant it?*

Stretched out on the daybed in her home office, a pale blue blanket draped over her legs, she was finally relaxed. Although it had taken some work to get there this morning, she was starting to deal with the myriad of thoughts and emotions that Dave's bombshell about wanting a child had evoked.

She had purposely started with her normal meditation and journaling, completed a light workout to release her tension, and then spent more time in conscious breath and meditation. At last, after several hours, she felt her mind clearing, her emotions settling down. She was grateful to feel connected to her higher self and centered.

As Sheryl took another deep breath, she looked around the room. She knew it was decorated in soft blues and cream, with an antique white desk and bookshelf. But even though it was mid-morning, the room was too dark to see more than shadows. She had lit a single white candle that burned on the side table, but it did little to dispel the gloominess of the day. She could hear the rain slashing against the window, driven by the wind in a cycle that ebbed and flowed in a harsh, uneven rhythm. When she had first gotten up, she had felt that the day matched her mood. Now, though, Sheryl smiled to herself. *There is something comforting about being snug and warm inside while a storm rages outside.*

Pondering the situation, she knew she needed to talk more with Dave, but not yet. She wriggled into a more comfortable position, then closed her eyes and slipped back into a semi-meditative state.

She allowed her thoughts to drift back. After she had dropped the wineglass on the floor, Dave had gently led her out of the room and cleaned up the mess. Seeming to know that she was not ready to continue the conversation, he had settled her on the sofa and made a light meal for the two of them. He had replaced her wine, and his Scotch, with a glass of water and, later, a mug of hot chamomile tea.

She had managed to have a desultory conversation with him about inconsequential things while they ate, but she couldn't remember a word of it now. After he cleaned up the kitchen, they had watched a light-hearted movie, which she also couldn't recall. She only knew that when she finally tumbled into bed, she had ached all over, a deep emotional pain that penetrated her bones. Sleep had been a long time coming.

Suddenly feeling Dave's presence in the doorway, she brought herself back to alertness.

"Sheryl?" he asked tentatively, as if unsure of his welcome.

"Hmmm," she answered, not opening her eyes.

"Are you okay? Can I get you anything?"

Annoyance and compassion struggled briefly for dominance. She sighed. That compassion won was a testament to the power of her morning practices. She had noticed that the longer she did them regularly, the calmer and more centered her reactions became.

"No, I'm okay," she murmured without moving.

Dave didn't respond, but she could sense him standing nervously on the threshold. She waited.

"Sheryl, I'm sorry," he finally said quietly. "I'm really worried about you. Can we talk, please?"

She opened her eyes, peering through the semi-darkness at him. All she could see was his tall, athletic frame outlined against the light in the hall.

"I'm not sure what to say at the moment," she admitted, pulling the blanket more closely around her.

He slipped into the room, moving cautiously, and settled on the daybed next to her. She felt the cushion dip and her body slide towards him. He reached out as if to steady her but withdrew his hand and laid it on his knee.

"Look, I'm sorry. I guess I shouldn't have told you that, but—"

"Of course you should have told me," she interrupted, unable to restrain the thread of anger lacing her words. "How can I deal with any of this if I don't know the whole story?"

Sheryl sat up, scooting back against the pillows and drawing her knees up to her chest. She stared at him over crossed arms, unable to read his expression in the dim light.

Her abrupt movement jostled Dave, and he steadied himself, settling farther on the bed near her feet. He stretched his hands to either side, palms up.

"What am I supposed to say now?" he asked, helplessly. "I want to make you feel better."

Her face flushed. "Well, you should have thought about that before you went spouting off about our personal lives to your friend Alisha," she retorted truthfully.

Dave dipped his head and ran his hand through his hair. "I know. I know I screwed up," he said. "I never thought . . ."

"Yeah, you never thought," Sheryl said with more bitterness than she'd have liked. "And now look where it's got you."

She paused. Closing her eyes while taking several deep breaths, she reined in her frustration. *Being snippy is not going to help the situation,* she scolded herself. She sought the centeredness she'd had moments ago.

Exhaling audibly, she opened her eyes. She leaned forward and looked at him searchingly.

"Dave, what in the world *were* you thinking when you told her you wanted a kid? She has to know that I'm too old to have children. What did you think she was going to think?" she asked, her voice calm but her eyes intense.

"I think we already established I wasn't thinking," he said wryly. "But I certainly never thought she'd take it the way she did . . . although it seems kind of obvious now."

Sheryl bit her lip. *At least he's taking responsibility.* "But where did this sudden need to have a child come from? I had no idea it was that important to you. I thought we were both okay with the decision we made years ago. Why didn't you say something?"

"Well, honestly, it's not something I thought a lot about until recently." He paused, his forehead creasing with deep thought. "I guess it's been Robert that has brought it up. He talks about his sons all the time, about playing basketball and doing other stuff with them. I don't know. It just kind of struck me that I would like that." He shrugged slightly, apologetically.

Sheryl unexpectedly felt the sting of tears in her eyes. *Dave would have made a great father.*

"Oh Dave, I'm sorry." She reached out and touched his arm. She was startled to see an answering sheen of tears mirrored in his eyes.

"I'm sorry too. I know it's too late for us now—and I wouldn't want to have kids with anyone but you," he said earnestly. "I really wouldn't."

"I wish we had talked about this before," she said wistfully.

"But we did talk about it," he said emphatically. "It just didn't seem that important ten years ago. We were happy. We both were busy with our careers. We had full lives."

"Yeah, and I couldn't seem to get pregnant," she reminded him softly.

"Right, and we didn't want to go through all the trauma of infertility treatments."

"Yeah," Sheryl sighed the word. "All that hassle Chris and Carol went through . . . and then nothing."

They had watched their close friends and neighbors struggle through years of treatment only to be disappointed again and again. Chris and Carol had finally given up, sold their house in the family-friendly neighborhood, and moved into an apartment in Philadelphia. They were over an hour away now, and Sheryl and Dave had largely lost touch with them.

Dave grimaced, and there was deep emotion in his voice as he agreed, "That was awful. We felt so bad for them. We didn't want to put ourselves through that."

He grabbed Sheryl's hand that was on his arm, holding it firmly. He looked at her, a question in his eyes. Nodding ever so slightly, she allowed him to pull her into an embrace. They held each other in shared regret and . . . *Is that grief?* She didn't know, but she melted into him and felt him melt into her.

After several minutes, Dave pulled back. "I'm really sorry, Sheryl," he said sincerely. "I really didn't mean for all of this to get so out of control."

Sheryl's lips tilted in a weak smile. "I know, but . . ."

"But where do we go from here?" He finished for her.

"Yeah, that."

"I guess the first question is can you forgive me?" Dave raised his eyebrows with the question.

Sheryl looked down at their entwined hands. Although she still felt traces of anger and hurt, her feelings now were overwhelmingly compassionate. *I know how much I love Dave. And he loves me, despite his foolishness, I do believe he deeply loves me.* She looked at him, looked into his eyes, and asked herself a vital question. *What's more important: our relationship or being right?*

"Sheryl?"

She could hear the anxiety in his voice, but there was still one big unanswered question.

"Dave, this whole situation has really hurt a lot," she said slowly, testing each word before she spoke. "First, you were so awful to me a few months ago, when I needed your support, and I still don't get that. Now, you've created a mess with another woman, however inadvertently. Even you admit that you were giving her mixed signals. Are you attracted to her? What are your feelings toward her? Do you know?"

Dave pulled his hands back and stood up, pacing back and forth across the small room. He stopped in front of her, his hands shoved deep in his pockets.

"I know I hurt you. I'm sorry. I guess I was feeling like you didn't need me this fall, that you were going your own way regardless of me and my feelings. That made me mad, and I lashed out. I was also afraid for you—"

Sheryl started to interrupt, but he held up a hand.

"No, listen. I *was* afraid. I didn't want you to lose your job. You've worked so hard for it, sacrificed so much. I didn't want to see you get hurt. You have to at least give me credit for that," he said passionately.

She nodded, bouncing her head from side to side. "Yeah, okay, I guess I can see that." It was the first time Dave had spoken these words, acknowledging her hard work and sacrifice—and his pigheadedness.

Dave raised his hands in a gesture of helplessness. "I know I handled it badly, but you wouldn't listen to me."

"I did listen," she protested. "I just didn't agree with you!"

He groaned and sank back onto the daybed. "Okay, okay. I'm just telling you how I felt. That's what you asked, right?"

She gave a self-deprecating laugh. "Yeah, it is," she admitted a bit grudgingly. "So how does Alisha fit in?"

He rubbed his left hand across the back of his neck.

"I guess, well, she was having trouble with Liam." Sheryl rolled her eyes but stayed quiet. "And, it felt good to be helping her out. She was listening to me, confiding in me, taking a lot of my advice."

"And you were flattered," Sheryl interjected.

Dave flushed and nodded sheepishly. "Yeah, I guess I was."

"Here's this young attractive woman who is hanging on your every word, while your mean old wife is ignoring you," Sheryl continued, rapidly filling in the gaps.

"Hey, I never said you were old," he objected. "You're still beautiful and very youthful."

Sheryl rolled her eyes again. "Nice recovery," she said, a hint of a smile curving her lips.

For a moment Dave's lips almost curved, but then he sobered again as he admitted, "But yeah, to some degree, you're right. And then I was envious of Robert and his relationship with his sons, so I guess that came out, too."

She lightly touched his arm but remained silent.

"I see that I overreacted—now," Dave said. "I didn't see that at the time, although, to be fair, Robert warned me."

Sheryl's face scrunched in surprise. "I knew I liked Robert," she said. "Why didn't you listen to him?"

"Because I thought he was just pushing my buttons, teasing me, like he always does." Dave gave her another wry look. "I guess he wasn't."

"So, what does Robert say about the situation now? Does he know?" Sheryl asked, her brow furrowing as she considered this angle.

Dave rubbed his jaw, his fingers scraping on the rough growth. He obviously hadn't shaved yet today.

"I'm sure he knows. HR was calling him in to interrogate him just as I left. I haven't talked to him since."

"Can you call him and find out?" Sheryl asked thoughtfully.

"Good question. I was told not to contact Alisha or any of my customers. I don't know about Robert. Elizabeth didn't mention him specifically."

"Hmmm. Maybe talking to him would taint the investigation?" she suggested, going into problem-solving mode.

"But they've already talked to him. It's not like we can compare stories now," he countered.

"Maybe you'd better wait. Maybe he'll call you," she said, thinking rapidly. "You'll need to be careful. You don't want Elizabeth to think you're going behind her back or trying to tamper with her process in any way."

"Thanks, that's a good point," Dave said, his shoulder relaxing as he responded to Sheryl's support.

She paused. *Do I dare ask him?* She squared her shoulders.

"Dave, *does* Alisha have anything to base her complaint on?" she asked intently. "And think hard before you answer that," she cautioned as he started to protest. "I'm serious."

Dave sat up straight. "No, she doesn't," he said adamantly, looking her straight in the eyes. "Despite the conversations I told you I had with her, I've never said anything directly about having a relationship with her. I never touched her inappropriately. If anything, she's the one who came on to me. She's obviously made a lot of assumptions from the things I have said, but there was nothing I did that was wrong. Yeah, maybe I showed poor judgment with what I shared about our relationship, but I was never disrespectful to her or made any inappropriate comments or anything."

"Okay, okay. I had to ask. I have to know what we're dealing with."

"We?" Dave asked hopefully.

Sheryl sighed. "Yes, we," she said. "No matter what's going on between us—and there clearly are things we still need to resolve—I can't just stand by and see your career ruined by false accusations. It's not fair. However, it is obvious that you used poor judgment, and that might make things tough."

He swallowed hard, relief flooding his face. "I don't deserve you," he said.

She laughed. "No, you don't, but you're stuck with me," she said pertly. But then her face and voice turned serious. "I'm willing to put the issues between us aside for now, but, Dave, we still have things to work through. It's going to take time and more conversations to make sure that we are truly on the same page with our relationship, our careers, and our lives. However, I have realized today that I own part of the blame for where we are, even though some of your actions of late have been pretty hard to take."

He turned somber as well. He held up a hand, palm forward. "I know they have, but I promise I'll work through this with you," he said firmly. "You hurt me, too, you know. But I realize now that I handled it all wrong."

Sheryl murmured an agreement and stood up, feeling determined and ready to do what she could to defend her husband.

"Come on," she said, grabbing Dave's hand. "Let's get some lunch and strategize. Whatever else happens, we can't let Alisha win."

Dave gave a half-hearted moan and followed her out of the room. She smiled at him over her shoulder, feeling lighter than she had in weeks. She knew that they still had work to do, still had wounds that needed healing, but she felt much more hopeful after this conversation—at least about their relationship.

On the other hand, she also knew that Dave was in serious trouble, much more than perhaps he even realized. Sexual harassment charges could be extremely damaging. *At least I could give him an honest, partial alibi, but that's not enough. We have to get him off the hook entirely—and fast.* She knew the longer this lingered, the more damage that could be done. *I wonder if I could call Robert.*

Her cell phone rang. She didn't recognize the number but answered it anyway on a hunch.

"Sheryl, it's Robert. I called on my wife's phone."

Sheryl chuckled softly. "I was just thinking about calling you."

She heard a deep answering chuckle. "Why am I not surprised?" Robert asked lightly, but then he paused. Sheryl held her breath.

"But I'm not sure why we're laughing," he continued, his voice deep and very serious. "Your boy, Dave? He's in deep shit."

Chapter 22

Dave leaned closer to Sheryl, barely able to hear Robert's voice coming from her phone. It felt strange and very uncomfortable to be merely an eavesdropper to the conversation, and it was even more odd to hear his friend's tone so serious.

He gripped the edge of the countertop hard as he listened to Sheryl ask very insightful questions. It was all he could do to keep himself from interrupting or getting up and walking out of the room. He strained to hear Robert's replies clearly. He hoped he wouldn't have to ask Sheryl to repeat much, but they had tacitly agreed not to put the phone on speaker. They wanted to preserve Robert's integrity as much as possible—and their own.

A few minutes later, after a sincere "Thank you," Sheryl tapped the end button and turned toward him. He saw the concern etched on her face. As brief as the call had been, Robert had taken a big risk in reaching out to her. Elizabeth Curtis had been clear: no contact with Dave or Alisha. Robert, being the loyal friend he was, had called Sheryl anyway, wanting to let her and Dave know what had been said during his "interview." Dave was extremely grateful, but he felt awful that Robert was now deeply involved in his own mess.

Dave sat on the stool shaking his head and suddenly dropped his face into his palms. "This is a nightmare," he said, his voice muffled. "A nightmare."

He heard the soft thuds of Sheryl's sneakers against the tile as she stepped toward him. He felt her hand touch his back and rub gently. She didn't speak, but he could sense that she concurred. *A nightmare.*

"At least we know more of what we're dealing with," she said, her voice calmer than he expected. But he could tell from her ashen face that she was shaken. He certainly was. Robert had been specific about the vehemence with which Barbara had attacked Dave in Robert's presence. He couldn't believe it. But at least Robert had reported that

Elizabeth seemed to be more balanced. *Still, "balanced" is a long way from her being on my side.*

Dave raised his head and looked at his wife, seeing his angst mirrored on her pale face. "What am I going to do?" he asked. "If they didn't believe Robert . . ."

"Hey, he didn't say that," Sheryl comforted him. "He said Elizabeth listened. And even you said Elizabeth seemed sympathetic. Isn't she the one who counts? She's this Barbara person's boss, isn't she?"

Dave nodded, putting his feet up on the rung of his stool, feeling a bit defeated despite Sheryl's encouraging words. He wasn't convinced this was going his way, even though Robert had told HR exactly the same story as Dave himself. Of course, Robert hadn't known all the details Dave did, not firsthand anyway, but it sounded like Robert had corroborated the information about the golf match as well as other comments of Alisha's that he had personally overheard.

Sheryl walked over to the cabinet and grabbed two glasses, filling them with water from the refrigerator door and setting them on the counter. She slid onto the stool next to him.

"Dave, I know this is hard, but you've got to keep a positive attitude. You have Robert firmly on your side—and me. We may not have the full story yet, but at least Robert gave us a sense of what Elizabeth and Barbara are thinking."

"Yeah, a sense that Barbara hates me," he groaned, taking a gulp of water then putting the glass back on the counter with a loud thunk. He saw Sheryl wince at the sound.

"He didn't say Barbara hates you. He just said that Barbara believes that you behaved inappropriately with Alisha," Sheryl corrected.

"What's the difference?" Dave snarled.

Sheryl took a deep breath, closing her eyes for a moment before looking at him with sympathy. "Dave, stop it," she said, her gray eyes gentle. "We've got to figure out how to defend you. Maybe we should find a lawyer."

Dave jerked back, feeling like she had punched him in the gut. "A lawyer? What do I need a lawyer for? I didn't DO anything!" He knew his voice was too loud, but damn it! *This whole thing is insane. What is Alisha doing to me?*

"Lawyers defend innocent people, you know," Sheryl pointed out.

Dave snorted, curling both hands around the water glass. His knuckles turned white.

Sheryl laid one hand on his wrist. "Barbara is just one person. There must be other people who know something about Alisha, something about Liam and Alisha, something . . ." Her voice rose. "Think, Dave. You need to calm down and think!"

He glared at her. "*Who* needs to calm down?"

She flushed. "Sorry. I'm just trying to get through to you," she said, her voice quieter. "You said this whole situation was precipitated by Liam's harassment of Alisha. Robert agrees with that. Who else knows about it? You and Robert can't be the only ones who have witnessed Liam's behavior. He can't have been that careful. Someone else must at least *suspect* something. Who might that be?" She paused, tilting her head thoughtfully. "Or maybe there's someone *else* he harassed?"

Dave mulled that over for a minute. "Those are good points, really good points," he said slowly. He tapped his fingers against the granite. "Who else *would* know something? It would have to be someone from that office, the one in San Jose where Liam and Alisha were based."

Sheryl nodded. "Good, good. Yes, who do you know in that office who might have seen something . . . and would be willing to help?"

Dave paused for a moment, his mind on his associates in California. He took a sip of water and then went back to tapping. He could see that Sheryl was itching to say something, but she only leaned toward him as silent encouragement.

He abruptly stopped tapping and snapped his fingers. "Olivia!" he exclaimed triumphantly.

"Olivia? Olivia who?"

"Olivia Perkins," Dave said, smiling for the first time since Robert's call. "She's been in that office a while. She's about the same age as Alisha, pretty, but not as, umm, striking as Alisha. Still, she's been there longer than Alisha. Maybe Liam came on to her. Or maybe she's seen Liam in action."

"What's her role there?" Sheryl asked, returning his smile cautiously.

"She was the office admin," Dave answered. "But I think she was promoted recently. She might be a sales assistant now. I'm not sure." He frowned, trying to remember exactly what Olivia's new role was. It escaped him.

"So, she's someone Liam might intimidate? He must be her boss, right?" Sheryl prompted.

"Yeah, he's her boss, and he does like to intimidate women," Dave acknowledged, trying to remember what he knew about Olivia. "I'm not in that office much, really. When I'm in California, I'm usually out at customer sites."

"Or playing golf," Sheryl muttered.

Dave shot her a dark look.

"Okay, sorry," she said, lifting one shoulder.

He shook his head. "Most of the other people in that office are guys. I'm not sure how much they'd pay attention. I'm sure they all noticed Alisha. Maybe . . ."

Sheryl wrinkled her nose. "Do you think they paid *enough* attention to see how Liam treated her? Did Liam make his interest in her obvious?"

"Who knows?" Dave said, his voice tight. "For me it was mostly that golf experience, when he'd been drinking, and it was uncomfortably obvious." Then he felt his face flush with anger. "But I can't talk to anyone anyway."

She nodded, deep in thought. "True. Hmm. That's why you need a lawyer. A lawyer would be able to talk to Olivia . . . and anyone else you can think of."

Dave suddenly slammed his fist against the counter. "I can't believe we're talking about lawyers," he growled.

He felt Sheryl run her hand down his arm. "Me either," she said with a huff.

That surprised Dave for a moment. He suddenly realized how difficult all this must be for her. He looked up at eyes, grasping her fingers.

"Sheryl, I'm so sorry about all of this. My God, I had no idea what a mess this would turn into." He exhaled. "You don't deserve this. I'm sorry."

As he looked at her, Dave saw a glint of tears in her eyes. Then she bit her lip. "Thank you," she said softly, her voice a bit breathy. "I do appreciate your apology." He felt the warmth of her when she squeezed his hand back.

Dave slid his free fingers down the side of her head, smoothing her hair before cupping her cheek. "I will make this up to you, somehow," he promised.

Sheryl nodded, and he saw her throat move as she swallowed hard. "Thanks, Dave," she said, her voice heavy with emotion. "I'm going to hold you to that," she finished with a bit of flippancy in her voice, as if trying to normalize things.

A quick smile crossed his lips, but then he sobered. "Okay. A lawyer," he said, grimacing. "You're probably right about that, although it makes me feel like I'm guilty of something."

Sheryl's look was sympathetic. "I know," she said, tightening her grip. "But I think you need to protect yourself. Robert thinks so, too."

Agitatedly, he ran his fingers through his hair. *How has it come to this? Where did everything go so wrong?*

"How do we go about that?" he finally asked. "I don't know any lawyers that specialize in employment law, do you? I mean, I guess that's who we need?"

Sheryl looked perplexed for a moment, then grabbed her cell phone. She started scrolling. *Is she looking through her contacts?*

"I'm going to call Janine," she said. "As an HR director, she must know someone who could at least point us in the right direction." She hesitated, looking at him with a question in her eyes. "Do you mind if I share what's going on with her? She might have some good advice."

Dave felt his face flush. "Oh geez, Sheryl. Do you have to? This is so . . ." He sighed. "Humiliating."

"Yes, Dave," Sheryl said firmly. "I think we do. We need all the help we can get. Janine will keep this confidential."

Dave frowned but nodded. "Go ahead then," he said, resigned to yet another person knowing about his big screwup. "Just do it. I'm going to go get a shower."

"Don't you want to be here? She may have questions I can't answer."

"I can't. I just can't listen to it all again. I need . . . I need a few minutes," he said, his voice rough. Suddenly Dave felt his anger resurface with a vengeance. He jumped up from the stool. "Damn Alisha. Just damn her!"

"Dave—"

"Not now," he begged as he stepped back from her outstretched hand. "I gotta move. I gotta breathe. After all I did for her, this is how she repays me? I can't believe it!"

He felt Sheryl's eyes watching him as he stomped furiously back and forth across the kitchen. His fists were clenched into tight balls, his whole body rigid with fury as the unfairness of Alisha's actions sank in. He was going to have to spend money to defend himself when all he had done was try to help. *Damn her to hell!*

"Why don't you go run on the treadmill?" Sheryl asked, looking a little alarmed at his outburst. "Get rid of some of that excess energy?"

Dave glanced out the window. *Still raining buckets. I'd rather run outside, but that's too much rain, even for me.*

He turned back to Sheryl. "Yeah, that's probably a good idea. I'm sorry."

"Dave, it's perfectly reasonable for you to be angry. I'd like to take a swipe at Miss Alisha myself right now. Unfortunately, it's not going to help anything. Go do a good workout, let off some of that steam. It'll be my turn next!" She gave him a tired smile. "In the meantime, I'll call Janine. We can regroup later."

He gave her a curt nod. "Yeah, okay, I'll do that."

"Go!" Sheryl smiled weakly.

He leaned over and kissed the top of her head. "Thank you," he said gruffly, before turning and heading upstairs to change. *A workout will feel good, and it's not like I can do much else right now.*

He heard Sheryl's voice just as he reached the bedroom door. He paused for a moment, then said a silent *Thank you* that she was being so understanding and helpful. *Most wives wouldn't be,* he thought, *especially after the way I've treated her. I just hope I* can *make it up to her . . . and that I get a chance to. What if she decides to believe Alisha, too? What if everyone at work believes it?* He couldn't help but have that deep, penetrating fear creep into his head. After all the hard work he had done at his job, after his years of striving to be excellent at communications, sales, and relationships, he couldn't believe how quickly that had all come to a head—or how quickly it could all come tumbling down. All of it.

Dave yanked his T-shirt over his head. He had to do everything possible to stop that from happening. Alisha had declared war. *And I'm going to fight. I'm going to fight that woman . . . and, I'm going to fucking fight for my wife.*

Chapter 23

Monday, December 13

Sheryl sat at the desk in her home office, rubbing her forehead again as she tried to concentrate on her work. She kept listening for Dave's voice from below, worried about how things might play out for him.

She shook her head. *Worrying is accomplishing nothing.* She took three long, slow breaths, centering herself. The buzz of her cell phone startled her. It was someone from the office.

"Hello?"

"Sheryl, it's Joaquin. You're not in the office today?"

"No," she answered quickly. "I've got some stuff going on at home, so I'm working from here." She paused briefly. "Is something wrong?"

"I'm not sure . . ." he said, concern threading the rich timbre of his voice. She'd always liked that he had a slight Spanish accent, which lent an exotic warmth to his words, even now.

"What's happening?" Sheryl prompted him.

"Rachel came to see me this morning," he said.

Oh boy, I should have called Joaquin on Friday! Ugh, Sheryl thought. She exhaled audibly. "I suspect she said something directly about Keisha," Sheryl responded, not even making it a question as she leaned on the desk with one elbow.

"You're right, she did. How did you know?" Joaquin asked.

"Keisha came to see me late Friday afternoon. Rachel had approached her and blamed the whole situation on Keisha overreacting. Keisha was quite upset by Rachel's attitude and, well, frankly . . . she full-out threatened Keisha. I was going to call you this morning to tell you, but you beat me to it," Sheryl said, an apologetic tone in her voice.

"Hmm, I see," Joaquin replied, his voice thoughtful. "Rachel mentioned something similar to me. In fact, she sounded a lot like Jim Leaders. I wonder if he put her up to it."

Sheryl hesitated. She was a little taken aback that Joaquin seemed to be confiding in her. She didn't know him all that well.

"Good question," she responded, cupping her chin in her hand. "I wouldn't be surprised. From what little I've seen, the two of them seem to be in close communication. Rachel telling Jim about my lunch with her is what seems to have prompted Jim to call that meeting with Todd and Janine—which led to you getting involved. I guess I don't know who's prompting whom."

"That's a good point," Joaquin agreed. "I told Rachel that it was a moot point, that the investigation was moving forward."

"And how did she react to that?" Sheryl asked, leaning back in her chair.

"Not well," he admitted. "Although she didn't say much. It was just the way she looked at me."

Sheryl chuckled. "The killer look?" she guessed.

Joaquin laughed. "Yeah, something like that. She just told me that it was critical to get the investigation done quickly so everyone could get back to work on the Portal Project. You'd think the entire company's future rests on that one project."

"Well, it is Rachel's project," Sheryl said wryly. "Her entire future probably does rest upon it—or at least her career at The Diamante." She paused after that last statement. *Is that true? Where had that idea come from?*

"How's Keisha?" Joaquin asked, interrupting her thoughts.

Sheryl pursed her lips in surprise and appreciation. "She's okay, I think. At least she was after we talked Friday and got it all out in the open. She had been holding it in, frankly, until she couldn't any longer. Thanks a lot for asking about her. I was going to check in with her after I talked to you."

"Good. Good," Joaquin said heartily, and Sheryl could almost see him nodding his head. "She certainly doesn't deserve Rachel threatening her," he continued.

"No, she doesn't," Sheryl agreed. Since Joaquin was being so forth-coming, she decided to ask for information herself. "So, how *is* the investigation going? Has the forensic database person started?"

"Yes, he started on Friday."

"Wow, quick work!" Sheryl exclaimed.

"I don't want this to linger," Joaquin said urgently. "We need to get this resolved quickly—and hopefully quietly—the importance of the project aside. The longer it goes on, the bigger the chance of a leak *or* the SEC stepping in. For now, they're letting us handle it on our own, but I don't know how long that will last. Which reminds me, do you know when the board meeting is?"

"Wednesday afternoon, I think. At least, that's what Todd is shooting for. He told me to hold time in my calendar. I'm sure he'll call you soon," Sheryl told him. "But what about Rachel? Is there any way you can tell her to leave Keisha alone—and everyone else on my team, for that matter?"

There was a moment of silence.

"Well, I did suggest that to her," he said slowly. "But I didn't demand it. I guess I could, but . . ."

"But you don't want to be too heavy-handed?" Sheryl finished for him.

He laughed. "No, not really. Not my style."

"Oh Joaquin, you shouldn't have become the compliance officer if you want to be the nice guy all the time."

This time, his laugh was full and hearty. "Yeah, I didn't think about that before I took the job." His voice dropped. "But yes, I will talk to Rachel if she crosses the line again. I can't allow her—or anyone else—to interfere with the investigation."

Sheryl cringed at the word. *Too many investigations going on right now.* "Sheryl?"

She refocused on Joaquin. "Yup, still here, and thank you. I'll let you know more promptly if she approaches Keisha or anyone else."

"Keisha can always call me herself," Joaquin offered, his voice slightly husky. "I don't mind."

Sheryl raised her eyebrows. *Does Joaquin have a thing for our Keisha?* The thought made her smile.

"Great, Joaquin, I'll let her know," Sheryl said, purposely keeping her tone even. "I'm sure she'll appreciate your support."

"Okay then," Joaquin said. "I'll let you know if I hear anything else . . . and you do the same."

"I will. Promise." Sheryl assured him, ending the call.

She gazed at the phone thoughtfully as she placed it back on her desk. *What is Rachel up to? Is Jim putting her up to this, or is she acting on her own?* Then she remembered Jim in her office, trying to get into her laptop. *No, it has to be Jim. Has to be.*

She bolted upright. "Oh geez, I didn't tell Joaquin about that," she said out loud, reaching for her phone, but it rang before she could dial.

By the time she finished that call, another one came in, and the thought of calling Joaquin slid from her mind.

Around eleven, she took a break and went down to check on Dave. It was so weird to have him home during the day . . . and not working. The last time that had happened had been when he was sick with the flu, almost two years ago. And he had been antsy to get back on the road the moment he started feeling better. She couldn't imagine how he felt now.

She found him sitting glumly at the kitchen counter, watching something on his iPad. He looked up when she walked in.

"How's it going?" she asked, lightly rubbing his shoulder.

"I need a phone," Dave said bluntly.

She blinked. "Oh yeah, I guess you do."

Sheryl now glanced at the phone in her hand, her work one. Her personal phone was still upstairs.

"It probably makes the most sense to add you to my personal account," she said.

He nodded. "That's what I thought. Do you have time to go to the Verizon store today?"

Glancing at her calendar, she saw that she was technically free until about 1:30. "Yes, but we'll have to be quick."

Dave gave her a half-hearted smile. "Thanks, should we go now?"

She scrunched up her nose but agreed. "We'd better get there before the lunch crowd," she suggested. "You'll drive?"

"Sure, why not? It'll give me something to do."

Sheryl shot a sympathetic look his way, but he was already rising.

"Let's go, then," he said, walking toward the closet where their raincoats were hung.

A few minutes later they were on their way, Sheryl settled comfortably in the passenger seat of Dave's SUV. *It's a good thing he doesn't have a company car now.*

"I talked to that lawyer, the one Janine recommended," Dave volunteered.

"And?"

"She asked me a lot of questions," he said, running his hand through his hair. He'd been doing that a lot since Friday, she noticed.

"Good questions?" Sheryl asked.

"I guess. She made me feel kind of stupid," Dave complained. "Not that I didn't feel stupid anyway . . . damn it, why does this have to be so complicated?"

Sheryl's heart went out to him. He looked more forlorn than when his favorite cousin had died a few years before. "I'm sorry," she said. "I'm sure the attorney is just doing her job. She needs all the information, even the stuff that's not so flattering."

"I know, but it's all so embarrassing," Dave said, maneuvering into the parking lot of the strip mall.

"What did she say the next steps are?" Sheryl asked.

"She's going to call Elizabeth. I don't know if that's good or bad."

"It's good," Sheryl encouraged him. "Elizabeth needs to know that you are serious about defending yourself. It will give her a strong signal that you believe in your innocence."

Dave pulled into a parking space in front of Verizon Wireless and turned to look at her doubtfully. The heavy rain continued to beat against the outside of the SUV, obscuring their view of the store.

"That's what Janine said," she reminded him. Janine had been a wealth of information. She had a good perspective on what Elizabeth might be looking for and what steps she would recommend taking next. The lawyer Janine had recommended was a relatively young woman, probably around Alisha's age, with a stellar reputation. "According to Janine, she defended someone else at The Diamante who was under investigation, and Janine was very impressed with her competence. In fact, Janine said she'd rather *not* have her as an adversary ever again."

"Did you tell her about Olivia Perkins in California?"

"Yeah, I told her everything we talked about," Dave assured her. "I was honest. I promise."

"I know you were," Sheryl said confidently. She unbuckled her seatbelt and shifted so she could face Dave across from her in the driver's seat. "What else did she say?"

"She said I should do nothing," he said with disgust in his voice. "*Nothing.* Like, what am I supposed to do now? Just sit here and wait?"

Sheryl pulled her hand from the door handle and looked Dave straight in the eye. "Yes. You need to do what she says, Dave," she said firmly. "I know it's hard, but cheer up. You have things on your to-do list at home."

Dave groaned. "Yeah, my honey-do list."

"Yup," she said cheerfully, a smile on her face. "Look at all the extra time you'll have to work on that!"

Dave glared at her as she hopped onto the sidewalk and flipped up the hood of her raincoat. She watched from the curb as he slowly slid out of his seat and locked the car behind him. He trudged up to her.

"Let's get this over with," he said, jerking his head toward the storefront.

She nodded, and they headed into the store. *I just hope this won't take too long.*

A frustrating forty-five minutes later, they were back in the SUV, heading home.

"Hey, all things considered, that didn't take too long," Dave said as Sheryl glanced at her watch again.

Sheryl's reply was interrupted by her phone ringing. It was the office again. She had already taken two calls while they were at the store. This time, she looked at Dave with a question in her eyes.

"Go ahead, get it," he said sardonically, nodding at the phone. "One of us needs to work."

She barely answered the call when she heard her name: "Sheryl." It was Joaquin again.

"Yes, Joaquin?"

"The investigator found something."

"Already?" Sheryl was amazed.

"Apparently it wasn't that hard," Joaquin said, his voice full of irony.

"No? What is it?"

"Keisha was right. Someone has been hiding fields in the database, and it definitely started around the time the Portal Project went into high gear," he answered.

Sheryl felt her jaw drop, and Dave glanced at her, concerned, as they got back on the highway. "Wow. Wow. Wow," she stuttered. "That's incredible! Does he know who did it?"

"Not yet, but he confirmed it wasn't anyone in IT. The changes were all made before anyone on your team had access to the database," Joaquin confirmed. "So, you and your team are off the hook. I thought you'd want to know that."

"I never thought we were *on* the hook," Sheryl retorted.

"Of course you were!" Joaquin laughed. "Everyone is on the hook until they are proven innocent."

"So, what now? What do you need from me?"

"I need you to stay alert. Keisha, too. The investigator thinks that whoever is behind this is likely to throw up a smoke screen. He's seen this before. He suggested that I warn you. And Keisha."

"A smoke screen . . . ? Like what?" Sheryl asked, puzzled, but she couldn't stop a shiver of dread that ran through her body. She felt more questioning looks from her husband as he drove, but she couldn't shift her full concentration from Joaquin's reply.

"He wasn't specific, but he said that people can do strange things when they think they might be exposed."

"Like trying to break into someone else's computer?" Sheryl muttered, only vaguely aware that Dave was now listening intently, too.

"What?" Joaquin returned sharply. "What are you talking about? Who tried to break into whose computer?"

Sheryl sighed. "Jim Leaders," she said reluctantly. "I caught him in my office, fingers on the keyboard at my desk early last week."

"And you didn't tell me?"

Sheryl wrinkled her nose. "Uh, no. I was going to . . . and then other stuff happened. In fact, I remembered right after we talked this morning. I started to call you back, but I got interrupted, and then I got sidetracked. I'm really sorry. I know I should have told you! The good news is he didn't get in, and I think my catching him scared him into not trying again. I've been careful to keep everything locked down since then."

"Sheryl!" Joaquin's voice was exasperated. "You *have* to tell me this stuff."

"I know. I know. I guess this looks bad for Jim."

"Yes, it does. I'll have to let the investigator know what happened. When exactly did you say you found Jim in your office?"

Sheryl quickly gave Joaquin the pertinent details, aware of Dave's shocked expression.

"Okay, got it. I'll fill him in. He may call you if he has other questions," Joaquin said crisply when she finished.

"I'll be available," Sheryl agreed. "Although I don't know what I have to add."

"Well, you've sure added a lot of new information already today," he said wryly.

Sheryl's phone dinged with another incoming call.

"Joaquin, I've got another call from the office. Call you back?"

She heard him say "Okay" as she switched to the other call.

"Sheryl, this is Tim from the data center. Your company identity has been compromised, maybe hacked. We've locked all your accounts and access, including your ID badge. You're going to need to come into the office right away to get this straightened out."

Sheryl looked at her phone in shock. *Wow! I didn't expect this . . . or this quickly. Is the investigator right? Is this the smoke screen? Or something else?*

"Yes, Tim, of course," she said, shaking her head to clear it. "How bad is it? Is any of my data missing? Did they steal the passwords or any sensitive systems? Not that I have that many, but still. Did they copy my emails? Do they have access to listen in on this call?"

"Sheryl, stop!" Tim jumped in when she took a breath. "I don't know. We just got a security alert about an unrecognized IP address, not one on the VPN. It's clear that there's been unauthorized access, but we don't know anything else yet. That's why we need to see your equipment."

"Okay. I'll come in as soon as I can." She glanced at Dave, catching his sidelong look. He nodded and accelerated slightly.

"Did you let Joaquin know?" Sheryl asked Tim.

"No, why? Compliance isn't usually involved with this kind of thing," Tim said, clearly confused.

"You need to call him!" Sheryl urged. "It's important that he knows right away." Sheryl was shaken by how rapidly the situation had escalated from a disturbing investigation to something suddenly complex and maybe downright dangerous.

"Okay, I will," Tim said. "But you're going to come in?"

"Yes, yes," Sheryl assured. "I'll be there within the hour. Just call Joaquin."

"On it. Just have the security guard call me when you get to the office," he said. "You'll have to bring your phone, laptop, tablet, and whatever else you have to the data center as soon as you get here."

"Yup, I will," Sheryl confirmed. "See you soon."

She slid the end button upward and took a deep, deep breath. She glanced at her husband, who looked stricken.

"That sounded really bad," Dave said, his voice deep with concern. "Are you okay?"

Sheryl shook her head. "No, I don't think I am," she said, feeling rattled and disoriented. "I can't believe how fast things have unraveled at work. This investigation . . ."

"The one about the Portal Project?" Dave asked.

"Yeah, that one."

"Sheryl, are you safe?" Dave's voice was thick with emotion.

"I honestly don't know," she said, shrugging her shoulders.

"Damn it. And you're having to deal with this on top of all my crap," he said with a mixture of disgust and regret. "I am *so* sorry, Sheryl."

"Thank you, but I can't even think about that now," Sheryl said absently. Her mind was whirling with all the things she might need to do next. Calling her team was at the top of that list.

"Do you want me to drive you to the office?" Dave asked, but she barely heard him. She was reaching for her phone again.

Joaquin's warning had clearly come a little too late. She had to warn Keisha . . . and Patrick. *And who else might be targeted?* Either this was a weird coincidence, or whoever was behind the database changes had just raised the stakes. A lot sooner than expected.

Chapter 24

"But why can't we figure out who is behind this?" Sheryl cried in frustration. She pushed her laptop roughly away and flopped back in her chair at the end of the small conference table. Three men arrayed around the table eyed her sympathetically, the same frustration written clearly on their faces.

It had been nearly two full days since Tim's shocking phone call to Sheryl. Since then, she had been closeted for long workdays with these three men: Rick Hutton, The Diamante's head of IT security, who was Tim's boss; Hye Park, forensic database expert and investigator; and, of course, Joaquin— trying to figure out exactly what had happened and who had done it. So far, unfortunately, they knew far more about what had happened than who had done it . . . or why. Although one thing had become apparent through Hye's research: the whole scheme had to involve more than a single person, including at least one who was outside of The Diamante.

It was Hye, seated to Sheryl's right, who finally responded. "Look, we had some quick breaks with this investigation, but people who put these schemes together are not stupid. The people involved made some rookie mistakes, which gave us a break, but these things take time." He looked grave, his dark almond-shaped eyes underscored with thick smudges of fatigue.

"Time we don't have, Hye," Joaquin said, looking at him severely from across the table.

Hye shrugged. "It's gonna take whatever time it takes," he said philosophically, clearly familiar with pressure from his clients. "I'm working as fast as I can, as is my team."

Joaquin acknowledged the comment with a curt nod, and he too leaned back in his chair.

Although the hotel conference room was well-lit, it seemed dark and airless to Sheryl. The bright modern artwork on the walls did little to disguise the lack of windows and institutional feel of the tiny room. The atmosphere only exacerbated the sense that they were dealing with something sinister.

The small group had convened in the hotel only this morning, aware that their ongoing huddle at the office had been noticed by other members of the Portal Project team, including members of Sheryl's staff and people from the sales organization. Sheryl had told her team only enough about the security breach to allow them to protect their own devices. Her accounts, newly secured, had been unlocked, but she encouraged everyone to be extra cautious. Needless to say, Sheryl's work with Joaquin and the mysterious investigator only heightened their curiosity, and she had agreed with Hye that it was better to take their work away from prying eyes and probing questions, friendly or otherwise.

Plus, Hye was convinced that whoever was behind this could too easily access information about the investigation if they stayed in the office building. The clandestine activities that had been discovered, along with the recent breach of security in Sheryl's case, had them all on edge.

Joaquin sighed. "Let's just walk through everything again," he said with resignation. "Maybe we'll pick up what we've been missing."

Sheryl eyed Hye appreciatively. He was shorter than Joaquin, thickly built, and to Sheryl, he looked like pure muscle. He had joked about being misnamed by his Korean parents, who had chosen the name Hye for its meaning, "intelligent," but Sheryl could see that they weren't wrong. He and Joaquin looked liked opposites, but both embodied a keen intelligence and eye for detail.

"Sounds like a good idea," Hye concurred, and he began to go over every detail again.

As he spoke, a thought occurred to Sheryl. "Should Blake Jones or Alex Thompson be helping us here?" she interrupted. "I mean, would they be able to see something that we aren't? After all, Blake is an accountant and the CFO. They're both on the board of directors, too. And Alex knows a lot about investments, seeing as he's the Chief Investment Officer."

Joaquin eyed her thoughtfully, considering, but the forensic investigator shook his head. "Not yet. Let's give ourselves a little more time before we bring more people in."

As Hye launched back into his recap, Sheryl listened with half an ear, letting her mind drift to her husband. Dave had been incredibly supportive in the last two days, checking in on her regularly from his new phone, making sure she ate the dinners he prepared, and serving as a sounding board for whatever information she felt free to share with him. It was such a huge departure from his behavior over the last few months that Sheryl found herself doubly grateful. She also felt guilty that she hadn't been able to be as supportive with him because her work had once again taken priority over his needs.

Rick, seemingly bored by the recitation of facts, pulled Sheryl's laptop closer to him and began scrolling through the logs once more, comparing them to information on his laptop beside it. His team, mostly Tim Newsome, had discovered Sheryl's laptop had been hacked by someone installing keystroke-logging software on it. None of them could understand how that had been accomplished, because not only were there safeguards in place to prevent it, but Sheryl couldn't remember a time when anyone would have had access to her laptop long enough to install it. Yes, Jim Leaders had been in her office, but as far as she could tell, it hadn't been for very long and her laptop's screen had still been locked when she reached it.

Even so, Jim was still the most likely candidate. All evidence and theories so far pointed to him. Of course, Rachel remained in question, but other than her threats and defensive behavior, they couldn't find anything specific to tie her to a bigger scheme.

Sheryl sat up abruptly as a thought struck her. "What about looking at their finances?" Sheryl asked, interrupting Hye's recitation.

"Whose finances?" Joaquin asked reflexively, but Hye looked at her with interest.

"Jim's and Rachel's, of course."

"We'd have to get warrants to do that," Hye said dismissively. "Not easy without getting the authorities involved."

"No, I don't think we do," Joaquin said slowly, catching up with Sheryl's thinking. "At least not for some of it."

Hye leaned forward, a glint of excitement in his eyes. "Oh, wait! As the compliance officer, you have access to their investment information, right?"

"Yes, exactly," Sheryl said, who'd already had to provide the compliance office with access to her own investment accounts—and Dave's since he resided in the same household. It was a requirement for employment at The Diamante, even for employees outside of the investment department. Everyone had to provide that information to Compliance as soon as they started.

Joaquin looked unhappy. "Yeah, I do. I could do that," he said reluctantly. "There's nothing to prevent that, except that I usually don't, unless—"

"Unless there's a red flag!" Sheryl interjected triumphantly.

Joaquin chuckled almost involuntarily at her tone. "Yeah, unless there's a red flag."

"Can you do that from here?" Hye asked bluntly, gesturing with his head toward Joaquin's laptop. "Not that I expect you to find anything in what Jim and Rachel provided the company."

"Yeah, I can do it from here," Joaquin said, opening the computer. "Give me a few minutes."

Rick piped up from the other end of the table, his white-blond hair almost glowing in the fluorescent lighting. "For what it's worth," he muttered, "I still don't think Jim Leaders is smart enough to do this."

Sheryl smiled at his comment. Rick was a valued member of Sheryl's team. He had been with The Diamante for a long time, and it was clear that he knew everyone at the office—even though he rarely left the data center. Sheryl wondered how he did it, but she had noticed previously that he had an opinion about everything and everyone.

"So, who *is* smart enough to do it, Rick?" Sheryl didn't really expect an answer since they had been over this ground before.

"Ha! There are lots of people at The Diamante who are smart enough," he prevaricated, turning back to the logs on her computer. He had already been through them several times. Sheryl had answered exhaustive questions the last two days about her activities, including excruciating detail about when and where she had accessed her laptop. They were focused on that, rather than her other devices, because that's where the keystroke logger had been found.

Sheryl frowned. She picked up her company cell phone and looked at it. *Is there a way?*

"Why are you staring at your phone, Sheryl?" Hye asked. "Expecting it to answer your questions?"

Sheryl tilted her head to the side. "Rick, what about the phone connection?"

Rick looked surprised by the question. "What about it?" he asked. "Your phone isn't tied directly to your laptop . . . or is it? You know we discourage that, Sheryl."

Sheryl flushed. "I know, but, well, it was just so convenient," she said apologetically.

Joaquin looked up from his laptop. "What are you two talking about?"

"Microsoft," Hye answered, humor softening his harsh features. "The ability to have your phone's message and calls pop up on your computer, right?"

Sheryl shifted uncomfortably as she nodded.

Rick frowned at her, disapproval in his ice-blue eyes. "And you're the head of IT, Sheryl. You should know better."

"What *are* you guys talking about?" Joaquin asked again, pushing his laptop aside.

"Well, Sheryl connected her phone to her laptop. So, that's another potential gateway into her system," Rick answered sarcastically. "Geez, Sheryl."

"I know, I know," Sheryl put her palms up. "I'm sorry, but is it something?"

"It could be," Rick agreed, holding out his hand for the phone.

Sheryl handed it over, gave him her passcode, and leaned back again, crossing her arms defensively across her chest. Joaquin studiously turned back to his laptop. Rick tapped furiously on her phone, but Hye watched her with renewed interest.

"Why were you bending the rules, Sheryl?"

Sheryl shrugged one shoulder. "I'm a technologist," she said ruefully. "I like to play with the toys too."

Rick snorted without looking up, but she caught the quick smile that crossed his face. Hye chuckled softly.

Sheryl was about to explain that she had connected her phone to her laptop one weekend about a month ago, when things were blowing up, when it rang in Rick's hands. Seeing the caller was Todd Fisher, Rick handed it back to her.

"Hello, Todd."

"Sheryl, where are you?" he asked without his customary courtesy. "I need to talk to you and Joaquin. The board meeting is this afternoon. I want to know what you two are presenting, and I haven't been able to find either of you. Anthony Russo is already pressuring me for details."

Sheryl flushed, knowing that they had deliberately not told Todd— or almost anyone else—that they were moving off-site at Hye's urging. At the time it seemed like a good idea, because, as Hye had said, no one was exempt from suspicion, but now . . .

"Uh, we're not in the office, Todd," Sheryl informed him, inwardly cringing. She had forgotten all about the board meeting. So had Joaquin, to judge from the look on his face.

"What? Why not? This is not the time for either one of you to be taking time off," Todd said sharply.

"What? Todd, no. We're not taking time off!"

"Well then, where the hell are you? And where's Joaquin?"

"We're together. We're working off-site because we don't want the investigation compromised at the office," Sheryl answered calmly, though her forehead wrinkled in confusion at Todd's apparent attack. Joaquin regarded her with concern.

"Compromised? Meaning what? Don't you need the resources here? Sheryl, this isn't making sense." Todd's voice was tight with anger.

Overhearing Todd's tone, Joaquin held out his hand for the phone, but Sheryl shook her head.

"Todd, what's wrong? We're fine. As a team, we're sorting through everything we've learned so far on the Portal Project and developing new strategies. We can work from here without the risk of being over-heard or walked in on," Sheryl answered in a smooth, measured voice, refusing to rise to Todd's baiting.

"What HAVE you learned so far?" Todd was shouting now. "I don't have a single clue, and yet we have this critical board meeting in just a few hours!"

"Todd, calm down," Sheryl said firmly but kindly. "You don't need to shout at me."

She heard Todd take a sharp breath, but he exhaled more slowly before speaking again.

"Okay, okay, I'm sorry. You're right," Todd said, lowering his volume but still speaking quickly. "When—"

"Todd, listen," Sheryl interrupted, wanting to expedite the call. "How about Joaquin and I meet you for lunch? We can fill you in on what we'll cover with the board in plenty of time for you to be comfortable." Sheryl went on to suggest a quiet restaurant about fifteen minutes away from the office and not far from the hotel.

"Noon?" Todd shot back, clearly annoyed.

Sheryl looked at Joaquin and mouthed the question. It was already close to eleven. He nodded, with a rueful sideways look at Hye.

"Fine. I'll see you there." Todd ended the call as abruptly as he had started it.

Sheryl handed her phone back to Rick.

"Is he always that, um, aggressive?" Hye asked curiously, leaning toward her. He looked slightly apologetic. Sheryl sensed that he felt sorry that she had been attacked because of following his recommendation.

"No, he's almost always more polished than that," Joaquin inter-jected, looking questioningly at Sheryl.

"Yeah, he is," she agreed, flipping her palms upward. "I don't know why he's so wound up today."

"The board meeting might do it," Rick interjected.

"Maybe, but he's had difficult board meetings before," Sheryl responded, thinking back to when *she* had been the direct cause of Todd's difficulties a few weeks ago. She ruefully watched Rick going through her phone, hoping she wasn't going to be the cause of more problems for Todd.

Joaquin nodded in agreement. "He does seem more agitated than usual. He's always so smooth, so, hmm, suave." His tone was almost admiring.

"Interesting," Hye observed. "You might want to probe *that* a bit at your lunch."

Sheryl grimaced, not liking the thought of interrogating the company president.

"You were pretty bold with Todd," Hye continued, still focused on the exchange. "Isn't he your boss?"

"Yes, he is." Sheryl was puzzled by the question.

"Well, people don't usually tell their bosses not to shout at them, especially . . ." His voice trailed off.

"Especially women, Hye? Is that what you were about to say?" Sheryl challenged him playfully.

Hye's sharp eyes dropped a little in embarrassment, but he directed them back at Sheryl when answering. "Yes, Sheryl, that's what I was about to say," he said dutifully. "Especially women."

Sheryl grinned. "I'm giving you a hard time. But seriously, being yelled at is one of my boundaries. I've had people do it in the past, and frankly I don't like it. So, I've learned to tell people to stop, calmly and respectfully, but, yeah, I stand up for myself. I wish more women would."

"More *people* would," Joaquin interjected strongly. "I know enough men who should do that, too, instead of either shouting back or passively putting up with it. Shouting is a power play."

"It is," Sheryl agreed thoughtfully, although she was taken aback by Joaquin's vehemence. "And one that Todd doesn't usually use."

"Really?" Hye asked, obviously intrigued. "That's very curious. Let's see what you find out at lunch or at the board meeting."

Sheryl and Joaquin both nodded. Sheryl remembered that she had seen the normally unflappable Todd let his agitation show twice now during this situation. It was odd—although it was a serious situation, and he could also be worried about Jim. After all, he had been the one to bring Jim into the company . . . *which would make Todd look bad if Jim happens to be at fault.* She shifted in her seat. *Todd must be worried about that,* Sheryl decided. *He's worried that Jim's behavior is going to reflect badly on him.*

Rick interrupted her thoughts. "Sheryl, who has had access to your phone?"

"I have no idea, Rick. Do you think that's the way my account got hacked?"

"I don't know," he admitted. "But I think it's important that we know who might have been able to get into your phone."

Frowning, Sheryl murmured, "Hmm, let me think about it."

A taut silence stretched across the room. Sheryl closed her eyes, thinking frantically. *Who?* She could hear Rick's fingers tapping on his keyboard. She could feel Hye's quiet observation. From several feet away, she sensed Joaquin's determined focus on his own research as he tried to ignore the elephant that just filled the room.

Sheryl deliberately took a slow, deep breath. Then another. Something tickled in her memory.

My phone. When have I been away from my phone?

She allowed awareness of her physical body to expand, focusing on the sensations moving through her rather than on her whirling thoughts. She visualized herself, and the three other occupants of the room, surrounded by light, and gave her mind the freedom to roam her memories.

No one spoke for a full minute.

"Rachel!" Joaquin and Sheryl broke the silence simultaneously.

"What about Rachel?" Hye asked, looking between them.

"Rachel had access to my phone, when we were at lunch, and—"

"—Rachel's financial records seem very incomplete," Joaquin finished.

They all looked at each other, wide-eyed. Sheryl struggled to wrap her mind around what she and Joaquin just revealed. Yes, Rachel had been aggressive with Keisha, but Sheryl never really thought . . .

"Could *Rachel* be the one behind all of this? Or is she covering for Jim? Or might she be *involved* with Jim?" Joaquin was the one who incredulously voiced the questions on everyone's mind.

No one answered, because Sheryl's phone rang again. She answered automatically, without identifying the caller.

"Sheryl." Dave's panicked voice jolted her out of her shock. "Sheryl, thank God. You gotta come home. Elizabeth just told my lawyer that someone else corroborated Alisha's story. I'm totally screwed now."

Chapter 25

Sheryl groaned audibly. *When is this going to stop?* Rick, Hye, and Joaquin all looked up from their work with concern written upon their faces.

"Dave, hang on a minute," she said quickly into the phone. Rising, she looked at the three men. "Sorry, you'll have to excuse me," she said hurriedly. "And no, the call is not related to the investigation."

She turned and rushed out of the room before they could respond, but she felt their curious eyes on her as she closed the conference room door behind her. Walking a few paces down the empty corridor, she spoke to Dave in a hushed voice, pushing her bangs back from her forehead. "What? How is that possible?" Sheryl said with more than a little anger in her voice. "I thought you said—"

"—I have no idea how it's possible," Dave cut in sharply. "I *did* say that none of it was true, if that's what you were going to say."

Sheryl paced to the end of the corridor, keeping a watchful eye for anyone entering the hallway. She took a deep breath and exhaled audibly, feeling some of her tension ease as she did. "Okay, I'm sorry," she said, her tone much more measured. "Tell me exactly what your lawyer said."

"Michelle said that Elizabeth told her that someone corroborated Alisha's story about us leaving the office together on Thursday night," Dave replied, his voice still tight and higher than usual. "And it seems that the same person saw us at TGI Fridays."

Sheryl turned back toward the conference room. Her pace slowed slightly, and she deliberately eased her tight grip on the phone. "But that's nothing new, is it?" she asked, starting to be puzzled by Dave's reaction. She heard him huff in exasperation.

"No, but what's new is that the person told Elizabeth that I was walking very close to Alisha and looking around as if I didn't want to be seen. He or she also told Elizabeth that we seemed very chummy at the restaurant, up until Alisha stormed out. Whoever it was assumed that Alisha was running away from *my* advances!"

"But, Dave, none of that is different than what you've already told her. It's just a different perspective with circumstantial information." *And boy, there's a lot of that going around, too,* she thought.

"But now Elizabeth thinks that I *was* the aggressor. That's what Michelle said," Dave insisted.

Michelle Ito was Dave's lawyer. Neither of them had met her in person, but Sheryl had been impressed with her astuteness on the call they had had with her on Monday evening.

"How does Michelle *know* that Elizabeth thinks that? Or was she just telling you what Elizabeth relayed to her?" Sheryl asked thoughtfully. "I mean, Elizabeth could be just giving Michelle the facts."

"Damn it, I don't know."

"Oh Dave, I'm sorry. I'm sorry Michelle upset you. I know this is really hard on you, especially when you have nothing to do but dwell on it," Sheryl commiserated.

"I just want to DO something!" he all but shouted.

"I know. I know how hard that is, not to be able to take action," Sheryl empathized as calmly as she could. She had felt the same way when all the layoffs had happened at The Diamante: helpless and unable to do anything useful.

"Damn it, Sheryl! Why—?"

"—How is Michelle doing with contacting Olivia or other people in the California office?" Sheryl broke into Dave's rant, trying to get him on a more positive track.

"She has made calls to people, but no responses yet," Dave said dejectedly. "Elizabeth told her that she would encourage Olivia to talk to Michelle—after she talks to her herself, of course."

"Dave, you have to let Elizabeth and Michelle do their jobs," Sheryl urged. "I know it's hard, but it's all you can do. Unless you can come up with some other witness or fact for Elizabeth to look at."

She paused and, turning, noticed that Joaquin had stepped out of the conference room and was gesturing her back with a great deal of urgency.

"Uh, Dave, I wish I had more time to talk, but I need to get back. Joaquin looks like he needs me—like right now."

"I know you're busy. I'm sorry. Thank you for listening," Dave said with grudging appreciation. "I'll let you go."

"I'll call you when I can," Sheryl promised. "Love you."

"Love you, too."

Sliding the call to an end, Sheryl halted in front of her agitated-looking colleague, tilting her head to look up at him. "What's up? Has something happened?"

Joaquin straightened. Even in a polo shirt and khakis, he could summon a commanding presence. "The lunch with Todd is off," he replied, his voice rough with urgency. "The SEC just showed up at the office. Todd is *livid*. We need to get back there ASAP."

"What?" she said, alarm bells ringing in her body. "I thought you had until Friday to get back to them."

"I think they found what we found about Rachel," he replied, grimacing. "I can't believe they found it so quickly."

"You mean the fact that her records are incomplete?" Sheryl asked, recalling what Joaquin had said just before Dave called.

"Yeah, except that after I did some more digging, it's not that they're incomplete," he responded, his voice rising in intensity. "It looks like she's taken a *lot* of assets out of The Diamante's funds over the past year. She took a bigger chunk than usual out just yesterday."

"Yesterday? Like, sold them?" Sheryl gasped, struggling to keep up with Joaquin's rapid-fire information.

They both started at the sound of a door opening at the far end of the corridor.

Joaquin gestured to the conference room. "We shouldn't be talking out here," he said as he opened the door and waved her inside. "Besides, we need to get going."

Sheryl preceded him into the room, still trying to piece together what he was saying. "But how would the SEC *know*?" she asked over her shoulder.

"I don't know," he said from behind her. "They must have started their own investigation . . . without telling us. Probably looking at all the senior people at The Diamante, especially those in Sales." Joaquin sounded quite chagrined.

Inside, Sheryl saw that Rick and Hye were already prepared to leave, and she hurried to gather her things. She started sliding her phone in her purse, then hesitated.

"Do you need my phone anymore?" she asked, looking at Rick.

He shook his head as he slung his backpack over his shoulder. "Not right now. From what I was able to research quickly, I'm pretty sure the hack couldn't have come through your phone." He looked at her point-edly but with a twinkle in his eye. "But you do know we have IT policies for a reason, right, Ms. CIO?"

She flushed and shrugged apologetically. "So, we still don't know where the hack came from?"

Rick shook his head. "We're trying to trace the IP—"

"The IP address," interrupted Hye. "My team is on it, too. We've fol-lowed it as far as the Bahamas, but we lost the trail there."

"Bahamas? But why—"

"Let's go," Joaquin snapped impatiently. "Todd and the SEC are wait-ing. We can talk about all that later."

"I'm outta here," quipped Rick, heading toward the door. Hye was close on his heels.

Sheryl rapidly shoved the rest of her things in her bag and grabbed her coat. "Coming now," she said, following Joaquin out into the corridor.

Shrugging into her winter coat as she walked, Sheryl glanced down at her attire, grateful that she had dressed formally despite the fact that they had planned to be out of the office all day. If she thought the board of directors was intimidating at times, she'd need every ounce of confidence and gravitas she could muster to face the SEC.

A blast of cold air hit her lean frame as she pushed through the lobby doors of the hotel, but it was the ominous sky that sent a real chill through her. All her senses were alert. Rachel's portfolio was one thing, but Sheryl had a sense of foreboding that went far beyond that. *What's really going on?* A twinge of unease trickled through her. *I trusted*

Rachel—at least before all this started. She held her belongings close against the cold air. *I can't believe it's her, but who else . . . ?* Sheryl reached her car and climbed in quickly, starting the engine to get the warmth flowing as soon as possible.

Pulling on her gloves before touching the cold steering wheel, she connected her phone and dialed Dave on the hands-free system before she was even out of the parking lot.

"That was fast," he answered.

"Yeah, big problem," she said shortly. "Folks from the SEC showed up at the office. We're heading back there now."

"Wow. That *is* big. This just keeps unraveling, doesn't it? What did they find?" Dave sounded concerned.

"Don't know yet," Sheryl replied. "But it's definitely not good. Joaquin was shaken, and he said Todd was livid."

"I'll bet he is," Dave answered, although Sheryl was unsure to which "he" Dave referred.

"So, are you okay?" Sheryl asked, picking up on their aborted conversation.

"Yeah, thanks for helping me put it in perspective," he said ruefully. "I'm just so on edge about all of this. Everything sounds like a disaster."

She murmured her agreement.

"But what you're dealing with is very serious too," Dave went on. "I'm sorry that I'm such a drag on you. You have enough on your plate."

"Dave," Sheryl chided. "You're never a drag. I wish I had more bandwidth to support you." She guided the car onto the off-ramp, noticing Joaquin just ahead of her.

"Hey, me too," Dave was saying.

"I'm about at the office," Sheryl told him. "I'm going to hang up. I'll call you as soon as I can, but I have no idea when that will be."

"Don't worry about me," Dave assured her. "I'll be fine. I'm going back to work on cleaning out the basement so I can expand our workout area."

Sheryl laughed. "Good! You've been wanting to do that for a while."

"Okay, my love. Good luck this afternoon," Dave said encouragingly.

"Thanks," Sheryl said softly as she hit the end button on the steering wheel. She sighed as she pulled into the parking lot. *What new drama is the afternoon going to bring?*

Her administrative assistant, Tina, was standing there to greet her after she had climbed the stairs to her third-floor office. "Todd said to go directly to his office," she said, holding out her hands for Sheryl's coat and belongings.

Sheryl gave her a wry smile and handed everything to her. "Yeah, I kind of figured that," she said, shrugging out of her coat and adding it to the pile. "Sorry about this."

Tina smiled. "No problem."

Shaking her head, Sheryl grabbed a notebook and pen and headed toward the elevator. Todd's office was only a floor above hers, but she didn't want to be the least bit out of breath when she arrived.

There was a knot of people gathered near Todd's conference table when Sheryl walked in shortly behind Joaquin. He looked calm and confident, but Sheryl sensed a deep unease beneath his bravado as they all shook hands and introduced names. It looked like Todd was at his suave and charming best, although Sheryl noticed him tugging at the knot of his tie.

She turned her attention to the SEC representatives: two men and one woman. Sheryl tried to get a sense of the energy emanating from them. She'd been getting more adept at reading people's energy. She'd had to. The woman had her lips pressed into a thin line and what seemed to be disdain in her eyes. Sheryl sensed some underlying sympathy from the younger of the two men, who had given her a slight smile, but the other man was enigmatic. She observed that Hye was the only one that looked at ease.

Todd nodded toward the conference table. "Let's all have a seat," he said.

Taking his position at the head of the table while the others arranged themselves around him, Todd looked at the SEC reps. "Okay, now that we're all present, would you like to explain *now* why you are here?"

The woman SEC agent, who had identified herself as Indira Shah, cleared her throat. "Thank you, Mr. Fisher," she started, stopping to look specifically at each person at the table. "We came here today because we made a disturbing discovery about the financial activities of a senior member of the sales team."

Sheryl watched Joaquin shift uncomfortably in his chair.

"Who?" Todd asked cautiously, raising an open palm as an invitation.

Indira's eyes narrowed, but she continued. "Jim Leaders. He has purchased a new home, and he liquidated assets to do so. Given the circumstances, we wanted to raise our concern."

Todd blanched. "Uh, he bought a vacation home," he said hesitantly. "In the Bahamas. Surely there's nothing unusual with that."

Sheryl, Hye, and Joaquin exchanged uneasy glances, but they all remained silent. *Oh boy, is that why the IP trail ended there?* Sheryl thought, certain that the others were thinking the same. *But it could just be a coincidence. No reason to bring it up to the SEC now.*

"No, sir, but it did seem odd given the circumstances. His asset sales were above the norm."

Todd subsided. A silence hung in the room.

"I didn't think his sale of assets was that much beyond the norm," Joaquin bravely interjected.

He must have decided that the IP thing is a coincidence, too, guessed Sheryl.

"And you would know this how?" Indira asked coldly.

"I've been reviewing the assets of people in question as part of our internal investigation," Joaquin said evenly.

Indira gave him a hard stare. "Have you found anything suspicious?"

At her question, Todd noticeably relaxed. Sheryl realized that the SEC people were on more of a fishing expedition than anything else, and apparently so did Todd. Even Joaquin's face appeared more confident as he spoke up.

"I'm still looking into it. It's too early to say," he prevaricated. "We've been reviewing things from a variety angles."

"And just who is doing this reviewing?" Indira asked pointedly.

Joaquin nodded toward Sheryl and Hye. Sheryl resisted the urge to shrink back in her chair under the woman's cold and penetrating gaze.

"But none of you was in the building when we arrived. You had to be summoned, I believe?" Indira shot back, her voice and demeanor quite haughty.

Hye spoke up, calmly and confidently. "We were at an off-site meeting I convened."

"And you are?"

"The investigator that The Diamante, specifically Mr. Gonzales, hired," Hye returned.

"Have we worked with you before?" The question came from the older man from the SEC, who had introduced himself as Joe Campbell. "You look familiar."

"Yes, sir," Hye said respectfully. "In fact, you and I worked on a project about two years ago."

"Ah yes," Joe conceded, his eyes sparking. "I remember now. The Jennison investigation. You were quite exceptional."

Hye smiled.

Indira looked at him with new respect. "Joe doesn't say that lightly. Tell me more about The Diamante investigation."

Giving her a long look, Hye recapped the steps they had taken with the investigation, omitting any specific references to Rachel's finances. "I've been impressed with the diligence and integrity of Mr. Gonzales and Ms. Simmons," he concluded.

Indira turned her gaze back on Sheryl. "Ms. Simmons?" she queried. "You are the one who initiated this investigation, yes?"

Sheryl gulped. "Yes, I was," she confirmed.

"Sheryl has always been proactive about making sure that we are aware of any inconsistencies," Todd interjected.

"Indeed?" Indira's look was disdainful again.

A flicker of anger whipped through Sheryl's body.

"So, Ms. Simmons, what prompted your concerns?"

Sheryl paused, now giving Indira a long look. "I would think you would know that, Ms. Shah," she countered. "I reported, through Mr. Gonzales, that one of my team members found some inconsistencies in the CRM database."

Eyes narrowed, Indira stared at Sheryl. "Of course," she finally acknowledged. "I do know."

Silence descended on the room. Sheryl kept her gaze even as she met Indira's stare. She made a silent plea to her higher self for balance and perspective.

Joe finally broke the long, tense silence. "So, what now? I understand there's a board meeting this afternoon."

Todd jerked in surprise. "Yes, yes, there is. In a matter of minutes, to be precise."

"Are any of the other directors involved? Besides Mr. Leaders, of course," Indira jumped back in.

"No, not that we know of," Hye answered quickly. Sheryl was grateful for his quick response so that this situation didn't get any further out of control.

"Hmmm, then what *do* you know?" Indira asked accusingly.

Hye gave her a deprecating smile. "Very little, as of now. But we have some theories and are actively pursuing them."

"Theories? I'd like to hear them. Now."

Hye raised his thick, dark eyebrows. "They're not worthy to share at the moment, Ms. Shah."

"Really? That's not what I asked!" Indira said indignantly, her eyes flashing.

Todd cleared his throat. "Ms. Shah, I appreciate that you want answers," he said firmly, although Sheryl detected a slight quaver in his voice. "So do we, but we also don't want to jump to any false conclusions. And we do have that meeting in a few minutes. Is there something we need to share with them about the SEC involvement?"

Joe answered, his tone light and even jovial as he ignored his colleague. "No, not at all. We needed to check out the information we had, but we are still content to leave the investigation with you . . . for now. Right, Indira?"

Indira shot him a dark look but nodded. "Of course. We don't have any other reason to intervene—yet," she added ominously.

"Great, great," Todd said, standing up. "Then we'll let you get on your way so we can get back to it."

Sheryl, Joaquin, Hye, Joe, and the younger SEC man stood up with alacrity. Indira followed more slowly.

"We'll leave you to your board meeting, then," she conceded, her eyes not leaving Todd's.

"Thank you," Todd said, back to his customary gracious ways. "Joaquin will keep you apprised of any developments in a timely manner."

Joaquin dipped his head in acquiescence.

Indira narrowed her eyes again but made no rebuttal. She turned and swept out of the room, her male colleagues in tow.

When they were gone, Todd closed the door and rounded on the rest of them.

"What the hell are you guys doing?" he demanded, his voice low and seething. "You'd better fill me in right now, because I'm going to have all of your heads—and your firm, Mr. Park—if I don't get answers right this minute."

Joaquin recoiled, his handsome face reflecting total confusion.

Sheryl looked at Todd in shock.

Only Hye remained unemotional, returning Todd's glare with a steady look.

"Perhaps you should tell us why you are so upset," he said to Todd. "You're the one who appears to be overreacting."

Todd slammed his palms onto the conference table as he leaned forward. "Who the hell do you think you are, Mr. Park?"

Sheryl watched, mesmerized, as Hye stood his ground. Joaquin's eyes widened.

"I'm the forensic investigator your team hired to get you out of this mess, Mr. Fisher," he said coolly. "Why does that bother you?"

Todd straightened, drawing himself up to his full height, which was shorter than Joaquin and taller than Hye and Sheryl. "I'm the president and CEO of this firm, Mr. Park, and I can fire you at any time."

"Go ahead," Hye challenged him evenly, looking him straight in the eye. Sheryl admired his calm confidence. "But I think you'll have an awkward time explaining that to the SEC."

Todd met his gaze with a hard stare, but his eyes dropped first.

"Mr. Fisher," Hye continued after a full minute of silence. "What are *you* hiding?"

Todd's whole body stiffened. He glared at Hye and opened his mouth to protest.

Hye raised a single thick eyebrow.

Sheryl was astonished to watch Todd's whole demeanor collapse.

"I'm not hiding anything," Todd said weakly. "But . . ." Todd's chin rested on his chest. He drew in a deep breath, then another.

"You're not?" Hye asked, but it was not much of a question. "I beg to differ," he continued firmly. "I think you had better tell us what's really going on, Todd. It's your only hope."

Todd raised his head, a helpless look in his eyes. "You all," he said, nodding toward Sheryl and Joaquin, "had better sit down."

Chapter 26

Sheryl strode out to her car as if it was any other day, holding her head high and her shoulders back. While she didn't exactly smile, she made sure she had a pleasant look to her features—pleasant enough to hide the level of strain she was feeling.

Confidence. It was important that she continue to exude confidence to her team and to everyone at the Diamante. So many people were relying on her, as she had been made aware by the numerous pairs of eyes that watched her every move the past few days—at least the sparse times she'd been in the office and not out handling the investigation and one crisis after another.

She had to be an example. With so many young people on her team, Sheryl knew the importance of strong leadership. She finally took in a deep breath as she buckled her seat belt and reached for her phone to connect it to . . . *nothing.* She muffled a curse as she gripped the steering wheel. *That phone is at the hotel. How could I have forgotten it?* she chastised herself. *I* never *leave my phones behind, either of them.*

A wave of exhaustion broke over her. Her shoulders sagged, and her head dropped onto the top of the steering wheel. Tears threatened, but only briefly. *I can't cry. I'm in The Diamante's parking lot, for goodness' sake!*

She started the car and carefully backed out of the parking spot, maintaining that caution as she drove through the spottily lit row. Unshed tears blurred her vision to the point she was afraid she might hit someone.

Making a right turn at the end of the driveway, she guided her car onto the road, which was dark except for the dim light of the quarter moon that hung low in the December sky. Her gloved fingers tightened again on the wheel. She felt uncertain, uncomfortable even.

Even since she was ten years old, Sheryl had been conscious, probably overly so, about not losing control. Far more than her friends, she had been careful not to drink too much, drive too fast, or allow herself the kinds of emotional outbursts that she witnessed regularly in her college dorm. This emotion now, when there was so much at stake, rattled her.

About a mile down the road, a park 'n ride lot appeared to her right. Thirty or so cars still lined the narrow lane, waiting for their owners to claim them and take them home. Impulsively, she pulled in and parked far at the back, away from any prying eyes, although she left the car running for warmth.

She sat for a long moment, struggling with what to do next, her breaths coming in shallow, uneven gasps.

"Help me, please!" she whispered into the quiet. "I'm not sure I can hang on any longer. And now this phone thing . . ." Tears filled her eyes. She blinked them back. "If I can't even remember my phone, how will I ever help solve this problem at work? And save my falsely-accused husband? I can't keep being strong for everyone . . . Dave, Keisha, Joaquin . . ."

Sheryl jumped as her work cell phone rang loudly through the car's sound system.

Glancing at the dashboard display, she gave a cry of disbelief as she realized it was her friend Cindy—one of the few people outside of work who had this number. Sheryl realized with a jolt that she hadn't talked to her best friend at all in nearly a month. *Why haven't I called her? And why is she calling now, on this phone?*

If it had been any other person on the planet, she wouldn't have picked up, but this was Cindy. Sheryl pressed the button to answer. "Cindy?"

"What's wrong?" her former college roommate asked without preamble, her voice full of worry. "I just got a sense that something is horribly wrong."

Cindy's concern washed over Sheryl, breaking the fragile hold that she had on her emotions. The torrent of tears she had been holding in check, for what suddenly seemed like weeks, released in a flood of salty water streaming down her face. The sound of her sobs filled the car.

"Sheryl. My God, Sheryl, what's going on? Do I need to call 911?" Cindy asked sharply.

"No," Sheryl gasped. "No 911." She gulped for air, her whole body shuddering with the effort. Why was it suddenly so hard to function now that the dam had finally cracked?

"Honey, what is it?" Cindy's voice had softened. "Tell me."

"It's everything," Sheryl blubbered. "Everything is falling apart."

"Your job? Dave?"

"Yes . . . yes . . . to both." Sheryl struggled to get her tears under control.

"Shh. It's okay. It'll be okay," Cindy soothed. "Breathe, all you need to do is breathe."

"Try . . . ing."

Cindy chuckled softly. There was a long pause with only the sound of Sheryl's soft cries echoing in the car. Suddenly, Cindy broke in more sharply again. "You're not driving, are you?"

"No," Sheryl affirmed. "Not . . . driving. Sitting . . . in the car." Another gasping breath. "At park 'n ride."

"Are you *safe* there?"

Cindy's alarm touched Sheryl deeply. *Finally, someone's worried about me.* The thought floated unbidden across her mind. She couldn't remember the last time someone had asked her about her.

"Safe enough," she managed to say. The sobs continued to wrack her body. "I can't do this. I'm so . . . ."

"Breathe, honey," Cindy cajoled her. "Just breathe. Whatever it is, it will be okay."

After another minute, maybe two, Sheryl felt the warmth of Cindy's love and reassurance begin to permeate her distress. Her tears began to subside. She dug in the glove compartment for a napkin and blew her nose. Leaning back against the plush leather seat, she sighed deeply.

"Better now?" Cindy asked.

"Yeah, better. Sorry about that," Sheryl replied, wiping her face with yet another napkin. "I guess everything is just catching up on me. I feel so . . . helpless? Overwhelmed? Hopeless?"

"All of the above?" Cindy teased gently. "I hadn't heard from you in a while. I suddenly felt the distinct impulse to call you."

"Thank God you did. You always know when I need a call."

"Like you do with me," Cindy agreed. "So, what's going on? Why is everything wrong?"

Sheryl sighed deeply again, pushing her bangs back. "I don't have time to go into all the details," she said. "But the short answer is work is a nightmare—*and* it's confidential, so I really can't talk about it as much as I want to—and Dave, well, Dave's been accused of sexual harassment."

She felt the hot flush of embarrassment spread across her cheeks. There. She'd finally said it out loud.

"What? Dave? No way," Cindy interjected indignantly. Sheryl felt a slight smile cross her lips. This was the same Cindy who had been ready to throw Dave to the wolves that last time they had talked. Had that really only been two weeks ago?

"Yeah way," Sheryl said wearily. "Alisha . . . something-or-other. She's the one that . . . that . . ."

"That Dave has been fooling around with?" Cindy finished the sentence pointedly. Sheryl wasn't surprised at her judgment. After all, Cindy had been the one who had planted that idea in Sheryl's head when Dave started staying away on weekends earlier that fall.

"He says no." Sheryl heard the tentativeness in her own voice. There was a pause.

"Do you believe him?"

"Yeah, mostly. He clearly crossed a line with her, but not physically. I think he was mostly trying to help her, but . . ." Sheryl stifled another sob. "But he did enough that she thought he was interested. She was . . . she was moving out here to be with him."

The enormity of what she was saying hit Sheryl hard. *Dave had done enough that Alisha thought he was truly interested.* A spurt of anger danced through her limbs, followed quickly by her honest dismay.

"Are you kidding me?" Cindy cried.

The tears started again, a trickle this time instead of a torrent. "No," Sheryl whispered. "No, I'm not."

"Did you kick his sorry ass to the curb?"

A small laugh broke through the tears. "No, no, I didn't."

"Why not?" Cindy demanded. "*I'm* going to kill him."

Cindy's husband had cheated on her, leaving her without warning about five years ago. That's why she was in Denver, not New Jersey. Of course she had no tolerance for anything resembling cheating.

"Hey, down, Fang," Sheryl said, a thread of warning creeping into her voice.

"Okay, okay, but seriously, girlfriend, why not?"

Sheryl thought back to her conversations with Dave. Yes, she had forgiven him, truly she had, but the fact that things had gone so far with Alisha still hurt. That pain was taking longer to heal. *And the stress now? With the accusations?* It was obviously taking a much bigger toll on her than she realized.

"Because he didn't really do anything wrong, except talk too much. He was frustrated and angry with me—"

"For no reason!"

Sheryl huffed, tucking her thumbs inside her fists. "Cindy, he did have some reasons. I'm not blameless in all of this," she admitted.

"Yeah, I know, but still, that has to hurt," Cindy conceded, her voice softening.

"Yeah, it hurt. I'm trying to be upbeat and supportive for Dave, because he really is devastated, but the timing couldn't be worse."

"The work thing that you can't talk about?"

"Yeah, let's just say it's *another* investigation. Cindy . . ." The breath went out of Sheryl in a long whoosh. "I'm so damn tired and wrung out."

"Have you been doing your spiritual practices? Journaling?"

"I have, and I'm doing a good job of keeping centered, but I feel like I've reached a breaking point. I was pretty much falling apart when you called. All of this sucks," Sheryl said, her voice tightening with frustration. She took a ragged breath as the tears started to flow again. She leaned her head against the steering wheel.

"That's it, let it out," Cindy encouraged her, letting her cry for a few moments. "It *sounds* like it sucks. But you know it doesn't help to judge it. It is what it is. Not good or bad. It just is."

"Ugh," Sheryl rolled her eyes, knowing Cindy was right. "I know. I know. Stop judging; it just is." She let out a long sigh, flopping back against the seat. "You know, that's so much easier said than done right now!"

"I know. I'm so sorry, Sheryl. I wish I was there to give you a hug."

"Me too, my friend, me too."

"So, what happened tonight? Why were you crying when I called?" Cindy asked.

Sheryl gave a self-deprecating laugh. "I left my personal cell phone at the hotel today," she said. "That's actually what set this whole meltdown off."

"You can only cover things up for so long, but you know everything will be okay, right? That this is all—"

"A gift and an opportunity," Sheryl dutifully finished the sentence. She and Cindy had had many conversations like this when the shoe was on Cindy's foot. "It sounds so freaking trite, but I *do* know that. And I know it's true. I guess I've lost sight of that because I can't really see the light at the end of the tunnel yet. It feels really—really dark."

A silence pervaded the car as Cindy took in Sheryl's feelings. "Yeah," she said kindly, "it sounds like it seems pretty dark right now." She paused. "How about we bring some light to the situation?"

Sheryl smiled, this time more genuinely, and nodded, forgetting for a moment that Cindy couldn't see her. "Ha! I knew you were going to say that! Yes, let's do that. And, just for the record, I can already see how the situation with Alisha has brought Dave and I closer together, a lot closer. It's been kind of nice."

"That's good," Cindy responded cautiously. "I know you guys have been struggling. Is he listening more?"

"Yeah, he is. Not only is he listening more, but he's also taking much more accountability for his actions . . . especially around younger women," Sheryl said thoughtfully. "And so am I, to be fair. I just need to have faith, right?" She sat up a little straighter as her path forward became clearer. "That's the bottom line. I got so wrapped up in every-thing that I lost sight of my faith tonight."

"It happens to the best of us," her friend assured her, her voice sincere and comforting. "So, about that light?"

242

Sheryl could see Cindy in her mind's eyes, leaning forward, her rounded chin on her hands, her big brown eyes filled with compassion. The image comforted her.

"Yeah, let's bring in the light," she responded, shifting in the seat to get into a more comfortable position. She closed her eyes.

"Okay then," came Cindy's voice over the sound system. "Take three deep breaths . . . inhale . . . and let it go . . . ."

Sheryl felt herself relax as Cindy talked her through the breathing exercise. Before Cindy even prompted her, she started visualizing a pure and brilliant white light above her head, connecting to her, surrounding her, pouring into her. Her breathing deepened.

"Now, let the light expand," Cindy was saying, and Sheryl felt the chamber of the car fill with light and warmth.

"It's warm tonight," she whispered to Cindy and heard her friend laugh softly. Sheryl felt her tension start to ease as she released her worries and feelings of inadequacy into the night.

"Yeah, for me too," Cindy agreed.

They sat in silence, letting the white light bathe them together, even though they were separated by thousands of miles. Sheryl felt the tension unwind, being replaced by calm and courage. She inhaled deeply, filling her lungs and her body with the peaceful essence that now filled the car.

Trust.

She heard the word from deep inside herself. *Trust.*

"Trust," Cindy breathed, echoing her thought, and it sent a chill of connection down Sheryl's spine.

Feeling her breath fall into rhythm with her friend's, Sheryl's felt the word reverberating between them. *Trust.*

Finally, after a long minute of silence, Sheryl slowly brought herself back to her surroundings.

"I'm back," she said softly, letting her friend know that their meditation was complete. It had only lasted a few minutes, but it felt as refreshing, maybe even restorative, as if it had been hours. "Thank you," she said, her voice growing stronger. "I needed that, needed to reconnect with my faith, to *believe* it."

"Exactly."

Sheryl exhaled, feeling somehow cleansed and refreshed and more focused than she had in days.

"Better now?" Cindy finally asked.

"Yeah. And thanks so, so much for the call. I'm so sorry I haven't been in touch. Everything crashed all at once, and I've been trying just to keep up."

"Hey, I get it. Don't worry about me. But you'd better call me and let me know what happens. You know I'm going to be dying of curiosity."

Sheryl laughed out loud. "Yes, I know you will."

"I'll also be holding space for you and sending you lots of love and light," Cindy promised.

"I know, and that means a lot. Thank you," Sheryl said, "but I've got to get going. Dave will be wondering where I am, and I still have to get my phone."

"Okay then, I'll let you go—for now," Cindy said, her tone implying worlds of support. "Sheryl, keep the faith. And *call* me, or I'll track you down again!"

"I will. Promise," Sheryl agreed.

"Love you, my friend."

"Love you too, Cindy."

Sheryl pressed the button on the steering wheel to disconnect the call. The peace she was feeling inside now was permeated with gratitude, as always, for Cindy's friendship.

She gently wiped her eyes, then pulled down the sun visor to peer into the vanity mirror. Miraculously, her eyes, while red and puffy, were not smeared with makeup. She patted her cheeks dry and applied fresh lipstick. *That's the best I can do for now.*

Starting the car, she selected a soothing spa-style playlist on Spotify and drove carefully through the deepening night to the hotel.

But as she drove, her earlier sense of unease gradually returned. *What is it about this hotel that's still bothering me? Or am I just imagining things?* Her lips quirked. Feeling more herself now and more deeply connected, she was prepared to deal with whatever came next, because there was no doubt that more drama was in store. *It's just a matter of when.*

Chapter 27

Alisha sat alone at the bar, nursing her second Cosmopolitan. It wasn't even six o'clock, and the evening crowd was just starting to build. Glancing over her shoulder, she saw about twenty people or so scattered across the lounge. She could hear the soft murmur of conversation around her, making her feel even more isolated.

She had left work early. She'd had to get away from the accusatory stares and cold shoulders she had been getting since Monday when the news had leaked about her sexual harassment claim against Dave. *Leaked? It had spread like wildfire through the company grapevine.* Other than Barbara, only two other women had cheered her actions. Everyone else . . .

Alisha hadn't realized how popular and well-liked Dave was. Of course, her experiences with him in the home office had been mostly one-on-one or with Robert. She hadn't seen him surrounded by the people who worked with him regularly. She had only seen the kind, supportive man that had come to her rescue. She had thought it was only her. Judging by the reactions in the office, she had been very wrong about that.

Realizing her drink was empty, Alisha signaled the bartender for another. The tall blonde, whose tattoo of a large snake slithering down her arm was visible in even the dim light, approached Alisha cautiously.

"You driving tonight?" the woman asked casually, although Alisha could tell the question was anything but casual.

Alisha defiantly pushed the glass toward her. "No, I'm staying here," she confirmed roughly.

The bartender's posture eased, but she slid a menu across the sleek aluminum bar. "You might want to get something to eat, though, or you'll regret it in the morning."

Alisha gave her a mirthless smile. *Why does everyone think they have to tell me what to do?* "Thanks," she said through gritted teeth. "I'll take a look."

The woman picked up the martini glass and turned away. Alisha hoped she would hurry. Her first drinks had eased her tension . . . but not enough. She desperately felt like she needed another one. She could take a hint, however, and she idly picked up the menu.

Her thoughts went back to Dave and her predicament. *This is all his wife's fault. Somehow, that woman has gotten her claws back into Dave and pulled him into her orbit—away from me!*

Alisha noticed a well-dressed older woman walking across the hotel lobby. *Probably another solo traveler,* she thought idly, admiring the woman's camel-hair coat and her confident gait. She looked back down the bar and then froze as another image crossed her mind. Her head swung back. *Wow! She looks a lot like the picture on Dave's phone.* She squinted as she tried to bring the woman's face into focus. *Oh my God, could that be* her? *Sheryl? What in the world is she doing here? What am I going to do?*

Body tensing, Alisha stared as the mirror image of Sheryl strode assuredly up to the bar. *Damned if she isn't just like I thought Sheryl would be, the skinny bitch. All prim and proper and professional,* Alisha thought with disgust as the woman leaned against the bar only a few feet away.

"Excuse me," the woman said, raising a slim hand to get the bartender's attention, and, of course, she did. The tall blonde promptly put down Alisha's drink and walked quickly toward the dark-haired woman, her tattoo seeming to stare menacingly at Alisha.

"I'm Sheryl Simmons," she overheard the woman say. "I'm here to pick up my cell phone. They told me that you would have it?"

Goddamn it! It IS her! Waves of shock and then anger crashed over Alisha, sending a shot of adrenaline to every muscle and nerve in her body. Dropping the menu, she catapulted off the barstool before she even had time to think.

"This is all your fault!" she hissed at Sheryl, her voice coming out much louder than she intended. The hum of conversation in the bar ceased, and some part of Alisha registered that all eyes were on her. But the momentum of her alcohol-fueled rage propelled her forward. She reached Sheryl in two strides.

"What have you done to him?" Alisha cried harshly, her face red and contorted. "You took him away from me! If it wasn't for you, none of this would be happening." She watched Sheryl recoil from her in horror and fear, and she leaned in closer to Sheryl's face. *Ha! Now I have my chance to tell her exactly what I think of her.* "Well, what do you have to say, *Mrs.* Simmons? You know your husband prefers me to you. He needs a *real* woman in his life, not some stuck-up, stick-in-the-mud CIO who cares more about her work than him!"

Alisha felt someone grab her arm and pull her back. Before they did, Alisha was pleased to see Sheryl's face flushed, her hands balled into tight fists.

"That's enough," the bartender said roughly, yanking Alisha's arm. "Time for you to go to your room. NOW."

She started to pull Alisha away from the bar, away from Sheryl.

"No, don't," came a firm voice. "I want to speak with her."

The bartender looked at Sheryl incredulously. "Ma'am, I don't think she's in any condition to speak rationally."

"I know," Sheryl said decisively. "But we need to speak regardless."

The moment Alisha felt the bartender's grip ease, she snatched her arm away. "Yes, we need to speak," she sneered, with an exaggerated echo of Sheryl's cultured tones.

"Perhaps you could get us some water . . . or coffee—maybe both," Sheryl said, casting a look at Alisha she couldn't discern.

"You're sure?" the bartender confirmed, looking between the two of them.

"Yeah, she's sure," Alisha said, impatiently. "Just go do your job and let me be." She found herself standing still, shaking with rage as the bartender slipped back behind the bar at Sheryl's nod. *Of course the bartender listens to her.* But in some tiny, partly rational part of her brain, Alisha had to admit that she admired Sheryl's commanding presence. It was clear that the older woman was used to being in charge.

The murmur of conversation picked up again, swirling around them, although Alisha barely noticed.

"You're Alisha, I presume," Sheryl stated, slipping her coat off. Alisha noticed Sheryl looking her over from head to toe. "I wish I could say it's nice to meet you, but . . ."

"Yeah, I guess it's not very nice to meet me . . ." Alisha broke in bitterly ". . . the woman who has upset your precious little life and threatened to take your husband away. I don't know what you've done to him, but he's *mine*. And I want him back."

Her barb was met with silence. Sheryl just looked at Alisha with a hard, perceptive stare. Somehow, the woman's gaze made Alisha feel lower than dirt.

"Don't look at me like that," she said defensively, crossing her arms across her chest. The pleasant buzz of the alcohol was dissipating quickly in the rush of her anger. The younger woman's senses sharpened as the reality of the situation began to sink in. *I am here. Talking to Dave's wife. What the hell?*

"Sorry," said Sheryl, glancing away, although Alicia noticed she didn't sound sorry.

The bartender returned with a glass of water and a cup of coffee, which she pushed toward them. "Everything okay?" she asked.

Alisha was dumbfounded when Sheryl responded with a tight nod, then proceeded to slide gracefully onto a barstool, draping her coat on the adjacent one. She gestured for Alisha to take a seat. *Wow! This woman has some nerve, acting like she's the hostess here or something. And what's she doing here anyway? She left her phone? Maybe she's stalking me.* Alisha slid onto the stool anyway.

A long moment of silence ensued. Alisha, watching Sheryl closely, saw her close her eyes and take several long, deep breaths before opening them again. *Guess she's not quite as calm, cool, and collected as she appears.*

"So, Alisha . . . may I call you that?" Sheryl asked gently.

Alisha just looked at her, then nodded grudgingly, completely off balance.

"I, um, I'm not quite sure what to say here. I'm sure my husband's lawyer would be appalled that I am even speaking to you, but since we're here . . ." Sheryl shrugged. "I guess we should take advantage of the opportunity."

"You mean *you* should take advantage of the opportunity," Alisha spat out. "I'm not taking advantage of anyone."

Sheryl remained calm, but she cocked her head to one side, her expression quizzical. Alisha suddenly felt like a bug under a microscope. She didn't like it.

"Hmm, that might have been a poor choice of words," Sheryl replied with a tinge of genuine regret in her voice. "I meant that perhaps we have the opportunity to get some things straightened out, between us."

"So, you're fighting Dave's battles for him now?" Alisha jeered quickly. "The wife riding to the rescue of the fallen hero?" She grinned when she saw Sheryl flush again. *Ha!*

"I wouldn't put it that way," Sheryl said mildly, although Alisha noticed her jaw tighten. "Dave is certainly capable of dealing with, um, *you* on his own. It seems logical for me to talk to you since I've suddenly been given this chance. After all, what are the odds that we would run into one another? Maybe it's meant to be."

"Hmph."

"You said that Dave is yours," Sheryl went on. "Would you please tell me why you think that since he is married to me?"

Alisha snorted. "Yeah? Well, you have a funny way of showing that, lady. He's been crying the blues on *my* shoulder for months about how you don't care about him. How you only care about your precious job."

Sheryl's head dipped, and Alisha watched her chest expand as she took a deep breath. She could help but compare Sheryl's slender form to her own more voluptuous one with a spark of triumph. She almost missed it when Sheryl spoke again.

"I know I have let my work interfere with our relationship recently," Sheryl acknowledged.

Alisha's eyes rounded as wide as humanly possible. *Wait a minute . . . what kind of game is this?*

Sheryl took a sip from her water glass. Alisha noticed with continuing satisfaction that her hand trembled slightly.

"But that's a lapse that can easily be corrected, and has been," Sheryl assured her. "I know you've needed Dave's help, and I'm proud of him for providing you with guidance and assistance. However, I'm afraid you've misinterpreted his intent."

"Yes. You should be afraid," Alisha shot back. "And not about my misinterpretation, because I didn't get it all wrong. He's attracted to me. I know that. *You* know that." Then she picked up her coffee and leaned back smugly. As she took a long sip, she peered past the rim of the cup and watched Sheryl's throat working. Suddenly she put the cup down with a clatter. "And, I can give him the children he wants," Alisha continued, crowing. "You're too old and shriveled up for that."

Sheryl stiffened and sat up so straight that Alisha thought she would topple off the barstool.

"That's a private matter between *my husband* and me," Sheryl said coldly. "He has no intention of having children with you . . . or anyone else."

Alisha smirked. Then Sheryl closed her eyes again, this time tipping her head back, her face tilted toward the ceiling. Alisha watched, curious. *Is she praying?*

At least a minute passed, maybe more. Finally, Sheryl opened her eyes, and Alisha saw that they were filled with . . . unmistakable compassion. She drew back in alarm, completely confused by Sheryl's behavior.

"Look, Alisha," Sheryl started, her voice now kind and gentle. "I know you've got yourself, well, all of us, in a bind. I know you're hurting, and I'm sorry for that. Truly I am. You've been through a difficult time with Liam, and now Dave has disappointed you by not meeting your expectations—"

"Liam," Alisha interrupted harshly, stunned that Sheryl had brought his name up—that she even knew his name. "What do you know about Liam?" she asked sharply.

"Only what Dave has told me," Sheryl responded softly. "Dave was quite upset by how Liam has been treating you. It sounds like he wasn't very nice to you."

Alisha gave a short laugh. "Yeah, you could say that. And you're right. Dave *was* upset about that because he *cares* for me."

Sheryl nodded, her eyes sympathetic. "Yes, Dave does care about you. He's concerned about any woman who is . . . abused, and he's said very complimentary things about your sales abilities."

"Abused?" Alisha snapped, trying to hold on to her anger. "Dave is the one that abused me!" Sheryl raised her eyebrows, silent. Alisha shifted uncomfortably as the pause stretched out until she thought she couldn't stand it any longer. *Wow! This woman is clearly a master at using silence.*

"Okay, Dave didn't abuse me," Alisha whispered, looking away as she folded under Sheryl's direct stare. "He just . . . he just . . ."

"He just disappointed you?" Sheryl suggested.

"Yeah, that too, but he hurt me," Alisha replied with some heat returning to her voice. "He led me on, and then he dropped me like a hot potato."

"I'm sure it felt like that," Sheryl agreed, as she reached out to touch Alisha's hand softly. Alisha jerked it back. "And he feels bad that you were hurt. He never intended that."

"How do you know that?" Alisha demanded, her face hot.

"Because he told me, Alisha. Dave has shared everything that happened with me."

"I don't think he would have told you everything . . ."

There was a pause, and then Sheryl's gray eyes held her gaze once more. "Yes, Alisha. Everything."

"Oh," Alisha replied with dismay, her face crumpling along with her resolve. "I didn't think he'd do that."

What am I doing? I wanted to get back at her, to make her feel bad. She's turning the tables without me even realizing it. Alisha sighed. She realized that she had been wrong about so much more than she thought. She shook her head. *Ugh.*

"Of course he did," Sheryl said, leaning toward her and catching her attention again. "Our marriage is not nearly as bad as you thought it was. Yes, we've been going through a rough patch, but that happens in all marriages, in all relationships. I'm just sorry that you've become a victim of our rough patch. Dave truly didn't mean for you to be hurt."

"Then what *did* he mean?" Alisha asked, becoming more and more bewildered by Sheryl's kindness and sympathy. "He was the one who wanted me to move here—to be with him!"

"Hm," responded Sheryl. "Is that what he said?" Sheryl's question was delivered mildly, but Alisha sensed a note of warning.

"Uh, well . . . not exactly," Alisha admitted, lowering her gaze to the floor.

"What exactly did he say, Alisha?"

"He, uh, he suggested that I should consider transferring here to get away from Liam," Alisha confessed, tugging on her ponytail. "Still, it seemed like an invitation."

Sheryl shifted back on the stool. "He suggested leaving because of Liam's behavior?"

Alisha nodded softly, still not looking up.

"Well, I'm a little curious, honestly. Why didn't you report Liam to Human Resources?"

Alisha was starting to feel like she was being interrogated. She looked up, a blaze of resentment in her eyes. "Why do you care?"

"Because, frankly, you reported my husband but not the man who really hurt you," Sheryl said sharply. "And I want to know why."

Alisha noticed that Sheryl's fists were clenched again. "Because *your husband* did harass me," Alisha said defiantly, sitting up straighter. "He basically attacked me at TGIF because I decided I didn't want to sleep with him after all."

Sheryl's face tightened, and she half-rose from the stool before looking around the bar. Alisha smirked in triumph before Sheryl shook her head and sat back down. She took a long drink from her water glass before turning to face Alisha again.

"That's a lie, Alisha," Sheryl said firmly but mildly, looking right into Alisha's eyes. "And you know it."

Alisha held her gaze for a minute before dropping her eyes.

"Alisha?"

Her eyes still on the floor, Alisha felt Sheryl's hand clasp her own.

"It's okay. It's going to be okay. If you tell the truth, I *will* help you. *Dave* will help you. We'll both be on your side. Both of us."

Feeling the urgency and commitment in the older woman's voice, Alisha looked up. She could see actual tears in Sheryl's eyes.

"Why?" she asked, bemused. "Why would you be on my side?"

"Because my husband *does* care about you. Dave thinks you're someone who's worthy of respect and support, and I trust his judgment. I support his friends, just like he supports mine."

"I don't understand you," Alisha said, pulling her hand away and giving Sheryl a dark look. "What's the catch? You just want me to confess to get Dave out of trouble, but then I'll be the one that's in trouble. I'll be the one who gets punished again, just like I always do."

Sheryl tilted her head to the side. "Who punishes you?"

"Oh, stop being so nice," Alisha snapped, pushing her coffee away. "You're trying to trick me. It's not normal to be this nice. Not normal. What's wrong with you, anyway?"

Sheryl shocked Alisha by laughing softly. "Oh, Alisha," she said compassionately. Her eyes, incredibly, seemed to be full of . . . love? "You haven't had much kindness in your life, have you?" Sheryl continued.

Something inside Alisha shattered. All the fear, hurt, guilt, anger let loose and spun through her body like a tornado. To her dismay, she burst into tears. She felt Sheryl's arms go around her, and she instinctively held onto the woman's shoulders. The tears flowed with great, gulping sobs. Sheryl just held her, murmuring soft words in her ear and rocking her gently.

When Alisha finally pulled back, she found a pile of napkins that the bartender had stacked by her hand. Grabbing a few, she blew her nose and wiped at the mascara she was sure was running down her cheeks. She noticed Sheryl wiping a few tears from her own face.

Alisha flushed with embarrassment. "I'm so sorry about that."

"No, don't be. Crying is good sometimes," Sheryl consoled her.

Alisha sat there. She had no idea what to do next. Here she'd been sobbing in her room the last few days until she was spent, not sharing her tears with anyone. Now she had just been crying in this woman's arms, for God's sake. *Sheryl. Dave's wife.* It was incomprehensible.

"So . . . what now? I mean, I don't even know what to do next," Alisha finally asked quietly, still sniffling. "I guess you caught me out, but . . ."

"It's really up to you, Alisha," Sheryl said frankly. "I can share our conversation, but without your cooperation it won't mean anything."

"I guess I can talk to . . . but Barbara is going to be so upset!"

"Barbara?"

The bartender approached, handing a cell phone to Sheryl. "This thing has been ringing off the hook," she said. "I thought you might want to get it."

Alisha was surprised when Sheryl gave her a questioning look. "It's probably Dave," she said. "Do you mind?"

"No, get it," Alisha agreed, waving her hand at the phone.

She listened as Sheryl explained to Dave that she had been held up at the hotel but would be leaving shortly—a fact she confirmed with Alisha using only her eyes. Alisha found herself nodding. *Who is this woman? Has she put some kind of spell on me?*

"Okay, I'll text you when I leave," she heard Sheryl say as she clicked off.

"Sorry, he was worried when I didn't get home on time," Sheryl explained.

Pain shot through her. Dave did care about his wife. The thought was sobering. "So, you're going to report all this to Dave's lawyer? I didn't even know he had hired a lawyer."

"He had to," Sheryl said simply. "His job and his reputation are on the line."

The words hung between them. Alisha's stomach churned with guilt. She dropped her head in her hands. "Oh God, this is such a mess!"

"That it is, Alisha," Sheryl said, but again her voice was calm and matter-of-fact.

Alisha was amazed by her graciousness. "You're kind of incredible, you know," she told Sheryl, looking up at her with grudging admiration on her face.

Sheryl smiled, "Thank you, but I've contributed to this mess too, as you know."

Alisha waited. She had no idea what to say to that.

"How about we all go to speak to Elizabeth Curtis together tomorrow morning? All three of us. No lawyers. No Barbara. Let's see if the four of us can work something out."

"Really? And how's that going to go?" The bitterness crept back into Alisha's voice. "There's no way this is going down without me getting in trouble, maybe losing my job. Besides, everyone knows what I did. They all hate me!"

"Look, I don't have all the answers right now, but you *were* a victim. Of Liam," Sheryl said firmly and confidently. "You deserve to get help because of that. Yes, you made a mistake when you accused Dave, but there are extenuating circumstances. I'm certain we can work something out."

Alisha felt a surge of hope.

"Okay," she whispered. "I'm willing to try. I, uh, I didn't mean to hurt Dave. I love him. I know you don't want to hear that, but I do."

Sheryl smiled again, her eyes glinting with tears. "I know you do. He's pretty lovable, but I don't think you love him the way you thought you did."

Alisha's protest stopped when Sheryl held up a hand.

"No, don't say anything. Just think about that," Sheryl cautioned.

Alisha decided that she had better just stop before she pissed Sheryl off again.

"Okay, I will," she agreed reluctantly. "But what now?"

"May I have your cell number?" Sheryl asked politely. Alisha could hardly believe the woman's courtesy. "I'll talk to Dave and Elizabeth to set up the meeting, then I'll call you and let you know. Is that okay?"

"You, not Dave?" Alisha couldn't help asking.

"I think under the circumstances, it had better be me," Sheryl said, a note of warning in her voice.

Alisha frowned, twisting her ponytail around her finger. "But . . ."

"Look, once this gets cleared up, you can talk to Dave again, if that's what *he* wants. But for now . . ." Sheryl playfully shook a finger at Alisha, but Alisha could tell that she was serious.

"Okay, got it," she said, feeling her stomach rumble as it loosened up for the first time in days.

Suddenly, Alisha realized that she felt hugely relieved. After days of anger and excruciating pain, she knew without a doubt that this was the right thing to do. She gave Sheryl a radiant smile, one that she could feel lighting up her whole face.

Sheryl looked startled but smiled in return. "Okay then, I'll get going. I'll call you later," she said, standing up and putting her coat on.

Alisha watched Sheryl start walking toward the door, then stop abruptly and turn back around. She tensed as Sheryl took a few steps to close the gap between them and then put her hands on Alisha's shoulders. Alisha felt that Sheryl's eyes looked straight into her soul.

"Thank you, Alisha. I promise I'll do everything I can to make things go well for you, and for you to get the help and support you need," Sheryl said.

Incredibly, Alisha believed her.

Chapter 28

Thursday, December 16

Either my wife is crazy, or she's a miracle worker, Dave thought as he drove to the office alone in his SUV. The winter sun was just peeking above the horizon, not yet in his eyes but casting a golden glow on the tops of the bare, frost-tipped trees lining the highway. He was still reeling from Sheryl's story about her conversation with Alisha, and the fact that they were about to walk into LSM's offices together.

Last evening, he had flipped out when Sheryl had been so late coming home. All he could think was that somehow she had left her phone at the same hotel where Alisha was staying. He shuddered as he remembered the panic roiling through him. And then, when she finally did get home . . . she confirmed that's exactly what had happened.

Dave shook his head again, picturing the wide grin on his wife's face when she told him about the meeting she had engineered. He still couldn't decide whether she was completely nuts, but . . . like everything else in this insane circus, the outcome was out of his control—again.

Upon reaching the parking lot, he waited while Sheryl parked her own car next to his. She needed to go straight from here to the office, where the investigative team was waiting, while he did . . . *What?* He wasn't sure. It all depended on the outcome of this meeting that his wife had orchestrated.

He watched Sheryl slide out of her car and walk a few steps across the parking lot toward him. *I don't deserve her,* he thought, admiring her powerful presence. *She has really bloomed in the last few months, and somehow, I've missed it.*

"Ready?" Sheryl asked, sliding her arm through his.

"Yeah, as ready as I'll ever be," he said, putting his free hand on top of hers.

They walked toward the building together. He was conscious of a few of his colleagues eyeing them curiously. With a knot in his stomach, he realized it reminded him of the day he left with Alisha, although there were far fewer people heading in at this hour. He straightened, not wanting to show any sign of weakness, but still found himself hesitating to make eye contact. *Who knows what rumors have been flying around in the last few days?*

Dave opened the building doors for Sheryl and ushered her inside, then guided her down the corridor to the Human Resources department, which was conveniently located on the first floor not far from the lobby. As they turned the corner into the department's tiny reception area, his stomach jolted. He saw Elizabeth standing outside her door, waiting. Barbara was standing by her side, her arms folded rigidly across her chest.

He glanced at Sheryl, noticing her jaw tighten as she observed the second woman, but she smiled warmly and held out her hand to Elizabeth. Dave was impressed that she had immediately determined which one was Elizabeth.

"Elizabeth?" Sheryl said in a friendly tone. "Thank you for meeting us. I'm Sheryl Simmons."

"Yes, of course," Elizabeth replied pleasantly, shaking Sheryl's hand. "You're welcome, although I must say that I was quite surprised that you requested this meeting."

Sheryl's smile turned into a grin. "I'm sure you were," she said cheerfully. "But I'm certain we'll be able to resolve everything this morning."

"Everything?" Barbara snarled. "Hardly."

Elizabeth frowned and shot a warning glance at her colleague. "Sheryl, this is Barbara Montgomery. She'll be sitting in on the meeting too."

Dave wasn't surprised when Sheryl stiffened. He did, too.

"No offense to Barbara, but I don't think that's a good idea," his wife stated. "Plus, I promised Alisha that it would just be the four of us," she went on, her voice pleasant but with an underlying thread of steel.

"That wasn't your promise to make," Elizabeth said coolly, drawing herself to her full height, which was several inches taller than Sheryl.

Uh oh, Dave thought, watching Sheryl straighten as well, and almost imperceptibly square her shoulders. She was going into "executive mode."

"Since I called the meeting," Sheryl said with a raised eyebrow, "I believe it is my call to make. You are going to want to hear what we have to say. You're welcome to invite Barbara in to join us once we've finished our initial discussion."

Dave watched a variety of emotions subtly cross Elizabeth's face as she weighed her options, while Barbara openly seethed beside her. Elizabeth clearly didn't want to concede to Sheryl, but Dave could see that the force of Sheryl's confident presence was impacting her.

Dave heard the tap of heels coming down the hall and turned his head to see Alisha hurry in, dressed in a demure suit. Her face was flushed, and she smiled hesitantly at Elizabeth, Sheryl and him as she was walking in. She came to an abrupt halt when she saw Barbara standing there, and Dave saw her already pale face blanch.

Elizabeth spoke first. "Alisha, thank you for joining us. Since we're all here, let's go into my office." She gave a quick, sharp shake of her head toward Barbara, causing the disgruntled woman's frown to deepen.

Alisha, who had not come any farther, turned stricken eyes toward Sheryl. Dave was reminded of the young woman he had seen facing Liam, unsure of herself and not confident in taking another step. Shocking everyone, including Dave, Sheryl quickly stepped over to Alisha and addressed her softly. "It's okay," she assured the younger woman. He watched his wife usher Alisha kindly toward Elizabeth. For a moment, he couldn't move. That was something he'd never dreamed of seeing. *Not in a million years.*

Dave, watching Barbara scowl angrily at Sheryl, felt his defensive instincts kick in. Before he could do or say anything, Barbara turned on her heel and marched the twenty feet down the corridor to her office, obviously understanding Elizabeth's signal. Dave's shoulders slid into a more relaxed position.

Elizabeth escorted them into her office and gestured for them to sit down. She quickly took the head of the table, as if afraid that

Sheryl would. Dave smiled to himself. *It won't matter where my wife is sitting, Elizabeth. She's the one in charge here . . . and you know it.* He felt a surge of pride.

"So, would you like to tell me what's going on *now?*" Elizabeth asked, facing Sheryl.

"I'm sorry I was so evasive on the phone last night," Sheryl apologized gracefully. "However, I thought we should all be together before we explained what has occurred."

"We?" Elizabeth asked, a skeptical look on her face.

"Alisha and I," Sheryl said calmly. "We had a good conversation last evening, and Alisha realized that she had allowed some misperceptions to, um, take on a life of their own, shall we say."

"Really?" Elizabeth said doubtfully.

Oh boy, Dave thought. Elizabeth was on a razor's edge. If Sheryl wasn't careful, Elizabeth might think she had orchestrated all of this and somehow strong-armed Alisha into meeting. He held his breath while Elizabeth turned to Alisha.

Dave watched in astonishment at what unfolded. Alisha nodded, and Sheryl shot her a look of encouragement. He saw Alisha's throat work as she swallowed hard. Still looking at Sheryl, she tugged on her ponytail and began talking hesitantly.

"Well, you see, um, when I talked to Barbara about moving and all that, I was kind of mad at Dave for not supporting me more. I felt rejected by him, because, um, well, I, uh, thought that . . ." Alisha's voice trailed off, and Dave watched her shift uncomfortably in the leather chair.

Sheryl nodded encouragingly. "You had different expectations of your relationship with Dave than he had," she prompted.

"Yeah, that," Alisha continued, her voice a little stronger, as she recounted her discussion with Barbara, emphasizing that she had thought the conversation was more personal than professional.

Turning his attention to Elizabeth, he noticed a slight tic near her right eye, but she remained otherwise impassive.

"And then, well . . ." Alisha paused, and Dave saw her look to Sheryl for support. *Amazing.*

After a small pause, which had everyone at the table leaning forward, Alisha continued.

"Um, Barbara started asking me questions about Dave and what he had done, and I was mad, so I kind of, uh, exaggerated what had happened, and—."

Exaggerated? Dave thought, stunned by her confession even though he had known it was coming. *I can't believe she's actually saying this. I'm going to be off the hook!* He glanced at his wife. *How did she pull this off?* He wondered, humbled by her graciousness.

"You mean you lied," Elizabeth broke in, her voice matter-of-fact. She looked at Alisha assessingly.

Alisha gulped and lowered her eyes. "Yeah, I guess." She took a deep breath, glancing at Dave, and her cheeks flushed a deep pink. "I guess I did kind of lie."

Dave was surprised to see Alisha square her shoulders and look right at Elizabeth.

"But Barbara encouraged me to make things sound worse than they were," Alisha said in a rush. "She put words in my mouth, and the next thing I knew she was talking about filing a complaint. I never even thought of doing that!"

Elizabeth reeled back in her chair. She looked at Alisha, then gave Sheryl a hard look.

"Barbara is a valued and trusted staff member," Elizabeth responded tightly, trying to maintain her professional demeanor. "Are you certain that's what happened? After all, I don't think you want to be throwing around *more* unfounded accusations."

Dave gave Alisha credit. This time, she held Elizabeth's gaze. He shifted in his chair, hearing the leather squeak as he tried to get more comfortable. *Oh, boy,* he thought, *now Elizabeth is pissed.*

There was a long silence while Elizabeth evaluated Alisha's statements, looking down at the notebook open in front of her but clearly not seeing it.

Finally, Sheryl broke the silence. "May I make a suggestion?" she asked respectfully.

Elizabeth looked up. "Please," she replied, her eyes narrowing.

"No, let me say something here," Dave broke in, feeling compelled to acknowledge his responsibility.

Elizabeth nodded.

"Yes, Alisha told Barbara things about me that weren't true, apparently with some encouragement from Barbara. However, Alisha *had* been misled by some of my behavior because I was trying to help her out. I was worried about her and how Liam was treating her. So, I did encourage her to move to New Jersey. During that time, we became friends, and I confided in her, a little more than I should have. She, understandably, took it the wrong way," Dave said bluntly, his cheeks pink-tinged with embarrassment. He cleared his throat. "I did hurt her, and I'm sorry about that. But I can see why it wasn't too hard for Barbara to glom onto what Alisha said and help her to exaggerate further."

He felt Sheryl gently squeeze his hand. He gave her a rueful look back.

"Is that correct, Alisha?" Elizabeth asked, turning toward the younger women with a softer expression.

"Yes, ma'am, it's true," Alisha said, nodding firmly. "In hindsight, I did read much more into Dave's actions than he meant. I'm really sorry about that." Her eyes dropped for a moment before she looked at Elizabeth again. Dave saw a faint sheen of tears in her eyes. "I really am sorry that I've caused all these problems." Her gaze swept to Dave and Sheryl, including them in the apology. Her cheeks were still pink, but she sat straighter in her chair.

Elizabeth took a sip from her coffee cup, staring into it for a moment. Dave thought that she seemed to be moved by Alisha's emotional apology.

"And this situation with Liam that Dave mentioned. What am I supposed to believe about that?" she asked a little gruffly.

Dave was surprised to see Alisha learn toward Elizabeth, meeting her eyes bravely.

"Liam is a bully and a lecher," she stated baldly.

Elizabeth paled. Alisha darted a quick glance at Sheryl, who nodded.

Then, the whole story about Liam poured out. Dave provided corroborating details, and Elizabeth finally leaned back with a stunned look on her face.

When Alisha finished, Elizabeth looked at Sheryl. "No wonder you didn't want to give me details last night."

Sheryl shrugged one shoulder. "It was her story to tell, not mine."

Elizabeth tapped one long finger on the table. "Okay, one step at a time," she said. "I want to know why neither of you"—she looked pointedly from Alisha to Dave—"or anyone else, for that matter, reported Liam to me."

"Because," Alisha blurted, "I was afraid that Liam would retaliate and make me the bad guy. He threatened to have me fired—or worse—if I reported him."

"What?" Dave exploded, half-rising. "You never told me that!"

Alisha looked chagrined. "I'm sorry," she said to him. "But I did tell you I was afraid to report him." She turned back to Elizabeth. "And I wouldn't let Dave or Robert report him either. I begged them both not to. I really *was* afraid."

Elizabeth leveled a long look at Dave. "You should have anyway," she said. "You've been here long enough. You know better."

Dave ducked his head in sheepish acknowledgement.

"So, I take it that you're officially dropping your charges against Dave?" Elizabeth asked Alisha.

"Yes, I am," Alisha said firmly, "and I'm really, really sorry that things got out of hand. Barbara—"

"We'll get back to Barbara later," Elizabeth interrupted her. "Let's focus on what happens now. Like why I shouldn't fire you for what you did to Dave, who, it appears, was only trying to help you out."

"Please—"

"Is that really necessary under the circumstances?" Sheryl said, talking over Alisha's plea.

"I'd rather you didn't," Dave said, firmly, just as he and Sheryl had discussed. "I think Alisha and I have both learned our lessons here."

Elizabeth looked among the three of them, shaking her head. "In all my years in HR, I've never seen anything like this," she said. "What a mess!"

Dave saw Sheryl reach out and lightly touch Elizabeth's arm. "I know. I've never seen anything like it either," she said. "But here's what I suggest."

Sheryl quickly laid out the plan that she had concocted with Dave's input. Dave and Alisha would both keep their jobs, with Alisha staying in New Jersey, and a clear understanding between the two of them on the boundaries of their relationship. Alisha would file charges against Liam, with Dave and Robert backing her up. And Sheryl promised that Dave would give Elizabeth any information that Michelle had turned up in talking to Olivia or other people in California to assist in the investigation.

"But what about Barbara?" Alisha asked, leaning forward, after Elizabeth had agreed to the plan.

Elizabeth shot her a dark look. "Let's leave Barbara to me," she said.

Chapter 29

Sheryl was pressing the call button on her phone before she even left the LSM building, responding to Joaquin's urgent text.

"Joaquin," she said breathlessly as she pushed open the door. "What do you mean some of the directors are going public with the investigation?"

"Where are you?" Joaquin shot back.

"I'm leaving Dave's office. I'm fifteen minutes away from the office, tops."

"We'll wait for you in my office," he said tersely. "Two of the outside board members have called for an emergency meeting—and Todd's resignation."

Sheryl groaned, as she slid into her car and pressed the ignition button. "Let me guess: Anthony Russo and the new guy, the one that replaced Hank?"

"Got it in one," Joaquin confirmed darkly.

"Why are they doing this? Why now? Do they have the votes? I can't imagine Jim would vote for that . . . nor would Blake."

"I don't know. All I know is that they are putting 'a lot of pressure' on Todd, his words, and threatening to go to the media before 'something leaks.' They claim they want to get ahead of things, and they blame Todd for the mess. He's the president *and* CEO."

Sheryl could hear the frustration in Joaquin's voice, as well as a layer of underlying panic. After all, his job would be on the line, too, if the board ousted Todd.

Hell, all of our jobs will be.

"Where are we with the investigation?" Sheryl asked, guiding her car onto the narrow two-lane road that was the quickest route to the office. Her hands clutched the steering wheel tightly. "Has Hye found anything?"

"Yes and no," Joaquin said. "We might have found something, but we want to go over it with you, too. That's why we need you here."

"Okay, I'm on my way," Sheryl said. "Let me focus on driving. I'll see you in a couple of minutes."

"Fine." Joaquin hung up.

Sheryl sighed and pushed her bangs back from her forehead. *What now? I'm jumping from one fire into the next.* Then she checked herself. *No, Dave is okay. Or I hope so.* She worried about leaving the meeting so abruptly, but she'd had to respond immediately to Joaquin's 9-1-1 text.

Using her car's voice system, she sent a quick text to Dave and told him that she'd call him as soon as she could. She also asked for any updates, but there was no reply. *He must still be in with Elizabeth and Alisha.*

She made it to the office in twelve minutes, driving above the speed limit and rolling through a couple of stop signs. It wasn't how she liked to drive, but at least she was there safely. She grabbed her purse and laptop bag and rushed into The Diamante, heading straight for Joaquin's office.

"What have you found?" she asked as she was opening the door. The air was thick in the room, and Hye was the only one who didn't appear to be wound tight as a spring.

Hye looked at her mildly and smiled. "You might want to sit down and take your coat off first," he said calmly.

Joaquin glared at him. Rick smirked.

"Well, you're awfully calm," Sheryl quipped, sliding her coat off and onto a nearby chair. She pulled her notebook out of her bag. "What have you got?"

Joaquin slid his open laptop across the conference table. He looked terrible. Dark circles underscored his eyes, and the creases around his mouth were noticeably deeper.

"Gracious, have you slept at all, Joaquin?" Sheryl asked, very concerned.

He shook his head. "Not much," he muttered.

Sheryl turned her attention to the laptop. "What am I looking at?"

Hye walked around the table to stand behind her. He leaned over and pointed to a column of numbers on the screen. "See that?" he asked. "That's a bank account—an offshore bank account."

"Wow! That's a lot of zeros. Am I reading this right? Millions! Whose account is it?"

Joaquin and Hye exchanged a look. "Rachel's—well, at least we think so," Joaquin answered.

"You think so? Why wouldn't you know?"

"It's in a corporate name, a shell company," Hye answered.

"Is this the money that Rachel took out of her investment accounts?" Sheryl asked, trying to recall the amounts Joaquin had shown her yesterday.

"Some. That's how we know." Hye pointed to the screen again. "Here, here, and here. Those numbers correspond to what Joaquin found in the compliance records."

"But that's only a small portion of the amount," Sheryl exclaimed. "There's so much more here. Where did it all come from?"

Joaquin looked grim. "We don't know yet. Hye's team is still trying to trace it."

"And you're sure it's Rachel?" Sheryl asked, perplexed. "Something doesn't feel right. That just doesn't seem like her."

"What do you mean by that, Sheryl?" Hye countered. He plopped into the chair next to her so that he could face her.

"I mean, I've always—well in the past, that is—I always thought Rachel was trustworthy," she said. She paused. "Could she be in some kind of trouble?"

Hye shrugged. "I guess it's possible. But right now, Sheryl, everything is pointing clearly to Rachel being behind this."

"What about Jim?"

Joaquin pulled his laptop back. "We've got nothing on him," he said. "Everything seems very transparent—with his finances, at least. We're going to have to go to Todd and report Rachel."

Sheryl took a deep breath, pausing and closing her eyes to let the information sink in. She kept breathing deeply, allowing herself to center.

She didn't know how to explain it, but something was wrong. She had to tap into her higher self. She didn't say anything for a couple of minutes.

"Sheryl?" Joaquin said sharply. "What are you doing?"

"Give me a minute," she murmured without opening her eyes. She felt Hye smile beside her and settle into his own quietness.

Sensing Joaquin's scrutiny and frustration, Sheryl took a few more deep breaths to tune him and his anxious energy out. Her breathing settled into a rhythm. A sense of peace and calm enveloped her. *What are we missing?* she asked silently.

Suddenly, an image of Hank Turner floated across her mind. His round, normally ruddy face turned bright red and angry, as it had been the last time she had seen him. He had been so infuriated that Sheryl impeded his desire to hire Layla Arch, the vicious female executive from one of the Diamante's partner banks. Layla had been considered a shoo-in by the other board members who were looking for a cost-conscious shark, but Sheryl had created a ruckus by disturbing the cultural norms . . . and objecting via her vote for the good of the team, she'd hoped. She just hadn't been prepared for the ensuing drama.

Her eyes shot open. "What about Hank Turner?" she asked.

"Hank? The former board member?" Joaquin looked puzzled. "What would *he* have to do with this?"

"I don't know," Sheryl said honestly. "But there's something there. I'm just realizing that at our last board meeting, which was just a few weeks ago, he was *way* too upset about us hiring Blake instead of Layla." Suddenly she stopped, a dawning energy of curiosity overtaking her. "She works for a bank, one with connections to The Diamante. Could she be involved?"

"Sheryl, you're grasping at straws," Joaquin said, his lips twisting into a condescending smile. "I know you felt some affinity Rachel in the past, but this is far-fetched."

Hye looked thoughtful. "Tell me what happened," he said. He was the only one in the room who looked curious and open-minded.

Sheryl quickly recounted the whole scene at the meeting in November, emphasizing how committed Hank and Anthony had been to Layla Arch rather than Blake Jones.

"I just had to speak up," Sheryl told Hye and Joaquin, who were listening avidly to her story. Rick listened idly at the other end of the table, as he had heard the story before. "I told them that the last thing we needed was a troublemaker like Layla. I had worked with her in my IT role, and so had other members of my team. Everyone hated her. She treated people like, um, nothing, like they were *worth* nothing. Of course, I was outvoted, so Hank thought that hiring Layla was a done deal."

"Then what happened?" Hye asked with rapt attention.

"Well, Jim Leaders and Alex Thompson both went to Todd after the meeting and told him they had second thoughts about hiring Layla and wanted to change their votes."

"Jim Leaders?" Hye broke in. "That's interesting."

"Yeah, I guess it is," Sheryl acknowledged before continuing. "Then Janine, as head of Human Resources, withdrew her support. Even though she doesn't get a vote, her opinion holds a lot of weight with hiring decisions. After that, even Todd rethought *his* position, and he called a special meeting for another vote."

"And Layla was out, and Blake was in." Hye concluded. "And Jim Leaders changed his vote? That's interesting."

"Yeah," Sheryl said. "And Hank lost it. I mean *really* lost it. He was forced to resign from the board because his behavior was so bad."

Joaquin whistled, his deep brown eyes wide. "¡Guau! I had heard there was some kind of altercation, but I had not heard exactly what happened. Good for you."

"I take it Hank's anger was focused on you?" Hye asked, a deep V forming between his dark eyes.

Sheryl nodded. "Yeah, he said some pretty awful things," she conceded, remembering that most awkward and uncomfortable day. "But he did apologize afterward."

Hye picked up his phone and called his team. Sheryl listened as he instructed whoever he was addressing to expand their search to Hank and Layla. Sheryl hoped she had done the right thing, but, well, nothing bad would turn up if she hadn't.

"Let's look into all of this further," Joaquin said, shutting down his laptop. "I'll let Todd know that we have some things to check out before we can meet with him. One o'clock okay?" He glanced at his phone. "That gives us three hours, almost."

Sheryl and Hye nodded. She would certainly feel more comfortable meeting with Todd if they had some hard facts.

Hye stood up. "I thought Todd was the chairman of board as well as the president and CEO," he said casually. "How could someone else call a board meeting?"

Sheryl, bent over her briefcase as she shoved her notebook back inside, looked up. "Technically, they can't, but they can request one. Any director can do that. Todd has to have a good reason not to call one, I'm sure, especially if the request is urgent."

"Should we be investigating Anthony Russo, too?" Rick asked, finally speaking up after observing the other three interact.

Hye gave him a sharp look. "Good point," he said, reaching for his phone. He was barking more orders as they headed out of the room, leaving Joaquin settling at his desk.

Sheryl gave Rick a grateful look. "Good thinking," she said. "See what you can find out on your end."

"You got it," Rick said, slinging the strap of his bag over his shoulder. He looked relieved that he would be heading back to the data center and away from the executive offices.

Walking slowly down the corridor to the elevator, Sheryl checked her phone. There was a thumbs-up text from Dave, which she took as a good sign. Her email inbox was full of new messages, but a quick scan showed nothing was urgent. *I have time to take care of a few things,* she thought. *And touch base with Keisha and the rest of the team. Not that I can tell them anything, but . . . at least I can make sure they're okay.*

At precisely one o'clock, she paused outside Todd's office, waiting for Joaquin to join her. They walked in together, both in somber, dark suits that somehow felt very appropriate today. She noticed that Hye hadn't appeared. *Where had he gone off to?*

Entering the office, she was surprised to see not only Jim Leaders but also Blake Jones and Alex Thompson in the room. They, along with Sheryl and Todd, made up the company's executive management team and were all members of the board. There were equal numbers of inside and outside board members, as required by law. Alex and Blake greeted her warmly, as they always did. Jim approached her more cautiously, holding his hand out to shake hers with a bit of hesitation. Sheryl guessed that he was still embarrassed about being caught in her office, but she smiled sincerely and greeted him amiably.

Todd started speaking, explaining that Anthony Russo and Paul Haven, Hank Turner's replacement and the newest director, had contacted him to formally request another meeting. They had been dissatisfied with what they had learned at the formal board briefing a few days ago, although they hadn't made a peep at the time. Anthony, who indicated that he was speaking on behalf of the investor group he and Paul represented, told Todd they felt that the executive team should go to the media now, so that the company could control the narrative rather than waiting for something to get out inadvertently.

"If they've already spoken to others in their group, *they* may be the cause of a leak," Alex observed.

"I agree," Todd responded, "and I've warned them about that. They swear they haven't told anyone else, but who knows."

"So, what do we do now?" Blake chimed in. "Where are we with the investigation? Do we have anything to hold them off?"

As if his words had conjured up the lead investigator, Hye hurried into the room, his forehead creased in a deeper frown than Sheryl had ever seen on his face.

"I'm not sure you can hold them off," Hye answered Blake's last question. "They are knee-deep in this embezzlement scheme, as is Hank Turner." He turned to Sheryl. "How did you know?"

Sheryl rocked back in her chair, stunned. "I d-d-didn't," she stuttered. "I just saw his face when . . . you know."

Hye gave her a knowing look and turned to Todd, who was looking at him with open-mouthed shock.

"Mr. Fisher—"

"—What do you mean they are knee-deep in this thing?" Todd rasped, his face ashen.

Everyone turned to look at him.

"I mean that Anthony and Hank are involved in the same illegal activity that Ms. Horowitz has been," Hye said.

Jim leapt up. "What? Rachel? It can't be Rachel! What are you talking about?"

Sheryl watched, stomach clenched, as Hye approached Jim.

"It appears that Rachel is involved somehow, Mr. Leaders. Unless you know something that we don't." There was a momentary pause.

"What?" Jim cried. "No. I don't know anything. I just know Rachel, and she wouldn't—"

"—Perhaps we should sit down and hear what Mr. Park has to say," Joaquin said with an authority Sheryl hadn't heard from him before.

"Yeah, sure," Jim said, sinking heavily into his chair. "I just hope he knows what he's talking about."

Sheryl bit her lip and observed Hye looking carefully at each face around the table, including hers, before sitting down next to Todd. No one spoke, but she could feel the tension and unease vibrating in the room.

"Mr. Park," Todd said evenly, having recovered his composure. "Please explain your statements."

"Are you sure you want everyone here?" Hye asked, glancing pointedly towards Jim and Alex. Sheryl felt her stomach tighten with dread. Todd's enormous office suddenly seemed to shrink to the narrow confines of the sleek, black conference table and the people arrayed around it.

"Is there a reason anyone shouldn't be here?" Todd countered, leaning forward on his elbows and steepling his hands in front of him.

Hye shook his head. "Not that I know of," he said. "But we don't have all the details yet."

Todd waited. Sheryl held her breath. *What is Hye up to?*

"Okay then," Hye said, leaning back comfortably in the leather chair. He was the only one that looked at ease. "I'll fill you all in, and then I think we're going to need to call the SEC and have them take over the investigation from here."

Joaquin visibly flinched. He wasn't the only one. Sheryl entwined her hands under the table.

"So, this is what we know," Hye began, grabbing everyone's rapt attention. He traced the investigation back to the fields in the CRM database that Keisha and Sheryl had correctly guessed were references to investment amounts that were not made with The Diamante. It turned out that those investments had been directed to another investment firm, a private one. The two salespeople were almost certainly responsible for introducing the investors to the other firm, and it was just as certain that someone inside The Diamante had created the database fields and facilitated their work. Rachel was the likely suspect in that endeavor, as she had access to the CRM database and prior knowledge of the salespeople from a previous employer, and because she seemed to have been directing some of her own money into the offshore account.

"But that doesn't make sense," Jim interrupted. "Why would she be putting her own money into an offshore company account . . . unless all the money in that account isn't hers? Is it?"

"No, it isn't," Hye agreed gravely. "And that's where this gets muddy. We traced the shell company back through several other shell companies to a company that's headed by none other than *Hank Turner*. Sheryl's guess about his involvement was the key to finding that link."

"How did you know, Sheryl?" Todd asked sharply, his eyes incredulous and his hands now clenched on the table.

Sheryl's eyes widened at his tone, and she shrugged. "I honestly don't know," she replied, putting a hand to her throat. "I just pictured his face at that last meeting in my mind, and something told me that his reaction was too strong for what happened."

"So, you had him investigated?" Todd snapped.

"No. I did," Hye said calmly. "The other two board members that are associated with him, also. Although the investigation is far from complete."

"That's right," Todd said, eyes narrowing menacingly.

Taken aback by her boss' reaction, Sheryl frowned inwardly. *Why is Todd acting so aggressively?*

"And you were going to tell us some tale about that, too, weren't you?" Todd continued.

"I was. I am," Hye replied, looking back at Todd with assessing eyes. "And I'll continue if you're ready."

Todd leaned back and nodded regally, but Blake spoke up first.

"What if Rachel is being forced to contribute to that offshore account? I agree with Jim that it doesn't seem likely that she'd put her own money there," he offered.

Hye nodded. "Could be. We don't know for sure that it is Rachel's money, but—"

He broke off as the office door swung open. Rachel Horowitz pushed her way past Todd's assistant. Sheryl suppressed a gasp.

"It *is* my money in that account, and Blake is correct. I am being forced," she said in a quavering voice. "And I'm not the only one."

A hush fell over the room. The door closed quietly behind her. Sheryl looked around. Everyone, except Hye, was staring at Rachel with shock, and Rachel was staring straight at Todd Fisher.

Chapter 30

"I am not involved!" Todd shouted. "Stop telling lies!"

Rachel, looking pale and frantic, her dark hair loose and disheveled, quivered at his rage. Looking around the room for an ally, her gaze zeroed in on Sheryl.

"I'm not lying. I'm not," she said urgently. "I'm . . ."

Tears started to fall down Rachel's narrow face, creating trails of black mascara. Sheryl cringed inwardly, feeling compassion for Rachel's obvious distress. She resisted the urge to rise and comfort her, though, understanding that Rachel was not innocent in the whole situation.

Rachel stood uncertainly halfway between the door and the table. After a long silent moment, Sheryl, seeing Rachel swaying unsteadily, finally did stand up and start toward her. *No one else is going to.*

"What are you doing?" bellowed Todd at Rachel. "She's the one making crazy accusations."

Sheryl hesitated for a beat before continuing toward Rachel.

"Get away from her, Sheryl. I'm warning you," Todd growled.

Sheryl shot an incredulous look at Todd. "Can't you see that she's about to fall down?" she shot back. "Let her sit down, and then we can sort out what she has to say."

Todd subsided back into his chair, although he continued to glare at Sheryl and Rachel. Sheryl noticed everyone else watching the interaction warily.

Sheryl put her hand on Rachel's arm, leading her toward an empty chair, which Blake, standing, had offered. It happened to be on the opposite end of the table from Todd. Sheryl sank down in her own chair, next to Rachel, keeping a watchful eye on Todd. She was astonished at how bad his behavior became when he was challenged. *Is it just now, in this situation, or is this normal for him?* Either way, he was making her very nervous.

Recovering from his shock, Todd stood up again and leaned toward Sheryl. "Just who the hell do you think you are?" he demanded. "This is my company, my office. You have . . . no . . . right."

Sheryl, along with almost everyone else, flinched at his tone, but she stood her ground.

"I'm just being civil, Todd," she said flatly. "Which is more than you are doing."

"You mean you want to protect her," Todd spat in Rachel's direction.

"Actually, I was thinking more about protecting the company," Sheryl said. "I thought we had decided to keep the investigation in-house and as private as possible."

Todd spluttered.

"She's right," Joaquin interjected, standing up to face Todd. "We need to listen to what Rachel has to say—fairly. Sheryl is protecting you as much as anyone else here."

"Protecting me? Why do I need protecting? She's the one who admitted that she created this mess, that she's behind the embezzling, if that's what you want to call it."

Joaquin gave Todd a level look. "And she's lying about your involvement?"

"Yes, she absolutely is," Todd said firmly.

Sheryl's gaze bounced back and forth between the two men, whose eyes were locked in a silent battle. Joaquin, standing on Todd's left, was a good four or five inches taller than Todd. He had donned a commanding presence that Sheryl hadn't seen in him before. On the other hand, Todd radiated power and passion, despite the height disadvantage. They looked like two angry bulls, squared off and ready to charge.

Hye intervened. "Why doesn't *everyone* sit down?" he asked calmly, but in a tone that brooked no dissent.

Todd glared at him but sat. Joaquin followed suit, directing a measured look at Hye. Sheryl wondered what they were communicating, even as she felt relief slide through her tense frame. She glanced at Rachel. The younger woman was still shaking.

Blake pulled a chair from in front of Todd's desk closer to the table, but Sheryl saw that he was still a short distance away. She also noticed that Alex and Jim were trying to slide back from the table a bit themselves. *They're getting out of the line of fire,* Sheryl thought, feeling like she had made herself a target by sitting right next to Rachel. She had a twinge of regret for her concern for Rachel.

Hye turned to Rachel, his face serious but not unkind.

"Do you want to fill us in on the details, Ms. Solowitz?" he asked gently.

Rachel looked at Sheryl, who couldn't fathom why Rachel was choosing her as an ally. Nevertheless, she nodded encouragingly at Rachel. *I want to hear this story too.*

"What? Why are you listening to her?" Todd exploded from the end of the table.

"She was the one who came to provide information," Sheryl responded, giving Todd a hard stare.

"Lies. She came to tell lies," Todd snapped back.

"Perhaps," Sheryl conceded. "But let's hear what she has to say."

There was a faint rustling as both Blake and Alex shifted uncomfortably in their chairs. Their faces clearly indicated that they'd rather not be there. Sheryl couldn't say that she disagreed, especially since she was not the one that was tackling Todd and his anger.

"It's not embezzling," Rachel began. "At least not from The Diamante."

Hye nodded thoughtfully. "No, you're just diverting funds from The Diamante," he stated.

Rachel dipped her head. "Yes, that's right. But it's not me. I didn't divert funds," she said in a pleading tone.

"Maybe not," Sheryl observed. "But you helped. You laid the groundwork with the database."

Rachel turned to glare at Sheryl. "If that stupid Keisha hadn't stuck her nose where it didn't belong," she all but growled.

Sheryl pulled back, stung by the sudden attack. But she took a calming breath and kept her face neutral.

"Keisha wouldn't have found anything if there hadn't been something to hide," Sheryl responded reasonably.

Rachel answered with a disgruntled look.

Sheryl noticed that Joaquin was taking notes while Todd stared malevolently at Sheryl and Rachel. Blake and Alex watched with silent interest.

"Why did you do it, Rachel?" Joaquin asked, looking up from his notes. The table only sat eight, so there was a level of intimacy with all but one chair filled.

"They made me," Rachel said, a trifle petulantly.

"Who made you, and how? How could they make you do anything?"

Rachel sighed, pushing her hair back from her face with both hands and tipping her head back. Sheryl saw that her hands were trembling.

"Hank and Anthony made me, sort of," she finally said.

"Hank Turner and Anthony Russo?" Hye clarified.

"Yes. I worked with Anthony before," Rachel glanced at Jim. "At Equitone, with Jim too."

Sheryl knew that Equitone was a smaller firm than The Diamante. Jim and Rachel had moved up when they came here.

"Did Todd work at Equitone too?" Hye was asking.

"No." Rachel shook her head. "I didn't know Todd before here. He had worked with Jim, though, at some other company. Neither Jim nor I were at Equitone very long."

"But that's where you met Anthony?" Joaquin asked.

Rachel nodded.

"Hank, too?" Sheryl jumped back into the conversation.

"No, I've never actually met Hank," she said. "I think he just tells Anthony what to do. At least that's what it appears when he's barking orders at me, always telling me how 'Hank is not pleased with this' and 'Hank is furious about that.'"

"So, what happened?" Joaquin blurted, clearly frustrated with the pace of the conversation.

Sheryl waited as impatiently as everyone else while Rachel gave him a long look, as if deciding what she should say. She glanced at Todd, who sat fuming with his arms folded across his chest.

"Well," she started. "Anthony came to me with this scheme . . ."

Once she got rolling, the whole story poured quickly out of Rachel. Anthony was the one who had convinced her to "join" this new investment company that they were just getting off the ground. It was all on the side because they didn't have enough capital to hire people full-time. Rachel had been suspicious but had been intrigued by the idea of being one of the founding members of the firm, getting in on the ground floor with the opportunity to really make it big. Anthony had encouraged her to invest her own money, a little at a time, so that she would have a larger equity stake.

"And you didn't ask to see the SEC filings? Or any paperwork?" Alex broke in.

"I did!" Rachel answered indignantly. "They looked like they were in order, but . . ."

"But they weren't," guessed Joaquin. "And you didn't check."

Rachel shook her head, and pink tinged her flushed cheeks even further. "Not until later. Until . . ."

"Until you were in too deep," Hye finished.

Rachel hung her head. "Yeah," she murmured.

Sheryl winced. *What a mess!*

"How is Todd involved?" Jim Leaders piped up for the first time. His face was flushed under his tan.

Rachel looked at him. "I'm sorry, Jim," she said. "I know you trusted me."

Jim shifted uncomfortably but didn't reply. Sheryl sensed he was deeply embarrassed by Rachel's actions. After all, he had been giving her the benefit of the doubt—far more than she deserved, apparently.

"Todd?" Hye prompted.

Rachel sighed. "Hank and Anthony convinced him to start investing," she said. "I don't think he knew at first, not until after everything blew up with Layla."

"What *happened* with Layla?" Sheryl asked, puzzled by how the situation with Layla fit into the picture.

"She was doing the accounting for the new investment firm," Rachel replied, looking grudgingly at Sheryl. "I'm not sure how she got recruited, but she wanted to be here."

That's for sure, thought Sheryl.

"Bigger role, more money, closer to the action," Rachel continued. "Hank promised her the job, I think."

"Did you know that?" Jim asked Todd sharply.

Todd shook his head. "I did not," he declared emphatically.

Rachel snorted.

Todd stared at her, but she didn't back down.

"He didn't know at first, but he sure knew after Sheryl made her little speech at the board meeting, forcing her off the list for consideration," Rachel said. "Even *I* heard about that."

"How close were you to what was going on?" Hye asked.

"What about Todd?" Jim interrupted. "I want to know what he's done."

"Todd was investing too," Rachel said. "Hank promised to merge the new company and The Diamante, make Todd the president of this huge new firm."

Sheryl gasped as that news sunk in. A deep and uncomfortable silence filled the room. Along with everyone else, Sheryl turned to look at Todd. Shock and dismay were on all their faces. Todd returned the stares defiantly, his eyes hard and stony, arms across his chest, but he said nothing.

"But did he know that it was all a sham?" Joaquin finally asked, directing his attention back to Rachel. "And when did you become aware of that?"

"I didn't know until I got here, and they wanted to create those fields in the database, start to divert money into their fund. They said why waste the money on investment advisors when we could just use The Diamante's? That's when they gave me a story about 'merging' the firms. It seemed reasonable, I guess, so I went along," she said, her cheeks red with embarrassment. She clearly recognized how flimsy that excuse sounded.

Sheryl felt her stomach clench. *Wow. I wonder how much trouble Rachel is in?* As she glanced around the table she thought that nearly everyone looked troubled except Todd, who sat there glaring at Rachel. *She'll surely lose her job, but could she go to jail too?*

At the other end of the table, Todd snorted. "What a fairy tale," he said with disgust.

Sheryl looked at him in amazement. *If what Rachel is saying is true, he could be losing his job, too. Doesn't he get that?*

"When did you figure out they were just stealing all the money?" Joaquin asked. "Even yours?"

"When Sheryl called for this investigation," Rachel answered.

Sheryl felt a shiver go down her spine. *Keisha's instincts were more accurate than we ever imagined.*

"When Anthony found out, he went ballistic," the younger woman continued. "That's when I found out that Hank was involved. They were afraid that everything would blow up before they could cover their tracks—or get out of Dodge."

"They were going to bolt?" Hye questioned her.

Rachel shrugged. "That's all I could guess," she answered. "But I've realized I don't know a whole hell of a lot." Her mouth twisted in a bitter smile. "In the meantime, I've lost all my savings."

"She's lost more than that," Todd muttered bitterly.

"Has she actually done anything illegal?" Jim asked. "I mean, those database fields are unethical, but are they illegal?"

"Good question," Joaquin replied thoughtfully. "That's not up to me to decide."

He nodded at Hye, who shrugged.

"Well, regardless, she's fired," Todd stated, standing up. "I've heard enough. Get her out of here. She's betrayed all of us in her greediness."

Sheryl raised her eyebrows. *Who is the greedy one here? It seems like Todd was just as greedy, if not more so.*

She caught Hye's eye. His lips twisted in a wry smile. *Guess I'm not the only one thinking that.*

Jim Leaders looked sorrowfully at Rachel and nodded. "Yeah, I agree. She can't stay here."

Sheryl watched Rachel's face crumple. Tears filled her eyes, but they didn't spill over. Despite Sheryl's understandable anger and disgust at the younger woman's behavior, she couldn't help but feel some compassion for her too. *Rachel's sure brought a whole heap of trouble on herself. It's a shame, because she's a bright woman who had a lot going for her . . . and now look at her.*

"We need her to stay until we get the SEC and probably the FBI in here," Joaquin countermanded, standing up himself and leveling a hard look at Todd. "And we still need to find out what Todd knew or knows."

"I don't know anything," Todd said again. "I'm as much of a victim as anyone else here. Hank fooled me too. He obviously fooled us all." Todd looked hard at Jim, Alex, and Sheryl, as if including them in the "all."

Joaquin and Hye looked at each other. Sheryl saw Hye shake his head, and Joaquin nodded in response. A tense silence descended on the room. Sheryl twisted her wedding ring on her finger. Jim looked down at his hands, which were clasped in his lap. Alex and Blake exchanged nervous glances.

Sheryl finally straightened in her chair. "So, now what?" she asked, directing the question to Joaquin and Hye.

As if on cue, a firm knock sounded on the door. Before anyone could move, the door was flung open and a trio of men and one woman, all clad in dark blue with the gold letters FBI embossed on their shirts, strode into the room. They fanned out across the room, with one man staying close to the door, as if to prevent an escape.

Even though she had done nothing wrong, Sheryl couldn't help but feel frightened. It was an intimidating display, reminding her uncomfortably of the guards that had fanned out on the day of the layoffs. She unconsciously shrank back into her chair, her gaze focused on the large FBI agent striding toward the table. With only fifteen feet or so to cross, it didn't take long for him to be standing right next to her—and Rachel.

"Mr. Gonzales?" he asked, looking accurately at Joaquin. "Senior Agent Spence."

"Agent Spence." Joaquin walked around the table and held out his hand. The agent shook it briskly.

"We're here for Ms. Solowitz," he said, looking between Rachel and Sheryl with a stern demeanor.

Sheryl cringed, instinctively pulling back further from Rachel's side.

"I'm Rachel Solowitz," the younger woman said, standing bravely.

The agent put his hand on her shoulder. "Sit down," he said. "I'll let you know when to move."

Rachel sat. Quickly.

"Mr. Gonzales, is there anything else you need to report?" Agent Spence asked.

Sheryl's breath caught. *When did Joaquin call them?* She saw Joaquin swallow hard.

"I'm not sure," Joaquin said, for the first time that afternoon appearing nervous.

"Not sure?" Agent Spence asked, his right eyebrow raised.

"Well, Ms. Solo—"

"Don't even think about it," Todd growled. "I swear to God, if you say another word—"

The female agent took a step toward Todd, her hand resting lightly on her gun. She was as tall as Todd, lean, and clearly in good shape. Todd took a step back.

Agent Spence held up a hand. "And you are?"

"Todd Fisher, President and CEO." The answer was crisp and confident, but Sheryl saw a tiny twitch above his left eye.

"I see. And you were threatening Mr. Gonzales about?"

"About repeating misinformation that Ms. Solowitz had given him," Todd said smoothly. Sheryl had to give him credit: he could be quite the chameleon.

"Really? Perhaps that's information we should hear," Agent Spence came back, just as smoothly.

"I'm sure that's not necessary," Todd parried.

"Mr. Gonzales, do you agree?"

Joaquin blanched.

Oh boy, Joaquin's in quite the spot. Still, he has to tell the FBI what Rachel said. He has to, doesn't he? I would, if I were him.

Hye stood up. "Agent Spence, Hye Park. I'm the forensic investigator that The Diamante hired."

Spence gave him an assessing look. "Mr. Park. We'll need all your findings."

Hye nodded. "Of course," he said. "I'll provide them to Mr. Gonzales first, though, as he technically commissioned them."

Spence quirked an eyebrow. Sheryl shivered. She quickly looked at her colleagues. Blake, Alex, and Jim all looked like they were about to jump out of their skins. She knew the feeling. *I'd rather be just about anywhere but here.*

The door burst open again.

"What the hell is going on in here?" Indira Shah, who Sheryl immediately remembered from the meeting with the SEC, said in a hard, cold voice. "This is *my* investigation. *I* decide when the FBI gets involved."

Agent Spence laughed out loud. "Not this time, Special Agent Shah. Mr. Gonzales called us first."

Special Agent Shah turned to glare at Joaquin, who merely shrugged.

"I called you both," he admitted.

The SEC agent turned to Agent Spence. "We'll be working this as a joint case," she demanded more than asked.

He nodded. "Of course," he said pleasantly. "As always."

Agent Shah narrowed her eyes and nodded imperiously.

"Let's go," Agent Spence said to his team. "We'll take Ms. Solowitz *and* Mr. Fisher . . . for now." Then he carefully made eye contact with everyone else, including Hye. "The rest of you had better keep quiet and available until further notice. We're not done with you yet."

Chapter 31

"—Breaking news. Todd Fisher, President and CEO of The Diamante investment firm, has been taken into FBI custody for questioning." Dave's heart seized as he listened to the report with disbelief. "The circumstances of the situation are still unfolding, but an anonymous source informed us that Rachel Solowitz, a client services executive, has also been detained. Early reports indicate that funds from The Diamante have been redirected into an apparent Ponzi scheme . . ."

Gripping the steering wheel tightly, Dave tried to keep his attention on the road as he absorbed the information. His thoughts rushed to his wife. *How is Sheryl doing? Has she been detained too? Oh no! I hope she's okay.*

"Siri, call Sheryl Simmons, work," he all but shouted, his body rigid.

Moments later, he heard his wife's breathless, slightly muffled voice. "Dave, is everything okay?"

"That's what I'm calling to ask you," he responded urgently. "I just heard the news on Bloomberg about Todd. He's been *arrested?*"

"Oh no!" Sheryl gasped. "I didn't realize it had gone public. Hold on."

He heard her murmur something but couldn't hear what she said.

"Sorry, I had to let Blake and Joaquin know," she said as her voice came back clearly. He could hear the extreme stress in her voice. "We were in a meeting, and . . ." He heard excited voices in the background. "Sorry, Alex just came back in with the news."

"What in the world is going on? Are you okay?" he asked, guiding the car into the right lane.

"Yes, I'm okay, but Dave ... things are crazy here. They haven't arrested Todd—yet. They took him in for questioning. We don't know what he's done," Sheryl replied, her words tumbling over one another in a rush. "And Rachel, they've detained Rachel, too. She confessed—"

"Hey, slow down," Dave broke in. "Do you need me to come to your office? What can I do?"

"No, no, don't come here—but thank you. We're still trying to sort things out. I'll call you in a bit. Sorry, honey, but I've got to go."

The call ended. There was a brief silence, then the disembodied voices of the Bloomberg announcers returned. They had moved on to another story in a mere three minutes. *What the hell?*

All Dave's earlier jubilation faded in the face of Sheryl's latest crisis. He had been feeling *so* good. Robert had slapped him heartily on the back when he made his way to the cubicle pod shortly before noon. His employment status had been restored to normal, his laptop and business cell phone returned to him. *Thank God.*

"You're back," Robert had cried, relief clear in his voice. "Man, I thought you were done for! How in the world did you...?"

"Sheryl," Dave had said very quietly, quickly explaining his wife's role in getting Alisha to confess. Truth be told, he was both embarrassed and proud that his wife had "rescued" him, and he knew that Robert deserved the full story.

His friend had been incredulous. "Wow, I would have loved to be a fly on the wall for *that* conversation," he said in an awe-filled voice.

"Yeah, me too," Dave had admitted, feeling guilty that he had put both women through that. He knew now that his actions had been irresponsible at best, and well, he didn't want to think about the worst. All he could do now was be more conscious of what he was saying and to whom.

"I guess Liam's in the line of fire now," Robert had observed correctly. "The grapevine is going crazy again."

"Yeah, and it's about time," Dave had agreed emphatically. "That guy is such a creep."

Robert's eyebrow had quirked. "Yeah, well—pot, meet kettle."

Dave had scowled at him. "Hey, I'm not a creep!" he protested vehemently.

Laughing, Robert had rolled his eyes. "Well, not as much as Liam," he teased, "but I told you that you were headed down a bad road with Alisha."

Biting back a sharp retort, Dave had flushed. "You're such a pain in my ass," he had muttered. "I *knew* you would have to get your 'I told you so' in."

Robert grinned. "Of course," he had said cheerfully.

Shaking his head, Dave had turned to sit down at his desk, meeting Robert's gaze in the process. Sudden gratitude for his friend's loyalty had filled his eyes, and a long look had passed between them. Dave had seen a flash of deep and genuine respect reflecting back in the other man's eyes.

Swallowing back a surge of emotion, Dave had merely nodded and sat down. Robert had done the same, but Dave had been left with a feeling of deep connection that stayed with him all day.

Well, until now, he thought as he paced the kitchen, waiting for his wife to arrive. He wasn't sure what to do to help her, but he was determined to be there for her . . . this time.

It was nearly 7:30 when Sheryl finally walked into the kitchen, her shoulders slumped and her face pale. Dave rushed to take her computer bag and help her with her coat.

"Sit," he ordered gently, pointing at the sofa, his heart in his throat. "I'll get you a glass of wine. I have a cheese plate ready. I wasn't sure . . ."

Sheryl looked at him, her look changing from weary to stricken.

"Oh god, I forgot to call you back. I'm so sorry, Dave. No, at this point, I'm not in any trouble—and don't feel in danger of it except for the fallout at work. This whole thing has been such a mess, and today, more than ever."

He just nodded mutely as Sheryl sank into the sofa, kicking off her shoes and curling her legs beneath her. He noticed that her makeup was smudged under her eyes, something that was becoming a more common occurrence. Striding quickly back into the kitchen, he poured a glass of her favorite Pinot Noir and picked up the platter arrayed with Brie, white cheddar, and some whole-wheat crackers. He'd added some carrot and celery sticks for good measure.

Sheryl reached for the wine glass with a wan smile. "Thanks," she said softly. "I need this tonight."

Picking up his own wine glass, which had been on the coffee table, he sat next to her. "Except for Bloomberg, the other networks are being pretty quiet—for the moment. Tell me what happened."

"It was really unbelievable," she said, her voice husky. "I don't even know where to start."

He listened in astonishment as she filled him in on the afternoon's events.

"And did they actually arrest Todd?" Dave probed as she wound the story down. He'd been feeling anxious since the preliminary news—especially when it hadn't come from Sheryl and he couldn't find much more in the way of details.

"No, no, just took him in for questioning. It's still unclear what his involvement is, if any. He was denying everything, even though Rachel insisted that he knew what was going on."

"Well, what do you feel about it, Sheryl? What is your gut telling you?"

Sheryl blinked. "Did you just ask me what my *gut* said?"

Giving her a sheepish grin, Dave nodded. She smirked in return, then sobered.

"Anyway, Todd was acting strange, no doubt about it, but do I think he was involved? My gut says no, not on any kind of significant level."

"Is what they did illegal? What are the consequences?" Dave had no idea. That part wasn't clear to him.

"According to Hye and Joaquin, what Hank and Anthony were doing is illegal. I'm sure they've been arrested by now," Sheryl answered. "With Rachel, it's less clear. It's certainly unethical, but in a lot of ways it feels to me that she was a victim." She grimaced. "She was greedy, Dave, I will tell you that. She'll lose her job—of course. So will the two financial advisors who were diverting some of the investments to the so-called new company. They all absolutely violated company policy. I'm sure they'll also lose their accreditations. They should! And, I doubt they'll ever be able to get jobs in the industry again."

"Wow." Dave whistled. "And Rachel, she'll lose her savings too? At least what she gave to Hank?"

"I don't know about that," Sheryl said, shaking her head. She took a gulp of wine. Dave noticed that her hand shook slightly as she continued, "It looked like most, if not all, of the money is still in the offshore account. It may be recoverable—for her and the other investors—although she could have fines to pay. We managed to catch them before Hank and Anthony skipped town, since that is what it seems they were planning on doing. Hye found out this morning that Hank had bought a place in Costa Rica! Can you believe it? It's like it's out of a movie—and it's my work. This whole thing has been crazy."

"Really? Why would he do that? Surely this bigwig Hank has enough money without stealing." Dave picked up a cracker and slathered it with the soft Brie. He handed it to Sheryl before preparing one for himself. "I mean, he's been in the news before, so even I've heard just how successful he's been in the investment world."

"That's what's really interesting," Sheryl said. "This afternoon the investigative team and I did a little more digging—not enough to interfere with the agencies, but enough to give us some indication of what's been going on. I told Joaquin and Alex that we have to have a little more information so we have *some* clue how to manage things. In doing so, we discovered Hank isn't nearly as successful as everyone thought. Hye found he's made a series of really bad investments in the last few years, in high-risk tech companies that have gone belly up. We're guessing that he lost almost everything he had. It seems that he was using Rachel to try to recoup his losses so that he could retire comfortably."

"How is Anthony involved?" Dave asked, still puzzled.

"I guess Hank brought him in on the same bad investments, although Hye doesn't think Anthony was quite as broke as Hank. He might have just been greedy, like Rachel. We're still in the process of sorting everything out except where our hands are tied by the SEC and FBI. They're asking for our cooperation but have made it *very clear* that they are in charge of the investigation now."

"What's the impact on The Diamante? Or you?" Dave frowned. "This can't be good for the firm."

Sheryl sighed, taking another sip of wine. "No, I'm sure it won't be," she said. "I really have no idea what's going to happen. But it's not like anyone who's invested with The Diamante will lose money. It's only the ones who invested in the 'fake' investment company."

Dave shook his head. "What a mess," he said. "I sure hope Todd isn't involved. That will make it even worse."

Sheryl nodded her agreement. "Yeah, I hope so too." She paused. "And poor Jim. You know, I didn't think I'd ever use those words together! Yet after talking with him at length this afternoon, it's obvious he's devastated about Rachel. He really trusted her. When we talked, I found out that it was *Rachel* who wanted him to break into my computer. Can you believe it—she told him that Keisha and I were falsifying information that could be used against them both!"

Dave's jaw dropped. "Wow, that's unbelievable." He shifted a little uncomfortably as the memory of his earlier accusations surfaced. *Rachel wasn't the only one blaming Keisha for things that weren't her fault,* he thought with chagrin.

Sheryl paused, and he noticed her rubbing her forehead as if she had a headache. "He apologized profusely," she explained, indignation and compassion warring for precedence in her voice. "I could tell that he was terribly shaken. He had no idea all this was going on." She made a face. "It's sad that he believed Rachel over me—and stupid—but I guess I can understand. I still can't condone his behavior, but . . ."

Dave felt his fists clench, anger at Jim Leaders spilling through him on his wife's behalf. He was about to voice his ire when it hit him that Jim's situation was not all that different from what he had just been facing with Barbara and Alisha. He shook his head. *It's so easy to believe things about others that aren't true, if we're not careful.*

He sighed. "How are you feeling about all this?" Dave asked, changing the subject a little, while reaching out to rub his wife's shoulder gently. She tipped her head into his hand and let him cradle it for a moment.

"I don't know," she said wearily. "But thanks for asking. I guess I'm most concerned about Todd. I'm sure that Hank promised him *something*. He must have known at least a bit about the fake investment company. That seems obvious, but how much he knew about the Ponzi scheme, if that's what it was, I don't know. He could have sincerely thought the company was legit, like Rachel did. That doesn't excuse his claiming complete innocence, however. It still has me flummoxed."

Dave increased the pressure of his hands on her shoulder. She hummed contentment as he hit a tense spot.

"What about the advisors who were talking clients into sending some of their money to this other company?" Dave probed further. "Did he know about them?"

"I don't think so," Sheryl replied. "I've been watching this whole thing carefully. He seemed genuinely shocked when we first brought that up. It's only very recently that he's become so angry and agitated— so different from his generally charming and suave self. Joaquin seems to think that Hank was putting pressure on Todd to stop the investigation after the board meeting. That may have been how he found out what was really going on."

"Either way, his leadership is compromised," Dave observed.

"True," Sheryl agreed reluctantly. "Alex Thompson is the acting head of the firm now, pending the completion of the investigation. He and Joaquin are going to have to sort all this out, along with the rest of the board."

"Which means you. Again," Dave added, reaching for her now empty glass. "More?"

"Yes, please."

He stood up and stepped around the sofa toward the kitchen, taking both their glasses with him. He heard the soft clink of utensils on the plate behind him, and he remembered the healthy meal he had waiting in the oven. He filled both glasses.

"I'll definitely be involved. In the meantime, there will need to be a lot of damage control—for keeping both our investors and our employees."

"Is Alex up to that?"

Sheryl paused, cocking her head as she considered his question. "You know, I think he is. He's a rock-solid guy. I think his presence will be very calming and comforting to people. He doesn't have Todd's flair, but he's got his own brand of quiet magnetism."

"What about Blake?" Dave asked, mentally running through the rest of the management team that Sheryl worked with.

"Thank God we hired Blake instead of Layla!" Sheryl exclaimed suddenly, appalled at the realization she'd just had. "Can you imagine? We'd be in serious trouble if she were on the board instead of Blake—especially since she's involved with Hank and Anthony. But Blake is such a good guy, with such a great reputation. He's going to be a big help."

"Will he stay or bail, though? I mean, he *just* started."

"I'm pretty sure he'll stay. For one thing, it won't ruin his reputation as this all came to light when he's so new—but also, Dave, he's just that kind of guy," Sheryl replied confidently. "And if Blake certifies the books, the investments, that will go a long way to helping our public image. I mean, The Diamante itself really isn't involved. Only Rachel and the two financial advisors—"

"—And Todd," Dave reminded her.

"Yeah, and Todd," Sheryl said sadly. She shook her head. "It's all so sad and disappointing. Alex has his work cut out for him, but I know that Jim, Blake, and I will support him. I'm sure the other board members will too."

They sat quietly on the sofa together for several minutes, each contemplating The Diamante predicament. Dave looked over at his wife. Despite her weariness, she was calm and poised. *She's a real trooper,* he thought. *All my drama . . . and this too. It's amazing that she's not only holding herself up, but she keeps helping everyone out—including me.*

"How are *you* doing?" he asked abruptly. "You're going through so much. What can I do to help you?"

Sheryl looked momentarily taken aback, but his reward was a grateful smile. She reached out and clasped his hand. "Thank you. I can't tell you how much I appreciate that. Just listening tonight is doing wonders—not to mention the wine and food."

He rolled his eyes. "Of course," he said simply. "I have dinner still on 'warm' in the oven—although you've hardly eaten over the last three weeks." Then he felt his face soften at the look in her eyes. "Honestly, it's the least I can do after you rescued me."

"How did that go?" she asked, shifting to face him more squarely. "I'm sorry. I didn't even ask about that since I left you and Alisha at Elizabeth's office this morning."

"It was pretty uneventful after you left," he replied. "Nothing like the drama you faced! Elizabeth took care of reinstating me pretty quickly. She gave Alisha one more lecture but didn't seem too hard on her. The best news of the day is that she started the official investigation into Liam."

"Really!" There was a flash of fire in Sheryl's eyes.

"Yeah. That's where we spent the most time. I think Liam's days are numbered."

"Well, they should be!" She paused. "What about Barbara?"

Dave laughed. "Oh, that part was kind of funny. You should have seen Barbara's face when Elizabeth called her in after you left and told her what had just gone down."

"Really? What did she say?"

"The woman kind of sputtered and blustered, defending herself," he said, just a slight curl to the corner of his lips. "Still, she folded fairly quickly, admitting that she *might* have misinterpreted what Alisha said. Elizabeth didn't say too much in front of Alisha and me, but I can guarantee Barbara was going to get quite the talking-to after we left! Elizabeth did assign her to investigate Liam, so Alisha was happy about that. Me too! Let that lioness jump on the next guy. She just kept glaring at me, as if she still thought I was getting away with something."

Sheryl chuckled. "You're going to have to watch your step."

Dave nodded, sobering. "Yeah, I really am. Elizabeth is none too happy with me, either," he admitted. "Even though I'm off the hook, Elizabeth made it clear that I had better be more careful in the future. Alisha too. She didn't let us off too easily. We were in her office for a good two hours after you left."

"I can understand that. You both deserved a bit of a lecture," Sheryl said sternly, but he was relieved to see that there was a glint of humor in her eyes.

"I know," he said sheepishly. "Have I told you how sorry I am? And how grateful? You've been so amazing through all of this, especially with all the crap going down with your own job." He paused, leaning forward to take the wineglass from her. He set both glasses on the coffee table.

Turning back to her, he took both her hands in his. When he spoke, his voice was deep and grave. "Seriously, Sheryl. I'm really sorry," he said sincerely. "I've behaved badly over the last few months, and I really have nothing in the way of excuses. I'm the one who made such poor choices. But please know that you are very, very important to me. I value our marriage, our relationship. I . . . I value *you*."

He watched his wife's eyes fill with tears. "Oh Dave, thank you," she breathed, her voice breaking. "I needed to hear that."

"I love you, and I want to make this up to you," he said. "I'm not sure how—"

"You're making a good start tonight. A really good start."

Chapter 32

Alisha slipped into the hotel bar and onto a barstool facing the lobby. She checked her phone. It was just after 6:00 pm on Thursday evening. She wasn't yet ready to slip off her coat, however. She was still getting used to the cold New Jersey nights.

Alisha glanced up to see the same bartender with the snake tattoo approaching her warily, searching the vicinity to see who else might be joining her for more drama.

"I'm alone," Alisha assured her, her cheeks tinged with pink. "No trouble tonight—I swear."

The woman grunted. "You didn't end up being *too* bad last night. A bit messy is all."

Alisha chuckled, and some of the awkwardness dissipated. "*Messy* is a good word for it."

The blonde slid a cocktail napkin toward Alisha. "What'll it be?"

"I'll have a light beer and a burger," Alisha responded. "Whatever's on tap."

"Coors Light okay?" the bartender asked, raising an eyebrow.

"That's fine, and I'll take the burger medium. Keeping it simple tonight."

The woman nodded approvingly and turned away, stopping to put the food order into the computer before filling a cold mug with the beer.

"What's your name?" Alisha asked when she returned, using her sales skills to her advantage. She was suddenly anxious to change her image in this woman's eyes. *I have to stay at this hotel for a while. It'll be better if I don't feel so uncomfortable whenever I see her.*

"Jenny," came the surprised reply.

"Thanks, Jenny," Alisha said. "I do want to apologize for last night. I'm sorry I caused you trouble."

"No worries. All's well, and all that," the woman said with a slight smirk. "Although I'd love to hear *that* story. From screaming to tears in only twenty minutes or so? Pretty interesting stuff."

Alisha blushed a deep red now. "Yeah, I guess."

Jenny paused, as if waiting for her to say more. When Alisha stayed silent, the bartender just shrugged and hurried down the bar to wait on a group of three men who were beckoning her. Alisha blew out a sharp breath, thankful that Jenny hadn't pressed. *I'm embarrassed enough as it is. I don't need to confess my stupidity to anyone else.*

Watching the bartender work, Alisha was startled when she felt someone slide onto the barstool behind her.

"You new around here?" a gravelly voice spoke softly.

Turning quickly, Alisha saw an attractive older man leaning toward her, his very nice head of hair speckled with a bit of gray. *Oh no—not going there again!*

"Not really," she said, her voice neutral.

"I could show you around," he said with a chuckle.

"Thanks, but no thanks," Alisha said, standing up and moving down several seats toward the middle of the bar. She caught Jenny's eye, and the blonde nodded and ambled over as the man approached her again.

"You don't have to move on my account," he was saying, his voice low and seductive. "I don't bite . . . unless you want me to."

"The lady said no," Jenny said firmly.

The man ignored her, keeping his focus solely on Alisha, who shuddered.

"Please leave me alone," she said forcefully, looking him in the eye. "I'm *not* interested." She felt Jenny tense, ready to step in again.

The man gave her a cold look and held up his hands. "Well, look at you, Ms. Hoity-Toity. Can't be bothered," he said, a slight slur to his words.

Alisha turned her back on the guy, hoping he'd just go away. She heard his heavy breathing too close to her ear for a moment but then felt him sidle off in the other direction. Alisha relaxed. *Phew.*

She smiled as Jenny nodded crisply and turned toward the kitchen.

Moments later, she pushed a plate with Alisha's burger and metal basket of fries across the bar.

"That guy was a little creepy," Alisha murmured.

Jenny shrugged. "He makes the rounds but usually doesn't push too hard."

Alisha nodded and picked up the burger. *I won't admit it to her, but just a few months ago, I might have fallen for that,* she thought. The man had been attractive, and of an age that she often found alluring. *Guess I'm growing up a little—finally, as Julie would say.*

She glanced at her phone again. *I should give Julie a call, fill her in on what happened.* She knew her friend would be thrilled by the outcome—*and* the fact that Alisha had come to her senses about Dave.

She sent a text. **R u there?**

Yes working, came the reply. **U ok?**

Yes. All good Alisha responded. Then she hesitated before typing. **Really good. Met Dave's wife.**

Three, two, one—the phone rang, as Alisha expected.

"What? When did you meet his wife?" Julie cried in a rush. "What happened?"

Laughing at her friend's intensity, Alisha filled Julie in on the events of the night prior and early that day.

"I can't believe all that," Julie said, her voice full of awe, when Alisha had finished. "Wow. Just wow. I want to hate her for your sake, but I gotta say . . . Sheryl sounds amazing."

"Yeah, she is," Alisha admitted. "Although I can't believe I'm even saying that! I'll be honest, I know I wouldn't have been nearly so gracious or compassionate if I were her."

"Me either," Julie replied thoughtfully. "But . . . maybe we should be. You know?"

"Yeah, I've thought about that," Alisha mused, tugging on her ponytail. "She believed me . . . and had this way of looking into my eyes without pity—just compassion. Well, at least after she got over her feisty, claws-out moment. She just . . . sort of took a breath, and then I saw that she was there, open, listening. I've never experienced anything like it. It takes a really special person to respond like she did. It pains me to say it, but I wouldn't mind being more like her—obviously when I grow up."

Julie laughed. "Me too."

Alisha took a bite of her burger with her phone balanced between her shoulder and her cheek, letting the silence linger.

"So, what next?" Julie asked. "Are you staying in New Jersey?"

"Yeah, I am going to stay," Alisha said definitively. "I met with my boss this afternoon. I had to confess everything, but . . . Brittany was actually really great about it, Julie, I mean, even really supportive—especially when I told her about Liam."

"Wow. That's awesome."

"She suggested that it would be better for me to stay in New Jersey, be away from Liam while the investigation is going on. Elizabeth, the HR lady, said the same thing. Plus, they both think it will be better for my career to stay near the home office. More opportunities for advancement—in the future."

"Wow, they're really talking about advancement? I'm surprised they didn't fire you!" Julie said frankly.

"Right?" Alisha cried. "Me too. I have Sheryl and Dave to thank for that," she admitted soberly. "They both went to bat for me. Honestly, I'm pretty blown away by their support. But I'm definitely going to have to watch my p's and q's for a long time to come."

"No messing with guys at work," Julie surmised.

"Yeah. That too. Maybe no messing with guys period for a while?" Alisha murmured, wondering if that made sense. She was nauseated just thinking about Liam, but even the guy at the bar had turned her stomach. Something inside her was changing.

She was surprised when Julie didn't laugh. "You know, that might be a good idea—for a little while, anyway. Give yourself some space to process all of this."

"Hmm . . . I think I might need some time. This has been a lot . . . especially the conversation with Sheryl."

"Yeah, it has been a lot," Julie agreed. "But it sounds like you are trying to learn from it. That's the important part."

"Then I'm going to do it—at least for now," Alisha answered resolutely.

Down the bar, Jenny sent her a questioning look. Alisha wasn't sure if it was about what she said or if she was questioning another beer. Alisha shook her head.

"Okay, my friend," Julie was saying. "I need to run, but keep me up to date. And . . . my friend?"

"Yeah?"

"I'm liking this new Alisha."

"Yeah, me too," Alisha said.

She finished her burger, mulling over Julie's words. *Can I be a new Alisha? And what does that look like?* She had a feeling that being in New Jersey, away from her constant disappointment in her father's responses, was going to be a good thing. It was time she grew up and faced the reality of that situation.

Her father was never going to fully accept her or give her the support she craved. Julie was right about that. *I guess it's time to stop trying to get his approval.* But what did that mean, and how would she approach things differently? She wasn't sure.

However, the one thing she *did* know for sure was that she was going to need to make an extra effort with her job. *I need to prove to myself and everyone else that I'm not just some flaky, guy-crazy blonde.*

I've been given a second chance at LSM, and I want to make the most of it.

Chapter 33

Friday, December 17

"The board wants Todd out," Alex said without preamble as he strode into Sheryl's office shortly after she arrived Friday morning.

Glancing at her watch, Sheryl made a face. "And good morning to you, too, Alex," she responded pertly. "How in the world would you know *that* at 7:30 am on a Friday?"

Alex sighed as he dropped into the chair in front of her desk, wearing an attractive gray suit. His sandy hair was mussed, and his light brown eyes looked uncharacteristically bloodshot. "I've been up half the night fielding their emails and calls," he answered wearily. "They're not even willing to wait to hear what his side of the story is."

"What are you going to do?" Sheryl asked. "Don't we *have* to give him a chance? Have you heard from him?"

Alex shook his head. "No to both questions . . . and I have no idea what I'm going to do about Todd," he said, his voice frustrated. "I can barely think, and we have that press conference at 8:45." The board wanted to get The Diamante's side out before the stock market opened.

"Is there anything I can help you with? Do you need any information from me for the press?" Sheryl's heart already ached for Alex. *This is so unfair to him.* Relieved that she wasn't in his shoes, she wanted to support him as much as possible.

"You don't need to brief me," Alex answered, with a curious look on his face. "You can just answer any questions about the IT piece that I can't directly,"

"Directly? Me?" Sheryl swallowed hard. "I didn't think you'd need me there."

"Of course I need you there." Alex looked incredulous. "You, Joaquin, and Hye *all* need to be there. I'm not going in there alone, although I'll make the opening statements."

"Oh." Sheryl paused. Thankfully she had dressed in a flattering navy suit with a peach silk blouse that morning, just in case. It seemed her foresight had been accurate once again. "If you need me . . . of course," she assured the man who was now her boss—at least temporarily.

Alex's boyish grin appeared briefly. He scrubbed his jaw absently with his hand. "Can you believe this mess?" he asked, but Sheryl knew it was rhetorical. Even after a long night with little sleep, the whole situation still seemed unreal.

"I'm going to need your help, Sheryl. Everyone's help, really, but especially yours," he continued earnestly. "You've shown such great leadership, even in the short time you've been on the executive committee and the board. The perspective you're brought has been refreshing, and . . ." Alex paused, seeming to search for the right word. "Honorable. Yeah, that's a good word. Honorable. We'll need that now more than ever if we want to keep The Diamante afloat."

A faint flush crept up her cheeks. "Thank you, Alex, but you've never been anything but honorable too—from what I've observed, anyway."

Alex shrugged.

"But, of course, I'll support and help you anyway I can. I know we're going to need everyone working together to overcome this . . . problem? I hesitate to call it a catastrophe, but . . ." She lifted her hands in a gesture of consternation.

"Okay then, I'll be off. I'll see you in the training room at 8:30." Alex pushed himself out of the chair and shot her a quick smile. "I know you are familiar with *that* room," he teased, reminding her of the 'memorial service' she had held there in October.

Sheryl smiled, learning back in her chair. "Yes, Alex, I am," she said laughingly, glad to have a little relief from the thick tension that had been smothering them.

By 8:30, Sheryl had reviewed all her notes about the investigation and Keisha's findings several times, even though she really knew them all by heart anyway. Having never participated in a press conference, she was understandably nervous. Ha! She hadn't even been on the executive team long enough to have received press training, something that she and Blake were scheduled for next week. *Lot of good that's going to do!*

But she knew her preparations were better, as she had also taken the time to do her pre-meeting meditation and visualization, just as she had done before all important meetings in the last few months. She carried the vision of herself surrounded by pure, white light as she walked confidently to the auditorium-style room.

The room was packed and loud, Sheryl saw the moment she entered. Men and women with still and video cameras lined the aisles, and it looked like every seat was taken. She could hardly squeeze through the throng to make her way to the front of the room, where Alex sat in a row of chairs that had been prepared for The Diamante team. Like her, Alex had clearly checked his grooming, as his sandy hair now lay neatly on his head. Even his eyes looked clearer. *The miracle of eye drops,* she guessed.

He murmured a greeting that she didn't quite catch over the chatter of the press representatives. as she sat down next to him. Joaquin and Hye pushed through the crowd moments later and joined them. They had barely sat down when Alex stood up and approached the microphones arrayed around the podium.

"Good morning," Alex said, looking carefully around the room. "Thank you all for coming . . ." He continued with a prepared statement that outlined, in general terms, the sequence of events leading up to yesterday's dramatic incident. "As of this time," he concluded, "no one employed at The Diamante, including Mr. Fisher and Ms. Solowitz, has been charged with any crimes. One board member, Mr. Anthony Russo, is being questioned, but I don't know what his status is. The remaining board members and executive team were not involved and will continue to operate The Diamante with the same integrity and meticulous care for our clients as we did before."

"That you know of," a male voice called out from someone near the back of the room. "You don't know yet if anyone else is involved."

Alex nodded curtly. "That I know of," he amended. "However, there is absolutely no evidence that we've uncovered in our internal investigation that indicates that anyone else was involved. Are there other questions?"

"How did the IT department know to look for hidden database fields?" a woman reporter in the front row asked.

Alex looked over at Sheryl, who rose gracefully and went to the podium. "We actually didn't know to look," she said confidently, looking only at the woman who asked the question. "One of the programmers on the team—her name is Keisha Smith— discovered the fields accidentally when she was reviewing the file layout. It was her diligence and attention to detail that made her bring the discrepancy to my attention."

"What made you ask for the SEC investigation?" came from another reporter near the front.

Sheryl smiled. "Well, I didn't ask for *that*," she responded. "I suggested an *internal* investigation because we weren't sure at the beginning how serious it was. However, I felt that there *was* enough irregularity to warrant more than just the IT department looking at it. Mr. Gonzales was the one who contacted the SEC."

Questions were then fired at Joaquin, who looked frankly besieged. As he stumbled through his answers, Sheryl had to jump in to clarify once or twice before the press finally turned their attention back to Alex. As they sat down, Sheryl saw Joaquin wipe a bead of sweat from his upper lip and gave him a reassuring smile.

"In closing," Alex finally said after the predetermined limit of twenty minutes, "I'd like to give special acknowledgement to Sheryl Simmons and her team, especially Ms. Smith, for their diligence, integrity, and competence in escalating this issue. It's people like them who are the backbone of The Diamante and are why we've been so successful in the past and will continue to be so in the future. Thank you very much."

Sheryl sat stunned in her chair, astonished by Alex's closing words, which she had not expected. *It was a brilliant move to reassure investors,* she thought. *But wow, to acknowledge Keisha and me like that.* She noticed that Joaquin and Hye were nodding in agreement. Alex had turned to face her and had a big smile on his face too. She blinked back tears as a swell of emotion rose through her.

The room emptied quickly as the press crews hurried out to broadcast the details of the conference to the world—at least those who hadn't been broadcasting live. As she stood up, the enormity of the coverage suddenly struck Sheryl hard. *I've just been on national news—maybe even international.* Her legs began shaking, and she sat back down. *Did I do okay?*

"Thank you, Sheryl. You did great!" Alex was saying as he strode back over to their little group.

"Yeah, Sheryl, you really bailed me out," Joaquin added gratefully. "How come you were so calm? You and Alex both. Have you done this before?"

Sheryl shook her head mutely, momentarily unable to speak.

Alex laughed. "*Now* you get nervous," he said, clearly amused. "But that's okay. Better now than before."

Smiling, Sheryl started to rise. "Yeah, I guess it just hit me all of sudden."

"Let's get out of here," Alex said, ushering her toward the door. "We've got lots more to do today."

Sobering, Sheryl preceded him out of the room, conscious of all that lay ahead. The press conference was the first step, but there was so much more yet to tackle.

Back in her office, she picked up her phone wanting to call Dave, then realized he was already calling her.

"Hello," she said breathlessly.

"You were amazing!" her husband exclaimed. "We watched the whole thing. And what Alex said at the end? You're the hero of the day. I'm so proud of you!"

"Yeah, me too," came Robert's voice in the background.

Collapsing in her chair, Sheryl let out a long breath. "Wow, I was shocked when Alex said that."

"I know. They panned to your face. You looked dumbfounded . . . but very beautiful," Dave replied. "It was actually perfect. You came across so *real*—polished and professional, but *real*."

"Yeah, Sheryl," Robert chimed in again. "You made The Diamante look really good. Alex did, too, but you stole the show."

"Especially when you were helping Joaquin out, poor guy. That was rough on him," Dave elaborated. "I am so proud of you, honey, I can't even tell you how much."

Tears welled in Sheryl's eyes again. To have her husband's support and accolades again was so gratifying. "Thank you," she said, her voice breaking. "I really appreciate that."

A soft knock sounded at the door, and Sheryl looked up to see Keisha hovering hesitantly in the doorway.

"Hey, I gotta go. Keisha's here. But thank you . . . and Robert too!" Ending the call, she waved Keisha in.

"Well, boss lady, who knew you were so great on camera?" the younger woman said with a grin.

Sheryl laughed. "I certainly didn't. Thank God, I kind of forgot that I was on camera."

Keisha rolled her eyes. "Unbelievable." Then, her face sobered. "But you didn't have to mention me," she said seriously. "I was . . . well, I was kind of blown away that you did."

"But you deserved it," Sheryl assured her. "We might not have found out about any of this if you hadn't dug into those missing fields. Someone else might have just ignored it. You didn't."

"Yeah, well, I'm always going to say if I think something is wrong," Keisha replied indignantly. "What else would I do?"

"Of course you would. That's who you are," Sheryl agreed firmly.

"But what's the deal with Rachel and Todd and those guys from the board?" Keisha asked in an anguished voice. Why did they do that? And the financial advisors? Were they really just greedy? It's disgusting!"

"I don't know," Sheryl said soothingly. "It seems that they were greedy . . . or maybe trying to make up for other mistakes they made. I don't know for sure. People don't always make good decisions."

"But those people were in leadership roles!" the younger woman cried. "They're supposed to be setting examples, not being criminals. How are we supposed to *trust* management if they do stuff like that?"

Frowning, Sheryl leaned toward her protégé. "Keisha, people are people. No one is perfect, even those in leadership. And don't forget, I am 'management,' too." She paused, grimacing and making air quotes. "But most of us in management have good intentions and are good people. People like Alex and Blake and Joaquin, even Jim Leaders."

"But Todd was the president!"

"Yes, and we don't know yet if Todd even did anything wrong."

Keisha shot her a skeptical look. "Well, he must have done *something* if he was taken into FBI custody."

"I don't know, Keisha, and I'm trying not to assume the worst," Sheryl told her, inwardly cringing. In reality, she was just as disgusted as Keisha was with the behavior of those involved, even Todd, who should have known better even if what he did wasn't illegal.

"You're making excuses for him? Hmph."

"No, Keisha, I'm not making excuses. It seems that Todd exercised poor judgment, but I don't know what else. I truly don't know. And, I'm not condoning him or anyone else." Sheryl looked the young programmer right in the eye. "But no matter what, you can't let what one person, or a few people do, color your opinion of everyone. You know, like people have done to you."

Sheryl watched Keisha's tawny face pale as that barb hit home.

"We all like to think that leaders have their act together, that they are always right," Sheryl continued gently but with conviction. "But it's not always true. The best leaders will admit when they don't know and get help. The best leaders have integrity. But it's naïve to assume that all of them do. I guess we just have to assume the best of people but be aware that no one is perfect. Right?"

"I guess," Keisha grumbled. "This is all confusing sometimes."

Chuckling softly, Sheryl agreed. "Yeah, well, you're not the only one."

That brought a smile back to Keisha's face. "Ugh. This is what you meant when we talked in September, right after the layoffs, isn't it? That things aren't always black and white."

"Yup, it is. We can't lose faith," Sheryl said, to herself as much as Keisha. "We have to be diligent—like you were—but we also have to trust the people we work with, until they give us reason to do otherwise."

Nodding thoughtfully, Keisha was silent for a minute. Sheryl could almost see the thoughts whirling through the younger woman's brain.

"You're right," Keisha finally conceded. "But I need to get my head around this a little more."

"Well, let me know when you do," Sheryl said wryly. "I'm not sure I always have my head around it."

Grinning, Keisha rose to go, but Sheryl held up a hand to stop her. Rising herself, she walked around her desk and grasped her protégé's shoulders.

"Keisha, thank you," she said sincerely. "Your integrity did uncover something that needed to be brought to light, and I really am appreciative of what you did and how you handled it. Alex was right when he said that people like you are part of what makes The Diamante great, and you should be very proud of yourself. Truly."

Deep red bloomed in Keisha's cheeks, and she reached out and gave Sheryl a big hug. "Thank you, boss," she whispered before hurrying out of the room.

Sheryl caught a glimpse of tears rolling down her cheeks as she left. Smiling to herself, she stepped back to her chair and sat down. *Now* that *was the highlight of my day.*

Epilogue

Saturday morning, Sheryl stood on the deck, watching the sunrise over the frosty yard. The trees along the back property line glittered in the golden light. She pulled the blanket closer around her, gripping her hot coffee mug firmly between her hands.

She had foregone her usual morning workout because she was frankly exhausted after the crazy week. And supplementing her morning meditation with some healing time in nature, despite the cold, seemed exactly what she needed to nourish herself today.

What a week, she thought, mentally reviewing the astonishing events that had unfolded. *My whole world is changing, and mostly for the better, I think.*

It certainly was better with Dave. He had been amazing since the meeting with Elizabeth and Alisha on Thursday morning. So attentive. So thoughtful. She felt like they were starting a whole new phase of their relationship, one that was stronger and more honest. Alisha had been a wake-up call for them both.

Sheryl took a sip of the hot brew, thinking about the younger woman with compassion. Clearly, Alisha has some work to do. *She had grabbed onto Dave like a lifeline, a role that no one could fulfill.* Sheryl shook her head. All she could do was pray that Alisha somehow got help and onto the right track. Confident that she had done all she could for the girl, Sheryl made her peace with that.

Her cell phone rang, startling her. *Who in the world would be calling now?* Although, it being December, the sunrise wasn't all that early.

Seeing that it was Alex, she reluctantly answered. He had inherited a huge mess when he became acting head of The Diamante, and she was committed to supporting him as much as she possibly could.

"Hey Alex," she answered, turning to go back inside. She couldn't juggle the coffee, phone, and blanket in the freezing temperatures.

"Sheryl, I didn't wake you?" Alex's deep voice rumbled with concern.

"No, not at all," Sheryl replied, slipping into the great room through the French doors. "I was just watching the sunrise."

Alex chuckled. "I haven't even looked. Stuck glued to my home computer, still drowning in emails." She heard him sigh deeply. "A lot of our investors are asking questions . . . and they're all directed to me."

"Oh Alex, I'm so sorry. That's got to be so difficult, but I'm sure you'll handle them all well."

He grunted. "I'm getting help from the public relations team," he muttered.

"So, how are you really, Alex? Yesterday was tough, but you did such a great job with the press conference."

"So did you," Alex shot back.

"Thanks," she said modestly. "I didn't expect that."

"Keisha's become something of a hero," Alex said with a smile in his voice.

"Yeah, and she has no idea what to make of it," Sheryl said, laughing. She sank onto the sofa. "Although I'm glad we were able to keep her out of the press conference directly. She really doesn't want to talk to the press."

"I don't blame her," Alex agreed. "I don't either. You never know how they're going to twist what you said."

"The coverage seems pretty balanced so far," Sheryl reminded him, peeling off her gloves.

"Yeah, for us. But they're crucifying Hank and Anthony."

"As they should!" Sheryl said indignantly. "I can't believe what they almost got away with."

"Me either," Alex said sorrowfully.

"What about Todd?" Sheryl asked curiously. She took another sip of her coffee.

"What *about* Todd?" Alex repeated with disgust. "We *still* don't really know what's going on with him. But that's actually why I called. Even *after* the press conference, all the other outside directors want him out. We'll have to have yet another board meeting on Monday." He groaned softly. "They want to officially confirm someone as the president, at least a temporary one."

"I'm sure that will be you," Sheryl said confidently, tucking her hair behind her ear. "And why not? You're a great candidate."

Alex huffed. "Thanks, but I'm not so sure about that. I'm not nearly as good as schmoozing as Todd is."

"Maybe that's a good thing," Sheryl countered. "Todd was a little too good at schmoozing, wasn't he? I'll certainly vote for you."

"I really appreciate your support, Sheryl. I'm glad I can count on you," he said appreciatively. "Not for your vote," he added. "But for the way you always put the company first."

"Of course," Sheryl responded. "What else would I do? And what about Blake? Is he staying?"

"Yeah, he said he would. He knows we need him now more than ever."

"That's really good," Sheryl said, her shoulders relaxing a bit with that news.

"It is," Alex said. "So, board meeting Monday afternoon. That will give us time to get an update from Agent Spence or Agent Shah. I'll call the investor group that Hank and Anthony were representing and see what they want to do."

"Wow, they really have egg on their faces. First Hank and the whole Layla situation, and now this! Will they back out?"

"No idea. I couldn't reach anyone from the group yesterday. I expect they are scrambling."

"Were they involved, or do they know anything?" Sheryl wondered.

"Doesn't seem like it," Alex said. "But who knows? Like everything else, we'll just have to wait and see."

"Okay, I'll be there on Monday. You know I'll do whatever you need, Alex," Sheryl assured him.

"I know. Thanks, Sheryl. Try to get some rest this weekend."

Sheryl laughed. "Sure, Alex. I will. You, too. I mean, the worst is over now, isn't it? The bad actors are all gone from the company. And now we can put the pieces back together. The Diamante will weather this storm, and you're the perfect person to lead us through it."

"Yeah, it seems like the worst is over. And, judging from the press coverage, we will get through it," Alex agreed. "They're not blaming the company, anyway. If anything, they're actually praising you and Keisha—and the company—for your diligence in finding the problem."

"I know. I've been pleasantly surprised with the coverage," Sheryl replied, thinking of the mostly truthful stories she had seen earlier on her smartphone.

"Plus, none of the emails I'm getting indicates that our clients are pulling out. They seem to be wanting reassurance but aren't threatening to leave, although it's early yet. It's possible that we'll lose some, but not probably too many, largely thanks to you and Keisha."

"It's a good thing that Keisha has a sharp eye," Sheryl agreed, thinking that her star programmer should be rewarded. She'd have to think about how best to do that next week.

"Okay, I'll let you go. See you Monday," Alex said. "Early."

"Got it. Thanks, Alex."

Sheryl hung up the phone, setting her coffee on the nearby table. She slid her Ugg boots off, tucking her feet beneath her. Sighing, she thought about everything that had unfolded. Even though she had been an active participant in the investigation, some of it still seemed unreal, especially Rachel's actions. *I guess we never really know other people.*

Grimacing softly, she reflected back on what she had told Keisha the day before: *"We all like to think that leaders have their act together, that they're always right." Well, they really don't, do they?*

Sheryl picked up her coffee and leaned against the soft cushions, resting her head on the back of the couch. She thought about the silver linings—Keisha's heroism and growing confidence, Joaquin's ethical approach to the investigation, Hye's incredible investigative work, and Alex having the chance to change the leadership landscape in the firm.

The Diamante would survive. So would she.

She felt really good about the part she had played and would continue to play. With Alex in charge, it was likely that she would have an even more prominent role in the firm. He respected IT. He respected her.

Her husband shuffled into the room, looking sleepy and rumpled.

"Where did you go?" he asked. "I woke up, and you were gone."

"It's late, sleepyhead," she teased him. "I was watching the sunrise."

"Brrr, it's too cold for that," he said, heading toward the coffee pot. "Do you need more?"

"Yes, please," Sheryl answered, smiling at him.

We've come a long way in a short time, she thought, watching him with a heart full of love.

"We can't let work come between us again," she said out loud, her voice reverent as if making a vow.

Dave handed her the coffee mug, full and steaming. He sat down next to her, wrapping his free arm around her. "No, we can't," he agreed. "We won't." He leaned over and kissed the top of her head, whispering "I love you" as he did.

She smiled and whispered it back.

Yes, I can count a lot of blessings coming from these crazy few weeks, she thought gratefully. *And I'm sure that, despite what new challenges are undoubtedly coming, we can take them on together.*

Acknowledgements

My heartfelt thanks to you, dear reader, for purchasing and reading this book. I hope you found it as entertaining and inspiring as I was during its creation.

Thank you to Bridget Cook-Burch and Hannah Lyons for their incredible support, editing, and suggestions in the creation of Pursuing Truth. My writing has been forever changed—for the better—by your insightful guidance.

I also want to thank Rebecca Hall Gruyter and the team at Inspired Legacy Publishing for guiding me through the process and helping me bring this book into the world.

My support team also continues to grow and evolve. I owe a huge debt of gratitude to Krista Mollion, Sally Anderson, Susan K. Younger, Brigitte Bojkowszky, Dara Myers, and, of course, my husband, Reed Heine. You've all made the process a lot lighter and more fun!

Stay tuned for Book Three of *The Ascending Ladders Series* in early spring of 2024.

About the Author

Karen Ann Bulluck is the author of the bestselling novel **Discovering Power**, an engaging and inspiring speaker, as well as a contributing author to three International Bestselling anthologies. Passionate about making a difference, Karen is a Risk-taking Coach and the founder of *DARING TO TRANSCEND*. She partners with women leaders to push beyond the limits of their leadership, career, and life so that they can make a bigger impact in their work and beyond. Through her proprietary methodology, Karen works with leaders to EXPLORE what matters, INTEGRATE the Whole Self, and FLOURISH in new dimensions.

The first woman promoted to Executive Vice President at AM Best Company, Karen's career was marked by taking risks to make many cross-disciplinary changes and have an impact across a wide variety of people and processes.

An ardent traveler, she loves to explore new cultures, new ideas and new ways of doing things while learning from and valuing the wisdom of the past and present. She lives in New Jersey with her husband and very spoiled cat.

Email: karen@daringtotranscend.com
LinkedIn: www.linkedin.com/in/karenannbulluck
Website: www.dareingtotranscend.com
Facebook: www.facebook.com/karenannbulluck
Ascending Ladders Series Information: www.ascendingladders.com

Reviews

"What a great book! By far the best I've read in the last 12 months. Captivating story, believable dialogue and a group of characters that just about anyone could easily identify with. Well done, Ms. Bulluck... well done. You've outdone yourself!"

Brian Hilliard

Popular Speaker & Coach

www.MorePaidSpeakingGigs.com

"Karen Ann Bulluck is a master at building suspense, providing surprise twists at every page turn. This story is filled with unsaid things, managing perceptions and the lengths people will go to hide the truth – even from themselves.
It demonstrates the impact of leaders who trust their gut and those who don't – at their own detriment. It recognizes the power of self-awareness, emotional control, and true self-mastery. A thoroughly enjoyable and suspenseful read."

Lisa Coletta

Founder/Managing Director, The Governance Collective

www.governancecollective.com

"Karen Ann Bulluck has done it again!!! Another masterful story that rings so true to life that you feel the emotions of the characters! You can't help but be drawn into the story!
Read one page of this book and I guarantee you won't be able to put it down!"

Misti Mazurik

Director of Operations, Your Purpose Driven Practice

"Life does not happen in the black-and-white extremes. Both ethics and relationships traverse the grayscale. Sheryl Simmon's journey poses some vital questions, highlighting the complexities of human relationships and decision-making dilemmas. Pursuing Truth will make you take a second look at your own journey!
Dr. Kasthuri Henry, PhD
CTP - Founder, Ennobled for Success Institute
International #1 Best Selling Author
www.kashenry.com

"*Pursuing Truth* pulls you into the story immediately and keeps you guessing right up until the end.
Our heroine from Discovering Power, Sheryl, is back, taking us deep into the complex and multifaceted world of her workplace with a big mystery to solve. But this time her marriage is also in the spotlight as she navigates an increasingly sticky situation of what may or may not be her husband, Dave's, affair.
Rich in storytelling and intrigue, this book was an absolute delight to read! To anyone wondering if they will enjoy this book, don't hesitate!"
Krista Mollion
Founder of From Zero 2 Six Academy
https://fromzero2six.com/

"Great characters, powerful story, exciting read. Karen Bulluck has done it again with her new book *Pursuing Truth: Book Two of The Ascending Ladders Series*. I loved the book."
Maureen Ryan Blake
Maureen Ryan Blake Media

"Seriously impressed how Karen can bring to life complicated real-life drama that challenges the boundaries of personal and professional relationships, all intertwined for the purposes of teaching the power of ethical behavior. It's got it all: dynamics around communication, responsibility, accountability, professionalism, trust, mutual respect, pushing the limits. The title sums it up: *Pursuing Truth*. It takes a skilled writer to bring real-life dynamics to life and have the reader really look at their own ethical boundaries. All of Karen's books have such a powerful underlying intention, they are enhancing the human condition for the betterment of humankind."
Sally Anderson
World Class Coach Intuitive
Sally Anderson International

"Karen Ann Bulluck's *Pursuing Truth* is a riveting standalone addition to her trilogy, delving into ethics, relationships, and personal growth. Vivid descriptions transport readers, while Sheryl and Dave's struggle amidst Alisha's entry creates a captivating journey. Thought-provoking and timely, the book addresses the dynamics of gender interactions at work, shedding light on women's treatment of one another and the broader issue of workplace conduct concerning women. Sheryl's conflict resolution skills inspire, and her leadership highlights the significance of women in executive roles. With exceptional storytelling, Bulluck keeps readers engaged, skillfully unraveling mysteries while leaving a lasting impression. A gripping must-read."
Brigitte Bojkowszky, PH.D.
Global & Personal Branding Strategist
BridgetBrands
www.bridgetbrands.com

"As an avid reader, I love books that combine intrigue with life lessons and redemption. In *Pursuing Truth*, author Karen Ann Bulluck gives us this and more. I highly recommend this page-turner."
Dr. Lori Leyden
Developer of The Grace Process®, Founder of Create Global Healing
www.DrLoriLeyden.com

"*Pursuing Truth* is a real page-turner. The second in the series by Karen Ann Bulluck, her character, Sheryl Simmons, explores her power, standing strong to be her best despite all things collapsing in life and colliding in business around her. The perspective of different characters helps us as readers see the uniqueness of individuals. What drives them to do good and evil. As the tale unravels, we want to understand if her marriage will survive and if the business is going to crumble. What risks is Sheryl willing to take to be fulfilled and have both succeed? Great storytelling."
Susan K. Younger
Relationship Architect – Engaging Humanity in the Workplace
Codebreaker Technologies Pro Certification

"I hope *Pursuing Truth,* although a fictional book, can make a non-fiction impact on how leaders see their role and responsibility of being more human and understanding in times of crisis."
Nikki Green
Life & Business Resiliency Expert, 4x Best-Selling Author
Green Chameleon Collective
https://thenikkigreen.com/

Made in the USA
Middletown, DE
04 November 2023

41784000R00179